IN A DARK WOOD

Marina Warner's most recent novel is *Indigo*. Her previous novel, *The Lost Father* was a Regional Winner of the Commonwealth Writers' Prize, Winner of the Macmillan Silver Pen Award, and shortlisted for the Booker Prize. She is a writer, critic and historian and besides two earlier novels, *In A Dark Wood* and *The Skating Party*, she is the author of three studies of mythology, *Alone of All Her Sex: the Myth and Cult of the Virgin Mary*, *Joan of Arc: the Image of Female Heroism* and *Monuments and Maidens: the Allegory of the Female Form* (Winner of the Fawcett Prize). She is currently working on a study of fairy tales, and has just finished the libretto for a children's opera, *The Queen of Sheba's Legs*, for the English National Opera.

Marina Warner lives in London with her husband, the painter John Dewe Mathews, and one son.

BY THE SAME AUTHOR

Fiction

The Skating Party
The Lost Father
Indigo

Non-Fiction

Joan of Arc:
the Image of Female Heroism

Dragon Empress:
The Life & Times of Tz'u-hsi

Alone of All Her Sex:
the Myth and Cult of the Virgin Mary

Monuments and Maidens:
the Allegory of the Female Form

Marina Warner

IN A DARK WOOD

VINTAGE

VINTAGE
20 Vauxhall Bridge Road, London SW1V 2SA

London Melbourne Sydney Auckland Johannesburg
and agencies throughout the world

First published by Weidenfeld & Nicolson, 1977
Vintage edition 1992

1 3 5 7 9 10 8 6 4 2

Printed and bound in Great Britain by
Cox & Wyman Ltd, Reading

ISBN 0 09 996220 9

FOR IRÈNE
cosi scintilla
come raggio di sole in acqua mera

I am soft sift
In an hourglass – at the wall
Fast, but mined with a motion, a drift,
And it crowds and it combs to the fall...
Gerard Manley Hopkins

It was almost noon. The emperor's parasol cast a precise pool at the hem of his robe. The attendants who surrounded him did not move. Now and then he withdrew one hand from his yellow sleeves to spread the fan that hung at his waist and wave it once, twice, three times in his face. Then tiring of it, he folded it again and let it drop to the end of its silken cord. The gesture was slow like an old man's, although the emperor was a boy of fifteen.

On the polished stone flags of the second innermost court-yard of the Forbidden City, between the pool of shadow in which the emperor stood and the knot of his official astrono-mers opposite, lay a copper rule. It was marked off in lengths, and two particular places were arrowed by ivory markers. A gnomon had been set up at right angles to the rule, projecting a shadow on to the copper. The knot of officials stood stiffly, in imitation of the emperor's stillness, but their eyes flickered from one another to the rule and back again, always returning to the shadow that crept along the measure on the ground, shrinking back into itself as the sun mounted, like the slow-motion retraction of a living tongue.

The astronomers stood apart from a group of three Euro-peans who were distinguished from them not by their clothes (though the embroidered plaques on their breasts proclaimed that the Europeans bore no rank or titles), but by long beards which set off their thinner Western lips. They stood close to-gether as if for support, and their eyes travelled to the emperor and to the decreasing shadow and back again. They were too proud to cast a look in the direction of their rivals. For they had placed their ivory marker closer to the gnomon than the astronomers of the court, and their enterprise in China depended on the exactitude of their prediction.

The shadow shrank along the rule. The pool at the emperor's hem diminished stealthily, like water burning up under a desert sun. It was almost noon, but time that day was being eked out in millimetres. The tongue of darkness contracted: it reached the first ivory marker. The group of astronomers stirred slightly. But the gong of noon did not sound in the courtyard, and the emperor's lids closed slowly, for the shadow slid past. He did not speak. The courtiers shifted on their feet, and dropping their eyes, glanced across at one another uneasily. Under his robes, the leader of the Europeans felt for his rosary and prayed that the shadow would continue its retreat. Only a half minute now to noon. The shadow seemed to him to stop between one marker and the other, as if the sun had been arrested in its ascent to the zenith. The astronomers began to titter, looking at the three Jesuit Fathers derisively. Their calculations had been at fault, perhaps, but then so it seemed had the Westerners'. They laughed at the shadow, in suspense between the two arrows, but the emperor did not smile with them.

The shadow on the rule stood at the point of the second marker. It seemed to hover, but then held, and perceptibly began to lengthen again. The emperor raised his hand, and the courtyard rang to the struck bronze of the midday gong. He turned to the three Europeans. 'It is noon,' he said, 'and yours is the true measurement.'

❧ CHAPTER 1

Jerome Namier rang his front door bell, and waited. Although he had a key to his home, he rarely remembered to move it from one jacket to another. A thin upright old lady let him in, and Jerome greeted her courteously. He set the package he was carrying down on the hall table. From the box inside the wrapping he lifted up a small golden cage and, holding it gingerly, wound a key at its base. A bronze-coloured bird perched on a spray of jade leaves of waxy green and rose began to warble and chirrup, its beak opening and closing as it sang, its jewel-crested head bobbing up and down. Bells on the bird's gem-studded branch rang to the movements of its head and its long enamelled tail opened like a fan.

'Oh, that's very pretty, very pretty indeed, I must say!' exclaimed the old lady with a gentle smile.

'It's for Gabriel,' said Jerome. 'At least it might be of interest to him. Is he still here?'

Jerome took off his coat and carried the clockwork nightingale into the drawing-room. He poured himself a large vodka, his favourite drink. He preferred a Polish kind, flavoured – or so it was said – with grass trampled by the last herd of bison in Europe. He had been introduced to it on a trip to Poland years ago, when he had written a long article on Polish cultural life for the *Review*. But it did not lift his spirits tonight, and he wound up the musical bird again and listened to its song, walking up and down between the sofa and the mantelpiece.

You are fortunate, Gabriel my brother, he thought, to have work that absorbs and completes you, that no one can take away. I should be the one engaged on an important work,

3

instead of frittering my time and my talent – such as it is – in criticism. He looked into the clear liquid in his glass and drank it greedily.

On an ordinary night, the sweet fallacious song of the clockwork nightingale would have lifted Jerome's heart like any cunning piece of art or craftsmanship, but this evening it left him dull and spiritless, and his thoughts turned from sour contemplation of his brother's fortune to the events of his own day.

This attack he had suffered was the most wounding of all the attacks he had suffered at the *Review*, and he knew, and was prepared to admit, as he closed his eyes and let the absurd gaiety of the music ripple over him, that his detractors were right. Yet he would not let them know it. Today, he had drafted measures and countermeasures he could take – under the guise of reading a 1000-page American bestseller about impending armageddon in Western capitalism. None of them had been adequate. He could not say that the revelations did not matter, that it was of no consequence that the Institute of Cultural Affairs turned out to be a front for the CIA and that *The Albion Review* had been subsidized by CIA funds. Personally, he was inclined to take this view since as editor of the *Review* for twelve years he had never once been approached by the Institute with an article it wished to be published or a book that it insisted should be reviewed. In a characteristic gesture Jerome Namier slapped the back of his left fist with his right hand. If the CIA had used his paper to peddle its point of view, Jerome knew only too well it would have used more covert channels. The trouble was, the ineptitude of the agency, as proven by so many books that the *Review* itself had gleefully discussed, made Jerome's position more embarrassing : for how could he have allowed himself to accept interested money ? How could he indeed ? He went over to the vodka bottle and refilled his glass, remembering now with loathing that excellent lunch in the Connaught with a quiet and tousled intellectual ten years ago. They had discussed whether the literary executors of a major poet who had recently died should publish his private correspondence, revealing his subterranean and unsavoury sex life. Then the American had said that the Institute of Cultural Affairs would be willing to contribute to the *Review*'s finances. After only two years of publication, he had stated with calm authoritativeness, the *Review* was already considered the finest critical organ in England, and by the most thoughtful communities of learning on the east coast. Jerome Namier had felt both flattered and scornful, and regarded the American benefactor as a schoolmaster regards an admiring pupil who does not interest him because he absorbs his teaching too unquestioningly.

Had a shadow of satisfaction passed over the lips of the American? Jerome tried to remember his expression, and with a movement of self-hatred recalled that at that moment he, Jerome, had bent his head to sniff luxuriantly at his bread and butter pudding.

Twice-over greed, he groaned. The worst of it was to be innocent. The *New Radical*'s article would be on the stands tomorrow, and it would inform all London that he should have known the money's origins. It would have been better to have known, thought Jerome miserably, to be corrupt rather than fooled.

He had spent the day composing a letter of reply to the *Radical* and had met the eyes of his staff with a certain over-stated geniality, puzzled as to whether they knew or not. The attack would appear in tomorrow's issue, he had been told by a friend on the *Radical*, but did his staff know as well? The look of disquiet shot at him by Ian Holmes, his newest and most talented editor, himself the son of a leading critic and already possessed of a growing reputation for rapier reviews, particularly troubled him: would he resign in protest, and shame Jerome into following suit? Literature, he could hear Ian proclaim, was a political act, just as all sexual intercourse mirrored sexist oppression in the West. There could be no refuge inside the whale anymore. Jerome stirred in his chair and raised his shoulders to try and lift the weight that troubled him.

When Gabriel walked into the room, the bird in its gilded cage had stopped warbling. Jerome stood up and with a sharp look at his brother, indicated the table. Gabriel blinked at him questioningly, but on seeing the bird his long frame twitched, and rapidly, with a caressing motion, he picked up the cage and scrutinized it.

He was half a head taller than his brother, and his thick

hair had kept its dark colour, but was cut short above his collar while Jerome's greying curls were swept back almost to his shoulders. His indifferent black suit hung emptily on his frame from shoulders set high in his body, so that his seamed and sallow face, with its black eyes often red-rimmed with hay fever, seemed forever thrust forward in concentration. His appearance was more striking than his brother's; sometimes hectic spots of colour suddenly appeared in his cheeks. Jerome wore glasses, with frames that were too heavy for his features, already softened by fleshiness round the nose and mouth. Gabriel's face, with its etched lines, remained vividly in the minds of people who knew Jerome better but somehow could not picture him.

Gabriel's hands prised off the bottom plate of the musical toy to examine the mechanism. They were white, far whiter than his face, and their tapering form was of a different order from Jerome's stubby fingers with their square nails. At Gabriel's evident delight in the bird, Jerome glowed with satisfaction. Again he beat the back of his hand.

'Interesting?' he asked.

'It could be da Rocha's work. It is possible.' Gabriel's voice was reedy and his breath short. He tapped the exposed clockwork parts. 'This way of cutting shallow teeth in the gear wheels, it could be him. He writes how pleased he was that he had devised this because it saved time, and the Emperor K'ang-hsi was demanding and wanted half a dozen musical boxes at a time. Da Rocha made him a dozen clockwork toys of one kind or another. Of course ...' His face clouded. 'It could be someone else's work. I shall have to check.' He looked at his brother. 'Did Wang find it?'

Jerome nodded. 'He was so excited he brought it round to the office. "Very interesting piece for Father Namier." He mimicked the Chinese antiquarian with a grin. 'I knew immediately it was something good. He let me borrow it to show to you, which was good of him.'

Gabriel wound the bird up again, and standing back to admire it, asked his brother for a drink.

'Help yourself,' said Jerome, with annoyance. 'You know where it is.'

Gabriel left the room and returned, carrying a bottle of wine and brushing the dust off the label with his sleeve.

'Cold for a nice burgundy,' he said. 'And really we should let it breathe. Still.' He poured himself a glass and sat down opposite Jerome, sipping at it with an air of concentration.

Jerome's good humour, inspired momentarily by the visible effect the toy had had on his brother, diminished as the old irritation at the priest's easy-going use of his house and cellar re-established itself, and reminded him of the unpleasantness of his day. He sank deeper into the cushions of his arm-chair and gave one of them an irritable punch to adjust its position behind his shoulder.

'Well?'

Gabriel did not reply at once. He looked at the bird, and thought, How close it brings me to Andrew. Andrew da Rocha, he repeated to himself slowly. Andrew da Rocha, SJ like myself, arriving in Peking on the mission to China in 1673, and making bibelots for the Emperor K'ang-hsi's pleasure – a golden cage with a golden bird that whistles and calls, several chiming clocks with ingenious figures, a magic lantern peep-show with wax figures delicately coloured by hand, and a spinet exquisitely inlaid with scenes of Italian topiary gardens. After five years' work at these trinkets Andrew wins an audience before the Dragon Throne and there begins to talk, not of God or Jesus Christ, but of the stars and the fate of man. Does it hang in the stars, in their movement and conjunction? But when the subject of Christ's passion is broached, the emperor waves his ringed fingers and declares that the audience is at an end. The eunuchs take the priest away.

Gabriel smiled drily to himself, still oblivious of Jerome's impatience.

On the shelves of the Jesuit archives in Lisbon lay a set of diaries that chronicled thirty-five years spent in China by Andrea da Rocha, SJ, one of the Portuguese priests in the Jesuits' China mission. The third son of a prosperous wine merchant, Andrew had joined the Society at the age of nineteen, and his account of his life as a missionary was one of the most thorough and revealing ever written by a Jesuit. Gabriel Namier, SJ, had been chosen to edit the diaries because he united in himself an extraordinary and appropriate set of circumstances. Henry Namier, Jerome and Gabriel's father, had built up a small Chinese trading empire first in Tientsin, only seventy miles down the Peiho river from Peking, and then in Shanghai; and in spite of the troubles that convulsed the country from 1906–21, the Namier family had a deep love for China and an intense respect – unusual in the treaty ports – for its people, its culture and its institutions. Both sons were intellectually gifted, but Gabriel, who was born in China in 1908 (Jerome was born in Sussex two years earlier, before the family left), displayed a special affinity with Chinese philosophy and language, and had practised Chinese calligraphy all his life. Although Henry Namier had no religion, he had married – to the horror of her parents – Catherine Staunton, daughter of a celebrated recusant family, so the sons were brought up Catholic. At the age of thirty-two, Gabriel had been ordained a priest of the Society of Jesus. 'It was a moment of profound importance,' the Father General had written to him, 'when the great wisdom of the Western world met the ancient civilization and wisdom of the East; our Society's missionaries were the instrument of this momentous encounter of cultures. You, my dear son in Christ, are now chosen to disseminate the story, because God in His wisdom has seen fit to grant you a knowledge of China and to call you to Himself as His representative.' It had been a long-cherished ambition of Gabriel's to use Andrew's papers for his biography and through it, to describe the Jesuit mission in China at the time. The Father General's approval had filled him with joy.

Gabriel looked at the bird, whose head dropped slowly as the clockwork unwound. For him, history was the writing of scents and sights and pain and joy, not the dry ordering of documents, and he felt he was working well only when his material leaped to life on the page. If Andrew had made the bird, it brought him into the room beside Gabriel in a way the diaries themselves did not. For the diaries were laborious; handwritten in Latin, with many abbreviations and quirks of style, they had taken several months to decode. Gabriel had now translated them all and was busy collating and arranging the immense range of material. For a time he had worked at the Jesuit headquarters in the centre of London, but he had found callers and other duties distracting, and had asked his brother Jerome for the use of a study in his house. Jerome felt that he could not refuse – the house was empty all day – and so the priest had moved in, to work undisturbed. Andrew's voice in the diaries spoke clearly enough through the silence, but the bird was more eloquent, thought Gabriel with a shiver, proclaiming so clearly the depths of triviality Andrew ha' plumbed to please the emperor.

'How powerfully that object evokes da Rocha,' he said carefully at last, noticing a certain reserve in his normally ebullient brother.

'Good,' said Jerome.

Jerome felt that he had gained a small advantage over his brother by presenting him with a clockwork toy that was a first-hand piece of evidence for his subject, but the pleasure had been dissipated for him by Gabriel's apparent coolness. This was not unusual, for the elder brother had always felt eclipsed by the self-possession of the younger. Jerome was jovial, talkative, gregarious and temperamental; at the *Review*, his staff knew how quickly he became inflamed, and how quickly soothed. But often the words Jerome spoke in anger were not forgotten by his victims outside the narrow circle of his old associates. Gabriel inspired greater reverence because he created less trouble for his companions; his even and distant manner seemed the product of an other-worldly intellect which people glibly attributed to his vocation, overlooking the marked worldliness of his tastes and habits. Of the two brothers, Gabriel was unanimously considered the cleverer, and it was fashionable in London literary circles to deplore Jerome's position. 'He is somehow an *unfinished* man,' one writer's wife would remark to a publisher at a party. 'Yes, he never really wrote anything worthwhile since *The Drowning of Phlebas*. Of course, it's far and away the best critique of twentieth-century English poetry. It's still *marvellous*, don't you think?'

Jerome felt his failure keenly. He had fled the demon of academic life, the sapping of creative power by too much teaching and too many administrative problems, only to find himself the quarry of another demon, journalism. Teresa had wanted him to leave Oxford. 'If I have to talk to another don's wife at another dreary dinner in another Charles Addams North Oxford house where the heating's broken down, I shall kill myself,' she said. Jerome understood, and they moved to London, where he wrote criticism for the Sunday papers and eventually became the editor of the *Review*, a literary monthly he began and financed himself with his close friend James Cunliffe. That was twelve years ago, and he had not written anything he cared for since. Gabriel could mask his appetite for recognition, as strong in him as in his brother, under his sacramental role; and by appearing not to care, reflected Jerome, he was applauded all the more.

Jerome knew that Gabriel would hear, probably tomorrow, of his ignominy. In bitterness, Jerome suppressed his desire to tell his brother, but it cost him an effort that ran contrary to his open nature. He continued to sit in silence, drinking vodka, while the sense of grievance grew like a thorn inside him.

The last light of day faded, and the old lady Rosie Murphy came in and began to pull the heavy damask curtains. Jerome would normally have helped his wife Teresa's old Irish nanny, and drawn the curtains together while she waited to adjust the edges and the folds neatly after him. But tonight he let her work on her own.

'Will you be staying for dinner, Father?' she asked Gabriel. He nodded and spread a hand. 'If that's not inconvenient, Nanny,' he said.

'An American ecologist is coming,' said Jerome, filled with resentment that Gabriel had not waited for his invitation. 'One of the new secular breed of doom-merchants.' He added, 'And Paula, I hope.'

'Teresa?' asked Gabriel.

'Later, she's rehearsing.'

'How is it going?' asked Gabriel with little interest.

'Very well, I think,' said Jerome, trying to show enthusiasm. 'It's always a pleasure for everyone when Teresa is working, isn't that so, Nanny?' He laughed.

Rosie Murphy was switching on the table lamps and the lights in the cabinets on either side of the mantelpiece, where Henry Namier's excellent collection of blue-and-white was displayed.

She nodded her head vigorously. 'When Tess isn't acting, I hear her go round and round and round upstairs, up and down her bedroom. It's very bad, she has so much energy. She needs to get out and about. That's a fact.'

'This part is marvellous for her amour-propre,' Jerome added. 'But not for much else, I think.'

'I've forgotten the play,' said Gabriel, drinking his burgundy with appreciation now that its temperature had begun to rise.

'*South Pacific*,' said Jerome, with a look of mischief. 'An updated revival. And *relevant*. That's the crucial factor for today.'

Gabriel's mouth puckered.

'Teresa is the native girl's mother who tries to force the American lieutenant to marry her. The racist theme is being stressed, I believe. But Teresa has a lot of important songs, and she's being given movement classes and lessons in yoga which she enjoys. She spends hours on the bathroom floor in the mornings in positions quite remarkable for a woman of her age.' Jerome laughed briefly. 'The main thing is, she's delighted.'

Gabriel shook his head. 'This contemporary enthusiasm for half-baked oriental mysticism – it is so undisciplined, so ignorant.'

You are pompous, thought Jerome, and you have never understood Teresa. He suffered from his wife's faddishness – the loom she had imported at immense cost from Finland that stood unattended and unused in the basement. But, like a writer who is prepared to denounce his own work but bridles ferociously at another's criticism, he could not tolerate others' aspersions on his wife.

'I'm going up to change,' he said aloud. He wanted to add: Today has been such an ordeal. But he controlled himself, and left the room.

Halfway up the stairs, he heard the tinkling song of the clockwork toy, and some lines of Yeats that he loved entered his mind:

> Once out of nature I shall never take
> My bodily form from any natural thing,
> But such a form as Grecian goldsmiths make
> Of hammered gold and gold enamelling

To keep a drowsy Emperor awake;
Or set upon a golden bough to sing
To lords and ladies of Byzantium
Of what is past, or passing, or to come.

He turned the words over slowly on his tongue, feeling them
work on his nerves like balm.

❧ CHAPTER 2

Gabriel sank himself into the blue and chalk-white patternings of the Namier drawing-room furniture and lit a small cigar between his long fingers. He had given up cigarettes altogether, except for the occasional box of Turkish No. 3 from Sullivan and Powell, and rarely smoked while reading or writing. He heard the doorbell ring and Nanny move slowly to answer it. The prospect of playing host to an American journalist bored him, so he was relieved when he heard her exclaim and laugh with pleasure.

A light rapid voice said, 'I must have left my tools here, Rosie. Have you seen them? And how's things with you today?'

Rosie Murphy said drily, 'Fair, as usual.'

'Can I have a look?' A young man moved with speed into the room where Gabriel was sitting, spun around, threw out a quick 'Hi' to the figure of the priest on the sofa and then pounced with a cry of delight on a square metal box half concealed under the harpsichord by the window.

'There you are, you little blighters.' He laughed. 'Thank God I've found you. I wouldn't know what to do without you.' He brushed his long blond hair out of his eyes, apologized with a smile to Gabriel for disturbing him and was gone.

The boy smiled without parting his lips, with a slow curving of his mouth and dimpling of his cheeks, and although Gabriel did not articulate the peculiarity in his mind, the smile stayed with him and caused the priest a spasm, not of pain, but of pleasure in pain, for the smile passed straight through his hard hide of lonely self-absorption.

He called, 'And who was that, Miss Murphy?' Gabriel could

be arch, but he was using Nanny's formal name on this occasion to conceal the serious edge of his curiosity.

She came in shaking her head and laughing, and told Gabriel his name, Oliver Summers, and his work, at the Institute of Baroque Music round the corner. 'He's a natural from cloud-cuckoo land,' she said indulgently, clasping her knotted hands together in mock exasperation.

Impatiently, Gabriel asked, 'What was his business here?'

'Haven't you seen him before?' She pointed to the harpsichord. 'He tunes it for Teresa, though she never plays. But if the whim comes upon her, and it's out of tune, we never hear the end of it.'

Gabriel nodded. 'I see,' he said non-committally.

But again within him some painful unremembered desire stirred a dull root and he tried to quell it. He knew that it had something to do with his relationship to Andrew da Rocha, the subject of almost all his waking thoughts. For as Gabriel sank himself deeper into the sensitive personality of the Jesuit missionary, he became more deeply disturbed by the conflict – between the pomp of courtly life in Peking and the austerity of the priestly vocation – which had caused Andrew acute mental anguish. Rocha's attitude to the world, the flesh and the Devil – a useful cliché in Gabriel's opinion – was forcing Gabriel himself to reconsider his own attitudes. Gabriel Namier had long justified his appetite for food and wine and other luxuries in two ways: first, he believed that he did not crave them and therefore was not yielding to desire, and second, that he enjoyed them in a way that ran silkily with the grain of his best nature and the gifts bestowed on him by God. He respected the *Tao Te Ching*, which declares that the sage should be empty of desire. To rein in his tastes would be to run counter to his own nature and exacerbate his desires. Such violence would bear no good results. Gabriel appreciated that this was a Taoist, and not a Christian – or at least Augustinian – point of view, but he believed that pessimistic and dualist theology was exhausted, and he followed, though not very closely, the new philosophical redefinitions of the nature of original sin. He never endorsed the view, even when he was an impressionable and passionate young seminarian and ascetic practices were encouraged, that the use of physical penances – the scourge, the spiked thong on the thigh, bare knees on stone while praying – could diminish the stain of evil on the human soul. There was a relationship between physical mortification and the mystical state of ecstasy, which he had explored in an early work on the Christian vision, but he did not see it as an important ethic on the moral plane.

Gabriel also justified his life of ease with the contemporary argument that priests should not be set above or apart from the laity by external marks of distinction, but should merge and mingle in order to proselytize with more effect. The deviousness of this argument was not lost on him, and he often chuckled at the nonsense written by progressive Catholics about whether or not priests should wear jeans or Jesuits live in rented lodgings instead of the security of the Order's great community houses. Gabriel himself had rarely worn a dog collar in his life. With comfortable arrogance, he expected people to know he was a priest without being informed.

Close study of Andrew da Rocha's papers had however begun to trouble Gabriel's equanimity. The Jesuit missionary in Peking continually reproached himself in his diaries for allowing the style of life of a Chinese mandarin, which he led when he was in the Emperor K'ang-hsi's favour, to seduce him into a Chinese way of thought. This was of its very nature inimical to the worship of a personal God. Andrew often cried out in pain and prayer for help from God, begging Him in the words of the psalms to guide His servant out of the abyss. The Jesuits had acquired magnificence, power, wealth, and Andrew was ashamed, although he often wore a hair shirt next to his skin under the silken robes and furs sent to him by the emperor.

In 1692, the Jesuit suit at court was successful: Christians became free to worship and their priests to preach openly. When Franciscan and Dominican missionaries began arriving in China, they were aghast to find the Jesuits arrayed in the embroidered and gilded costumes of the mandarins, living in vermilion and lacquered and gold villas in the Tartar City under the Imperial City walls, with trains of servants, litters to carry them about the streets, and outriders running before them with the emblems of their rank. In bare feet and home-spun robes the friars stood in the fetid sewage of Peking's alleys and brandished their wooden crucifixes, preaching aloud in Italian, Spanish, Latin, whichever language they chose, to the astonished passers-by. They were soon rounded up by the authorities, who found such behaviour, no matter how lunatic, seditious and rabble-rousing. The Jesuits up-braided the friars for jeopardizing the Christian mission in China by their rashness. But the friars protested that they at least followed the ideals of Christ and were not betraying Him in satin.

Andrew da Rocha felt such attacks keenly, and although he reported to his superior in Macao the high comedy of the friars' antics, he confided serious doubts to his diary. The boundary between priest and mandarin in himself was being worn down, and he prayed in torment for help to shore it up again.

Gabriel was deeply moved by his subject's pleas, and it be-came impossible for him to avoid applying them to himself. It did not make him refrain from drinking his brother's best wines or commit him to any abstinence, but it opened him to outside experience and offered up the quivering quick inside him to a new world from which he shrank, like a clam prised open by a boy's penknife. Gabriel took no action upon his anxiety and had not yet even discussed it with fellow members of the Society. But he was considering doing so. The one area he dared not even contemplate was Andrew da Rocha's relation to the servant whom he kept by his side to attend to all his personal needs. A fellow Jesuit, the Frenchman Father Joachim Pernet, wrote a confidential letter to the superior in Macao accusing da Rocha of unnatural conduct. Gabriel found the enmity of one Jesuit for another in the tiny inflamed community of Peking normal enough, though the virulence of Pernet's de-nunciation was unpleasant; but he was more troubled by the issue of Rocha's homosexuality, and he was finding it difficult to tackle the chapter of his book in which he must discuss it.

The doorbell of Jerome's house rang again, but Gabriel did not move. He heard his brother come downstairs hurriedly and open the door. Together, Jerome and Larry Marks entered the room. The American ecologist was swarthy, with prominent teeth and heavy-rimmed glasses. He shook Gabriel's languid hand and introduced himself. Jerome offered him vodka, but he asked for a soft drink.

'Who was that earlier?' asked Jerome. 'I thought it might be Paula, though she has a key, I believe.' Looking over his shoulder at Gabriel, he handed Larry Marks his drink.

Gabriel replied stiffly, 'It was a young man who had left something behind. He tuned the harpsichord, I believe.'

Jerome nodded. 'Oliver Summers, good, good. Teresa should be pleased.' He turned to the American. 'My wife Teresa plays the piano, but she now has got it into her head that she prefers the harpsichord. I like the sound better myself. But the damn thing's never in tune, and she used to spend hours fiddling with bits and pieces of leather and nail scissors trying to tune it herself until she was too exhausted to play. Do you play anything yourself?'

Marks was about to reply, but Jerome continued, heartily, 'As good luck would have it, the curator of the instruments next door in the Institute of Baroque Music – it's a fine collection, by the way, you should look in on it – is a delightful young chap, and most obliging, and he comes in to play here from time to time and tunes it.'

Gabriel lifted his eyebrows. 'He's young for the job, isn't he?'

Jerome chuckled. 'We're old, and everyone looks young.' He paused, and then added, 'Besides, baroque instruments – it's not a big field.' His eyes twinkled for a moment behind his glasses, then darkened. 'Not like the world of letters.' He looked across at the American, who shook his head in sympathy but turned immediately to Gabriel, speaking rapidly.

'Father,' he began, surprising Gabriel, who was not accustomed to the use of the word by his brother's friends, 'I am one of your most devoted admirers. Your book *Vision and Prophecy* is a masterwork.' His face glowed with eagerness. 'You have a great following back home, you know.'

Gabriel brushed the compliment aside with a wave of his slender hand. 'My dear sir, you are too kind.' *Vision and Prophecy*, which Gabriel had written just after the war, had recently been re-issued in paperback with a psychedelic cover, and the ensuing correspondence from psychics and would-be seers in America and England had tried Gabriel's patience more than stupidity usually did. The response in his view consisted for the most part of nothing but tiresome reminiscences of déjà-vu incidents, tedious accounts of coincidences, of fulfilled dreams, of puerile dabblings at planchette and spiritualism. Gabriel hoped Larry Marks would not engage him in conversation of the fashionable occult order, and so he asked him what work he himself was doing. The American attributed the priest's evasion to humility and thought how refreshing it was to meet an author who did not want to talk about his own books at length.

Marks was describing his study of the whaling industry and the disappearance of the world's largest mammal when Paula, Jerome's younger daughter, strode into the room, and unzipping herself quickly out of a tight quilted patchwork jacket, flopped onto the sofa, her long legs stretched out in front of her. She pulled off the knitted cap she was wearing and ran her fingers through her dark spiky hair which then stood out untidily in tufts. Her chin was pointed and her steady grey eyes turned up at the corners giving her an eldritch air; but even in repose, a crease of anxiety and concentration persisted between her brows. She had a way of glancing sidelong and grinning before saying something. It was one of her methods of provocation, and it was captivating. But Paula was trying not to be captivating, and her manner was deliberately offhand, as if to say, 'I'm not trying to be liked, to be charming,' although she craved to be both.

'Am I late?' she said. 'What's happening?'

She reached across to Gabriel, and squeezed his hand. 'How's the Pope?' Gabriel smiled with a slight twitch of his upper lip. Her father she acknowledged silently.

'Like a glass of wine, darling?'

She accepted with a grin, noticing unusual reticence in his manner. He introduced her to Larry Marks.

'You Namiers are quite something,' said Marks, affecting the wowed American and scratching his head.

Jerome chuckled. 'I used to be known as Henry's son. Then, when I married my wife, I became Tess Henson's young man – though God knows I've never been young. Later, when Gabriel sprang to fame as the next best thing to Gerard Manley Hopkins, I became known as his brother. Now people come up to me and say, "You must be Paula's father" or "What does it feel like to have a daughter married to David Clark?" He's a war photographer, my daughter Francesca's husband.'

Larry Marks nodded. 'I know his work. It's great.'

Jerome chuckled and drank his vodka.

Paula eyed him and said, 'He sees himself as King Lear, really. And neither I nor my sister is Cordelia, I can tell you.' She laughed and her steady eyes caught her father's, but he blinked and did not respond.

She turned on the sofa and tucking her lanky limbs under her rocked forward on her hands.

'I walked over.' She threw her arms wide. 'It was so peaceful on the Heath. Neither dark nor light, but halfway between. Beautiful.'

> 'The moon is up, and yet it is not night.
> Sunset divides the sky with her . . .'

Jerome recited quietly. 'But I wish you wouldn't at this late hour, darling, I really do.'

'Rats,' said Paula. She shook her head crossly. 'You just can't go around being suspicious of everybody all the time. We'd never move out of our houses. Anyway, going in a car, that's suicide.' She was headstrong, and would never have admitted to her father that there had been a time on the Heath when a gaggle of teenage boys surrounded her and squirted her with Jif lemon juice and she had fought it out of her eyes determined not to weep though the smarting was terrible and fear was clamped under her ribs.

'Do you live far?' asked Marks.

Paula had the garden flat of a Victorian house on the other side of the Heath. She had a large room facing west where she could paint and draw, and a bedroom beside it with windows giving onto a flight of rickety wooden steps into a small wild garden which she sporadically tended. She had rented the flat from friends, a painter and his wife who had left for the west coast on an exchange fellowship. Paula took it because when she heard they needed a tenant she realized at last that her two-year-long affair with the man with whom she lived was over and that she was hungry for solitude. To mark her new condition, she had cut her hair shorter than any male contemporary, given up make-up and felt every muscle in her body hum with new vitality.

Jerome was pleased the affair had ended, because, as he put it, 'the fellow wasn't up to much – he was always asleep whenever I called.' But after the separation he observed Paula with solicitude, to which she responded with an airy smile of well-being. She was much too proud to admit any hurt; and she considered public display of unhappiness a crime against society. She had seen at a circus a clown in whiteface pin a paper heart to his shirt and heard the crowd sigh with sentiment; but such sympathy was worse in Paula's view than none at all, and she hid her wounds. No one knew therefore what she felt about the failure of her love for John, and they worried impotently about her resolute and breezy manner.

Nanny came in; dinner was ready. She was not sitting with them in the dining-room, because Larry Marks was an outsider and a guest, and Jerome looked at her apologetically, upset once again that his wife's theatrical career forced work on the old lady who had brought her up. Against the walls stood Henry Namier's fine coromandel screens. They gave the room an inner framework of ebony and gold and oxblood lacquer, where rain dragons pursued each other in the heavens and sages composed poems in eyries perched on dreaming cloud-swathed crags. It was a dark, wine-coloured room; as children Paula and Francesca had played ghosts and hidden behind the screens and under the floorlength velvet tablecloth. As they sat down to dinner now, Jerome asked his daughter how she was and how her work was going. But she left the room to help Nanny in the kitchen, tossing her head and replying impatiently, 'Fine, fine.' There was nothing Paula found more irritating than her father's doting interest in her; yet the driving force behind her life continued to be thirst for approval, especially from him.

Paula was twenty-three, and her father's favourite. He had called her Paula because he had been convinced that she would be a boy, and he overcame his disappointment by schooling her in amazonian ideals, telling her with relish of Paula, the Roman patrician who had joined his namesake Saint Jerome's ascetic circle and had founded one of the first convents. Jerome Namier had escaped the circumstances that made his brother a priest, and since the age of eighteen, he had not been to church except to sightsee. But he admired nuns: in his eyes they were courageous, resourceful, and selfless.

For him Saint Jerome's Paula was a woman of spirit, capable of throwing over the traces of a conventional matron's life in order to sail across the Mediterranean to the Holy Land with a half-crazed scholar-hermit who was leaving Rome because he was offended that he had not been elected Pope. 'Haha!' Jerome would cry, understanding well the bitterness of failed ambition.

Although Paula Namier knew this private version of female heroism so well that she was sick of it, his lessons about strong-willed women had penetrated deep into her when she was a child and she continued to strive to find ways of imposing her wishes on circumstance. The move to her new flat was an example of her wilfulness.

'What work do you do?' asked Marks, picking up his host's question as Paula, going round the table, handed him a plate.

She told him she was illustrating a dictionary of mythology for twelve- to sixteen-year-olds. The American looked at her with interest. 'That sounds fascinating.' He then added with solemnity, 'Myth has universal application, and in my field for instance, I am constantly struck by the relevance ...' (Gabriel caught Jerome's eye and smiled). '... of certain stories.' He had put down his fork and gestured in the air. 'That kid on a dolphin, what's his name – Arion – well, that reveals the Greeks' attitude of reciprocity and trust with the animal kingdom, which we unfortunately have lost.'

Paula nodded. He waved away the chicken dish she offered him, muttering he was a vegetarian.

'My dear chap, I'm so sorry,' interposed Jerome. 'Would you like an omelette? Rosie ... Paula ...'

But Marks plunged on unconcerned. 'The myth of Orpheus who stills the beasts with music – why that just shows that the spear and the bow and arrow and the harpoon gun and the bludgeon ...' The colour was rising to his cheeks. 'They're not the only means we have of relating to the other inhabitants of this spaceship earth.'

Paula laughed. 'We could hardly have gone exploring in Africa armed with harps and lutes, could we?'

'No, no,' said the American, forking some broccoli into his mouth. 'Myth should not be taken literally.'

Jerome laid a hand on Gabriel's arm.

'This talk of harps and lutes has reminded me of something I wanted to tell you earlier. That young fellow, Summers, you saw here earlier is an expert instrument-maker. Wasn't your man da Rocha in that line as well?'

Before his brother had finished, Gabriel understood the connection between himself and Oliver as vividly as the afterimage of a dream on waking. He laughed to himself. Of course, da Rocha had made a spinet for the Emperor K'ang-hsi, composed a handbook about its construction and methods of play, in Chinese 'so that I might improve my writing style a little'. Da Rocha had deeply impressed the young emperor when on the softly sounding keyboard he reproduced the Chinese melody played to him beforehand by the court's musicians. A vermilion decree had followed, naming da Rocha to the fourth grade of mandarin, which permitted him outriders and heralds when he rode through the streets and placed a lapis lazuli button in his cap and embroidered a wild goose on his breast. The emperor commanded him to create three more 'nightingale tables' for the Dragon Throne. Naturally, Andrew felt obliged to refuse the mandarin's rank, but the emperor considered his refusal a rebuff, and Andrew had to comply ... Gabriel felt a sense of relief that his response to Oliver Summers was so simple, and a flush of pleasure at the links that connect one human being to another. But the feeling did not unbind the knot of discomfort that still remained in the pit of his stomach. A second image struck Gabriel as precisely and as sharply as a bell rung in the still air of a convent precinct, and it was more profoundly disturbing; as he recalled the young man's slow smile, he was pierced again but this time by the memory of the angel in the *Virgin of the Rocks* in the National Gallery, who smiles and yet does not smile, while the light emanating from the Christ Child suffuses his composed and seraphic features. Some time ago, Gabriel had contemplated the painting for an afternoon, fascinated at first by the orientalism of the peaks and needles of rock rising out of the translucent blue cavern of the background and wondering how Leonardo could have dreamed up the unique configuration of the Yangtze river's pinnacled gorges. Then he remembered – or had he imagined it? – the psychological interpretation that the jagged background represented the cave of the womb, the *vagina dentata*, which Christ had escaped through birth from a virgin whose womb was never opened, from a mother who was never a yawning abyss into which a man falls and is swallowed up. At first the Virgin's sweetness and tranquillity abrogated for Gabriel this nightmare netherworld, but gradually it was the angel kneeling by the mother and her child who came to epitomize for him an ideal. His features became engraved on Gabriel's imagination, so that although the memory had slept now for a decade or more, it was still as sharply defined on his retina as if he held it under a glass. With annoyance, he tried to drive it away, ashamed at the seriousness with which he was taking the encounter.

Jerome was saying, 'He could probably comment intelligently on da Rocha's work. He is something of a musical historian. Why don't you consult him?'

'I might,' said Gabriel cautiously. 'It's an idea.'

Jerome sat back, listening to Larry and Paula's conversation. He felt too burdened by the problem of the *Review* to take part, but he was pleased that once again he had asserted himself as a guide to his brother's researches.

'The cosmos no longer belongs to man to use for his own pleasure or to satisfy his greed,' Larry Marks was saying. 'He is just one among the creatures, *primus inter pares* perhaps, but one among many. I remember going for a walk when I was a kid, and nature was still a very mysterious lady to me. It was in North Carolina, Cape Hatteras. Beautiful long dunes and sedge and seabirds. I was walking in a wood and I came across this sign: "You are in cottonmouth country. In this land, man is a trespasser." It went on that if harm came to anyone it was their own fault. Well, I guess some crazy farmer put it up to warn people off his land. The cottonmouth is a really deadly snake named, you see, for the white venom that foams around its mouth. So it was a pretty effective notice.' He laughed, baring his own prominent teeth, and Paula shuddered. 'That was the first time I realized man wasn't king of the universe.'

Paula looked across at her uncle, who was half listening to the conversation. 'Gabriel,' she began in a bantering tone, 'what do you say to that? At school I was told God had created everything and given Adam and Eve dominion over it ... How does it go, something about subduing ...?'

'Yes,' said Gabriel, laconically. 'Be fruitful and multiply, and replenish the earth and subdue it, and have dominion over the fish of the sea, and over the fowl of the air, and over every living thing that moveth upon the earth.' His voice was melancholy. 'Man is the centre of the Christian universe, the only creature made in the image of God.'

'But that doesn't necessarily imply that man has to exploit everything for his own ends,' protested Marks.

'Genesis doesn't have to be taken literally either,' said Gabriel with a warning gleam in his small bright eyes. 'Nevertheless, I do not think it will bear an ecological interpretation.'

'My uncle is famous for his liberal attitude to scripture,' said Paula. 'You don't have to believe any of it according to him.'

Gabriel winced. 'Not so, as you very well know.' But his tone was kindly.

Larry Marks would have liked to pursue the theme, but he sensed a difficulty in the atmosphere that he could not define. Gabriel looked over at Paula. He thought, She has her mother's vivacity, but her intelligence is keener. He liked her for it. Under the gawky bohemianism he recognized an alert liveliness, and unwittingly she had fingered one of the crucial distinctions that in Gabriel's view existed between Christianity's personal God, who is the apex of a formal and hierarchical universe, and Chinese pantheism's sense of the unity of all creation and equality of all in the flux of things. Gabriel's studies of the activities of his Order in China had led him to find, as Andrew da Rocha had found, much that was very attractive in Chinese religious philosophy. But it was dangerous territory for him to wander in, as Gabriel recognized, having found his way there the first time through his book on Christian visionaries, whose mysticism also often had a strong pantheistic bent. He must talk to his niece at a later stage. Her mind is quick and fresh and sceptical, he thought. She might inadvertently illuminate something for me.

'What drives me mad in the myths I'm illustrating,' continued Paula, 'is the hatred of women which constantly turns up in the stories. It may be rooted in fear, but it comes out in sheer savagery. When the women aren't being raped, they're being abandoned or destroyed or sometimes both at once. Listen, in the dictionary, A is for Ariadne. She's dumped on a rock in mid-ocean after rescuing Theseus. She's a drag, OK, she's in love, and she's adhesive. But A is also for Andromeda – another girl left on a wretched rock, "naked for the birds to peck." Charming. A is also for Amazon – all massacred by Hercules as one of his labours. I tell you it's disgusting.'

Larry Marks could not help laughing. But Jerome looked at his daughter with concern for her vehemence.

Gabriel too noted the sudden coarseness of her language, and decided that it reflected a straining in her thought which dulled the lucidity and humour he had appreciated earlier.

'It is time for our generation to see the fulfilment of women,' began Marks recovering his solemnity. 'Feminism is a big thing in the States right now. Is it here?'

Paula shot him a quick look, marvelling at his lack of wit, and then turned a bright eye on her father and uncle, challenging them to answer.

'What about goddesses?' said her father, without much enthusiasm. He was finding it difficult to concentrate on the talk around him. 'Aphrodite, Athene, Artemis – they're pretty powerful in themselves, aren't they?'

Gabriel decided to make an effort for the sake of Paula's earlier understanding, and he spoke before she could reply. 'It is important to disentangle the historical and ritual elements of myth from the superficial narrative.' He tapped the table with his fork. 'Andromeda is an account of a sacrifice made to appease the gods – I forgot what exactly had happened. But all the myths you mention contain memories of a barbaric age of bloodshed and human sacrifice to primitive gods who were feared by men. We overcame this long ago – with the New Testament, the Good News of Christ. The psychological attitudes revealed in such myths concern men's relations with the gods, not the relations between men and women. And it

25

would be a mistake to interpret the societies in which they lived from their myths.' He paused. 'There is however an element of truth in what you say.' He smiled at Paula, his thin and sallow face lighting up with surprising warmth. 'Because Theseus is the epitome of the heroic warrior, the new male superman, if you like, the paragon of a military race, who comes to dominate the ancient peaceful agricultural society and overthrow the fertility goddesses and the earth mothers of ancient worship.'

Paula observed her uncle with excitement, and did not answer except to incline her head in acknowledgement. It was a long and committed speech for Gabriel, who normally sat in silence at the Namier dinner table, and she was surprised and flattered by his attention.

'I have always maintained – as you well know my darling – ' said Jerome, 'that women are superior to men in every aspect. Beauty – men are revolting in appearance after their first youth. Look at the present company – you will forgive me, Mr Marks.' He laughed. 'As for brains and goodness, men cannot hold a candle to the female sex. It's men who torture, kill, fight . . .'

Paula shrugged her shoulders impatiently. 'You know that's not the point, Daddy.'

She hesitated, wondering whether it was worth proceeding with a topic on which all men and especially her father were purblind. 'It's a reflection of the same problem,' she said hastily, 'to say women are better than men. It's the same as saying men are better than women because . . .'

She was interrupted by the entrance of her mother, closely followed by a wand-like young man in painted gym shoes, then by Rosie who was pleading with her former charge, Teresa Namier (stage name Henson) to eat some dinner.

Teresa shook her head, and then smiled and said : 'All right, Nanny, all right, I'll have a yoghurt.' She turned to the young man. 'Would you like one too, Wayne?'

'Fine,' he said in a flat voice. He moved around the table with a springy tight step, his hands thrust down into his donkey-jacket pockets, his head poked forward.

'This,' said Teresa, 'is my family. Husband.' She pointed at Jerome. 'Brother-in-law. Younger daughter. And?' She looked enquiringly at Larry Marks. 'Don't know you,' she said. 'Husband's friend. This is Wayne Dupree, my movement teacher.'

Wayne Dupree sank his head deeper into his coat and pulling out some liquorice papers and tobacco, deftly rolled himself a black cigarette.

'Want one?' he said, holding it up to Paula's face.

'No, thanks,' she said.

Teresa pulled up a chair to the table. She was a very thin woman, with black curly hair pinned up with studied untidiness on the top of her head. She looked like one of Bonnard's bathing studies. It was from her mother that Paula had inherited her high cheekbones and pointed chin. Teresa's nose was thin and pronounced. 'It ruined my career in films,' she would wail. 'When I turned my head this nose of mine suddenly appeared full length for all to see, like a Sicilian stiletto.' Her eyes which were ringed in mascara and kohl, were even now, in her fifties, as moody and expressive as they had been in adolescence, but her voice had developed a theatrical huskiness. It represented a considerable change from the rounded ladylike tones that had made her, despite the nose, the darling of wartime films, in which she had appeared as a nurse or a WAAF, always virtuous, if coquettish. Jerome used to call her 'My beauty', a name which caught for him both the voluptuousness of her dream image and the stoniness of her rare desire. Teresa's veiled eyes when he first saw her reminded him of Baudelaire's lines:

> Car j'ai pour fasciner ces dociles amants,
> De purs miroirs qui font toutes choses plus belles:
> Mes yeux, mes larges yeux aux clartés éternelles!

He wanted to talk to her alone, to retire upstairs to their bedroom and sit while she wiped her face with cream and smoothed it off with tissue in the mirror where he could see her three times reflected, and tell her of his troubles at the *Review*. Her theatrical friends always reminded him how excluded he was from the world she truly loved; and even in his old age he felt jealous fear as keenly as he had in his thirties, looking now at Wayne Dupree and noting with repugnance his flaccid face, the hoop in one ear, the full bottom lip.

Teresa picked up his irritation and rebelled against what she considered her husband's tiresome proprietary stance. And he's been drinking, I bet, she thought. With an exaggerated semblance of casual youthfulness she tipped back her chair (he was extremely fond of his delicate set) and announced: 'I'm whacked, but it's a fabulous feeling. How was your dinner?' She ·looked purposefully away from her husband to Paula and Gabriel.

Jerome pushed back his chair and said harshly, 'Let's adjourn. Paula, make some coffee, please. I don't like Nanny doing everything.' He looked over at his wife reproachfully, but she did not move.

When Paula returned with the tray, Wayne Dupree sniffed and twirled a strand of hair between his fingers.

'What are you?' he asked Larry Marks.

'What am I? I'm a kind of scientist . . .'

'He means, "What sign are you born under?" ' interrupted Paula with a smile.

'Ah,' said Marks. 'Pisces.'

'And your old man?' Wayne asked Paula.

'Taurus.'

'Far out,' said Wayne. 'But it figures. And you? Let me see.' He rolled his eyes and placed a finger on his lips. 'You have to be Aquarius.'

'No.' said Paula, 'I'm Virgo, Virgo the Virgin.' She laughed.

'Yeah?' said Wayne. 'Well your mother is Gemini, like all great actresses, aren't you, darling?'

'Two natures aren't enough, darling,' said Teresa, echoing him with a gaiety intended to grate on her husband, whose ill-temper was growing fast. 'I am multi-faceted, aren't I?' She turned to Jerome. He hesitated, then produced his handkerchief and wiped his mouth, clearing his throat in an effort at polite laughter. He leant down to Gabriel, in an armchair drinking his coffee, and his brother's evident apathy stung him.

'Why do I have to allow this in my own house?' he said under his breath.

Paula started. 'Daddy,' she said warningly.

Jerome ignored her. 'Why don't you go roaming around picturesque Soho, my dear,' he walked up to his wife, 'with your fine friends who are so much more amusing than your old husband, and explore your several personalities?' His eyes sought hers, the plea in them contradicting his violence.

Teresa turned away from him, but without resolution. She

looked at her daughter and then at Wayne.

'He's jealous,' she said in a sing-song, and poked Wayne with her foot where he had squatted down in front of Paula to read her hand. 'Tell him there's no reason, do.'

Jerome glared at them both. 'I'm going up,' he said, producing his handkerchief again.

Larry Marks sprang to his feet, bubbling gratitude for the evening. Jerome waved him goodbye, and catching a shadow of concern pass over his daughter's face, said gently, 'Darling, if there's ever anything you need, for your flat or anything else, let me know.'

Paula bridled, angry that her own anxiety had been fobbed off by his.

Wayne Dupree wove a serpentine path round the room and finally settled cross-legged on the carpet with one neat swivelling motion of his hips. Hugging his plimsolled feet, he leant forward and spoke to Gabriel who, savouring the smoke of one of his brother's after-dinner cigars, was viewing the room through half-closed eyes.

'Get this, man, you must be Scorpio, through and through.'

Gabriel exhaled lightly. 'I think not.'

'When were you born then?'

'June the fifth.'

'Far out,' said Wayne Dupree. 'Another Gemini.'

'And what does it tell you?' asked Teresa. 'About old Gabs, I mean.' She took a cigarette Wayne offered her and lit it.

'Gemini are devious.' He threw back his head and laughed. 'Like when they seem to be one thing, then they're really something else. Like Steppenwolf. Secret lives.'

Gabriel urged a faint smile to his lips. He thought, Why do the young like Hesse, amongst all soi-disant metaphysical writers? Why Hesse?

Paula began pulling tobacco from the packet Wayne had thrown down on the coffee table. 'I've just about given up giving up,' she said to herself. She breathed in thankfully and looked at her uncle.

'Didn't you tell me once,' she asked thoughtfully, 'that your Jesuits in China insinuated themselves into the emperor's favour because they were such good astrologers?'

Gabriel did not open his eyes. 'Astronomers,' he said with quiet emphasis.

'What's the difference, man? It's all in the stars, anyway, my lovely.' Wayne Dupree folded his arms behind his head and tucked his feet over his knees lotus-style.

'Seriously,' said Paula, 'what is the difference?'

Her uncle looked at her sharply. 'I'm enjoying an excellent burgundy and a splendid cigar and you want me to repeat lessons you should have learned at your mother's knee.'

Teresa replied gaily, 'But I think you're ducking the question.'

Gabriel opened his eyes and leant forward, drawing scrolls of smoke in the air as he gestured. 'It is true, the seventeenth century did not draw the boundary between the two disciplines.' His voice came down with light sarcasm on the word. 'Not as clearly as we do. But astronomy is a science; astrology the superstitious application of the science.'

'Not superstitious. That's not fair. Religious, spiritual. Like you, darling,' exclaimed Wayne, pouting and casting up his eyes in reproof at Gabriel.

Gabriel eyed the anaemic-looking dancer with unconcealed dislike and said nothing. Paula pressed on, ignoring Wayne. She was used to her mother's entourage. 'But what did the Jesuits in China do? Where did they draw the distinction? What did your man, what's-his-name, what did he think of it?'

Gabriel wondered if the pointedness of Paula's questions arose from ignorant curiosity, or from special percipience on her part and, with unaccustomed humility, he spoke gently in reply:

'There, my dear, you have touched on the central dilemma of the Jesuit mission in China. They hoped to convert China from the top by converting the emperor, the symbolic and political heart of the people. They were prepared to yield up all the scientific and mechanical knowledge of the West into Chinese hands in order to gain access to his ear. The Chinese and later the Manchu rulers desired above all to possess the Jesuits' mathematical skills, because they wanted to apply them to the study of the heavens. You cannot overestimate how important astronomy was to the Empire: every night for three thousand years observers watched the skies from platforms in the southern capital of Nanking and the northern capital of Peking. Five mathematicians watched the movements of the heavens, one facing the zenith, four others facing the points of the compass, a quincunx at the top of each observatory tower . . .'

Wayne Dupree whistled under his breath. 'Too much,' he said softly, shaking his hair. Gabriel ignored him and continued, eyes half-closed as he smoked.

'Although the Chinese kept astonishing records of their observations, their astronomy had become very inaccurate, partly because they had clumsy instruments, and partly because they knew no geometry. The Jesuits who volunteered for the China mission were trained in these arts.' Gabriel paused. 'You can still see in Peking the instruments they made, on the city wall, where they stood to watch the stars.' He looked hard at the group in front of him. 'The Jesuits only became court astronomers in order to convert the Chinese to Christianity; but throughout the Chinese used their astronomy to predict lucky and unlucky days, propitious times for the emperor to marry or issue forth on a tour of inspection; in short, they applied the science to their own superstitions. Or . . .' He looked at Wayne Dupree, and added with an effort, 'Or religion, if you wish.'

'Wow,' said Wayne, shaking his head. 'Why didn't I go to school?'

Paula smiled at Gabriel. 'It's very sad.'

'Yes,' he replied. 'But they came quite close to their goal at one stage.' He stubbed out his cigar and handed her the ashtray. 'Take it to the kitchen, my dear. It does make the room smell so.'

He got to his feet with a heavy movement, and held a hand to his chest momentarily to catch his breath. Then he extended it to Wayne Dupree ceremoniously. 'It is interesting to historians like myself when ancient ideas endure.' He did not add, However bastardized their modern forms.

He waved two limp fingers in Teresa's direction, as if conferring on her an absent-minded benediction.

In the hall, Paula picked up his coat and helped him on with it. 'Is Daddy all right?' she asked.

'I think so,' said Gabriel. 'Your mother tries his temper, which as you know has never been good.'

Paula pulled on her jacket and left the house beside him. Outside, as they walked out into Grove Lane, she said on an impulse: 'Walk home with me. It's not late, and it's such a bore to get a cab.' She looked up at him. 'Walking is good for insomnia, it tires you out.' She kicked one booted heel against her toe. 'And it's a bit late to walk alone.' She kept her eyes down, ashamed at her admission.

'I've been told that before,' said Gabriel indifferently. 'Nothing has helped me sleep though – except prayer. And that only rarely.'

He smiled down at her. Gabriel liked to wander among the city's streets when a thought proved difficult to form or the words would not come. In the summer, hay fever kept him indoors, but it was April now and tonight he felt that diamond awakeness that presaged a white night.

'Yes,' he said, 'there is a fine sky.'

The priest and his niece turned their faces to the stars and then to each other. With a rapid smile, Paula slipped her arm through his and they turned down the street together towards the pond on the hill and the Heath that lay beyond.

❧ CHAPTER 3

'It is quite a long walk,' said Paula apologetically, as they approached the Whitestone Pond. At that time of year it lay empty, like the listening dish of a radar plant. Paula had rarely been alone in the company of her uncle, and her curiosity was aroused. 'It will do me good, no doubt,' he said cheerfully.

They crossed the junction. At the steep descent towards the Vale of Health, Paula said, 'I'll lead, I know the way.' It was sandy underfoot and bumpy. Away from the street lamps her eyes quickly became accustomed to the night, and she stepped surely down the narrow path towards the willows in the hollow. But the eyes of Gabriel Namier were older and he stumbled in the darkness.

'Careful,' she said.

It was mild for an April night; the air was soft but dry. Two of the willows were split open, their branches collapsed from the bole, but symmetrically, so that they seemed to Paula the ribbons of a maypole after the dancers have let them fall whirling towards the central trunk. Two weeks ago she had sat down beside a bush and drawn them until her numbed fingers could no longer move her pencil on the page.

'Look, Gabriel,' she said, taking his arm as he caught her up on the level ground, 'look at those willow trees.'

'I can hardly see,' he said. Then, after a pause, 'Yes, what happened?'

'I don't know, perhaps they were too weak for a storm.' She released his arm and walked on.

Both the girl and the Jesuit were now aware of the shadows which played under the trees, rapid as light flecks in water,

33

and filled with sounds. They had reached a beech grove where the ground was almost polished underfoot it was so bare, and the smooth-skinned trunks glistened as the light of the night sky penetrated the branches and projected a tangled trellis of black shadows. Paula looked up through the scaffolding of the trees and Gabriel followed her gaze.

'Look,' she cried, as the moon, almost full and lying low on the horizon, broke out and dyed the contours of the clouds around it an inky blue. 'How huge it is.'

'An illusion,' said Gabriel drily. 'The closer the moon lies to the horizon, the larger it seems. As it rises it appears to shrink but if you raised a pencil and measured it – as artists used to do – ' he smiled at her with a trace of mockery 'you would see that it is always the same size.'

'But I'm glad it looks huge,' said Paula, without petulance, although she had been taught the effect in her first art class. She felt flattered by his unusual informativeness, not rebuffed.

They were passing a hollow beech which she had spent many days sketching from every angle of the copse where it stood the proud master, because in its warrior trunk and twisted roots strange configurations of men and women could be deciphered. Tourists and other walkers on the Heath had passed while Paula drew, and most, without looking at her pad, had stopped when they too noticed the figures in the tree. The shapes changed with the light and the time of day, and in mounting excitement Paula chronicled a week of the beech's life until its metamorphoses had come to frighten her. In the first drawing a stately procession, as if of priestesses, had emerged from the gnarls and fissures of the trunk. In measured file they paced, one behind the other, away from the gaping wound of the tree's empty heart, and stretching out their arms like tribute-bearers on a triumphal column in Rome. But as she worked, the forms lost their dignity and their restraint: whorls became open mouths, knots faces distorted with pain, clefts abysses into which men were hurled. In her last drawing, a stream of creatures fell convulsed downwards towards the tree's roots, and grappled for footholds and clutched one another, heads flung back and eyes staring. Paula shivered a little as she looked again at the beech.

'I've drawn it many times,' she told her uncle, not wishing

to add more. 'It has a life of its own. Very strong mana, as some people would say.'

'Would you?' asked Gabriel. 'Are you a follower of – what do the book shops now call it – the Occult?' He smiled deprecatingly. 'The search for the spirit in a heap of . . .', his hand gestured, 'of flummery.'

'No, no,' said Paula. 'You shouldn't sneer. At least they're looking for something. Isn't that better in your eyes than materialism? Surely you prefer a freak who'll only eat soya beans and meditate to an ad man who believes in nothing at all?'

'I'm not sure,' said Gabriel. 'I feel a deep personal dislike for people like your mother's friend tonight. I would definitely prefer the company of the ad man to him.' He laughed drily. 'Of course this is a fairly traditional characteristic of the Church. We have pursued the heretic who was closest to us in belief and fervour with far more zeal than the indifferent sceptic. After Bernard of Clairvaux had toured the strongholds of the Cathar heretics in France, he said, "Their vision is pure and no morals are purer than theirs." But we lit the bonfires of the Inquisition all over Languedoc to exterminate them. If their hearts had been empty of God and they had observed the externals, as so many do, going to church like everyone else, no one would have set a torch to them. And we have persecuted one another. As you know, the Society was suppressed by the Pope, after long years of controversy, some of which arose from disputes about our methods of converting the Chinese.'

Paula looked at him in surprise. He was breathing hard. She wanted to ask him how he reconciled such observations with his faith, but she did not know how to phrase the question. Like many other people, she was intimidated by her uncle's reputation and did not want to appear foolish in his eyes.

So she said only, 'How terrible,' and looked down at her boots. Then she added, 'I think religion has got to be a belief in ghosts and spirits and supernatural powers. Trying to make it rational or reasonable is stupid. It's got everything to do with magic and ritual, and nothing to do with practicalities or logic. When you're up there in your splendid vestments muttering words over the bread and wine, you're not a professor of moral philosophy or a man of science. It's obvious you're a shaman, a witch doctor just like in Papua or wherever. Surely?' She looked at him, her pointed face glowing after her outburst, somewhat scared that she had overstated her case.

Gabriel did not answer for a time. Then he said solemnly, 'You don't believe any more?' His sharp eyes sought hers, but she dropped her gaze and stammered, 'Sure don't,' with deliberate frivolity.

'Perhaps you will come back,' said Gabriel, kindly. 'As all institutions crumble, the Church will again seem a source of strength to your generation.'

'I never really was a Catholic, not really.'

'I can hardly believe that, my dear,' said Gabriel. 'You know what they say, "Once a Catholic always a Catholic". There's some truth in it, you know.'

'But,' Paula faltered. She did not want to be rude to him, and tell him how appalled she was by most of the Church's decisions.

'That's why it's important for families to practise together,' said Gabriel. 'You didn't get the right example from your father.' He swallowed, and then continued, 'Or from your mother.'

'I'm glad of it.' Then sharply, she added, 'You don't like Ma, do you?'

'Oh, I'm not one to have likes or dislikes,' said Gabriel. His tone was suddenly cold.

'Why not? And why duck the question?'

'Your mother and I have never really hit it off – I expect that's the expression you'd use. But it has never worried me, such things don't.'

But what about her? thought Paula for a moment. Instead she said, 'I'm the first to run Ma down and find her irritating and stupid and crazy. But if someone else does, I want to fly at their throats.'

Gabriel laughed drily.

Paula went on, 'You see Ma treats the world with a kind of rough justice which in the end lets everyone get on with their own lives, even though she is so greedy for attention and praise. And in the end that's better for me, for Franny, and for you too than if she clung devotedly to every one of us.'

'You should love her, it's a child's duty.'

Isn't it more than that? thought Paula, but again, taking refuge in her brand of inconsequential boldness, she asked instead, 'Do you have a duty to love? I mean as a priest, are you meant to, or not?' She faltered and giggled slightly in embarrassment.

But Gabriel did not mock her. The corners of his tight mouth turned down. 'Ah, you're asking a great deal, my dear. Should I, as a priest, love? I should love God . . . but I should never put the love of anyone above God.' He coughed. 'It hasn't been a hardship.'

Paula eyed him, noting the chilliness of his voice. She felt more pity for him because he had not found his rejection of love a hardship than if he had told her he had suffered from it all his life.

They had left the woods and were walking across the open sports ground towards the bank, over which lay the rolling expanse of Parliament Hill and its flanking fields. Paula's spirits lifted as they emerged into the open, on the thick grass still spongy from earlier rain.

A figure with a dog was walking towards them. Paula drew nearer the priest; her silence was tense. She broke it suddenly, whispering, 'The Romans were right to fear woods, weren't they?' The dog, a Doberman pinscher, trotted past; its pink-lidded eyes gleamed in the dark. The owner made a sound in his throat as he passed Paula and Gabriel; a greeting, it challenged them like a wrestler's grunt. But he was a lightly built man. He was wearing narrow trousers and he carried the dog's lead in his hand like a riding crop.

'I thought you weren't afraid on the Heath,' said Gabriel, teasing.

'That's just brave talk I put on for Daddy. He fusses so much, it drives me crazy. I'm scared really, but I think it's silly so I try and overcome it. But I'm safe here compared to you – that man for instance . . .' She tossed her head backwards. 'He's not interested in me.' She laughed. 'But the emptiness here and the noise, that's what scares me. A million things creeping and staring, munching and grazing, and all quite invisible.' She giggled nervously and reached for her uncle's arm. 'But one must look the Devil in the face to make him go away. Isn't that right?'

'St Teresa recommended splashing him with holy water. She said it was more effective than prayer or the crucifix.'

Again Paula quivered at the priest's cynicism, and again she dared not probe as she would have liked. Instead she asked tentatively, 'You wrote about her in *Vision and Prophecy*, didn't you? I'm afraid I haven't . . .'

Gabriel interrupted. 'Families never read their members' works. It cost me a huge effort to apply myself to Jerome's *Phlebas*. I liked it.' His tone was colourless. 'As for Teresa of Avila, she is the greatest visionary of all. Have you read her *Life*? It is essential reading for any woman of character, my dear. Especially one with your views. If those views you were expressing at dinner are yours.' He caught her eye.

'Yes, yes, I'm a feminist. But that doesn't mean I'm a Women's Libber. Whatever that is . . .' she added warily.

Inwardly, Gabriel mocked her. How the young were terrified of being labelled the wrong way, of being allocated the incorrect social role. And how powerful the social orthodoxies were, making a student of Gabriel's flinch in genuine dismay when Gabriel described the Jesuits as an élite, making his niece gib at one denomination and yet adopt another.

Paula started up the bank and turned to help her uncle. He avoided her outstretched hand and gripped her forearm instead. At the top, breathing heavily, he stopped and faced across the gentle swelling sweep of Parliament Hill. He took a puffer from his pocket and sprayed the back of his throat. Paula waited beside him, watching with embarrassment. The darkness welled out of the dip where the meadow fell away to the south, but the bright stars and the scudding moon illuminated the hedgerows and the groups of trees that guarded the empty park benches under their branches like enchanted sentinels.

'How still it is,' murmured Paula. Hearing her uncle's breathing, she looked at him, 'It's still quite far, I'm sorry.'

'That's quite all right.' said Gabriel, laying his hand on his chest. 'It's not the season for hay fever, and I never have an asthma attack without it.'

'I'd forgotten, I'm sorry,' she said again.

'It's just that scramble up the slope, and my lungs.'

'Too many cigars?' Paula tried to laugh.

'Perhaps.' Gabriel's voice, through his slower gasps, was neutral.

'I thought people grew out of hay fever.'

'I never have.'

They began walking slowly together over the damp grass. Paula looked up. 'Are the stars different in China? When you were a child, can you remember what they were like?'

'Yes and no. I can't remember, but China and Europe are in the same hemisphere, so broadly speaking the heavens are the same. But the Chinese had very different ideas about the heavens and did not distinguish any of the constellations as we do. With the exception of the Great Bear, which they called the Bushel. Otherwise they discerned different patterns in the sky and few if any of the names and images correspond.'

'How odd. Like a child's game of Join the Dots and Find the Horse. They found elephants.'

'Perhaps.'

Gabriel's mind was elsewhere. Deep within him he felt a burning, a fire he knew and had felt earlier that evening when his brother Jerome had shown him the nightingale in its golden cage. In his brain there took place a sudden implosion of time and circumstance and an exquisite sensation, sweet and toothsome as honey, overwhelmed him.

He said, 'Let's sit down, it's so beautiful.'

They found a bench on the downy shoulder of the hill overlooking the dark stains of the bathing ponds, and sat down side by side. Gabriel sensed Andrew da Rocha brushing past him in the night. He smiled to himself. And he laid a burning coal on my lips to purify me, like Isaiah, so I should write the truth, he dreamed. Not quite, for I'm not writing revelation, but close. This experience is the essence of good writing, this closeness, this commingling of two natures. Was it on a night like this in 1685, Andrew, when you sat on the plains of Tartary beside the Emperor K'ang-hsi after a day's hunting? It was April then too, or was it May? Did the stars glint as fiercely, and the night well as deeply from the ground? Gabriel remembered the diary: the emperor had summoned Andrew to his side. Some of his huntsmen came to his tent with the message. Hurriedly he smoothed the tunic he had worn in the saddle all day and adjusted his fur cap. By the emperor's tent Andrew stopped and the guards entered and announced him. As he waited, he saw the emperor lift the yellow silk curtain at the opening, so he fell to the ground and knocked his face nine times on the hard earth and made three bows as was customary. Only twice before had Andrew entered the emperor's presence: in Peking on his arrival, then five years later. On this occasion, there were few formalities, for K'ang-hsi signalled that he should approach. In his diary Andrew described him: 'The emperor is uncommonly tall for a Chinaman, with a most pleasing visage, though it is heavily marked by the pox. His brow is lofty, his eyes small and slanted after the Chinese fashion, but luminous with wisdom, his nose is fine but somewhat crooked, the lower portion of his face is handsome in every respect. He is heavier than a man of his age in Europe, but bears himself as a god among men, which, in his own country, he is.'

Together, the emperor and Andrew da Rocha then left the camp where bright fires burned. They reached a hillside which was covered in such darkness that the stars could be clearly observed. K'ang-hsi ordered one of the Tartar viceroys accompanying him to follow, and invited two children in his suite, the sons of southern governors, to come too. The Manchu guards spread animal skins on the ground, and the emperor sat down cross-legged in the Chinese fashion and beckoned to Andrew to do the same. But he could not manage the position, so the emperor excused him and he squatted on his haunches.

Gabriel exclaimed to himself, laughing, How uncomfortable for a man of your age! The emperor was just thirty years old, but you were forty. I haven't been able to sit cross-legged since I was a boy.

The emperor motioned the guards away, as a pledge of his trust in the Christian. Their torches flaring and smoking, they turned back to the camp. Then the emperor took out a star-map that Andrew da Rocha had prepared for him and tapped it with his finger. Andrew noted that his hands were white and supple, and that he wore an archer's ring of white jade on his left thumb. 'Tell me,' he spoke to Andrew using his Chinese name, 'tell me, Ta Ling-hsing, if I interpret the stars correctly?

Here is the pole star round which the heavens move, indicated by this group of stars you call the Little Bear, but which we call the Western Hedge.' His gestures were slow, and the silken cuff of his hunting jacket fell over his wrists as he pointed out the stars and turned for confirmation to the Jesuit beside him.

Gabriel smiled to himself with pleasure. K'ang-hsi found Capella burning bright, and Aldebaran the fiercest star in Taurus lying on the western horizon, and Vega burning in the east. Andrew approved every word he said, because, as he wrote later in his diaries, 'This method pleases oriental princes; they enjoy it and it disposes them to receive the creed which has God through whom all knowledge comes.'

Gabriel looked up at the starlit sky and addressed Andrew da Rocha, his subject and his friend, silently across the three centuries that separated them. 'Then you pointed to other stars, using their European names and identifying them for the emperor: Alpheratz and Markab diagonally opposed in Pegasus, Aquarius below, Altair, Rosalhague, and Alpheca. Was the night as velvety as this in the year 1685?

'Andrew, you sat on the furs and you taught K'ang-hsi the use of a nocturnal you had made. You flattered his aptitude and his grasp. In your diary, you write that you considered then whether you should seize your opportunity and talk of the blood of Jesus and the redemption of the Cross. But you remembered the advice of the great pioneer and architect of the Jesuit mission in China, Father Matteo Ricci, who had counselled restraint in discussing the mysteries of our religion: "It is always best to avoid the subjects of the Incarnation and the Passion and Crucifixion of Our Lord because such mysteries are alien to the Chinese. They will reply, 'How can a man be a God when he suffered the lot of a common criminal in the times of the Han dynasty?' Concentrate rather on the learning and skill Westerners have achieved and emphasize its relation to the philosophy they follow. In this way, the minds of the Chinese can be influenced and won."

'But it seemed to you that your moment of intimacy in the Tartary night warranted some venture on your part. So you said, "The order of the heavens is worthy of praise, is it not?" The emperor nodded. "And its author worthy of worship?"

K'ang-hsi nodded again. Then a gleam of humour brightened his eye. "I myself," he said, "perform the sacrifices to the Supreme Ruler of Heaven every year. You and your fellows perform sacrifices to Him daily, I am told."

' "The Supreme Ruler of Heaven is the highest power in the universe and the creator of all." You used the same word as the emperor – *Shang-Ti* – because it had been approved by your predecessor Ricci as the correct appellation of God. But even as you used it, you hesitated at the ambiguity, you sensed that the emperor meant something different by his "Supreme Ruler". The Pope had already ruled against the term *Shang-Ti* for God, but our Order had ignored the papal ban.

' "Yes," K'ang-hsi replied, "His will is manifest in everything." His hand described an arc through the surrounding space and then pointed to the sky. "Human affairs are involved in the phenomena of the heavens, and of eclipses in particular. Because we can now calculate them with absolute precision, it does not follow that we must not make the necessary reforms in order to avoid trouble and obtain the peace and well-being of the people." His intelligent eyes rested on yours: "Things may seem determined in our lives, but there are these and other ways in which man's power can develop heaven's work."

'You were deeply struck with admiration at K'ang-hsi's words, thought Gabriel, because they seemed to depart in no way from Christian orthodoxy . . .'

Gabriel contemplated the vaulted blackness above him; there wheeled the universe, bearing on its course the sparkling diadems of the constellations in tier upon tier; his eye found one star that danced merrily as a candle flame on a summer night when the windows are flung open and the soft night air blows in. It flashed in his eye as if signalling to him. 'Consider,' it blinked at him, 'the power that created me and moves me and fills me with fire. Consider His mighty breath and His strong arm that sustains me here, floating in an infinity of light and air.' Gabriel smiled at the star, the visible proof of God's order. Its liveliness made him light-headed, as if his own spirit were spinning up and up and up through the darkness towards the magnetic field round the star's coruscation.

Paula stirred beside Gabriel, wondering what on earth he was thinking. In the darkness his long-lined face seemed to her graven like a saint in a Crivelli altarpiece; the etched seams in the impasto running from brow to nose, from nostril to lip, from ear round the sharp jawbone to the chin. The freshness of the night penetrated her quilted jacket and her boots. She laid a hand gently on her uncle's arm. He stood up.

'You were in a dream,' she said.

'Yes,' said Gabriel, smiling. Then he added: 'Shall I tell you a funny thought that just struck me? Looking at the night made me remember something.'

'Do,' said Paula, 'But let's move.'

Gabriel looked up again at the wheeling heavens, and chuckled. Then he spoke: 'The Jesuits never scrupled to use Chinese beliefs for their own ends, particularly the Chinese belief that they could rely on the stars for guidance. When the Emperor Shun Chih was dying – ' he turned to her, 'he was the Emperor K'ang-hsi's father and predecessor – the Buddhist monks at court had gained great influence over him during his last years, and they clustered around him on his deathbed. Adam Schall was then the Jesuit director of the Board of Astronomy, and had once been much loved by the emperor who even called him Ma Fa, or Father. He informed the emperor that some spots had appeared on the face of the sun, a most evil omen, and that these sunspots signified that the Buddhists were trying to obscure the emperor's glory.'

Paula laughed, although once again she felt a twinge of surprise. 'What happened?' she asked. 'Did it work? Did he believe it?'

But Gabriel was thinking, I shall work well tomorrow. His earlier curiosity about Paula had been swept aside by his inspiration on the Heath in the darkness. He was above all an historian; contemporaries could rarely rival the past for his attentions.

'What did you say?' he replied eventually.

'Nothing.'

'Oh yes,' said Gabriel. 'Unfortunately not. Shun Chih died a convinced Buddhist.'

They continued across Parliament Hill, down the slope towards the ponds. The high diving board loomed white against the blackness of the wood beyond, and the surface of the water flashed. They kept the ponds to their left, and continued down the slope.

'Do you remember China? From when you were small? Daddy does, of course.' Paula hesitated.

'Not really,' said Gabriel. He was lying. Memories of Tientsin grew each year more vivid, ever since he had turned sixty. There were times when he feared for his memory because the decades of his middle years had become a blank, while the years of childhood and adolescence were filling his brain to the brim, pushing all else beyond recall. Silly things happened to him now; in Gerrard Street the other day he had almost lost consciousness, so turbulent were the sensations provoked by the smell of peanut oil and soy and the faintly acrid spice of ginger mingling with sesame emanating from dozens of restaurants. 'You know the story, surely?' he said slowly. 'I stayed behind in England when the others went back. I was eight, or perhaps nine.' His voice was sharp. 'I remember very little, really. I did not know we were leaving China. It was 1917, and Father had been called home. We – that is your father, me, and our mother – went on ahead, on the steamer to Hong Kong and then London. We were expecting to return.' He paused. 'But I never saw China again.'

Paula threw a look over her shoulder at the ponds, and sensing a discomfort in Gabriel, coughed and changed the subject. 'Segregated bathing, huh,' she said. 'Just to keep everyone in order. You'd think women were all seducers the way these old rules stick.'

Gabriel was still silent.

'We're nearly there,' she said. 'We've hardly seen a soul.'

'Quite a walk,' said Gabriel. He was thinking, if I had known I would never see China again, would it have been any different? The summer of that last year reverberated in his mind. After his mother, Jerome and he had docked at Tilbury, they went to stay with their grandmother in Dorset near the Stour, in a tall-chimneyed red brick house where the fireplaces were so wide and deep Gabriel and Jerome wanted to pull their beds into the inglenook and sleep there by the embers. The garden was wild and rank, neglected by the only gardener so that the dry skeletons of last year's cow parsley filled the undergrowth in the woods where daffodils used to grow and last

44

year's apples squelched underfoot in the abandoned orchard. Huge climbing roses trailed over the sills and fell in natural swags across the windows. Jerome and Gabriel played all that June, trying to stone the frogs in the pond, watching the fledglings in the thorn hedgerow at the bottom of the garden learn to fly, and pouring salt on slugs to watch them boil and die. One day they made a wooden cart from one of the tea chests their father had used to send back his porcelain. They sawed it in half, and then stole shafts from the stables and took off the wheels from the gardener's cart. What fun we had with it, exclaimed Gabriel, what fun.

There was a grass clearing in the woods behind the house and they dragged the contraption they had made over there one day and pulled it to the top of the slope. First Jerome flung himself into the cart and hurtled to the bottom, bumping and flying over the grass the whole way down, and shrieking with joy. Then Gabriel ran down to haul it up again. At the top, he threw himself onto it and Jerome gave him a push. Helter skelter over the turf, the trees flew past in a blur and a rush of green. Gabriel crowed with fright and with delight. Then suddenly, the cart struck a tussock in the earth and flew sideways, turning up on end and hurling Gabriel out and under the shaft. His leg stuck out to one side, and he knew instantly, he'd broken it. But he remembered now he had felt no pain, though the angle his outstretched limb made with his pelvis frightened him. He was numb and the leaves above him shook and glittered like sequins in the bright June light and he heard the rushing noise they made as they moved. There was a halo round the edge of his eyes, but the centre had gone black and he could no longer see anything but looming shapes and heard nothing but a straining sweet call in his ears. He remembered that he thought then, I'm dying. He could not breathe, he could not breathe. He had thought then, If I ever breathe again, I won't be here anymore. I'll have burst if I can't squeeze the air out of me. The last thing he saw before he blacked was Jerome's scared face. Later, Jerome squealed, 'You were bright puce, you really were.' I wonder, thought Gabriel, if I had been able to return to China with the rest of them after that summer, would I now be in the Church as I am or, like Jerome, would I be a sceptic? He felt a pang of grief again as he recalled it, and he said slowly to Paula, appealing to her under-standing, 'It was the asthma, you see. They discovered I had asthma. Mother thought I should stay in England, because China is so dry and dusty, especially in the north, and she wanted me to be near the right doctors.'

'Of course I know,' said Paula gently. 'You were brought up by my great-grandmamma.' She paused, and attempted a light tone. 'She sounds quite an amazing lady.'

'She was.' Gabriel's voice was dry.

'Didn't she wear crinolines to go out shopping, right up to the Thirties?'

'Yes, almost.' Gabriel recovered his humour. 'She once came to see me at Oxford. It was 1925, I think, and she must have been already eighty or thereabouts. Her dress was of scarlet velvet and swept the floor; its edges were bedraggled and grimy. On her head she had a huge hat, with a spray of feathers – mangy feathers, that had seen better days as well. Coward that I am, when I caught sight of her, I hid in a doorway in the quad for a full ten minutes before I could swallow my embarrassment and greet her.' He laughed in his throat. 'She was a grand old lady, one of the old school. That's where your father gets his memory, and where I get my cloth.' He tapped his chest. 'She was very close to God, in her own way. She liked to have priests around her, and so I met many wise and saintly men when I was a child in her house.'

They reached the pathway leading from the Heath through a collection of houses, where the light of the street lamps blotted out the stars.

'We really are nearly there now,' said Paula.

When they reached her house, she found the key in the pocket of her jacket and turned to Gabriel.

He said, 'I'll come in and call a cab.'

'I've got lots of numbers; they push the cards through the door.'

'Coffee?' she offered, as she flicked on the light in the kitchen. There was no food stacked on the shelves. The only visible sign of an occupant was the jar of instant coffee and a bowl of apples.

'No brandy?' he said with a smile. 'Will you telephone for me?'

'Sit down,' she said, pointing to a kitchen chair of bright yellow. It'll be five minutes.'

She looked into her uncle's sallow face. It was expressionless, but his body was uneasy in the unfamiliar flat. When he felt her eyes upon him, he smiled thinly and said, 'I actually enjoyed that.'

Yet Paula felt that she had been greatly praised, and she grinned back, tousling her short hair with her fingers. 'Good,' she said, 'I hope it'll help you sleep.'

After Gabriel had gone, Paula noticed with pleasure her solitude and the counsel the flat kept of her life. She thought of John, asleep in the bed they had shared, and she snorted. Like a young girl in the first grip of a new love, her imagination was filled with thoughts of Gabriel, and beside him others looked insignificant. Niggardly as he had been with his confidences – she blamed herself for her lack of courage in questioning him – she felt deeply flattered by their long walk together in the darkness, and privileged to hear the stories of a man whom her own father had always greatly envied. It was because Jerome Namier's relationship with his brother was so contorted and painful that Paula had shunned the company of her uncle while her own attitude to her father had been hostile. But with the disappearance of John from her life, a rapprochement with her father had fulfilled a need, and with her new friendship for her father came a new fascination with her uncle. As she turned out the light that night, she smiled delightedly to herself in bed, thinking, Gabriel, Gabriel, shall we be friends?

❦ *CHAPTER* 4

Teresa Namier could hear her husband moving about upstairs making the sharp noises of a man who wishes to be heard. She tossed her head, and said to Wayne, 'He's dying for me to join him. He can't bear to be left out of anything. Doesn't like my friends, doesn't like me having fun.' Her head lolled a bit and she raised her black-rimmed eyes slowly to his face as he offered her another drag from the joint he had just rolled.

They were alone in the drawing-room now, and both were sitting cross-legged on the carpet. The American ecologist had taken his leave soon after Paula and Gabriel had left, and Rosie at the stroke of eleven had crossly announced that she was going to bed, as all sensible people should. Wayne and Teresa, left to themselves, ran over the day's incidents at the theatre, exclaiming and giggling at the quirks of the director, the flat-footed waddle of one of the principals, the intense seriousness of the juv. lead's diet, the wrists . . . the hair . . . the liquid eyes of the Eurasian girl who is loved by the American lieutenant. 'Leeeou . . .' mouthed Wayne. 'No, no,' shrieked Teresa, 'Loooo . . .'

'But darling, which one do *you* fancy?' cried Teresa, clinging to Wayne's arm with tears of laughter gleaming on her sooty eyelashes. She felt safe with Wayne. He allowed her to play the child. With him, four nursery walls came down and enclosed her and she became the darling centre of a subjective world. Also, his affectations were so extreme that her own artificial youthfulness seemed natural and easy. Teresa often complained that other friends did not have time to do nothing, to waste away the hours with her. With Jerome there were always matters to discuss, or stories to listen to, or memories to hear again. Teresa found the literary talk of her husband's world exhausting and barren. She would rather giggle with Wayne any day, because she considered him human, by contrast to the Namiers.

'Darling, I saw such a super T-shirt today.' Wayne cupped his hands to his face, smothering his laughter. 'Really good. It had the Queen on it, with a moustache pencilled in and one tooth blacked out.'

'And you didn't get it?'

'I should have done.' He sucked at the joint and handed it to her.

'You're so dressy!' Teresa exclaimed with emphasis. 'You remind me of my uncle. Do you know what I did to him?' She shifted herself forward on her hands till her head was very close to his. 'He had seventy pairs of shoes, I swear. One day when he was out, I removed one, and then I switched all the others in the cupboard. When he came back, I said to him . . .' She mimicked the simpering face of innocent adolescence and went on; 'I said, "Uncle, you have sixty-nine and a half pairs of shoes now." Oh God, I swear he must have been up in his bedroom five hours trying to find which one I'd taken.' She threw her head back, laughing.

'Oh, darling, you *couldn't*,' Wayne squealed, giggling behind his hands.

Jerome Namier heard Wayne's cackle and his wife's lower contralto with intense and increasing fury. It was unforgivable; he was deeply wronged. His wife should sense the crisis into which he was plunged, sense it spontaneously. Why don't you understand? he thought. Why don't you pay attention to me anymore? I have worked all my life to please you. I left Oxford for your sake because it bored you and you had nothing to say to the wives of other dons – oh God, you never tried! In his reproaches Jerome glossed over his failure to be elected Warden of his college and his own subsequent bitterness and desire to leave. I have tolerated your appalling friends in London, he thought, attended your appalling plays and smiled when praise was lavished on you and laid your weeping face on my shoulder when it was not. Why can't you give me some return for this? Self-pity welled up in him. The attachment he experienced for Teresa when he first grew to love her had never been loosened, because he was a man who lived inside his own imagination and the changing realities of the outside world impinged little on his feeling. But for her the bond was slack; as he had grown older and more bulky, and she had become taut and wiry, it had seemed to her that their very bodies evinced their incompatibility. She felt that they were miscast for marriage, though not in her fancy for the roles of guardian and ward in a restoration comedy about romance and money. In her own eyes, she belonged to her daughters' generation, and looked upon her husband as an aged and irksome warder who checked her spirit. Her waywardness was exacerbated by Jerome's ready irritation, but when he repented, as he did after each stormy exchange, she was bored by the repetitiousness of his moods, and remained cold to his demonstrations. He wanted to delight her, but Teresa, who could not express the pride she felt in his cleverness and could not acknowledge her dependence upon him and the authority he exercised, felt compelled to rebel. If Jerome wanted to make love to her, her insomnia became acute and she refused him, saying sleep was more precious to her than water in the desert.

That night Jerome felt special pain. When he left the others downstairs, he went up to the study lately usurped by Gabriel, by his manuscripts, notes, possessions. Under a map of China, made by the Jesuits in the early eighteenth century, Jerome dialled James Cunliffe at the terraced house near the river in Chelsea to which he had recently moved. As the bell rang at the other end, Jerome's eye wandered up the wind-curved line of China's eastern coast: Pei-hai, Lei-chou, Kuang-hou-wan, Macao, Hong Kong, Swatow, Nan-ao, Hsia-men, Ning-po, Ting-hsi. The names tolled in his brain; the sweltering train-rides of his youth; a slim dark figure in his bedroom beating a punkah to cool him as he lay, ten years old, under the milky veiling of the mosquito net; posts his father had held in the treaty ports of the south; the clippers gliding by so swiftly, nosing so skilfully into their harbour berths with the English officers stiffly formal on deck while the Chinese hands in turbans and rolled-up black cotton pantaloons hung monkey-like from the rigging and grinned and spat from betel-stained teeth and lips as their boat slipped through the crowded waters.

The telephone went on ringing. James was taking a long time to answer, if he was in. Jerome half hoped he wasn't. His eye travelled inland. Yes, the mountains of Shensi. That was where his father had hunted the Golden Takin in the autumn of 1911. The noble head with its large and tender eyes had hung in the hall of the Shanghai house all his childhood. Where was it now? Jerome wondered with a stab of nostalgia. His father always said, when visitors commented upon it, 'My first and only Takin! I shall never forget the moment when I first saw that herd of great yellow forms moving among the rocks on the far side of the basin. I fancy their colour is what struck me more than anything. It was the reincarnation of the Golden Fleece.' The Golden Fleece, thought Jerome. What magnificence!

Then, he was riding with his tutor along the Bund in his father's imported two-horse carriage, fairly belting along. It was March 1921, or 1922. He was sixteen and his tutor not much older, just out of Cambridge, a pale sweaty youth who took pills for dyspepsia. But he and Jerome warmed to each other. Together they dreamed of Paris and the Left Bank, where they both longed to live. As they went clipping down the Bund, the tutor expanded on the delights of Montparnasse – he had been there. He waved his long white hands in excitement. The Place de la Contrescarpe with its smoking oil lamps, and its ancient plane trees, where Nerval walked his lobster on a golden string. Nerval. Here am I, Jerome thought, prince of a crumbling tower. How bitter and how true it is. *Je suis le ténébreux, le veuf, l'inconsolé* . . . Jerome's mind turned again. Paris was what he had shared with James. Where was James?

At that moment, the number answered, and James's breathless voice came over clearly. Jerome started.

'Hello, my dear chap,' said James. 'You've caught us on our way in. We just came through the front door. Beatrice said she heard it ringing, and we were frightened it would stop just as we picked it up. That's what always happens. How good of you to call.'

Jerome let James's geniality run its course. His friend was a troubled man of minor talents which he had attempted to exploit without success. One of many heirs to an American tobacco fortune, he was still by English standards immensely rich. Philanthropic but rudderless, he gave generously to many projects – mainly artistic – in a haphazard way. He tried to write, and through his many contacts in the London literary world, he had published a slight and boring novel, about himself and the collapse of his second marriage. Beatrice was his third wife, of recent date. Jerome had suggested the title *The Rainy Country* – James's melancholy brought to mind Baudelaire's monarch – but the novel had not sold anywhere except in the Mount Street Bookshop where it was highly recommended to the socially minded clientèle. Most knew Cunliffe, and the rest knew who he was. Jerome had been at Oxford with him, and as neither of them had spent much time in England before their undergraduate days, they were drawn together by the sympathy an Anglophile Virginian feels for a member of the empire's official class. Together they cut an exotic figure, and the barriers of Oxford in the Twenties had come down before their blend of money, wit, and eccentricity. Side by side they lounged in a Gridiron Club photograph Jerome still kept.

Jerome spoke with unmistakable seriousness: 'James, do you remember the money the *Review* got – in the early days – from the Institute of Cultural Affairs in Washington?'

There was a pause. 'Oh no,' James said. He had a light, drawling voice, but now it sounded strained.

'What do you mean, oh no?' countered Jerome sharply. 'You never thought . . .'

'Hold on, old boy,' said James, 'what are you telling me?'

'The *Radical*'s publishing an article tomorrow.' Jerome briefly told him the contents. Cunliffe sighed. 'How on earth did the *Radders* arrive at that opinion?' He did not stop. 'The minute you said Washington, I guessed it.'

'Why?' Jerome groaned. 'Damn it, I was going to say why didn't you guess it before, but why, why didn't *I*?'

The two men were quiet. From the sitting-room came a shrill squeal of delight and fragments of conversation. 'Ooh . . . his legs, his legs,' he heard.

James said: 'Are you there?'

'Of course I am!' snapped Jerome.

'What shall we do?' Jerome gritted his teeth at his friend's usual ineffectiveness.

'Let's meet. First thing tomorrow. Where? Here?'

'My club,' said Cunliffe. 'I'd like to be down in the West End tomorrow, and it's dead as a doornail in the morning. No one'll disturb us.'

'All right, James,' said Jerome. 'Ten o'clock sharp.'

He clicked down the phone, and sat for a few moments longer in the chair facing Gabriel's notes. On one side lay his looseleaf files, numbered in Roman numerals, which contained Gabriel's translation of Andrew da Rocha's diaries. Jerome dropped his head into his hands. Did James know – had he always known that the Institute of Cultural Affairs was a CIA cover? He thought over the telephone conversation. James had been pretty quick off the mark remembering the money, while Jerome himself had almost forgotten it altogether. He rubbed his eyes. To be fooled by an American agent at the Connaught was bad enough, but duped by James, the muddler, the failure, the ineffectual poor little rich boy . . . such a failure he'd bungle his own suicide, that was the joke. Jerome cursed. He looked again at the piles of his brother's work and thought bitterly, Why is Gabriel the China historian, not me? Why is he acclaimed for his learning when it was I who was brought up there, while he was pampered by that priest-ridden old harridan? He is congratulated everywhere – Gabriel Namier sj, the Sinologist – while I . . . A wave of laughter assaulted him again from downstairs, and he rose to his feet and stamped heavily on the floor. Then he bellowed, 'Teresa.'

Silence followed. Jerome waited, but as no footsteps came up the stairs he lunged down them himself, his heavy weight rocking the banisters in their sockets.

'Teresa!' he shouted again.

From the doorway he saw Wayne and his wife doubled up on the floor, each with both hands clapped over their mouths as they stifled their giggles. But at the sight of Jerome's flushed face, Teresa straightened herself and became calm. The sprawling evening suddenly acquired precise definition, as the camera freezes the churning motion of the sea, and the atmosphere in the room, previously so unstructured, was all at once compressed and alert. Jerome said simply, 'It's late.'

Teresa replied, 'I know.' She got to her feet, and found her shoes. The balance of power was altered, and Jerome, appeased that he could still exercise authority, softened a little. Wayne Dupree in his gym shoes padded over to Teresa, and with defiance whispered, 'Bad vibes, darling. I'll be getting along.' She did not smile encouragement, but said only with some haughtiness, 'Goodnight.'

Jerome picked up the overspilling ashtrays and silently removed them from the room to the kitchen. When he returned, his wife was standing heavily, trying to shake off the daze that gripped her mind.

'Wayne's grass is very good,' she said, conciliatory.

'You smoke too much,' her husband answered, but without anger. He did not reproach her, because this aspect of his disapproval was understood.

'Perhaps I do,' said Teresa. 'It makes me laugh. I wish you laughed. Why don't you try it . . .' She stopped in mid-sentence and started slowly up the stairs. Then, leaning against the banisters with one hip, she turned languorously towards Jerome behind her and said petulantly: 'You were in a really foul mood this evening, weren't you?'

Jerome put his hand on hers. 'We both were,' he said. She withdrew her hand and continued up the stairs.

'Something rather terrible has happened,' continued Jerome. His manner was diffident. Teresa disliked problems.

'Tell me.' She was very sleepy. She sat on her dressing-table stool, and gazed into the mirror, smoothing with a finger the lines on her forehead and round her mouth. Methodically, she took out her contact lenses and laid them in a tiny silver box. 'Tell me,' she said again. 'I'm sorry I was horrid.'

Jerome sat on the bed and told her briefly. He made it seem less serious than he knew it to be, and described it as an interjournalistic squabble, arising from jealousy between the *Review* and the *Radical*. As he outlined the story, it came to seem plausible, and he wondered if he could use it to discredit his critics.

'Have you got a copy? Can I read it?' Teresa drew her black blouse over her head and slipped off her black velvet jeans; her necklaces fell with a chinking sound on the veneered dressing table. She pulled on a voluminous nightshirt, which made her light-boned frame seem touchingly frail, and tucked herself up under the sheets on the other side from where Jerome was sitting.

'I could have got one.' Jerome spoke hesitantly. 'To tell you the truth, I couldn't bear to go. It meant going round to the *Radical*'s offices in person, because I didn't want to send anyone on the staff. I suppose I am too proud.'

Very slowly, in a voice already thick with sleep, Teresa answered: 'That young turk, what's his name? He wants to get rid of you. This is the big putsch, my boy. That one you like, Ian something, he's a bad lot. I saw it the first time he came here. He's after you, he's after everything, poor old Jerry-derry, how sad.'

Jerome opened his hands in a gesture of disbelief. 'He's got nothing to do with the *Radical* or the CIA or anything. Teresa . . .'

Teresa turned her face into the pillow. 'You will have to resign, darling,' she said.

Jerome looked down on her sleeping form. How could she say that? Why didn't she stand by him and urge him to fight tooth and claw, and promise to confront all his enemies by his side? Why didn't she say, in that husky voice, What nonsense – let them try. He threw himself back on to the pillows beside her and reached an arm across the shallow mound his wife made under the bedclothes. A faint greasy tang touched with orange peel came from her creamed face. The *Review* was his whole life, and she could tell him in a few brief words that he must renounce it. A wave of anger passed over him again. She had never appreciated him; she did not understand that everything she took for granted – the wine in the cellar, the house, the trips abroad – would be forfeited if he could no longer run the *Review*. She would be sorry when they had to move. Jerome checked his train of thought. It was unthinkable that they should leave Admiral's Walk. In his self-pity he could entertain such forebodings about his livelihood, but his common sense restrained him. Although he never admitted it in public, he knew that his style of life had never been financed by the *Review*, even though the paper had been surprisingly successful and earned him, as a major proprietor, a good extra income. But the money from the *Review* supported only a few of the comforts he expected; Henry Namier's judicious and prescient investments saw to the rest. Of course, if the market continued its present fall ... Jerome forced himself to abandon the vision of his distressed future, and returned to his wife. Teresa was shrewd; he cursed her for it. 'You will have to resign, darling. You will have to resign, darling.' Oh God, he thought, Will you make fun of me then? Will Gabriel compress his lips in that thin deprecatory smile that for over fifty years has rebuked me? He visualised his brother's long and trenchered face, and then thought again of Teresa. But he saw her with his heart's eye, not as she lay beside him. Like many people who love, he saw the object of his passion as she was when he first felt it and she was London's toast and the pin-up of soldiers on leave: Teresa Henson the selfless, the courageous, the pert and independent WAAF of *The Path of the Stars*, 1942, starring David Snow and John Cotton. Of course Tess, as the boys called her, stole the film. Jerome still felt salt prick his eyes – absurd, his own sentimentality angered him – as he recalled the scene in which she offered a pilot a cup of tea. The man's face had been burned away; only his eyes, darting reptilian in that flayed and monstrous deathmask, betrayed the life within him still. Teresa was in her twenties then, a pixie with a wickedly direct approach. Jerome had met her at a party, and they were married in '44 when he was home on leave.

Jerome turned his face to the pillow. She was so silly, so empty, she never read a book, she never looked at the *Review*; even at the beginning she'd only glanced at it. Yet she was shrewd. He lumbered off the bed and stood looking at her asleep. With a characteristic mental tic, he raked his store of memories for a few lines to describe his state. What was it Eliot had written about old age? Gradually he retrieved the verses:

> First, the cold friction of expiring sense
> Without enchantment, offering no promise
> But bitter tastelessness of shadow fruit
> As body and soul begin to fall asunder.

Not bad, but Yeats was always better, and he began undressing as he whispered:

> Never had I more
> Excited, passionate, fantastical
> Imagination . . .

If Teresa was right, he was not going to yield with expected docility to the young and vigorous. He was still brimful of heat and sensation; though age had dimmed his ardour – he coughed wryly as he thought of Teresa's once Ledaean body – there was life in him yet, by God. He had pursued delight in all the forms he understood it to exist, in the beauty and ingenuity of man-made things and the subtlety of nature's gentler strokes. His aesthetic of luxury depended on his continued work as arbiter of London literary opinion, and it was not going to be stolen from him by some self-styled Prometheus brandishing a biro for a hollow stalk, while he, Jerome, felt the fingers of that cold friction steal over his body and his soul.

He brushed his teeth and spat with determination. He would not give in.

> Never had I more
> Excited, passionate, fantastical . . .

he began again. He would not resign. Gabriel should never see him fall so signally; Teresa would have to learn the value that he at least attached to his work. If he was to be an outcast, he was going to have to be cast out.

❦ CHAPTER 5

Gabriel arrived at his brother's house the following morning in a mood of intense irritation. It was past noon, and he had not yet been able to address himself to Andrew da Rocha's diaries, although he had risen at six in order to meet all his other duties – Mass and the recital of his breviary – and clear the morning for work. Instead he had been summoned to his Father Superior's cold and tidy office, asked to sit down, and then involved in what Father Superior described a 'delicate mission'.

Father handed over his desk a duplicated newsletter on cheap blue paper. '*The Good News of Our Lady of the Olive Grove*', read Gabriel, scanning the pages rapidly. It was a circular, put out from an address in NW6, and it analysed a recent message of the Virgin Mary, given in a village in Sicily called Selinunte in the spring of 1970. 'The eschatological meaning of the words of Our Blessed Lady is a warning to us all. "The cup is full," she said. "Soon it will be brimming over. Penitence. Penitence. Do penance for your sins." ' Gabriel read with dull interest. The jargon was familiar, the phrases hackneyed. Three children, all girls, and all, as far as he could make out, called Maria and aged about fourteen, claimed to have seen the Virgin Mary several times in an olive grove. Miracles, conversions, prodigies had followed. Prophecies had been made. Gabriel privately decided it was a ridiculous rigmarole.

'Surely, Father,' he objected, 'this matter comes under the diocesan authorities. Selinunte? Where is it? It was a colony of Syracuse in classical times, I seem to remember. Isn't it for the Archbishop of Syracuse to decide about the visions?'

'The Archbishop hasn't given the visions his approval.'

Father Superior spoke slowly, with precision. 'The matter rests with him still. Higher examination of the visions' authenticity and the sincerity of the young visionaries themselves cannot therefore be undertaken.' His manner was grave, and he rubbed his long dry fingers together above the blotter on his desk as he looked Gabriel in the eye. 'But we have been requested – privately – by the Commission of Inquiry into the Faith of the People in Rome to pursue some investigations ourselves. There is . . .' his tone was weary '. . . a growing lay apostolate for Our Lady of the Olive Grove, particularly in this country, in Ireland, and in France. Her popularity is marked.' He tapped the news-letter. 'This is issued *weekly*, you understand.'

Gabriel shook his head. 'I have heard nothing about it at all.'

'As I was saying,' continued Father Superior, 'the popularity of Our Lady at Selinunte is intertwined with protests against the decisions, and particularly the liturgical reforms, of Vatican II. Her "messages" have been interpreted as criticisms of the new Mass and of progressive elements in the Church.' A note of sarcasm crept into his voice. 'That is why you might have heard of it.' He smiled thinly, and then added, as if casually, 'You are to prepare a report and submit it to me – within a month. Everyone is most anxious to have further guidelines for the faithful in this matter.'

Gabriel was horrified, but his family would have been surprised at his humility towards his superior. And his book? What would happen to his masterpiece? He could not abandon it for a month, just as it was burning so bright in his brain. He calculated rapidly. If he lived another five years, he would have completed his natural span. A month represented what? A sixtieth of the time allotted to him. But he bit back his protest and folding his hands on his thin knees, asked only, 'May I know who "everyone" is? For whom am I preparing the report?'

'Let it be said, for me.' Father Superior smiled, acknowledging his silent appreciation of Gabriel's obedience. He ran a finger under his collar, where it pinched the greyish folds of his drawn neck and chin. 'I have given you a month only, because I am aware that you have a great deal of work of your own to complete. You will enjoy it, you know. Sicily in the spring. I half wish I could go myself.'

'I am to go?' Gabriel was taken aback.

'Of course.' Father Superior leant forward. 'You are to interview the children who have seen Our Lady, and their parents, their teachers, pilgrims to the shrine, and, of course, their confessors.'

Numbly Gabriel asked, 'But when?'

'As soon as possible. Your visit will not be an official one. In fact you are to appear as a priest with genuine personal curiosity about the apparitions and the cult they have attracted.' He rose and went over to a filing cabinet, and pulling out the contents of a drawer, handed a sheaf of papers to Gabriel. 'Here are other English and Italian newsletters about Selinunte, and related materials. I forget, can you manage Italian?'

Gabriel gave a half nod.

'I will tell Father Ambrose to prepare you a ticket and expenses and arrange some lodgings in the village, if possible. I believe it is usually crowded – with pilgrims.' He looked at Gabriel, and said cheerfully, 'You'll enjoy yourself, I hope.'

Gabriel gathered up the papers, and sneezed.

'Bless you,' said Father Superior, ironic.

'It's the dust,' said Gabriel, sneezing once more.

Father Superior held the door for him. 'Read the material, keep an open mind, and come and see me here before you leave.' As Gabriel passed, he added, 'By the way, how is the Chinese book?'

Gabriel nodded, but without a smile. Father Superior looked into his eyes and said calmly, 'Keep your distance from it. Never let any subject no matter how interesting crowd your mind till you forget all else.'

Gabriel piled the Selinunte material in his room at Xavier Hall and then sat down on his bed, weak with impatience. Reminding himself first of his early fascination with visions, then of the beauty of Sicily, and thirdly of his duties to his Order and to his God, he forced himself to kneel down at his prie-dieu and, sinking his head into his hand, began to meditate on the sensible and simple instruction of his founder, St Ignatius. 'Our Lord did not set much store by the ploughs and the yokes for oxen,' he recited, 'which St Justin says he made in Joseph's workshop for eighteen years. In themselves they were not worth a God's while. What gave them value was the Person who made them, and the spirit in which they were wrought.' Gabriel pondered the familiar text until its homely texture became limpid, as if each letter were written in bright air. It does not matter what I do, he thought, but who I am. 'God cares less for what we do than for what we are, His children in the state of grace. One of Satan's commonest temptations, under the appearance of greater good, is to inspire disgust at our present office and occupations, as too paltry for persons of our capabilities. Certainly we should be greater than our occupations, but we should busy ourselves about them with none the less zeal for that.' Gabriel went over the passage carefully and slowly, letting its glow transfuse him. He knelt motionless and its grace seeped through him and illuminated him within, driving out demons of dissatisfaction. He felt then, in his complete and glad resignation, as if a draught of spring water had been splashed on his forehead.

But the lateness of the hour dispelled his brief pleasure. He had lost the clearest, most eloquent part of the working day, and after a night when he had been filled with inspiration and energy. When he arrived, the house was empty, except for Rosie, who brought him a large cup of instant coffee. She liked to stop and chat to him now and then, discussing such matters as the canonization prospects of Matt Talbot, a fellow Dubliner who had spent the latter half of his life in chains in order to expiate the alcoholism of his youth. But she sensed Gabriel's impatience on this occasion, and left him. In his urgency to set to work he let the cup of coffee grow cold.

Gabriel sat down firmly at the desk, which looked through the wide-paned sash window over the small untidy lawn outside fringed by lilac and planted with apple. The mauve blossoms hung in grape clusters on the trees, their colour blurred to grey by the falling rain. It was too early in the season for white lilac, and cresting the budding branches were dried-up brown spires of last year's flowering. Soon, Gabriel reflected, the apple trees too would be flocked white, fleecy as lambs' skins.

He bent his face to the papers before him, and unlocked the left-hand drawer where he kept the originals of Andrew's diaries. They were octavo volumes, leatherbound and closely inscribed in serried line after serried line of black ink impressed on to the paper with a graceful boldness of stroke that must have been influenced by Rocha's study of Chinese calligraphy. Gabriel loved them, in spite of the difficulties they presented. He felt the sap rise in him at the mere look of them. Then, from the looseleaf file, he took his own manuscript and began to check the last ten pages he had edited and translated, from the days of April 1685, after the Emperor K'ang-hsi and the Jesuit had sat together in the Tartar night under the stars.

'It was a star that long ago led the three kings to adore the true God,' wrote Andrew da Rocha. 'In the same way the science of the stars will lead the rulers of the Orient, little by little, to know and adore the Lord. Our most sacred religion itself, invested in the star-studded mantle of our astronomy . . .' Gabriel paused. That's clumsy, he thought. He looked at the original. '*Imo ipsa sacra Religio stelligeram Astronomiae pallam passim induta* . . .' Revise it, he decided, and made a mark in the margin of his manuscript to remind himself.

He continued to read, skimming his translation rapidly. 'The Son of Heaven will be brought to the knowledge of the True Lord of Heaven, I know, because there is no ruler in the world who can match him for wisdom and intelligence. He called me over today as he rode past, and reined up beside me. A bird flashed by at that moment, and he asked me its name. I had forgotten, so I apologized. He smiled and said to me: "One of your colleagues told me many years ago its name in the Latin tongue." Then he laughed, and told me its name. Truly, there can be few emperors possessed of such a memory. He spurred his horse and sprang away from me. I was shamed by my own ignorance.'

Gabriel skipped a few pages, and began reading again: 'April 18, 1685. We left the environs of Liaoyuan today before dawn, and headed north-east towards the ancient Manchu city of Kirin. The emperor sent word to my tent the night before that he wished me to ride with the hunt, and so I rose before the first light and prepared myself. I do not carry arms, and I believe that I was the only man present today who went unarmed. The emperor ordered five of his personal Tartar bodyguard to watch over me carefully to see that I came to no harm. He looks upon me with increasing favour and benevolence, and for this I thank the Lord my God. Only yesterday he sent me food from his table, which is a mark of the highest degree, and he remembered our days of abstinence and did not embarrass me with fine fare during this Lenten season. He merely gave me some young greens cooked with a little porridge of millet, a grain much used in this northern climate. He ordered ten horses to be set aside for my use today, so that I might change my mount as soon as it was tired. These Mongol ponies are puny by our standards, and would not pass in our country as suitable for a common knight, but they are surefooted in this rocky wilderness, though they are not shod, and for myself, I prefer their small size and their steady step.

'The empress mother and the emperor's three wives with their suites had not yet stirred when we set forth. Their camp lay still, with the morning mist drifting lazily between the tents, gleaming nacreous in the first colourless and chill rays of the sun. We rode past, raising a duststorm on the hard and barren earth so thick that I could no longer see the horseman who rode abreast with me three men along. I could only hear the thunder of the hooves. We were three thousand strong. The wind blew keenly in our faces. Behind, more soldiers brought up the spare horses – ten thousand of them – in a cloud such as I imagined greeted Pharaoh's men when the Israelites were delivered from their hands. For two miles we rode beyond the camp, passing through a steep defile and then rising onto the wider Manchurian plain where it is watered by the great Sungari river. All around were strewn huge rocks, but the terrain is thickly wooded with pine and oak that have been growing here untended for hundreds of years. We passed a family's squalid settlement, erected among the stone ruins of a village that was razed together with many others by a former Tartar ruler of these regions who had engaged in war with China. It had been his wish that his soldiers should no longer have homes or fields to draw them away from fighting. War here is cruel, but no crueller than in our country, I believe.'

Gabriel pursed his lips: the strong stomachs of his predecessors often made brutalities acceptable.

He continued reading: 'When we reached the open plain, we paused and gradually the dust settled and we saw one another. It was a brave sight! For as far as the eye could see, horsemen in bright tunics were deployed and their javelins glinted in the morning sun. Since the emperor has united the whole of China under his control, he undertakes these hunts in order to keep his army exercised; he does not like his garrisons to stand idle, tasting the voluptuous pleasures of peace. He himself is admirably abstemious and frugal in his tastes, so each year he organizes a three-month hunting expedition north of the Great Wall in order to train the army, and also to warn the ever-turbulent Tartars of his mighty presence.

'As we stood waiting this morning, officers suddenly streaked out from the phalanx in which we stood and galloped across the field to the flanks of the cavalry in order to deploy us in the formation prescribed by the emperor. For this is the fashion of hunting in China. The horsemen – all three thousand of them – fan out in a wide circle. I gauged its diameter at three thousand paces. Behind us, forming an outer circle, march the footsoldiers, some carrying staves to fend off the wild beasts, should any escape slaughter, others leading dogs. To the sound of trumpets and the beat of gongs we move forward at a trotting pace, and the circle is drawn tighter and tighter as we ride closer together, as if pulling tight a long noose to throttle the prey. Gradually the space between us diminishes until only three hundred paces separate each man from his furthest companion. In this circus – for the scene resembles an arena, much like the Colosseum – the animals are driven. They rush hither and thither, scrambling over one another, veering and wheeling as the huntsmen block their escape routes. Then, at a signal, the horsemen let fly from their longbows, setting arrow upon arrow from the quivers they wear on their backs into the mighty string, aiming with precise skill and extraordinary swiftness at the game tumbling before them. They bear down on the animals, so that the mêlée justly resembles a battle. The horses rear and circle, and the deer, wolves, foxes and hare fall squealing at their feet. Sweat laces the animals' steaming sides; saliva flecks the rim of their slackening mouths.

'Usually the animals are transfixed through the throat by the huntsmen's deadly barbs, and the footsoldiers who bring up the rear have little to do to finish them off. Though I took no part in the killing – it is not for a man of peace to take up arms against God's creatures – I felt the thrill of the chase. I saw one hind race straight towards me. Her eye was filled with terror, foam hung from her jaws and sweat matted her golden coat. Fear pricked my neck and my shoulders and my head throbbed. Just before she reached me, a bowman felled her with an arrow, and she stumbled to her knees, a few yards from where I sat.

'The greater game – boar, bear, tiger – is despatched in a different fashion, and the huntsmen defer to the emperor, driving the game before them into the centre of the circle where he rides. He sets great store by skill in marksmanship and valour, and he himself gives the best example. He can shoot from both sides, left and right, with equal ease, and he bends a greater bow than any of his men. But with the big game, the arquebus is used.

'I saw K'ang-hsi today fell a tiger at close range. I was at his side. Crying aloud, the huntsmen urged on a tiger they had raised from its lair. It doubled back as they began to surround it and, with head down and tail stretched long and stiff behind it, it loped slowly back through the scrub towards the emperor's position. Then the big cat broke step and started to bound towards us. I sat rigid in the saddle, and felt as if darkness had fallen on the earth. "Now," said the emperor. I was plucked from my terror by his single word. As he gave me the order, his teeth gleamed in his face. I knew what I was to do. I took the lighted taper a huntsman handed up to me and set it to the emperor's gun. The powder sparked and flashed. Three times I did this, and three times the retorts jarred the emperor's straight back but neither his mount nor mine flinched. The tiger's look was wild, and his eyes rolled as his massive head jerked back and his limbs buckled and flung his great coiled weight of fur and flesh to earth.

' "Good," said the emperor, swinging his gun over his back and picking up his reins of yellow silk. "We have done well, Ta Ling-hsing." With that he smiled at me, and again I saw the brightness of his teeth in his face, which runnels of sweat and the day's dust had patterned like baked clay.'

Gabriel smiled to himself. To think K'ang-hsi died of a cold caught while out hunting like this forty years later. He opened a later volume of Andrew's diaries to locate another entry about sport in the emperor's court which he wished to edit together with the description of the hunt. But as he leafed through, his mind wandered, and with piercing definition his inner ear picked up a whisper heard nearly sixty years ago outside the door of the room he and his brother Jerome shared as children in Tientsin when he was six, perhaps seven years old.

In the spring of 1915, thrills running through him, Gabriel sat up in bed. 'What is it?' he cried hoarsely. A gentle voice answered him, '*Sai, sai*, it is me, Number Two Boy.'

Gabriel jumped out of bed and felt the fur rug under his bare feet and then the cold floorboards beyond. He opened the door quietly, filled with excitement. Jerome was now sitting up too, eyes shining with anticipation.

'Number Two, Number Two!' Jerome hissed, keeping his voice down and beating the bedclothes with both fists to show his delight.

'I have come to tell you a story,' said the Number Two house-boy of the Namier ménage. He set the small oil lamp he carried on the floor, and dropping the pidgin he used earlier to announce himself, spoke to the two children in Chinese.

'Yes, yes.' Gabriel remembered how they had cried out and then, stifling their voices and laughter, had clapped their hands over their mouths and buried their heads in the bedclothes. Emerging, they looked over at Number Two with glittering eyes. He was wearing a short grey tunic over black pyjama trousers – the long surcoat reaching the floor was reserved for the Number One Boy – and he settled himself down cross-legged on the floor.

'Which story shall I tell you tonight?' He rolled his eyes and placed a finger to his lips with exaggerated care. He must have been forty-five, Gabriel now calculated at a distance of sixty years, and at that time he seemed Methuselah to us, and twice as wise.

'Tell us the one about the White-Haired Ghost,' Jerome hissed from his bed.

'Or the one about the Pagoda that Flew Away,' Gabriel echoed him.

'No,' said Number Two, his voice already dropping into his storyteller's slow murmur. 'Tonight I shall tell you a new tale.' He stretched out one leg, and with his toes played with the fur of the rug between the boys' beds. 'It concerns this wolfskin.' He withdrew his foot quickly and tucked it under him, looking fiercely at the rug and wrinkling his high forehead in a scowl.

Gabriel quivered at the memory. A wolfskin from Tartary, hunted by the Mongol horsemen from the plains where K'anghsi had hunted. Or was it his father's trophy? Did Henry Namier hunt wolves? He could not remember. The gloomy stuffed heads that hung in the hall filled him with horror and dread, and he had always passed quickly by, glad he did not know what the animals were or where his father had hunted them. But Jerome had been fascinated, he remembered.

Number Two described the capture of the wolf. He made a graceful gesture with his hand, the formal gesture of a story-teller beginning his story. 'It was icy winter,' he whispered, 'and the snow lay in a white pall across the face of the godfor-saken world. The nomads shivered in their mean tents and the children died from the cold.' He paused, 'All around them they heard a pack of wolves howling, "Aaaahoooo, Aaaaaaahoooo."' Number Two threw back his head and mimicked them, his lips like a trumpet. 'Aaaaaa hoooo, Aaaaaaahoooo.' Jerome and Gabriel hugged themselves, squealing with delighted terror. 'And the Mongols set out to catch the wolves ...' Soon, the children were galloping beside the horsemen as they bore down on the wolves. 'But,' said Number Two with bated breath, 'as they came upon them, they realized that this was no pack of ordinary wolves. These wolves were possessed by spirits; as they raced along they struck sparks from the frozen ground and their long thick coats glowed as if with unearthly fire. Then the nomads knew it was the Pack that Never Dies. Weapons could have no effect upon them.

'So they debated amongst themselves what to do to save their lives and their children's lives.' Number Two's voice, quiet now as a prayer, held the two boys like a roar. 'And they decided they must catch the wolves alive. They cast a hunter's net over one and drew it in tight, then over another, and then another. In this way they captured three of the enchanted beasts; the others flashed away over the snow into the night.

'In the camp, they did not try to kill the captives, because they knew they could not be killed. Instead the chief and his sons made a circle around the fire and in the centre of the circle they set up a wooden frame with four legs. To this frame they tied one of the wolves they had taken, making each of his legs fast to a post so that he could not move. And then . . .' Number Two raised the oil lamp to his chin so that the shadows played grotesquely over his features and his nostrils glowed scarlet. 'Then,' he said, 'they flayed the wolf alive.' His voice sank to a barely audible hum, and he leaned forward towards the boys who craned towards him to catch every word. 'This they did with each of the three savage beasts in their haul. But the skins of members of that Pack that Never Dies live on for ever. And that is why the wolfskin at your feet is always on the move. It will always give warning when danger approaches. Then it will rear up as if in a wind, and howl, "Aaaaaaaahooooo, Aaaaaaaahooooo!" ' Number Two moaned under his breath and with that, he blew out the lamp and plunged the children into total darkness.

How they had buried themselves deep in the bedclothes! Gabriel laughed to himself, recalling the unrivalled pleasure of that scare. Number Two came to recite to me, he thought, because he cared for me, the youngest, more than he cared for Jerome. Jerome knew it, even then, I can attract where he cannot.

Noticing the rain streaming down the window pane in front of him, Gabriel pulled himself together. I must stop daydreaming as if I were a foolish old man out in the sun. He bent his head once more to his books, and began writing a commentary on the scene of the hunt, pointing out with asperity that Andrew always put the most favourable construction on K'ang-hsi's character, and that the benevolence the emperor showed the Jesuits was the customary courtesy of the Manchu despot, and was extended to countless minor mandarins. K'ang-hsi was inspired by his desire to secure the Jesuits' assistance in his astronomical and mathematical learning. 'Andrew and a colleague', wrote Gabriel rapidly, 'went a total of twenty-two times to the Forbidden City in Peking during the month following K'ang-hsi's return from the hunt in Tartary, in order "to enquire after the emperor's health". He ordered other officials to receive them and convey his thanks for their solicitude. He himself saw them only once, in order to ask them to manufacture a telescope to fit a lens he had been given by another Jesuit, posted in the south. It was strictly the scientist in Andrew and not the man of God that created his appeal to K'ang-hsi, but Andrew in 1685 had not yet faced this bitter fact.'

Gabriel turned to the passage in Andrew's diaries, dated 23 April, following the description of the hunt. 'I baptized my servant today,' he said. 'He took the name of Francis Xavier after our beloved saint. He is an upstanding boy who shows greater virtue each day. Truly we must have more missionaries to China to accomplish our work.'

At this point Gabriel rubbed his eyes, and passed quickly on. A letter followed, a draft of a plea Andrew was preparing to send to the Father General of the Society in Lisbon. 'In the whole of China,' read the draft, 'there are only thirteen or fifteen members of our Society. It is as if in the whole of Europe we had one priest in Rome, another in Turin, another in Madrid, another in Paris, a fifth in Vienna, a sixth in Brussels in order to keep all Europe true to the Faith. "*Quod, quaeso, valet unus miles tot hostium agmine circumcinctus ... ?*" And what, I ask, is the worth of a solitary soldier surrounded by such a host of the enemy?' Andrew went on to argue the grandeur of the mission in China, as a special calling with special privileges. Gabriel compressed his dry lips together in repugnance at the bearing of Andrew's thought. The missionary stressed the martyrdom of the China mission, and extolled the hardships of the journey from Europe, the dangers presented by pirates, shipwreck, disease, as well as the perils within China itself. Although the emperor smiled with favour at present upon Christian missionaries, Andrew wrote, not many years had passed since the Jesuits had been persecuted, loaded with chains, and thrown into the dungeons of Peking. Even Father Adam Schall, an old man bowed with age and illness, had been sentenced to death by the slicing process for high treason. Gabriel rebelled against the relish with which Andrew recounted the outrages and torments suffered by the priests, and the joyous manner in which he used them as bait for missionaries to China, arguing that a priest who merely died on the way to the East should be counted amongst the martyrs. Gabriel sniffed and rubbed his eyes. All this to attract greater numbers of missionaries, he thought. He found repellent the strong tradition of martyrdom within the Society to which he belonged. He was suspicious of the urge to immolate oneself, and too world-weary to tolerate fanaticism of any kind. Sometimes he had seen the martyr's spirit possess one of his pupils or younger colleagues. In the confessional he discouraged such thoughts, and privately he doubted whether the thirst for the glory of a gory death was sent by God. But Gabriel found it easy to meditate on the lives of the saints of the distant past. He did not associate that avid appetite for death with St Peter or St Paul. The fascination with torture that he glimpsed in his own contemporaries and in Andrew da Rocha's diaries was of a different order. The martyrs of the early Christian persecutions seemed pure; but the second age of martyrs – the Catholic dead of the Reformation and the overseas missions – provoked uncomfortable questions. He was still uplifted by the marvellous beginning of St Teresa's life, when she and her brother, hungry for the martyr's crown, set off from Avila hand in hand to seek death amongst the heathen Moors. But such desires were to be avoided, as she herself seemed to acknowledge by her subsequent life of practical reform and administrative business. In *Vision and Prophecy*, Gabriel had tried to show how wrong he thought St John of the Cross to be when he wrote: 'For until the desires are lulled to sleep through the mortification of our sensual nature, and until at last the sensual nature is at rest from them, so that they make not war upon the spirit, the soul goes not forth to true liberty for the enjoyment of union with its Beloved.' He loved and profoundly respected John of the Cross, but he was convinced that the physical austerities he prescribed were harmful, and that they fanned rather than extinguished the flames of desire. He had hidden the wellspring of his conviction from the readers of *Vision and Prophecy*. It had not been the place to discuss it; but concealment had not wiped out memory.

When Gabriel first entered the noviciate, he had confessed his early sin with much effort, and the sacrament had afforded him some relief. But he had never felt that the penance given him by his confessor matched the seriousness of the deed. He had told him so, begging him for a greater penance, but the priest made Gabriel admit – unwillingly – that the importance he attached to his childhood sin sprang from pride; he wanted even his sins to be more important than they were. For the confessor, Gabriel's story was common enough, and his troubled conscience proof of his contrition. But to Gabriel ... Gabriel could not exorcize it, and Andrew da Rocha's naive thirst for pain and death unsettled in him once more the deposit of anxiety that had lain still in him so long.

At the time, he had been eight years old, and Jerome ten. It was 1917, the year before the family left Tientsin for Shanghai, the year Gabriel sailed from China never to see it again. The two boys had been to the local Sunday School, run by the mild-mannered wife of a Protestant minister, because the boys' mother dismissed as total foolishness the notion that Protestants were damned and their churches unholy. Besides, the Catholics' classes were in French. 'How shameful it is,' she would cry, 'that the Chinese see our endless quarrelling, Protestant against Catholic, priest against friar.' She would shrug her shoulders and shake her head, adding, 'Henry is a very good man, for all he's a Protestant. My family could never understand that.'

At Sunday School that day, Mrs Midhurst, the minister's wife – or was it Middleton? Gabriel couldn't remember – had read the handful of children the stories of several martyrdoms: Sebastian transfixed by arrows, Perpetua and Felicity torn apart by lions, Cecilia asphyxiated in the baths of her own villa and slit through the throat. Mrs Midhurst then made the conventional comparison between these martyrs' sufferings and the Passion of Our Lord. 'Be good, children,' she said. (Her voice still cut Gabriel like cheesewire.) 'Because Jesus was scourged, mocked, beaten, crowned with thorns and crucified, just for you.' Then she sent them home.

Jerome and Gabriel were very excited by Mrs Midhurst's stories. She had none of Number Two's pitch or imagination; in fact, she was dull. But the very dullness of her tone made her stories seem real. Terribly real. Gabriel was frightened that the wolfskin would leap on him, or snap as he jumped into bed, and he and Jerome enjoyed playing on each other's fears as they lay side by side. 'I saw it move.' 'No you didn't.' 'Yes I did.' But they knew all along the rug was a rug; Number Two told fairy-tales. But Mrs Midhurst's prosaic style belonged to the real, live world. If she told them the rug was baying at the moon, they would have believed her in a way they did not believe Number Two. So Jerome and Gabriel were very quiet as they sat under the canopy in the family carriage bringing them home after the lesson, while Number Two ran beside them to keep up.

'I think we should punish ourselves, like the martyrs,' said Gabriel in a soft voice to his brother. He could still recall his feeling of fear and anticipation. Jerome, easily led as he had always been, agreed, but a puzzled furrow appeared between his eyes. Yes, thought Gabriel, Paula has inherited that look of perplexity.

Their parents were sitting on the verandah in the shade when the children returned, drinking cold tea with some friends while one of the houseboys methodically swung the fan above them. The boys bowed politely, pulling off their caps. Their mother asked them if they'd enjoyed school, and what Mrs Midhurst had taught them. Jerome would have given her a full account – on any ordinary Sunday. But that day he was silent, and the two brothers were told to run along and play.

Together Jerome and Gabriel made for their hideaway in the garden, deep behind a line of thuya that screened the house from the north winds blowing down on Tientsin from Manchuria, and into a clump of rhododendron bushes that grew twelve feet or more in height and left smooth clearings in the centre, under the dark branches. They had not said much to each other; it had not been necessary. Gabriel's lips twisted at the memory. 'You go first,' said Jerome. 'No, you go,' said Gabriel. 'We'll go together,' he added, when Jerome seemed reluctant. Gabriel was already excited. He pulled off his shirt and then his socks and shoes and trousers. It was damp under the bushes, in spite of the heat of the day outside and he shivered as he waited there without clothes. Jerome stood opposite him, naked too except for his underpants. Gabriel stripped a small branch from the bushes that covered them, and pulling off the twigs and leaves, handed it to his brother.

'Bags you go first,' he said.

'S'pose so,' said Jerome. He took precedence, as the eldest. 'I think we should pray first.'

They knelt down. Gabriel was trembling. Then Jerome beat himself with the twig, uttering sudden snorts of pain, and Gabriel watched him until his teeth chattered with fright and his whole body was stiff with joy. When it came to his turn, he lashed himself across the shoulders and shins and thighs until the twig snapped. Then he asked Jerome to do it to him, and throwing himself on his back on the damp earth, begged him to beat him harder, longing, though he dared not say so, that his brother would hit his genitals with the switch. Jerome beat him until his face was red and sweat stood out on his forehead and on his chest and back. Gabriel saw the branches meshed black above him against the dun sky, and twisted about, moaning. Then Jerome suddenly threw away the rod and fell down beside Gabriel and burst into tears. Gabriel wept too as they lay beside one another till the sobs exhausted them and they fell asleep. When they woke, they did not speak of it; they never returned to the hideaway.

Half a century later, Gabriel felt the memory grip him again. Shame, shame mixed with excitement held him fast as it had done then. It still troubled him, far, far more than the sin – if it was a sin indeed – required. And Gabriel knew the reason, though he tried to push it out of his mind: the perversion he sensed in this childish imitation of Christ told him something important about his faith, something he didn't want to face. It stirred doubts about the idea of the Passion of Christ Himself.

Later in Andrew's diaries, Gabriel remembered that the Emperor K'ang-hsi asked the Jesuit why God, if He was all-powerful and all-merciful, did not choose to forgive His son instead of sacrificing Him. Andrew had answered that the Redemption could not have taken place without a holocaust, but this answer did not satisfy K'ang-hsi. Indeed, thought Gabriel, it must have been quite incomprehensible to him. And it did not satisfy Gabriel either. But why, he thought miserably, rubbing his eyes, why am I not satisfied, why am I dry and dull now when I think of the Passion and the Cross? . . . His thought stumbled. It can't be true, he said to himself, it can't be true . . . He hesitated again, and then looked up sharply through the window at the steadily falling rain. This is hopeless, he thought. The day is ruined. I can't work.

He left the room. Downstairs, Rosie greeted him warmly

and followed him into the sitting-room. He sank into one of the soft armchairs.

'The phone hasn't stopped all day.'

'Thank God it's turned off upstairs.'

'Everyone wanted Doctor Namier. Every paper in England, it seemed to me. I told all of them there was nobody here but me, and that I wouldn't say anything even if they wanted me to.' She held her hands neatly together in front of her waist. The skin on them was pink and shiny, from years of work in hard water.

Gabriel showed no curiosity, which disappointed Rosie though it did not surprise her, since the priest usually seemed preoccupied. 'That's very good of you, Nanny,' he said absently. 'You mustn't let anyone know I'm here, when I'm working. It's difficult enough to work as it is, without additional interference.'

'No one asked for you, Father,' said Rosie pointedly, arranging a cushion on another armchair.

Gabriel looked at her dully. Then a thought crossed his mind, and he asked: 'Have you heard of some visions of Our Lady that took place recently in Sicily?'

'In Italy, Father? Yes, indeed.' Rosie put her head to one side. 'Why?'

'You believe in them – that they are genuine?' As soon as he had said it, Gabriel realized the question was unnecessary. The old lady looked hurt, and her back became straighter than ever. 'Why, of course, Father,' she said. 'Who would lie about a holy thing like that?'

They talked some more, because Gabriel felt he had offended in an area where a priest should not offend. Rosie told him all she knew from her local congregation and her friends in the Irish community in Kilburn, and mollified by his interest made him a tray of sandwiches and coffee for his lunch.

When he returned to his study, Gabriel found himself envying her, for her trust, her simplicity, the fierce heat of her belief. How dry, how constricted he was by comparison! He groaned and looked out of the window. It was still raining, but a walk would clear his mind.

It was chilly outside, and he clutched his black jacket to himself, bending his thin frame against the drizzle. He started down the lane, but at the end he faltered. Perhaps it was too wet for the Heath. He looked up and down the street and registered the mellow red-brick lines of the Institute of Baroque Music to his right. Then he remembered the young man who had swooped into the sitting-room the night before. Without further thought, Gabriel passed through the wrought-iron gates and, brushing the rain from his shoulders, entered the Institute.

There was no one in the hall, but he heard the sound of playing elsewhere, and so he walked softly through the first room filled with instruments and stood in the doorway beyond. In the window to his left Oliver Summers sat at a harpsichord of fragile inlay veneer. Gabriel did not move, but leant against the jamb and half closed his sore eyes. The notes fell in gentle cascades over him, following each other with tinkling symmetry – now soft, now louder, but never loud, an austere music, almost impassive in its formal purity. The rain veiled the large sash windows, and the light in the room was alkaline, it was so soft and clinging. Oliver was framed against the window, and his profile, running in a smooth curve from forehead to nose over a high bridge, again stabbed Gabriel's memory of Leonardo's smiling angel at the Virgin's left hand. He thought, I must move, but he stood where he was and let the notes' cool arithmetic steady him. Oliver's hands came to rest, and he too remained still, in contemplation of the instrument.

There was at that moment a pause, like a catch in the breath, between the two people, the young man and the old priest, as they stayed silent and still in the milkily-lit room. It was brief, but it marked a change of theme in Gabriel's life, just as a composer with an interval of silence stresses the melody more surely than with a clash of cymbals. Then Oliver rose from the stool, and became aware for the first time of Gabriel Namier in the doorway.

'Hi,' he said, throwing his hair out of his eyes with a sideways toss of his head, and coming towards him with a slow smile of greeting. 'I didn't know there was anyone here. The rain, you know, it keeps people away.'

'Don't stop because of me,' said Gabriel, removing himself from the doorpost.

'Oh, I've finished,' said Oliver. 'And I'm not much good at it anyway. Fingers fumble – full of mistakes.' He laughed. 'But it's the feeling between us two that counts.' He turned back to the instrument. 'Isn't she beautiful? What a song she makes, what a song.' Oliver Summers's world was entirely animate – for him even stones had life and formed part of the huge breathing, feeling, ungovernable, inchoate flux of which he felt himself to be a cheerful and equally disorganized counterpart. He knew that there was more than volition to the playing of an instrument; there was a spirit abroad, not only in the player, but also in the machine; Oliver never considered anything, not even a cash register let alone a harpsichord, a machine without a soul.

Gabriel nodded at him. He did not quite know how to deal with the young man's directness. Stiffly he asked, 'What were you playing?'

'Couperin,' said Oliver. 'One of the preludes. A pretty piece.'

He looked ardently at the harpsichord and then back again at Gabriel. Close to, Gabriel could see that Oliver was not as young as his rapid movements and childishly fair hair made him appear from a distance. He had creases round his mouth where he smiled, and fine lines round his eyes, which were a light hazel and unremarkable, except for a certain mischievous gleam that appeared in them from time to time. He gave Gabriel such a look at that moment, filled with an impish friendliness that displayed full awareness of the attraction he was exerting over the older man, the serene knowledge of someone who has possessed beauty and grace in abundance all his life, and has not hesitated to use them. A few years before, Oliver had let the full tide of his charms flow over the old queer who had looked after the Institute's instruments. He had been recommended for the job as his successor. But Oliver's opportunism was unsophisticated, and Gabriel, who usually felt dominant in any encounter through his gifts and status, relented towards it and allowed the younger man's startling, naive and open manner to draw him into a conversation such as he would never normally have had.

'On a day like this,' said Oliver, 'my spirit rises so high, feels so full, that I have to play . . . even badly. You see, I love rain. I can't understand why no one else does. It blurs everything and makes it beautiful, impressionistic, changeable. Which is of course the way things really are.' He laughed, because Gabriel, normally so imperturbable, was showing his dismay. 'You're Jerome's brother,' continued Oliver. 'The priest.' He looked intently at Gabriel and said, 'I've always thought that it must be the loneliest possible existence. I spend my life – I will spend my life – looking for someone to share it with, someone who'll love and understand.' He laughed again. 'Of course I make lots of terrible mistakes, but I keep trying. You – you haven't even got the hope of that. Apart from the fact that I suppose it's too late for you now anyway. I don't know how you can bear it, honestly.' He went over to the harpsichord and, with a gentle movement, closed its lid and covered the keyboard. 'What brought you round here?'

Gabriel cleared his throat painfully. 'My brother told me you were an expert on harpsichords.' But as he described his work on Andrew da Rocha, he relaxed. He told Oliver about the spinet – the 'nightingale table' – and K'ang-hsi's pleasure in the Jesuit's ingenuity.

Oliver was interested, but ignorant of any such instrument. 'Come on,' he cried, leaping up the stairs. 'We'll look him up in the library. It's only small, but we should find something.'

Gabriel followed Oliver into a panelled room at the top of the stairs, the Institute's reference library. There was no one else there. Oliver pulled down one book after another, and riffled the pages rapidly, while the lively torrent of explanations he offered, half reading, half talking, poured uncomprehended over Gabriel. Equal temperament, unequal temperament, the comma of Pythagoras, tuning registers of the Italians, the Flemish, the English, diagrams of the kind of spinets current in the late seventeenth century, with their characteristic jacks and keyboards, the contrasting textures of tone in different instruments, the greater merits of pearwood, the importance of real condor feathers for the quills which plucked the strings, allegories on exquisitely painted cabinets – it all made very little sense.

'You will have to explain much more slowly,' he said, smiling because Oliver's enthusiasm was infectious. 'Perhaps you could lend me the books you think might be of help.' Oliver looked up, worried. 'Well, if not, perhaps you could write out the references and let me come here and read them when I can.'

'I'd lend you anything, of course. But the Institute makes us swear on pain of death not to let a book out of the building. They never come back.' He pulled out a chair and began writing in a small, surprisingly neat hand with sharp italic angles. 'These are the main reference works, I think, and they'll give you other leads.' He smiled up at Gabriel. 'Do you want to start now, or shall I show you – I'd really like to – how a spinet works? Much better than reading old books, to see the real thing.' His energy amused Gabriel, who nodded slightly. 'Come on then, back down again we go.'

On the stairs, Oliver turned. 'I'll be your teacher. That's a turn-up for the books isn't it? When were you last taught, not teaching?'

'I'm far too old,' said Gabriel, drily. But he was enjoying himself.

'Never,' said Oliver. 'You might as well be dead if you think that.'

'I am almost.' Gabriel laughed as he said it, so much so that he opened his mouth and his small dark teeth showed. It was unusual for his face to soften; his lips were usually pressed tightly together.

Oliver sat down at a spinet in a smaller room adjoining the large drawing-room where Gabriel had found him playing. He waved Gabriel towards the stool he drew up beside him. 'Come, sit down,' he said firmly. The instrument was pentagonal, and made of cypress wood, inlaid with scrolls and formal flowers of ebony. 'It's dated 1742, here on the highest key,' Oliver showed him, 'which makes it later than your man. Also, this is an English instrument, and its five-octave compass, starting from GG, is very rare elsewhere, so I doubt your fellow used it in China.' He played a few fast scales up the keyboard. 'Sit down,' he said again. He stood up and placed Gabriel's stool in the centre.

Oliver's manner was so artless that it was difficult to withstand, and submissively Gabriel sat down. Oliver leant over him and lowered the stool.

'You're a longer man than me,' he said, smiling. 'OK. Now place your hands on the keys. Like this.' He picked up Gabriel's right hand from where it lay on his bony knee and placed it on the ivories. 'You must feel it, if you're going to write anything about it. You must feel the way the sound is made, the way the string is plucked, the tension between the player's fingers and the music inside the instrument. Go on, play it, gently. Doesn't matter that you don't know how. There's no one here to hear you. Except me, and I don't think that I'll complain that you can't render a perfect pavane or galliard.'

'Really, no,' said Gabriel protesting and making to move to his feet.

'No,' said Oliver. He laid one hand on Gabriel's and the other on his shoulder and, leaning over, played a scale slowly, to show him. Gabriel noticed with surprise that Oliver's thumb was disfigured by a large callus. Oliver followed his eyes and laughed merrily. 'That's from cutting up the bits of leather one needs to tune them. A right sight, isn't it?' The exchange broke some of Gabriel's resistance: the blemish on the young man's thumb somehow helped to undo the spell his behaviour and appearance had cast on Gabriel. Clumsily he imitated the movement of Oliver's hand over the board.

'Good, good,' said Oliver. 'Now as I play, look inside and you'll see how she works. That way you'll understand what your man was up to when he was making one. Won't he, love?' Oliver tapped the flank of the instrument lightly and bent his face to the keyboard. Then he tossed his hair out of his eyes again and smiled up at Gabriel.

'I wonder what they think, all these instruments?' He paused. 'Are you enjoying your lesson, Father?' His voice was light, but Gabriel did not feel mocked. He smiled back, and his long, furrowed face acquired a sudden air of gaiety.

'Well, I'm learning.'

❧ *CHAPTER 6*

Jerome Namier rose as the first anoerexic light of day began to seep out of the edges of the swollen clouds. He moved silently in the curtained room with the blind skills of a man accustomed to dressing quietly in the dark. He kissed the sleeping Teresa on the forehead with moistened lips but she did not move, and with the feeling of annoyance at her neglect which he had experienced almost every morning of their marriage, he left the bedroom and went downstairs.

'Good morning, good morning, Nanny.' She was waiting for him in the kitchen, with tea standing hot by the stove. Jerome paced up and down, every nerve tensed for the sound of the letterbox opening as the papers were pushed through it.

Rosie broke an egg into the pan and tilted it gently round and round so that the white would form a smooth circle about the yolk. She laid a plate in front of Jerome and poured him some strong tea, returned to the stove, and dusted the egg with black pepper. Jerome looked at her with glazed attention; but he was hardly aware of the rich smell of the bacon sizzling under the grill. He thanked her automatically, as he always did, with a feeling of guilt that she had ended up caring for him, and then ate his breakfast quickly, hoping that his speed might work sympathetic magic on the delivery boy. But he came to the end of his meal, and still the bundle of newspapers had not thudded to the floor. Jerome soaked up the remainder of the yolk with his last piece of toast and chewed it deliberately. Then, with silence from the front door, he went to the lavatory. While he was still there, he heard the papers arrive; he hurried out and snatched them with sudden rudeness from Rosie's hands. She looked aggrieved and her back stiffened, but she said nothing.

It was the same fear, Jerome remembered, that he had felt as a young man over the results of Schools, and the moment before he had met his examiners to defend his doctorate in 1936, so many years ago. He had acquitted himself gloriously then, so why not now? He whipped through the *New Radical* and found the page – page 3, the leading article – where the piece by Christopher Shaw was headlined 'The Fortunes of the *Review*'. He skimmed the article for his own name, just as he had run his eye over the class lists, first the Thirds, his heart beating faster, surely not there, no, then the Seconds, could it be, yes, thank God, but then the disappointment: he could have got a First, everyone said so, and the college would never have given him a fellowship if they hadn't recognized it. But the fact was he didn't.

He saw his name now in the *New Radical*. It jumped out at him over and over again, as if it were printed in caps. 'Dictatorial Jerome Namier, who has run the *Review* as if it were his family's dry-goods business . . .' What did they mean by that? Then later, 'The Namier family fortunes largely floated the *Review* in its early years. They consist of the proceeds of Henry Namier's commercial enterprises in China during the last days of the Empire, when opium was the European traders' most lucrative source of revenue.' I see, thought Jerome, a slur or two to blacken me the more. Heat snaked up his back and his forehead burned. Rosie watched him anxiously, as she washed up the breakfast things and wiped the stove.

His eyes continued down the page to the end, where he read: 'It is impossible to believe Jerome Namier could not have suspected the political affiliations of the Institute of Cultural Affairs and the nature of the commitment to the "Free World". If he did, his negligence cannot be condoned, and if he did not, his naivety cannot be excused.' Jerome groaned, and retired to the sitting-room to read the article through, word by word, from the beginning.

'The building at 3500, 14th St NW, Washington DC, looks like any other office block, and through the swing doors, above the potted tropical palms, between the lifts, hangs a guide to the businesses represented in the building as it does in any other large block in an American city. But 3500, 14th St NW is unusual because it houses a dozen or more CIA cover and feeder companies. The Pacific Air Company and the North-West Pacific Freight Company are two cargo airlines owned and run by the CIA to carry out operations in the Far East; Air America, the CIA passenger airline, and one of the five largest fleets in the world, has its central office here; South-East Asia Commercial Enterprises, Inc. and Four Winds Trading Company are simply two more screens erected by the CIA over its activities abroad.

'The sixth floor of the building houses the Institute of Cultural Affairs. The list of organs and centres funded by the Institute reads like an anthology of liberal orthodox causes of the Sixties.' Jerome's eye skipped on. 'And the Institute boasts a galaxy of honorary presidents, including the eminent philosopher Jacques Maritain and the theologian Reinhold Niebuhr.' Actually it is a remarkable and reputable list, thought Jerome.

'But what the receptionist', the article continued, 'shows you with the greatest pride of all is the latest copy of the *London Review of Books*, and the cabinet behind her in which she keeps the back numbers since 1961, the date of its foundation.

'During the late Fifties, the CIA used every device at its command to fight for the allegiance of European intellectuals who were turning away from the CIA's chief concerns and its conception of democracy and the Free World. The Agency was aware of the dangers to its own interests presented by Marxist sympathizers among the French intelligentsia who emerged during the late Fifties with the existentialists, and it did not want the pattern to be repeated anywhere in Western Europe, and certainly not in England.

'Since May 1963 – eighteen months after its inception – the *Review* has received 10,000 dollars a year from the Institute of Cultural Affairs.' Jerome heaved indignantly, God damn it, that hardly pays for my secretary. If they only knew the running costs of a paper like the *Review*. What the hell is 10,000 dollars?

'The CIA does not pay the money directly to the Institute. It has set up an elaborate structure of bogus subsidiary companies through which the money is laundered. The Institute of Cultural Affairs thus receives its funds from the Ranke Foundation, which on enquiry turns out to be a numbered account in Zurich. The Ranke Foundation in turn receives its funds from the Weissman-Drosser Corporation, which unsurprisingly – if you have followed the story so far – also turns out to be numbered account in a different Swiss bank, this time in Geneva.'

Jerome was interested. It is possible, he thought, that the American with whom I lunched didn't know the origin of the funds he was offering me. If the CIA covers its tracks so thoroughly that it's taken twelve years for Shaw to come up with the story, then maybe the men employed by the Institute were in the dark as well. But Jerome was sarcastic; he knew that even if it were so, he himself would still be culpable of 'naivety'.

Here came the attack. 'Jerome Namier is the editor of the *Review*. Indeed, in the eyes of many, he *is* the *Review*. He embodies the qualities of urbane intellectualism, solidly rooted in a European and specifically Francophile tradition. The *Review* has been known to run a 6,000-word article on its front page about a book by Gaston Perreyve called *L'Humanisme de Nicolas de Cuse et le Cercle Néo-Platoniste Cusain au Quinzième Siècle*. The *Review* is nothing if not sure of itself. "The reader is the last person you're writing for," Jerome Namier has been heard to say. "Do you think Dante thought about the man in the street who'd buy his poem? No."' Jerome chuckled to himself. Quite right, why not? Then a cloud crossed his mind. Was this just London gossip, or had someone been feeding the *Radical*? Teresa's words of the night before jolted him, and her suspicions rankled. He returned to his reading.

'Namier believes snobbery of all kinds is one of humanity's driving forces. "They'll read it, they won't understand it, but others will see them read it, and that's what they care about." This particularly nasty brand of elitism' – Jerome twisted in his chair – 'does not reflect democratic principles, but then neither do the activities of the CIA in alleged support of democracy and freedom. In Jerome Namier the Institute of Cultural Affairs found a hidebound, unenquiring subscriber to a prevailing intellectual orthodoxy – a man who belongs to no political party, but only to the ivory tower of privilege, jealously guarding his own interests, and therefore intimately trapped by the status quo which provides him and his enterprise with paymasters.'

Jerome clenched his teeth. I'll sue him, he thought. The fucking bastard. He did not swear much, so the words were unfamiliar to him. Damn the young punk. Rage swelled the blood in his neck, and he undid the top button of his collar. Hidebound, indeed. Paymasters. Privilege. Hadn't he worked? Hadn't he seen through and exposed dozens of political injustices, from here to Cracow?

He bent back to the paper. The brief description of the Namier Company's proceedings in China and Hong Kong from 1870 to 1925 followed, making what Jerome considered honest Victorian enterprise sound like piracy on the high seas. Then Shaw stated: 'The influence of the CIA on the *Review* remains to be analysed, and a breakdown of contents should be undertaken. But it is hardly necessary to point out that its intellectual standing marked the frequent political articles it published as unimpeachable, and that it consequently provided a cunning and watertight showcase for CIA opinion.' Jerome thought back over the years. He had always considered that the *Review* had no political affiliations, and that writers of all persuasions had freely contributed to it. Surely the impartiality and variety of its forum was its chief source of strength? He had always sought to provide the most well-informed opinion on any subject, regardless of its political colour. If anything, the greater number of liberal writers had made the *Review* leftish, he would have thought.

Jerome came to the end of the article, which contained a direct challenge to his continued editorship of the *Review*. But his rage had abated. He did not seize the telephone and ring his solicitors, but sat heavily brooding. He thought of ringing Shaw himself – whom he had met here and there in London, and remembered to be a seedy-looking young man with his shirt half out of his trousers and thinning lank hair – but he checked himself, and thought, No, first I'll grill James about what he knows, and then I'll have a good look through the files. He felt almost calm, and faced the ordeal of the day with resolution.

As he prepared to leave the house, he cast himself for a moment as Julius Caesar. Was Christopher Shaw the messenger of doom? Was today his Ides of March?

From the front door, Rosie Murphy called after him: 'You'll be soaked.' But Jerome shrugged his shoulders and did not turn back for the umbrella she proffered him. Does the man on a tumbril need an overcoat? he thought, with a fresh burst of gallows humour.

But when he emerged from the tube, he regretted it. He ran, with a heavy but powerful lollop, keeping his feet close to the ground to minimize splashing, towards the arcades of the Ritz. His hair was soon wet, and its dripping ends found their way under his collar. Cursing, he waited at the corner for the rain to stop. The newsvendor beside him called out: 'Looks set all day.' Jerome looked up at the sky through his rain-streaked glasses, and nodded agreement.

'Good morning, sir,' said the porter of Brooks's when he reached the door. He was shown to a battered black leather sofa in a flagged room under the stairs. 'There's a good fire burning,' the man said. Jerome nodded gratefully and stood before the flames, lifting one foot then the other to dry off his shoes, and polishing his glasses on his handkerchief.

'Jerome, my dear fellow,' he heard James behind him. 'Come, let's go to the Subscription Room. We shall have complete privacy there.' He shook Jerome's hand, and with his other hand took his arm lightly. 'They'll bring us coffee, too, but it's a pretty thin brew.'

Jerome passed him the *Radical*, limp from the rain. 'Read it,' he said. 'Before we talk.'

Jerome looked at his friend as he read. He was wearing a sports jacket of a large tweed in greys and blues, which came no doubt from Huntsmans'. Apart from this strident note, he was immaculately turned out. A fine figure of a man, thought Jerome with irritation, who hasn't been rained on, because he got a taxi.

Cunliffe was thinner than his contemporary and had the careful, puckered face of a man of great personal vanity. One felt while talking to him that he was conscious of every expression. Though past the glow that made him, as a young man at Oxford, the gossip of connoisseur high tables, he was still handsome. Jerome laughed now at his friend's vanity, but he admired his easy big-boned grace and his confident need to be looked at (hence the sports jacket). Jerome wished, as he had done as a young man, that he could keep his own trousers uncreased for more than a morning, and that the flaps of his jacket would hang straight and not split open over his backside, that his hair would stop thinning at the temples and over his crown. Soon, he reflected with abhorrence, I shall have to part my hair behind.

James sat with one leg resting on his other knee, and exhibited his strong profile to Jerome. Jerome wondered about him. Sitting there, he looked too crass, too much the blue-eyed boy in his frank narcissism ever to practise a deception of such magnitude on his oldest friend. Jerome's assumption of authority over James had come naturally for a long time, as if the latter were a pretty, vapid woman to whom everything had to be explained at enjoyably long lunches. As an undergraduate James had been enthusiastic in the way English cynics think is quintessentially Yankee, and Jerome had never reassessed his friend's character.

James handed the *Radical* back to Jerome with a studied look of sympathy.

'Well, what do you think?' asked Jerome, impatient.

'It's a bit over the top, isn't it? That stuff about the family. In rather poor taste, I'd say. The *Radical* goes in for this mixture of journalism and pamphleteering. I find it . . .'

Jerome cut him short. 'Apart from that,' he snapped, 'would you say it's correct?'

'That the money from the Institute came from the CIA?'

'You're being obtuse, James,' said Jerome quietly. 'That is obviously so. Whoever did the research, Shaw or someone else, did a thorough job. The money is undoubtedly CIA money. The question is, was the *Review* influenced by the funds, and if so, how?'

'Ahem,' said James, changing the position of his legs, but looking as statuesque as before. 'I would have thought you were a better judge of that than I.' He paused, then added, 'Listen, Jerome, we've known each other for years. You're my oldest friend.' He laid one hand, adorned with a family signet ring of chalcedony, on the table between them. 'CIA doesn't in my view demand a great return for its investments in this type of thing. It's not on a one-to-one basis. The article makes it quite plain that the Agency was delighted to have the *Review* in its portfolio, so to speak.' Jerome winced. 'I don't think you need worry at all about whether your editorship was somehow subverted by the funds you were receiving.' He laughed, showing his even teeth.

Jerome felt miserable. Something in James's speech jarred

horribly. He tried to locate it. Yes, 'CIA', without the definite article. He spoke cautiously, and as he did so, he tried to remember writers James had suggested to him in the past, but as he did so, a tide of greater misery began sweeping over him.

'The Institute of Cultural Affairs' identity was pretty well camouflaged, wouldn't you say?' he asked, slowly.

'Oh yes indeed,' said James heartily. 'There was no way you could have known its origins.' He tapped the *Radical*.

'Could you?' Jerome's voice was low.

'I *am* still American, old boy,' said James with that starry smile again. 'But I didn't know.'

Jerome shifted and felt anger heat his chest and rise in his gullet.

'You didn't?'

'We have a feeling for these things – I mean, we Americans. But I didn't know.' The smile had vanished.

'You knew.'

James was silent.

'For ten thousand dollars a year.' Jerome groaned and beat his hands together over and over again, palm hitting fist, palm hitting fist. He was too wretched to be angry. 'We didn't need it. God knows we didn't need it. Why?'

James was still silent. Then, as Jerome's anguished eyes searched his, he said deliberately, 'I own fifty percent of the *Review*, and I have no quarrel with the principles CIA is fighting to preserve.'

Jerome flung himself back in his chair and closed his eyes. 'James, James, Brutus killed Caesar out of principle so he's a hero. But Judas sold Christ, so he's a villain. God damn it, I can't think straight, but you could have defended the Free World . . . I could have laid down my life for democracy . . . the *Review* could have been the most jingoistic rubbish week after week – but not for ten thousand dollars a year.'

Jerome heard himself wailing and disgust suddenly snapped the bond that kept him by his old friend's side. His brown eyes glittered as he stood up and with a formal movement turned squarely to face James.

For once in his life, his reading did not come to his assistance. The phrases that formed and reformed in his head were each more trite than the other. He wanted to say things like, 'But we were up together, how could you do it?' for it seemed to him almost as great a betrayal of their shared education as of his own person. He thought of Mark, James's son to whom he stood as godfather, and of asking James, 'What will Mark think when he knows what his father has done?' He wanted to round on James and rail, 'You have ruined me and betrayed our friendship.' But he swallowed the melodramatic words in the same way as he bit back his reproaches to his wife.

'There is nothing more to say,' he said, and turned without offering James his hand.

Jerome no longer noticed the rain. He was suffocating, pain coiled round him like a whip. A thousand ties which bound him to James had been slashed, and he mourned in deep bewilderment at the loss. His association with James was part of the fabric of his life; they were meshed together by a thousand shared experiences. With a certain dulled shock, his connectedness to James passed before him in fragments of past experience. What was it they had written to each other at the end of their letters? Yes, 'Thine is the kingdom.' He smiled at the memory. He remembered seeing James for the first time in Hall during their first term at Oxford, and their first tentative excursions and conversations; walking in Christ Church Meadow at twilight by the brightly canopied barges of the Rowing Clubs and James's emphatic vow, 'I shall never do what my parents want me to do, I shall never go into Wall Street or a law firm or any of the professions.' His blue eyes had blazed with defiance. 'I shall write.'

Jerome had been jealous when James was the first to marry, before the war. They had a difficult drink together in some hotel in wartime London when he met James's wife; Jerome was back on leave, and was perplexed and hurt by the lack of interest people showed in the progress of the distant fighting in Africa and the East. Later Jerome was an embarrassed witness at James's second marriage; and throughout Jerome had helped to get James published, offering him review space and telling his contacts about James's novel. He could not believe that this ordered relationship had been turned upside down, and that he, Jerome, had been used by James and tricked.

His hurt pride deflected all his thoughts from the question of the *Review*'s finances. Could James be an agent? It hardly seemed possible. Maybe he had cooperated out of misguided patriotism because he was perhaps ashamed he had abandoned his country; and then later duped Jerome into furthering his co-operation. That must be the case, thought Jerome. He could not endure a more sinister metamorphosis of the easy-going companion of his youth. They had shared so much together, and as Jerome cast his mind back for clues to the hard-headed side of James's character, his humiliation grew more painful. He recalled evenings at his house, where over a decanter or two of claret he, Jerome, had held forth about the state of the world, the role of the press, the independence of editors. It filled him now with self-loathing; how he had pontificated, making large gestures, heavy emphases; how James must have mocked him inwardly, knowing he was fooling him and that Jerome's much-vaunted freedom to wield influence was itself curtailed by other influence. James had always seemed so compliant and so admiring – it made Jerome burn. His bitterness turned to anger as he remembered other evenings spent listening to James's expatiations on the problem of his lost identity – an American in Britain, neither Yank nor true Brit.; he had heard James out at length on his continual mishaps with marriage and women, whom he used, Jerome told him, as mirrors for his vanity. This weakness, and James's dilettantism had made it so easy for Jerome to patronize him. He almost turned now to find him again and reproach him face to face. But he kept on down the street, oblivious of all else. For as in many friendships and marriages, the partner who seems the strongest is often the weakest because he depends utterly on the other's acquiescence and respect, so Jerome now felt cast off to drift, rudderless.

Squirming, he remembered a dinner long ago in Paris when James and he travelled there together one vac from Oxford. He had shown James his favourite haunts, and enjoyed being his guide, playing that James was his amanuensis, filling him in on anecdotes and literary gossip. 'This is one of the cafés Apollinaire sat in when he wrote *Le Flâneur des Quais;* this the Rue de Fleurus where Gertrude Stein ate her way through Alice B. Toklas and others.' In the Orangerie, he identified one by one the poets and men of letters in Fantin-Latour's group portrait. They had laughed and laughed when Jerome told James that George Sand was addressed as Madame when dressed as a man, and Monsieur when in female attire. And, walking across the Tuileries one day, 'James, when Mary Wollstonecraft, that staunch revolutionary, walked here, the soft earth gave way under her foot, and she turned pale because when she looked down she saw that it was soaked with blood.'

They had talked endlessly, sometimes stimulated by hashish they bought near St Sulpice from an Arab youth, but more often by *porto* drunk in cafés till the small hours. Jerome always preserved jealously his role as the leader of the dance, directing the conversations of James and other friends. He was the acknowledged master, who had read more and had the imagination to experience his reading more vividly. It was Jerome, already thick in the waist and always shabby, who had moulded James in the image of a dandy of the Nineties, as if his friend's handsomeness could compensate for his own lack of it.

On one particular night – it still made him wince – a dinner was to be held to celebrate James's twenty-third birthday. They were meeting in a small ancient restaurant behind the church of St Germain's granite grey spire. Jerome, in order to please his friend (and also to prove his worldly wisdom in another way) had with great difficulty procured two young *midinettes* to dine with them. It was his birthday present to James, and a generous one – in the days before his father died, Jerome lived on an allowance which was intended to cut out extravagances like women. But when he arrived with the two girls – they clung together and clasped each other throughout, he remembered – James was sulky and silent. He stared at the menu with lack of interest and finally ordered something ordinary. 'But you can have that anywhere, any time,' Jerome complained. And then after a pause James with his clear blue gaze said, 'Everything is spoiled. *Tout est gâché.*' Jerome looked at his friend with amazement, and James, with an offended air, got up and left the table, leaving Jerome alone with the two young girls, who were still whispering together in their own dream where young Englishmen were invisible. At first Jerome was enraged by such petulance, and the waste of the birthday party he had prepared. He ate his way miserably through the meal, and took the girls back to the hotel with him and went to bed with both of them. They talked to each other throughout in a murmur of *patois* of which Jerome could only catch a phrase here and there. They did not talk to him at all, but about him, to each other. And they examined his body as if it were a clinical specimen. At times as they bent over him and held him stiff between their fingers, looking intently into his face, he fancied he saw white masks up to their eyes over their mouths and noses, and the doctor's frown of concern appear on their brow; and all the while the murmur as they spoke to each other and the soft laughter as he moaned with pleasure or expelled his breath harshly as he climaxed under their fingers. Soon after he fell asleep from exhaustion, he woke remembering James with sudden concern. Every limb weighted with lead, he left his bed and fumbled downstairs to James's room. He knocked hard on his friend's door. James was still up. He was in a silk jacket, and his blue gaze was now purplish with drink and smoke.

'I thought we were going to be alone,' he said unsteadily, and rumpled his thick hair. 'You don't have to find me women.'

Jerome remembered the incident because then as now, the balance of their friendship had been rudely altered. For a brief space, he had glimpsed a firmness in James's character which he had always wanted to overlook. But Jerome never extended this knowledge gained so long before and he never learned to respect James's erotic life, but remained amused by his troubles. He thought with shame, I've known him forty years and taken him at face value. And this sense of shame fuelled his anger. To be deceived by someone crafty and dangerous is tolerable, he railed, but by someone so soft, so foppish . . .

A vein of fear began to bleed deep within him. His worth had never been appreciated. Gabriel acquired the esteem of others without effort and was deferred to in almost any company. But not he, not Jerome. In 1960 he had left Oxford because his college had not appointed him on the death of the Warden. He had been the obvious choice; on his own intellectual merits as well as by right of seniority he outran everyone else. He thought contemptuously of the shrivelled chemist for whom they had passed him over. How dim and unforthcoming he was. High table must be unbearable with him presiding, correcting A-level chemistry papers in his lap no doubt.

Teresa had told him it simply proved her opinion of Oxford,

that it was a community more shrewish and rivalrous than the theatre, and that was saying something. Jerome was the victim of a complex of jealousies and petty ambitions which was the essence of Oxford and which he had always refused to recognize. It gave the lie to its pretensions that it belonged to a grand humanist tradition, she sniffed. Besides, there wasn't a spark of fun in the place.

It had been hard, leaving Oxford after so many years – he had been a don since the end of the war – very hard. Jerome had walked back from the Senior Common Room and taken a stroll under the mulberry trees along the raised bank that overlooked the grassy fields beyond the Fellows' Garden. He had stopped to look at the sundial, but the day was shadowless and dull, a sunless spring morning, with the night dew still hanging in the turf and weighing down the slender blades. So he could not tell the time from the dial. The pastorale beyond the place where he had stood remained in his retina like a familiar engraving, the monochrome of an English unlit landscape, damp seeping everywhere, photosynthesis of the leaves overtaken by hydraulics, one of the highest water tables in England, this valley where the Thames and her tributaries splash themselves over fields and through cities, nourishing the ever fertile mulch that makes the landscape of England so enticing, so velvety, so uncompromisingly green. He had felt as he stood there in the postdiluvian light that he must choose whether to remain at Oxford, a don for ever, or to go.

He had made Teresa happy, and left. Her pleasure had not sweetened his sense of failure. To fail was a grievous personal fault: Henry Namier had schooled his eldest son well. When they went snipe-shooting in the marshes upriver from Shanghai, his cold anger when Jerome failed to bring down a bird or more with two cracks left and right had filled his son with dread; similarly, he could even now hear his father bellow over the high wind on one of the Yangtze's streams, 'Reef that sail, you little fool.' Henry Namier's face was splashed and gleaming red, the wind tore the sound out of his empty mouth, but Jerome understood only too well. Fingers rigid with the streaming wet, he picked at the ropes and tugged, swaying at the boom, until his frozen and insensible hands managed to twist the ties around the soaked sail. His father had taught him aim and marksmanship, endurance and navigation and other skills, to which Jerome had added later. His failure could not be explained away as ineptitude, but was something more profound. James's betrayal epitomized his inadequacy. He had never been able to command allegiance, either among the fellows of his college or among his oldest friends like James. Jerome groaned. The rhythm of life eluded him, like a complicated dance step attempted by a man wearing a deaf aid. I stumble against the metre, he thought, I cannot make my days scan. It may be funny for others, like bad poetry, like MacGonagall. But it's not funny for MacGonagall.

As he passed along the newspaper-strewn corridor of the *Review*'s offices, his staff looked at him expectantly, but their expectation was dazed and lustreless. Naturally they had been talking – he saw several copies of the *Radical* on different desks – but his encounter with James had disarmed him, and in sudden cowardice he ignored the crisis and passed rapidly down the dark book-lined corridor, into his office in the corner turret of the building overlooking the British Museum's soot-covered portico.

'Rosemary,' he called, as he sat down at his desk and saw that his correspondence was not lying on the blotter as usual, 'Where is the post?'

The office mouser sidled in, and settled on a pile of newspapers in a corner of the room with a complacent air. 'Ah, Lion,' said Jerome, 'I expect that for you things are quite pleasant today.'

Outside his door, the staff's dismay grew perceptibly, and only after a long pause did Jerome hear Rosemary moving.

'It's been a late start,' she said apologetically in the doorway. Jerome looked up at her with a warning light in his bright eyes, and she did not give him the sympathy she had planned. Instead she took her seat in silence at her desk just outside his glass door and began slitting open the mail and cutting the string on the many parcels with a small sharp knife. Jerome knew that she would like to say something, but did not dare. She was a bookish iron-haired woman in her late forties who had worked for him since the start of the *Review* and knew everything about him and Teresa, including their tax accounts which she helped him prepare. Her taste in books, especially novels, was broad-based and sensible, and Jerome valued her patience and her humour, particularly because these qualities of hers increased in inverse ratio to his impatience and temper. She had bowed shoulders from too many years of typing, and they gave her a cringing look far from her natural character. Her slow ironic smile when Jerome was exploding over something had often helped to check his rage and recover his own good spirits. He would talk to her later about the *Radical*, he decided, but for the present he continued the business of the week as if nothing had taken place. He needed more time to think.

Through the glass pane of his door he saw the figure of Ian Holmes look at some books on the shelves outside. But Jerome knew he was looking in at him. A Gauloise was stuck into the corner of Ian's wide rubbery mouth, and his right eye screwed up to avoid the smoke; his thick black hair sprouted in all directions. His grey eyes slid past Jerome's door and then into his office to focus for a brief moment on the editor at his desk. Jerome submitted uneasily to his scrutiny and did not acknowledge it, but kept his head down over the proofs.

'Come on, Lion,' he pleaded. 'Inspiration, please.' The cat came silently and jumped on to Jerome's desk. It tested the pile of correspondence tenderly with a paw, and finding it solid, climbed on to it and stretched out in the light of the angle-poise, like an urbanite under a sun lamp. Jerome pulled some clean paper towards him, and began taking notes from the filing cabinet of back numbers he kept in his office. Now and then, coming across a famous writer's denunciation of American foreign policy, he would mutter to the cat, 'Unimpeachable, Lion, wouldn't you agree?'

On a rough check, it seemed to Jerome that his paper's view-point on the US role in South-East Asia had escaped all CIA taint – unless the agency were embarked on an elaborate double bluff, fostering criticism in one quarter in order to stiffen prejudice in another, just as it had used provocateurs to stir up violence on the campuses until all anti-war opinion was associated with student riots, and peace-loving intellectuals slurred by extension. But Jerome did not think that the *Review* had played a part in this strategy: it had refrained from printing do-it-yourself bomb kits with diagrams. Its coverage of the Vietnam war had been indignant, even anguished; but the contributors were sober spokesmen.

Over Eastern Europe, Jerome was more perturbed. Dissidents and refugees received interested, if not favourable treatment, and their books were prominently reviewed. There was no equivalent attention paid to pro-regime authors from any of the Communist countries. In 1968, the *Review* had issued a special number on Dubcek's experiment. Headlined 'Socialism with a Human Face?', it had included articles both by leading Czechs in the movement from Prague and Bratislava, and by British academics. The verdict of their combined voices had been an enthusiastic, almost rhapsodic, endorsement. In 1970, after the Russian invasion, the *Review* echoed the earlier issue with another, dramatically banded in mourning, and entitled 'Prague Winter'.

The difficulty was, thought Jerome, reaching for the scruff of Lion's neck, that the paper's policy would have been identical if the CIA had not invested in it. He knew from the experience of his own visits to Poland and Hungary – ah, those morning shots of cognac on the coffee tray! – how profound was the disillusion of intellectuals and artists with the development of socialism in their respective countries, and he was convinced that no alien agencies were needed to foment their complaints. It might indeed be an unpleasant ordeal, to look around at a meeting and see the colour of one's support, but should it make one shift or abandon position?

Jerome's feeling of vindication increased with a burgeoning sense of pride as he surveyed the achievment of the *Review*. The paper had been fertile, varied, and imaginative. He had combined reviewers and reviewed with wit and probity, and an occasional good dose of literary malice. Acquaintances had demolished each other's work in his pages and wrangled in his Letters column. In one issue, an eminent professor of criminology – an émigré from one of the Eastern European countries, as it turned out – had been given the month's pulp crime list to analyse. Of course he was a friend of James, but then James extended hospitality to so many exiles. He felt the expatriate's affinity. Jerome twisted moodily, then dismissed James's influence from his mind. The criminologist's article had no political content.

Jerome Namier was a famous name, not only for the superciliousness and snobbery attacked in the *Radical*. His attention to detail, his deliberate vetting of each article as it came in, his conversations with authors in which he stimulated their ideas and encouraged their ambitions were justly considered to provide a model of the editorial role . . . Or so he told himself.

When Ian Holmes entered Jerome's office around four o'clock that afternoon, Jerome's sense of injury was at its height. He looked defiantly at the young man, brushed the cat off his desk with an impatient blow and tossed an ashtray in Holmes's direction.

'Are you going to make a statement to the papers?' Ian's voice was low and subtle as he faced Jerome, narrowing his eyes over the curling smoke. 'Because if you're not, I am. I've spent all day controlling myself because I believe that you, as editor of "the leading critical weekly" should be first to speak, but I cannot contain myself any longer. Naturally I knew nothing about this CIA connection and I am disgusted. I shall resign, but out of simple curiosity, I am waiting for you to do so first.'

A rehearsed speech, thought Jerome. He brought his hands together on his knees and his voice matched the quiet deliberateness of Ian as he began, 'You are going to resign, are you? So high-minded, such a man of integrity, you're outraged by the revelation that the paper you work for has been receiving ten thousand dollars a year from the CIA? Your mean little spirit can't bear it; oh no, it offends your cherished self-importance. How much do you earn? Ten thousand dollars a year perhaps? And how quickly are you going to be back here shopping for a job when I've safely resigned and been put out to grass? Huh? Perhaps we could just let you resign and then say the CIA was paying your salary?' Jerome's face was mottled, his eyes glistened. Clenching his fists on the desk, he leant towards Ian. A small weak smile flickered on the face of the younger man, camouflaging his own anger. 'I have edited the paper for twelve years without a shadow of influence falling across anything I've written or asked people to write for me. I have been grossly let down – no, betrayed – by one of my closest friends, a man whom I would never have suspected capable of deceiving me, and then on top of it, I have to cope with upstarts like you holding the torch of your self-righteousness in my face and shining like new-born angels who've never seen ...'

Holmes spread his hands. 'Jerome,' he interrupted, putting his head slowly to one side, 'You know you never get anywhere by losing your temper.'

'God damn you,' shouted Jerome. 'Where would you be without me? Still writing profiles of film stars and their vintage cars?' He stood up.

'Rage doesn't get us anywhere.' Ian gave a brief laugh. 'And in your situation, I'd cultivate my strong points. I'm not going to leave the room until I know what's going on and what you're doing about it. Perhaps you could tell me.' He leant back in the chair, but kept his gaze on Jerome, still standing above him. 'It is important for us all, you know, not just for you.'

Jerome subsided, blowing hard. His mouth was wet, and as he spoke, his lips hardly moved. 'Of course I had nothing to do with the money. I knew it came from the Institute of Cultural Affairs but I accepted it to be what they said it was – no doubt foolishly.' His tone was filled with dislike of himself, and with hostility towards Ian. Cutting himself loose from his role as Jerome's protégé, Ian had become another enemy boring through his thin tolerance. The cigarette between Ian's lips, the flat vowels intended to disguise class but betraying instead a class-ridden self consciousness had never caught his notice before. Now they inspired fury. And he had thought him promising, this youth, this weathercock, obviously turned by every cause that came his way. 'I accepted that the Institute was a philanthropically funded American foundation dedicated to the promotion of education and culture all over the world. Perhaps it was negligent of me not to pursue enquiries, but in 1963, before former agents began unburdening themselves to the press, I doubt that it would have been possible to unravel the tangle of mother foundations through which the money was channelled to us. Secondly, I do not believe that the contents of the *Review* have been materially affected by the connection. I am going to call on James Cunliffe to sell his share of the paper to me. Somewhere, I'll find the money. Naturally all further funds from the Institute will be refused and I shall be lodging a strong protest against its part in the affair. And of course, I'll be replying to the *Radical*.' Jerome paused and sucked in his breath. 'And after that we will resume work – as before.' He got up and walked over to the door, then turned to where Ian still sat back in his chair, waiting for more. 'Now I have a lot to do, so if you would, please inform the rest of the staff.' The veins in his neck throbbed painfully, and his chest hurt. He was getting too old to lose his temper.

Holmes swivelled to look at Jerome, and did not rise. 'But what is there to tell them? You haven't said a thing.' He chuckled softly and paused. From the doorway Jerome could see Rosemary crouched over her desk with her head in her hands. Her thin shoulders quaked.

Overcome with penitence, he turned back. 'Oh God,' he said, and sat down heavily at his desk again. Looking up at Ian in exhaustion, he shut his eyes slowly. 'Ask everyone to come in, please, and we'll discuss it together.'

❧ CHAPTER 7

Paula woke up with a sense of purpose and clarity.

'Fran,' she said on the telephone to her sister, 'I wish you'd been home last night. It was fascinating.' She sounded excited.

'Oh yeah,' said Francesca. She was cool, as subdued as her younger sister Paula was high-spirited.

'Come on,' said Paula in a crushed voice. 'Don't be like that. What are you doing today?'

'Nothing much,' said Francesca. 'David's gone into the *News*. I'm here with Tilly. She's getting ill, it's too bad. There's chicken pox going around but I rang Ma and she says it's a good thing to get it over with. She brought round a bottle of camomile. According to Ma the only important thing is not to let Tilly scratch because the marks stay. She just whizzed in and out, because of rehearsals. So I'm here, minding the baby.' There was little laughter in her tone. Francesca had trained as a silversmith at a different art school from Paula, but since the birth of her daughter two years before, she had been unable to get out to workshops to practise her craft. Although she did not complain – she rarely described her states of mind – her frustration was evident.

'Listen,' said Paula briskly, 'can I come round to lunch?'

Francesca told her there wasn't much to eat.

'You know I don't eat much anyway.'

'See you then.'

'See you.' Paula hung up, with the feeling of dissatisfaction her encounters with her sister usually brought her. Talking to Francesca was like trying to talk underwater. She turned to her drawing board.

D for Dejanira. Paula forgot Francesca and ticked off the elements of the story in her mind: first Dejanira was Hercules's prize from her father for a horse race. Then the centaur Nessus fancied her and tried to rape her while ferrying her across a stream. Hercules didn't care for this, so he murdered Nessus with a poisoned arrow. But Nessus avenged himself, giving Dejanira the tunic he was wearing, soaked in his blood and Hercules's poison. He told her it would keep her husband faithful for ever. So when Hercules went off with someone, Dejanira used the robe and tried to get him back. He put it on and it clung to him, burning like poison ivy so badly he couldn't bear it: he threw himself on to his own funeral pyre and was snatched up to heaven by the gods.

Paula huffed when she first read it. Yet another piece of sexist trash, she thought, with all the ingredients: woman as prize, as victim, as sex symbol, as cheated but loving wife, finally as death-dealer – and she wasn't even given the credit for murder, because the poor little fool did her husband to death unwittingly. But the idea of Nessus, half-man, half-beast, appealed to her, and by contrast she felt nauseated by Hercules, the superman. She therefore began to try and express in her drawing the nobility of Nessus's union of human intelligence with animal passion. That Hercules was represented in the story as the just protector of his wife's chastity enraged her more than the attempted rape. What's his stupid gallantry but the proprietor's instinct? thought Paula. She mapped out in pencil the bank on which Hercules stood waiting, with the figure of the centaur in the foreground, breasting the stream while Dejanira held on, her arms flung round the centaur's chest. She inked in the line with her rapidograph, cross-hatching the shadows as if it were an engraving. She felt absorbed and happy, and as she worked her mind turned to the events of the night before. Her walk with her uncle still filled her with delight and she did not give a thought to her mother or Wayne or the interest she had aroused in the American or the unusual quietness of her father. She said to herself briskly, Friendship is really the key to everything. The lack of friendship is the problem with our whole society. If only women were friends with each other more than they are, instead of being forced into rivalries. But they're taught that getting a man is the only important thing in life, and they become dependent on that man for their livelihood and the livelihood of their children ... if only children were friends with their parents, lovers friends instead of, well, lovers, then it would all be different. But how? She jabbed with her pen at Hercules's musculature. I'm going to make a break for it. OK? I shall work on becoming friends with my family. With my parents (this made her a little less optimistic). Then with my sister. Yes. And with Gabriel, too. She thought over his name silently. She had not used it very often. A girl's name, she thought and laughed. I'll have to work at it because he's a reserved and difficult old man, and because anyway friendship is a rare phenomenon. But I shall try.

Paula caught a glimpse of her watch and, grabbing her shoulderbag, flew out of the house. When she reached the pavement, she realized she could not use her bike – it was raining too hard – and so she rushed back into the flat to telephone Francesca.

'Don't bother to come,' said her sister; again Paula felt wounded by her indifference.

'But I want to. Don't you want to see me?'

'Of course I do,' said Francesca, impatient of her sister's hunger for reassurance. 'I just thought it would be a bore for you to get over here in the rain.'

Paula set off on foot, and half an hour later, her pixie head soaking wet, she arrived at Francesca's flat. She held out a copy of the *Evening Standard*, and numbly watched her sister as she read the front page.

Francesca Namier, now Clark, had a long, almost severe face with a finely shaped straight nose that tilted very slightly at the end, giving a piquancy to a face that might otherwise have been too solemn. Her eyes were clear, almost like water, for their blueness reflected blueness around her and on a summer's day seemed deeper than the sky itself. She was given to long, enigmatic silences which, together with the serenity of her features, exercised a powerfully unsettling influence over people she met. Men hurried to be of service to her, to cause a flicker of interest or amusement to cross her grave eyes and immobile face. Through her remoteness she could make a group of people feel graceless and ill at ease; as a result, she attracted men, but had few friends. But Paula liked her and didn't like the way she was alone all day with Tilly; so she visited her sister often.

'Lord!' said Francesca. 'What is this?' She read the *Standard*'s headline – 'CIA Funds *Review*' – and her eye passed down the columns. Paula flopped on to the sofa and looked listlessly at Tilly, who tottered up to her, wrinkling her face as if with one more effort she could produce a really big howl.

'Please don't,' said Paula to the child, and turning her round sat her on her knee. 'Poor Daddy. It's pretty bad, isn't it?'

Francesca said slowly, 'Do you believe it?'

'I'd believe anything of the CIA, wouldn't you?'

'No, the part about Dad. Did he know?' Francesca looked at the article again. 'He hasn't said anything himself. It's the morning edition, maybe they didn't have time to ask him.'

'Let's ring him up.'

'Yes.'

'You do it.'

'You get on better with him,' said Francesca, pulling her long light-brown hair tighter and pinning it up.

'Hardly.' Paula shifted. 'I'll do it, you're right.'

She dialled the *Review*, and was put through to Rosemary. The two sisters' voices were very similar in timbre, though Paula spoke far more rapidly than Francesca. Rosemary hesitated until Paula identified herself.

'We don't know what to think,' said Rosemary quietly. 'Your father hasn't said anything to us, and he won't take any calls.' Paula could hear that the secretary was close to tears, and the frown between her eyebrows deepened in sympathy.

'Everyone's in a state here, and your father's just shut himself up. Ian Holmes is insisting on a confrontation, as he puts it. The papers keep on ringing up and asking for a statement and I have to say, "The Editor has no comment." Oh, God.' She was frantic.

'Can I talk to him?' Paula interrupted. She put her hand over the receiver, and whispered to Francesca. 'They're doing their nuts over there.'

'Tephelone,' said Tilly.

Francesca shook her head seriously.

'Hello, Daddy,' said Paula forcing cheerfulness into her voice. 'I'm over at Franny's and ...' Her father cut in. 'No, Tilly's fine. She's better. I really rang up because . . . well . . . have you seen the *Standard*?'

'No,' said Jerome. 'But your mother just rang me from the theatre. She wants you to go round to watch rehearsals today. She says she'd like some outside advice, some *sympathetic* outside advice at this stage . . .'

'Daddy,' said Paula in a tight voice. 'Please don't . . . Isn't it rather important?'

Jerome listened to his daughter's strained tone and felt afraid. Alone, he was arguing away the seriousness of his position, but when he heard the anxiety in the voices of others, or saw doubts engraved in the lines of their faces, he felt fear raw and indigestible lying on his stomach.

'I am dealing with it, darling,' he said, and Paula grimaced at the hesitation in his normally bluff manner. 'Of course I knew nothing about the money. But from my point of view that makes it almost worse.' He mocked himself. 'Oedipus couldn't exactly get away with it, saying, "Well, I didn't know", could he?'

Paula made a sound, but could not articulate. She thought, God, this is really going to feed Daddy's sense of drama.

'Don't worry about me, darling,' he said. 'It would only make my problems worse, to know I've made you anxious on my account.'

This was more than Paula could bear, and in a thick voice she said, 'Well, I shan't. I swear.' She put the telephone down.

'Don't you start crying too,' said Francesca languidly. 'You'll only make Tilly compete. How did he sound?'

'Terrible,' said Paula and sniffed. She recomposed her face, and tugged at her short hair. 'Spiritless and indecisive. And all noble. God knows why I'm upset. It's fucking stupid to cry. What good does it do?'

She walked into the kitchen and opened the fridge. 'Can I grab myself something to eat? All this has made me feel quite hollow.'

'Go ahead,' said Francesca. 'There's the remains of last night's stew.'

Paula began eating it from the saucepan with a spoon.

'For Chrissake, heat it up.'

'Can't be bothered,' said Paula. 'Anyway it's good cold.'

She sat down with characteristic abruptness on the sofa with the saucepan on her knees and, between spoonfuls, eyed her sister and Tilly pensively, eyebrows knitted. A gradual feeling of excitement, born of her irrepressible elation earlier in the day, began to take over from the panic she had felt when she first read the story about her father in the paper.

'It's really rather an interesting situation,' she said. 'Would you ever have thought that the stuffy old *Review* was in the hands of spies. Oooh!' she shrieked at Tilly, waving her spoon. 'Grandpa's a spy, Grandpa's a spy. He sows terror and revolution all over the world.' Tilly laughed too, with a bubbling wide-mouthed baby laugh, her eyes glancing up and sideways at her mother to see if she was laughing too. Francesca smiled serenely down at her.

'I think it would be a good thing if Dad packed in the *Review* anyway. He's been doing it too long. He's stale, and it must be a bore by now. This way he can go out with some dramatic flourish. Ma can provide background histrionics.'

Paula stamped her booted feet on the ground, looking at Tilly, and then trumpeted with her lips. The child screwed up her face in alarm. 'Oh no you don't,' said Paula, looking pleadingly at her sister. 'I've had enough aunty stuff for one day. Have you got a fag?'

Francesca nodded. 'There are some of David's upstairs.'

'Great,' said Paula, springing up and dumping the saucepan back in the kitchen.

The two sisters forgot about their father. Not out of hard-heartedness, but because the complicity between them that day made worry seem out of place for a time. Paula was happy. She rummaged about Francesca's dressing table, found the cigarettes, and returned, smoking. She enjoyed her sister's company: her remoteness seemed so admirably self-sufficient, and appeared to be free of the craving to be liked. 'Tell me, what you think, what you really think – deep down – of Uncle Gabriel?' Her voice wobbled a bit, because she cared far more about the question than she wanted to admit.

Francesca looked up in surprise, her blue eyes wide. 'What makes you ask that, all of a sudden?' Her voice was sharp, and she wiped Tilly's mouth with a hanky and felt her forehead with the back of her hand. 'Damn,' she said, 'she's hot.' She was more annoyed at Paula's tension.

'Why don't you get the doctor?' said Paula, impatient with her sister for not replying. She added, brightening, 'Why don't you put her to bed?'

'I've tried,' said Francesca dully, readjusting the tortoiseshell clip in her long hair once more. After a pause she said, her grave eyes scanning Paula's face, 'I've always thought him – that's Uncle Gabriel – an awfully cold fish. And not my idea of a priest. The idea of telling *him* one's sins. Ugh.' She shivered. 'He wouldn't understand anything. All he understands is which is Dad's best bottle of wine. He sits there in Dad's sitting-room drinking and smoking and not saying anything and everyone commits hara-kiri – no I mean that other oriental thing – everyone kowtows to fetch and carry for him, and exclaim at his words of wisdom when he says, "Today's Tuesday." Actually it makes me sick.'

Francesca spoke with uncommon energy, and Paula thought, Gabriel stirs strong feelings, that's a good sign anyway. She also smiled to herself, because she often had to defend Francesca's own reserve, especially to people who noticed her sphinx-like silences and felt reproved by them. 'She sits there looking all *fatale*,' said one friend of Paula's. 'And everyone falls about as if the Mona Lisa had walked into the room.'

'I don't think Gabriel's cold,' said Paula. 'In fact I think he's full of all sorts of complicated feelings and passions.'

'My arse, as David would say,' retorted Francesca. 'And what's more, you're welcome to them all. He's got as much passion as . . .' She looked around for a simile and her eyes caught the fridge, 'as the freezing compartment in that fridge.'

'Well, that's quite powerful,' said Paula, laughing. 'At least it does something. I think he does freeze it all up actually, but it is all there. There must be something to him for you to get so steamed up.'

'Surely not,' said Francesca. 'He's been a dried-up, juiceless bore all his life, pompous, conceited, tyrannizing everyone, Dad included, because of his great reputation, though God knows how he got it in the first place.' She smoothed down her child's hair and kissed her. 'He epitomizes for me everything that's sterile, that's the opposite of real, or good. He's a Jesuit, of course he is, what else could he be? Elitist, superior, intellectual

105

in that ghastly arid way that means he's all books and nothing else. I sometimes think David and he should be locked up together for a day, for Gabriel to learn what the world out there is like, what people have to put up with when they're not shut up in institutions with every comfort, praying. Ugh, it fills me with disgust, honestly. What is the point of a life like his?' Francesca pulled down the corners of her mouth and sucked in her cheeks to imitate the grooved face of her uncle. "I wouldn't say so, my dear.' She mimicked his short breathy voice. "That is hardly the case, Jerome." Bah! He pisses me off, and he upsets Dad. I don't see why you don't feel the same way – you've seen him and Dad together and you're the one who's closest to Dad anyway.'

Paula's shoulders shook, half in amusement at her sister's extraordinary animation, half in embarrassment at her vehemence. 'Yes,' she said. 'Well, yes.'

Francesca laughed back. 'Come on, I can't believe you aren't going to launch a counter-attack. You're not going to knuckle under for once, are you?'

Paula shrugged slightly, then squatting on the floor, looked up at her sister and wrapped Tilly's little hand round her middle finger. 'I felt sorry for him last night. He sounded sad about lots of things. Bitter about the Church, sad about leaving China when he was young. Plus he's not well, and that always makes me feel bad. He's been ill for years, and it must have been rotten when he was left behind with doctors while Dad went shooting from sampans or whatever it was they got up to. Anyways I like him.' Paula was resolute. She admired Gabriel because his priesthood represented to her an uncompromising, unconditional, unambiguous surrender to a particular role which she was unable to make. She did not like him because he was a priest, but because he had been able to choose something. She always felt feeble and vacillating – two years with John, not because she loved him, but because she couldn't make up her mind whether she loved him. She despised herself for what she considered weakness of will, and saw in Gabriel the attraction of a man possessed of a definite sense of purpose.

'Balls,' said Francesca, calmly. 'All that stuff about asthma – a typical attention-seeking ploy. It's like Tilly crying when I'm talking to someone else; Gabriel wheezes and sneezes so everyone looks at him. And so is his priesthood. He's no more a priest than I'm the Tower of Pisa. It's just another ploy he uses to seem special.'

Paula frowned, then lit up. Was that a Freudian slip? Did Francesca know people called her the Mona Lisa? Cole Porter's lyric ran through her head and she sang offkey: 'You're the Nile, You're the Tower of Pisa, You're the smile on the Mona Lisa.'

Francesca yielded to her sister's teasing; their eyes met, and both understood. It was Gabriel's turn to be forgotten. 'I'm sorry,' said Francesca, 'I don't care about him one way or the other. I just think people have an exaggerated opinion of him. I'm tense because . . .' She paused and rocking Tilly gently on her knee for the little girl was struggling, said softly, 'I'm all tensed up because I think . . .' her voice dropped until it was almost inaudible, '. . . David's going to be sent off again. Anyway he's been longing to go for months – ever since he came back.' She laughed, a dry laugh, and looked squarely at Paula, her clear eyes clouding. 'Damn it all, honestly.'

'I'm sorry,' said Paula in a small voice. But she knew from experience that Francesca resented sympathy about her husband's assignments abroad. 'It's exciting – for him.'

'Oh yeah,' said her sister, 'He'll be over the moon.'

David found the two sisters silent when he returned from the *News* offices. He tossed two yellow cartons of film on to the sofa and picked up his child off his wife's lap, kissed her, put her down, and then put his arms round Francesca so that she suddenly seemed angular and small. She clutched at the clip in her hair, and pulled it free. Defensive, she did not return David's hug. He held her and said, 'Yes, Froggy, I'm off again.' He had called her Froggy ever since she had told him when they started going out that her name could mean 'the French girl.' Few people, looking at Francesca's clear small face, understood why.

'Tomorrow morning,' he added. 'Singapore Airlines direct to Bangkok, then a short wait, then Saigon.' His voice was flat. He accented the first syllable of Saigon, a quirk of people who know the place, but he usually avoided the jocular abbreviations in vogue with American pressmen with military pretensions, and he never called the country Nam. 'John Delaney's coming with me. He's good, so I'm pleased about that.'

Francesca was used to David's sudden departures; when she met him he was already established as a combat photographer of skill and nerve. But her voice quivered and a muscle in her cheek gave the lie to her still face.

'I'll start packing for you, shall I?'

'How long will you be away?' asked Paula, realizing immediately that it was the wrong question.

'Dunno,' said David. He never did know, but he added, for Francesca's sake, 'Not more than a month, in any case.'

'Poor Tilly,' said Francesca, picking up the little girl and hoisting her on to her hip. 'You're very tired and it tickles doesn't it? Nasty pox.' She left the room and went upstairs without another look at David or Paula. When she was afraid, she closed the doors on her private world, where Tilly was the only other human creature allowed, and remained walled up in numb and silent hurt.

David, looking embarrassed, pulled a cigarette from the packet. 'Vietnam,' he said slowly, 'Vietnam.' The word was astonishing to him, it sang like the greatest measure of heroic verse.

Paula looked at him and smiled wryly, ruffling her damp hair and letting her eyes drop. David Clark was strongly built, and the tension of his limbs showed through the jeans and jeans jacket he was wearing, a mirror image of Paula's usual clothes. His head was compact and his hair short, not because he preferred it so, but because a close crop was more comfortable in the steaming climates where he often worked. Also, he disliked being thought a long-hair, with the label's connotations for the people whom he photographed. His face was not handsome, but pleasant; sardonic mouth and frank sharp eyes that held his interlocutors fully and openly; when he smiled, he showed a broken front tooth which gave him a self-mocking, roguish look. Paula liked her brother-in-law, and had done so from the beginning when her parents were all too ready to find him 'not good enough for Francesca', just as they had condemned John, for different reasons. Paula admired David Clark's work. It was immediate, brave and often utterly devastating. He was often criticized for being a voyeur who disguised opportunism, sensationalism, even sadism, under a false mask of compassion. He sought out atrocities, said some people, because he got off on them. But Paula knew that David's hunger for battle was not nearly as basic as that. It was a kind of savagery in him, but it wasn't a cheap urban form of it, as one finds in rubber-gear shops. He had – for a moment it flashed through her – Nessus's kind of savagery. Because he reacted quickly, violently and ardently. That was why he took photographs no one else could take, even if present at the same battle. It was David who, when two American reporters came running out from a wood blasted by fire, shouted, 'Where's the third man?' The other two looked around them, horrified. 'He was behind,' they shouted back. 'Where the hell is he now?' screamed David, breaking out for the wood until he saw him, lying full of shrapnel under a tree. He dragged the man out, keeping his head down under the raking cross-fire. He was prompt, thought Paula, the most important part of courage. Without him the third reporter would have died. But it wasn't David who told the story afterwards; and when asked about it, he only grinned and shook his head, saying, 'There he was, full of shrapnel. It was bad, very bad.'

From the sofa, holding his cigarette between his teeth, David said to Paula, 'Polo, tell me, how's things with you?'

He gave her a look of mocking disapproval when she told him she'd been working. 'You're looking good. I meant you in yourself, I mean are you great here?' He laid his hands on his chest. 'Or for that matter there.' He pointed at Paula's crotch and laughed.

'Dirty bastard,' said Paula. 'Prize MCP, you'd win the big scarlet one at the Hampshire Agricultural Fair, wouldn't you?' Then she laughed. 'I don't care about men anymore. I'm off them. Actually if you must know about my private life, I've got the hots for my Uncle Gabriel.' She pulled at her hair and grimaced at David, trying to hide what she felt with playacting.

Puzzled, David looked at her, and then down at the cuffs of his jacket. He unpopped one wrist and pulling up the sleeve, scratched his arm thoughtfully. 'Polo, you're lovely, but you live too much in your head. You can't just decide things like that and make them come out as you plan them. Your uncle ... he's another person who's all head, and no heart. Not that you're heartless. You just try to be, so as you won't get hurt. Bad scene, Polo, believe me.'

Paula hit one heel against the toe of her boot and then took another cigarette. She was hurt, but she couldn't see any way out. 'But David,' she began, 'you see there isn't anyone . . .'

'I know.' David stood up and stretched. 'There never is anyone till you meet them, and then you don't want them.' He yawned. 'What's all this about your dad I've been hearing at the office?'

Paula's mournfulness increased. She told him what she knew.

David said, 'Does it matter? Isn't the *Review* the same paper it was before people knew the CIA supported it?' He thought, head down, for a moment. 'It reminds me of forgeries. Everyone buys some brilliant faker because they just love art, and then he turns out to be D. Jones and not Van Eyck and suddenly the same paintings are all trash and D. Jones is strung up from the nearest lamppost.'

'Like Chatterton,' said Paula. Then she added in a serious tone, 'It does matter – about the CIA, because it's all been underhand and no one knows how much the *Review* might have been manipulated. It must be ghastly for Daddy if he really didn't know.' Her grey eyes looked appealingly at David.

'I've no love, no love at all for the CIA,' he said deliberately. 'After Vietnam . . .' He shook his head. 'But this is peanuts.' He looked sharply at Paula, strong hands resting on his knees, cigarette in his mouth. The crease between her brows deepened and she glanced sidelong at him, her concern for what he would say doing visible battle with her attraction to him as a man. Both of them enjoyed the pleasure each had in the other, and were able to set light feet on the dangerous territory of their mutual liking because each felt the other was 'safe'. David for me, thought Paula looking at him appreciatively, is like Wayne for Ma. She chuckled at the thought. Both men are safe for us because they're unobtainable – for different reasons, of course. She continued smiling to herself, and David looked at her enquiringly.

'I'm sorry,' she said. 'I was thinking of something else.'

'There's the rub,' said David gently. 'When it comes to Vietnam, everyone, even you, Polo, starts thinking about something else.'

'You're right,' said Paula meekly. She did not give voice to her thoughts in order to excuse herself, because she knew that the flavour of her flirtation with her brother-in-law depended on the unspoken quality of the conspiracy between them. She urged him to go on talking.

'Jesus,' said David, shaking his powerful head. 'The thought of those literary lions all out for blood because their favourite poncy rag turns out to be connected with the CIA. Oooh, ugh. Nasty.' He imitated a high-pitched squeal and wiped imaginary turds off his shoes. 'It makes me puke. It's so fucking self-righteous. When you think that every one of us – you, me, Tilly, Frog, everyone, is being manipulated the whole time in ways far more fundamental and serious than your old man's oh-so-chic-nobody's-even-heard-of-it-in-Brixton piece of classy rubbish.' This was one of David's favourite themes; when drunk, he would worry at it for hours, shouting more and more slowly and heavily that television and advertising were warping the mind of his child. Paula knew it all from him, and largely agreed. So she waved it aside, and said, 'But it'll be the end of Daddy. The shame will get to him. He's too old to face the pack any more.'

David got up, reaching for another cigarette from his buttoned-down breast pocket. 'He'll be OK. It'll be good for him. He might even enjoy it.' He went towards the stairs. Paula followed him.

'I'll just say goodbye to Fran. And to you too, of course.' She gave him a small smile. 'You'll take care, won't you? No daredevilry.'

They found Francesca in the bedroom, with David's open suitcase on the floor, and Tilly, a soft rag clutched to her mouth, crying to herself behind a chair.

'Come now. I'll do it,' said David, taking a pair of socks from his wife's hands.

Paula saw then, with sudden clarity, the way her life was interspun with the lives of these others, how the single skein of her immediate family was looped in such a way that distant distorted faces staring out of newspapers, close problems of philosophy puzzled out long ago in a distant place, even the character of a Chinese emperor and his court, were gathered in so that these small and unreverberating dramas – Tilly's illness, David's packing – were performed against a background of greater breadth and business. The flash filled her with a sense of wonder, and of tenderness.

'I'm off,' she said gently, and turned abruptly on her heel, for she felt superstitious about kissing David.

From the bottom of the stairs she shouted up: 'I'll go and see Ma at the theatre.'

'Damn this rain,' she muttered, as she walked rapidly to the nearest tube.

Although Francesca concealed her personal feelings under the enigmatic passivity of her face and her movements, Paula could gauge that her sister was increasingly terrified by David's work, and that habit, far from diminishing her fear, exacerbated it, rather as fear of aeroplanes grows with each journey. It was tough on Francesca, thought Paula, although she advocated marriages in which the partners led independent lives. When she saw her sister living alone with her two-year-old and nothing but letters from David – infrequent and often delayed – and telephone calls from the Foreign Editor assuring her he was well, Paula was angry, frustrated by a pity she felt and did not want to feel, because the pity of a single and childless woman insulted Francesca, and other mothers, tied at home like her. Yet the drudgery was obvious, and with David absent, the ordeals were sometimes excruciating. Once, in her dreamy laconic way, Francesca told Paula that she had received a telephone call from the paper David was working for at the time. 'The man on the Foreign desk rang. He said, "Hello, Franny?" I said, "Yes." – I'm always scared when they ring, though I know they'd probably come in person if anything happened. He said, "Don't worry about a thing. David is doing a superb job, a really great job. He's right out there in the front line, sending back the most amazing stuff. It would turn a rhino's stomach . . ." "Thank you," I said, "I'm so pleased".' Paula had screamed, 'Bloody thugs, God! I can't believe it.' But Francesca remonstrated with her gently. 'He was right, you know. From David's point of view, that's what matters. The story, and nothing else. That's why he's so good . . .' Her voice faltered and Paula swam for a moment in the brimming blue of her sister's sad eyes. But then Francesca turned away, and when she next looked at her, Paula saw nothing but the long, mysteriously solemn face of her sister, concealing herself as usual.

Paula frowned hard at the memory. Of course, she realized

Francesca doesn't need attention and assiduous love the way some people do, like Ma. She's self-possessed and marks out her own boundaries, separating the likes from the don't-likes without the hunger that makes some people like anyone who likes them. In fact Francesca doesn't really need people at all. Not like me. She tossed her head and felt her hair, wet once again from the rain.

She reached her mother's rehearsal room in a building above a morning market. The rotting leaves and fruit strewn on the pavement and in the gutters fleshed out the rain-smell in the air with a ripe sweetness. Paula sucked it in appreciatively, a sudden compost scent in the dead concrete of the city. Then she turned into the doorway, and leapt up the stone stairs to the rehearsal rooms at the top. She pushed open the door quietly, and signalled to her mother, who was standing in the centre of the room wearing leg warmers, surrounded by a chorus of strutting, bending, flexing figures, all similarly wrapped in thick wool. They were predominantly male, with taut necks and ramrod backs, and Paula wished she had brought her materials to draw them. Her mother waved a hand, and continued discussing something with the man beside her, whom Paula took to be the director, as he was wearing ordinary clothes and leather shoes. She found a seat at the back against the wall.

'Hi, darling,' said Wayne Dupree, wagging a hand at her. She nodded back, smiling.

'OK, OK, everybody,' said the director, and spread his hands, walking backwards from the throng.

'Now boys,' said Wayne. He signalled to the old lady in spectacles at the grand in the corner. 'One two three four *and* one two three four *and* . . .'

'There is nothing like a dame,' shouted the chorus, knees bending and arms flexing. 'There is nothing like a dame!'

'Put some chutzpah into it. Come on. None of this gay stuff. You're meant to be MEN with a capital M,' the director exhorted them. 'I know it's out of fashion with you, but the coach trade still like it. Give me some brawn! Come on, Marvin, look Strong, look Virile!'

The dancers strode about, flinging their arms wide and filling their chests with air. On the beat, they snapped into position. 'There is nothing like a dame!'

Paula had a spasm of horror: this charade in front of her was supposed to be Vietnam.

'Lovely, darlings, lovely!' said the director, silencing the pianist with a clap of his hands and bringing the actors to a standstill. 'Teresa dear, I want you to move forward gradually through the GIs so that as soon as this number finishes you are centre stage, eyeball to eyeball with our young hero.' He ferried Teresa through the crowd towards the blonde juv. lead. 'You're all doing fine, though it's still much too restrained. I want it very free, strong, raucous. But the movement's your department, Wayne. Will you see to it everyone loosens up?' He looked at him expectantly. 'Good. Time for tea.'

The dancers stopped stretching and pointing their woollen limbs, and padded on out-turned feet towards the urn that stood on a trestle table to one side of the room.

Teresa came over to Paula, pulling off her headband and shaking her hair loose. 'Oof,' she said, sitting down beside her daughter, 'was I all right?'

'I didn't see much. Of course it's just wonderful. Vietnam!' She scoffed. 'How can you take it?'

Teresa's black eyes darkened and her mouth quivered. 'You have no idea, Miss Know-All, how much trouble and compassion . . .' she stressed the two words, 'have gone into making this the Vietnamese *South Pacific*. The estate kicked up a terrible fuss about changing some of the words, so that Bali Hai for instance becomes Phu Quoc Isle in one of the songs I sing, you know, the famous "Bali Hai may call you . . ."' Teresa hummed, pouting her lips, and moving her head to the music. 'But eventually the gnomes understood that the play could say something important about things now. I think it's awfully good myself, to change the girl into a Vietnamese. You know there are hundreds, no, thousands of babies born to Vietnamese girls by GIs. To show an inter-racial love-affair in Saigon now is very significant. And the soldiers in this version aren't clean-living, lantern-jawed young men hung about with medals. They're mixed-up psychopaths and pacifists and cowards. The hero questions what's he's doing all the time. It's been extensively re-written, in the light of everything we now understand about war.'

Paula looked at her mother sideways, a wave of hysterical laughter surging up from her stomach and fighting the other feeling lodged there, of sickness. 'Mummy, please,' she said, trying to control herself, and pulling wildly at her hair to stop herself blathering. 'You honestly can't make a musical like *South Pacific* about the horrors of Vietnam. It won't do, it's like . . . It's nothing but camp. *Springtime for Hitler*.'

'You know nothing about the theatre,' said Teresa with dignity, adjusting her headband again in the reflection in the window. 'This show will be seen by millions.'

Paula decided it was useless. When her mother had work she was always dedicated to it, and nothing could ignite her critical faculty. And when she didn't, there wasn't much on in London that could come up to her standards.

Paula sighed, 'Anyway I came about Daddy.' She added, in order to wound her mother's vanity, 'I know I'll have to sit through the play later.'

'Your father didn't sound too bad,' said Teresa, in a distant tone. 'But I got the shock of my life when I saw the billboards. Imagine Jerome in headlines!'

'So he's fine is he?' Paula retorted with bitterness.

'We can have a council of war later, at home,' breathed Teresa, getting up. 'Tell Francesca to come.'

'David's off to Vietnam. The real one.'

'Not again,' said her mother, making a wry mouth. The director beckoned her to her place.

'You come then, darling,' said Teresa as she returned to her position. 'We'll sort it all out together.' She smiled vividly, with self-conscious attractiveness, as if she were taking a curtain call.

Outside the door, Paula stamped her foot, gritting her teeth so she wouldn't cry. Her mother's husky voice followed her as she tramped stolidly down one step at a time. 'In your heart,' sang Teresa, 'You'll hear it call you. Come away, come away.'

❧ *CHAPTER 8*

The small room at Xavier House was filled with a harsh sucking sound as Gabriel breathed. Or rather tried to breathe. He lay on the narrow bed with his head flung back on a rubber bolster, for he was allergic to feathers and had not used pillows since he was a boy. The white thinness of his neck was exposed against the whiteness of the sheets. His dry lips hung open as he forced the air in, out, in, out, down the resisting passages from his swollen lungs. The breathing was greedy, menacing, like a fissure in a rock that gulps greedily at the rising sea then spews it back with a hiss of foam. Sometimes Gabriel's painful exhalations struck a high note, like the wheeze of a schoolboy blowing on a comb wrapped in paper. But such comic effects were few; the sound on the whole was terrifying, and invaded everything in the room, making it share the sleeper's suffering.

Gabriel was dreaming. He was in a dark wood, and he was running. Brambles tore at his legs like barbed wire, branches of thorn trees grabbed his chest and gashed his cheek as if they were live hands reaching for him. They bore open, scented flowers in deceptive meekness, like garlands. The ground was steep and stony, it broke his feet through his shoes. Through the thatch of branches overhead the thin light spattered the ground crashing past him. He was finding it hard to breathe and his chest hurt, but he kept on running because behind him, he could hear four hounds giving chase. He heard them, careering almost gaily through the scrub that obstructed him so cruelly, and he knew they were gaining on him, because their howls of pleasure broke through the snapping twigs and undergrowth and the rasping sound of his harshly taken breath, and were getting closer all the time. He named them to himself for what they were, the hounds of the angel Gabriel, his patron saint and his guardian; he knew without having to turn around that the first, bounding in front, was Justice, the second leaping at his tail, Fortitude, and then neck and neck behind, Temperance and Prudence. He heard the angel huntsman blast on his golden horn, chasing fast behind them. The branches lashed at his face and his eyes wept from their whip on his cheeks. The hounds of virtue were after him. They were coming to claim him: no, coming to reclaim him. Tears fell burning on his cheeks though they were already hot from running. A root caught him and flung him on his face. As he hit the ground he thought, Now I must go back, go back to the virtue I've been flying from. The first dog pounced on his back and pinned him down. He saw the red rim of its mouth and the glitter of its teeth as it stood panting astride him; a drop of the dog's warm saliva fell on his cheek.

On the narrow bed in the darkened room the thin figure of the old man cried out and one arm thrust out crookedly to push the dog away. He moaned, with a rasping sound in his throat and struggled under the bedclothes. And so he woke.

For some minutes after opening his eyes, Gabriel lay stiff with terror. The twisted trees carrying their thousand instruments of torture still forested his room and the dog's weight crushed his breath. He forced himself to open his eyes wide and then, slowly sit up. He scanned the room and made a slow and careful inventory of its familiar objects. Trying to ease his gasps, he noted, Desk, yes, prie-dieu, yes, chair, yes, bookshelves in order, crucifix still on the wall. He looked up at it and his mouth twisted. The wrong, the wrong. It was not difficult to see the meaning in the dream. He had been intemperate and weak, imprudent and foolish; above all, weak. What had held him in Oliver's company? How frivolous, how empty, how vain ... to imagine he could ever learn the harpsichord and waste time like that. He had been carried away; but that didn't excuse it. Then later, at the pub, why had he stayed to have a drink? He had listened to him talk – no, prattle, that was the word – with indulgence. Why? Gabriel closed his eyes tightly and groaned. Behind him the dogs crashed through the dark wood once more, but more quietly now. His terror lessened; as his swollen eyes became used to the night, he began to be able to pick out the colour of his surroundings which restored normality to them and banished the darkness. It was his central flaw, this always too easy susceptibility, this quick attachment of the senses, which distanced him from God's mercy and goodness just as he was about to reach out and grasp it. Ignatius, Ignatius, he prayed, what did you write? That a man who seeks to be true to Christ must not experience attachment to anything or anyone except Christ. Oh, I need help, help me.

Gabriel got shakily to his feet and walked over the cold floor to the window. He parted the curtains. A sulphurous light filled the sky above the street lamp. How appropriate, his mind told him: the chemical of hell. And how different from the clarity of the night when Andrew sat with the emperor, when I discovered him sitting on the Heath beside me. Gabriel sucked on his puffer and felt some relief. He left his room and turned down the corridor to the bathroom at the end. There he splashed his face with cold water, feeling again as he pressed his hands to his cheeks how the stinging thorns had lashed him. His eyes darkened as he remembered how he ran, and he walked slowly back to his room keeping to the side of the passage like a man seeking the shelter of doorways in a storm.

The fear stayed with him when he lay down again. He tried to fasten his mind on the cross on the wall beside him, but he could not, and soon the dogs were at his heels again and the wood grabbed at him with its barbed fingers. Only the returning weight of sleep began to warm his limbs and drive the dream away. He lay rigid, eyes closed, arms by his side, waiting to be cast off from wakefulness. But as he lay, images of his life flickered past his retina.

Gabriel was dreaming once again. It was the dreaming that comes in the penumbra that passes as sleep for insomniacs, it was the dreaming halfway down the long slope into the serene nothingness of real sleep. Gabriel saw his grandmother standing at the entrance of his room. She was holding the door ajar and the light from the lamp turned her single long plait over her shoulder the colour of flame against the azure of the Chinese dressing gown – the one that had arrived in a trunk from Shanghai a few months before. She was listening, and Gabriel, lying in the nursery and pushing at the merciless air trapped in his lungs, turned to bury his face in the bolster so she should not hear his gasp. He could not bear being weak, being waited on in this household of women, a thirteen-year-old boy alone among old ladies. And there was a letter from Jerome in Shanghai:

'We went snipe-shooting today. We got a good big bag. Snipe are brown and spotted, with long bills, and are scrumptious to eat. Papa nearly got a hundred by himself. I helped him and took the stand on his left. There is terrific sport in China. We all hope you are well. It is very hot here, like midday at midnight. Mama says you wouldn't like it, so it's just as well you are in England. Love to Gran. Your brother Jerome Namier.'

Gabriel cried when he read the letter. He hated his brother, he hated him for having fun, he hated him for having health. He pressed his face hard into the bed, thinking of China.

But his grandmother heard him twist and entered the room. The silken rustle of her dressing gown came nearer. He shut his eyes tight and concentrated on his breathing. Let it come back, let it come back, he prayed. But she came over: 'My lamb,' she said. 'Is it bad?'

He kept still, trying hard to pretend he was asleep. His shoulders heaved with the effort and she bent down over him. She lit a coil of incense by his bed to help his breathing. He smelt her perfume, the warm, hidden, woman scent of she who gaoled him. She slid an arm under him, 'Try and sit up, it'll ease you.'

Gabriel stirred in the twilit world of his half-sleep. He felt his grandmother's hand on his forehead brush back his damp hair and cool him. Suddenly he no longer dreamed of her as his female demon, but relaxed to her touch. His dry lips twitched in a smile in his sleep. It was a sweet touch, fresh and cool. He surrendered to it, turning over; the child he once was, imitated by the old man on a bed of the same spartan narrowness, and his breathing grew quieter. His grandmother's candlelit face faded and another smiled at him through half-parted lips slowly curving, and looked at him with merry eyes.

'You might as well be dead,' said the eyes, mocking, full of affection. Or so it seemed to Gabriel. One arm reached out again in sleep with a gentle, sweeping gesture. He was breathing regularly now, slipping down down the long slope. The creased sourness round his mouth had altogether gone. 'My angel,' he mouthed as he drifted down.

The next day, the dreaming of the previous night stayed with Gabriel, like an internal wound seeping through his whole shattered frame. The asthma attack had weakened him, and he moved slowly, going through the movements of the Mass (it meant little to him, for the dreaming dominated), and assembling his papers for work in Jerome's house.

His brother had already left and Gabriel knew nothing of the charges in the *Radical*. Teresa had not yet left for rehearsal; a forlorn Rosie greeted him, assumed that he knew, and when he said nothing, felt she should not mention it.

His brother's difficulties would not have distracted Gabriel very much from his own thoughts; but as it was, the dreams of the night occupied his mind unopposed. They overcame his attempts to concentrate; they oppressed his chest and his head burst with the darkness and the crashing undergrowth and the tearing branches. He was frightened that they had the power to hold him, that he could not dissect them calmly in a mood of placid concentration, though he knew such scrutiny might set him free. And so the dreams continued to flash through him, now the lash of the trees, now the weight of the dog, now the scarlet rim of its mouth, then the cool hand, and the smile of Oliver.

He addressed himself to Andrew's diaries, resolved to work now on another section, and avoid the emperor's hunt – obviously the immediate source of his nightmare. He chose the part of his book which dealt with the distaste the Jesuits felt for Buddhists, particularly Lamas – but he was still in the night's grip: the text became a palimpsest before his eyes and under the letters he found the dark wood.

It was a crucial chapter in the book and Gabriel was excited by it. But he was the prisoner of a high and perfect state of subjectivity, so that all experience, however remote – even the seventeenth century in China – became meshed with the immediate circumstances of his life. He struggled to blot himself out so that he could feel once again the times and the man he was writing about. But he could not, and history became interwoven with his own imaginings.

The Order, his Order, from the early days of Matteo Ricci's

pioneer mission in Peking, had rejected Buddhism, which was popular in China, for Confucianism, the establishment religion, also widespread. This choice was seen by the Jesuits of the time as the proper rejecton of superstition in favour of a system based on the sovereign law of reason, a highly developed social code of good behaviour which oiled the machinery of the family and of the larger family of the emperor and his people. In the Jesuit view, Confucian ethics could not be faulted. It was not a religion, the Jesuits decided, not a challenge to Christianity, but a monotheistic philosophy which could be reconciled with the highest principles of the Catholic Church. Thus, Andrew da Rocha stated firmly: 'The Confucian Chinese have their own classical authors, and interpreters of classical texts from antiquity, that are received throughout the Empire, and these are filled with moral doctrines and contain nothing against our faith or good conduct.' Gabriel read the entry again, slowly, '*Nihil continent contra fidem et bonos mores.*' He smiled, ironic. How eager Andrew was to accommodate the Chinese! Bend, bend, he thought. If only he could bend as easily.

Of course, to most Christians who had not fallen under the Chinese spell – why have I fallen under it? thought Gabriel, his mouth twisting. Because I was taken away and Jerome was left behind? – it was obvious that Confucianism involved religious rituals, and could not be safely relegated to the category of philosophy without great mental agility. The Peking Fathers had used plenty of that, God knew. They overlooked so much: the rites to Confucius and to the ancestors demanded incense, and also sacrifices of animals – rabbits, hares, chicken. Yet Father da Rocha, and other Fathers with him, claimed in all honesty that these ceremonies were not religious, but civil and secular remembrance rites to the departed. The celebrants fasted before they performed the rites; the hair or feathers and the blood, of the sacrificial victims were buried afterwards; wine was poured in libation on the effigy; the family prostrated itself before the altar and begged for benefits, chanting in the prescribed manner the prescribed words. And yet Andrew believed that these rites could be performed by Christians and permitted in Christian families because they had nothing to do with divine worship! Gabriel smiled, but ruefully. If only he could believe as firmly as Andrew must have done. If only he could believe in the face of the evidence. That was a good test. Would he ever pass it? Here was Andrew, a man of faith; would he, Gabriel, have stood his ground like him?

The expediency of the China missionaries did not shock him; it awed him, when it did not merely amuse him. He knew that the Jesuit Fathers had assessed the political situation wisely: if the Confucian ancestral rites were forbidden to Christian converts, there would be fewer converts, if any. Ancestor worship linked each Chinese to another tight and fast; by refusing to perform the rites, a Chinese renounced his race and became a stranger to his own, an unnatural and a renegade. There was a further risk too, that if Christianity denounced the Confucian rites, Christianity itself would become a threat to traditional Chinese society, and be proscribed as dangerous. The Society's members had won ground millimetre by millimetre through hardship and persecution to consolidate their extraordinary position of influence as astronomers-royal and mathematicians in the Emperor K'ang-hsi's court. It was more than they could bear, to endanger this achievement by rejecting what they saw as nothing more than a code of social behaviour thoroughly Christian in its values and ideals.

Gabriel battled again with the sensation of cold lying heavy on his chest as, a fugitive once more, he fled through the tangled wood. But Andrew's Confucianism was helping him to distance himself, and his concentration was returning. Gabriel savoured Andrew's logic: the Ruler of All, *Shang-ti*, was none other than the one true God whom the Chinese, without the benefit of revelation, had recognized for themselves all along, *through natural reason*, intuitively. Now that missionaries had brought them the Gospels, the Chinese would recognize the identity of their supreme being and the Christian God as one and the same. St Paul himself after all had preached in Athens that the Unknown God in the Areopagus was the Christian deity.

Gabriel's mouth pursed at Andrew's optimism, but he was entertained by it nonetheless, remembering earlier Jesuit missionaries' warnings not to discuss the Christian mysteries of the Incarnation and the Redemption with educated Chinese. *Shang-ti* could never be reconciled with the incarnate God; Gabriel knew, and so he suspected did Andrew himself, that *Shang-ti* and Christ made flesh were incompatible. But in his fervour to convert the Chinese race, Andrew waived the problem and hurried on with his exposition that everything the Chinese believed in was fundamentally Christian already.

Gabriel coughed drily. He was ashamed of his own cynicism, and a part of him – the serious part of him – was disturbed by Andrew's eagerness to hug all of Chinese wisdom to his Christian breast. Such transparent accommodation embarrassed him but it wounded him more deeply because ... this was complicated, and Gabriel pushed his hands into his eyes, keeping his head bowed down low over his desk, trying to darken all the other pictures in his head and focus on this single thought which was plucking at him. He searched in the darkness and the blindness suddenly lifted.

Yes, he realized, that is it, the aspects of Christianity which Andrew evaded because the Chinese would have found them repugnant are the very doctrines I consider – and rightly – to be central to my faith. And yet, and here he paused as he tried to finger the exact spot where his thought stumbled, I feel in sympathy with Andrew on this point. I mock his attitudes to the Confucian rites and the rites to the ancestors because they were obviously sacred rituals and he refused to admit it. But I cannot mock his desire to identify *Shang-ti* with my God. I can't leave out 'Jesus Christ, the Word made flesh, who suffered under Pontius Pilate, was crucified dead and buried, on the third day rose again from the dead ...' Yet I feel his embarrassment when K'ang-hsi turned to him and said ... Gabriel quickly turned over the pages of Andrew's diary to an entry made in 1705, in which Andrew told the story of his disastrous attempt to discuss the Redemption with the emperor: ' "Why did God not forgive His son and the sins of the world without making him die?" the emperor asked me. I could find no answer but that the sacrifice was necessary. My God, I cry to you now in the words of your only-begotten son, why did you forsake me then, when I was in such need of your help and inspiration?'

Gabriel read Andrew's torment and frowned. 'When I could find no other words, the emperor spoke to me and his words were full of contempt for your servant, "Some of your words are no different from the wild and improper teachings of Buddhists and Taoists, so why should they be treated differently?" The emperor looked at me coldly when he spoke thus and then dismissed me.'

His head in his hands, Gabriel remembered: at first, K'ang-hsi had accepted the Jesuits' definition of their religion as akin to Confucianism, and was gratified by the similarity. On these grounds, in 1692 he had granted toleration of Christianity in the Empire. When Dominicans and Franciscans, arriving to preach in China as a result of the edict, began to question the Jesuit acceptance of the Confucian rites, the Jesuits petitioned the emperor himself to justify their claims. The Peking mission, including Andrew, memorialized the emperor, asking him to confirm that (Gabriel found the document) 'Confucius is honoured in China as a legislator' (i.e. not a deity). 'That it is to this end and solely with this in view that the ceremonies established in his honour are performed.' Making them something like laying a wreath on the tomb of the Unknown Soldier, thought Gabriel. 'We believe that the Rites which are performed to the Ancestors are established only with a view to communicating the love in which the latter are held and to consecrating the memory of the good they accomplished in their lifetime.' (Flowers on the grave, thought Gabriel again.)

'As for the sacrifices to Heaven (T'ien), we believe that they are addressed not to the visible Heavens that we see above us, but to the Supreme Ruler, Author and Preserver of Heaven and Earth and of all that they contain.'

To this the emperor had replied with a rescript appended in vermilion ink: 'What is written here is without fault. It conforms to our holy doctrine. To honour Heaven, to serve the prince and parents, to honour one's master and one's superior is the universal doctrine of the Empire. In all this petition there is not one word which needs changing. Respect this.'

Gabriel shook his head slowly. The breach between the Chinese and the Christians was fundamental, nevertheless. In 1705 Andrew's painful interview with the emperor clearly revealed their incompatibility. Moreover, the Jesuits' position was being undermined by Rome, where criticism of their proselytizing methods was clamorous. In Peking however, the cracks in the structure were still very fine, and until his death in 1708 Andrew continued to go daily to the palace, rising at dawn to give the emperor, his sons, or whatever officials he cared to send, tuition in mathematics, geometry and astronomy. Still, during the last six years of Andrew's life cracks were appearing, because K'ang-hsi in his shrewdness had come to a realization that was to be disastrous to Christianity's progress in China. And that was ... Gabriel, struggling to unravel the knot of his argument, held his eyes tight shut till the blackness sparkled ... that Christianity had much more in common with Buddhism, a religion of mystery and magic, and less in common with Confucianism, the sober philosophy of state. K'ang-hsi had entertained Jesuits for nearly thirty years in his court, he had exploited their knowledge of the sciences, and in spite of all their cunning readings of the Chinese classics, he had lit upon Christianity's essential mystical and otherworldly character. 'Some of your words are no different from the wild and improper teachings of Buddhists and Taoists, so why should they be treated differently?'

Gabriel felt a sudden surge of admiration for the emperor's perspicacity. There was no nonsense suffered in that quarter. How practical he was, how level-headed! But to Andrew the kinship between Buddhism and Christianity was abhorrent, if indeed he had ever recognized it at all. It made nonsense of the Order's argument that Christian doctrine was the luminous product of natural reason, and relegated it instead to a twilit world that was despised by the Chinese literati, in which miracles were believed and the gods thought to intervene in man's affairs, in which the divine presence was considered to inhabit a man, and celibacy was deemed a greater virtue than reproduction. In the same painful interview of 1705, K'ang-hsi told Andrew that he would gladly witness a miracle such as the priest had described to him. 'But none are forthcoming?' he added with asperity when Andrew, flustered, tried to explain that miracles could not be performed on demand.

Yet Andrew himself years before had played a trick during a hunting expedition to Tartary, in order to excite belief among the emperor's soldiers and followers. He had boasted he could freeze water over fire. He was sitting with the soldiers round a bonfire, and so, when he was challenged, he hung a cauldron of water over the flames and just as it was coming to the boil, and the assembled company began to laugh at the vection beginning at the sides, Andrew slipped some nitre from his full sleeve into the water. It froze instantly. But he could hardly do the same for the emperor when he asked for a miracle.

Gabriel's mouth twisted beneath his hands. Now that he had pursued his thoughts so far, he had still found no consolation. The fact that he could recognize – without the dread that it seemed to inspire in Andrew – that Buddhism and Christianity were philosophically connected afforded him no relief at all. He groaned silently, and feeling the hollowness in his stomach and the cold grip of the dream on his chest return, he pushed back his chair and went downstairs to ask Rosie to make him a cup of tea.

Would he ever finish the work? He doubted it, and slumping into a chair in the sitting-room, he tried to drive away the new trouble that afflicted him. He sank his long and haggard face into his thin chest, waiting for Rosie. And moreover, he had to go to Sicily. He was sweating, and the palms of his hands were damp.

He muttered a brief thank you to the old nanny when she brought him his tea, but she sensed his trouble and left him to himself, darting an anxious glance as she did so at the withered figure in his loose black clothes. He coughed and shivered a little, and she pulled her cardigan round herself in sympathy.

All that afternoon, Gabriel struggled on between the wood and the baying dogs, and collated Andrew da Rocha's passages on Buddhism, while unease continued to grow cancerously inside him. He copied out part of the account of the expedition of 1685 to Tartary, when Andrew returned independently to Peking. On his way back, Andrew had encountered a party of Lamas. The emperor's uncle, who at the emperor's orders was accompanying the priest back to the capital, knew and esteemed the head Lama, and to Andrew's disgust received him in their camp with the greatest marks of respect.

'The mighty prince,' wrote Andrew, 'was offered a little packet of a certain powder, which I think was the ashes of something which the Grand Lama has used, or maybe even his powdered excrement, which the Mongols hold in such high regard that they carry it strung around their necks in little sachets like the most precious of relics, capable of preserving them from all mishap and of curing them of all kinds of illnesses.

'The Lamas were on horseback, and most of them were clothed in a material of saffron silk, with long red scarves wound around their bodies. There was one amongst them, a well-favoured young man with round cheeks and a complexion so white and so delicate that I thought he must be a woman. He was the leader of the group, and was distinguished by a hat made of I know not what material, gilded all over, and rising to a peak with a very wide brim . . .' Gabriel's eyes darkened, and the fresh face of the young Lama overlapped, like a second screen printed over the first, with the face of his dream, smiling and dimpled and confidently healing. He ran his hands through his short hair and closed his eyes, but the image stayed, laughing on his horse under a large-brimmed golden hat and holding up his reins with a graceful but firm gesture of his hands.

All at once at that moment Gabriel was released from the problem that had worried him throughout the day. The horseman in saffron, his face shaded by the glittering hat, receded; the cool touch of a hand on his damp forehead the night before receded too; the sounds of the snapping branches and the howling dogs were silent within him, and he understood something clearly that had eluded him during long hours of doubt and pain.

The Chinese God did not have a face, a body, a touch, sight, or smell, he could not be 'born of a woman', could not laugh, cry, or bleed. He was pure spirit – *T'ai ch'i* – blowing through the universe, the life force itself that informs all things. And the humanity of Christ? What was it but a mechanism to arouse all the conflicting emotions that had tormented Gabriel in the wood, that had been stirred when the face of the angel had become someone else's: the Lama leader's on his pony, the face of Oliver? Was the naked broken body of a young man only a device to channel the strong tide of passion towards the divine? 'Why did God not forgive His son before he died?' K'ang-hsi had asked. Why not? Because it was necessary to use the imagery of flesh and skin and eye and nose and muscle and blood to move the hearts of the faithful, just as it had been expedient to concentrate on the abstract conception of the Almighty when the hearts of the faithful Chinese seemed inclined to abstract conceptions.

The groan that was wrung from Gabriel's dry throat at that moment took possession of the study just as his strangled breath had seemed part of his room the night before. Don't leave me, he prayed, don't. He tried to fight his way back to the time when he had not understood, and get away from the light pouring into his muddled head. Don't leave me, he prayed again. Don't.

Then, suddenly floating free from the old man who sat huddled at his desk with his hands folded over his bent head poring over his papers, Gabriel laughed. He recovered his normal cynicism and he laughed. Crisis of faith indeed, he mocked. Taking doubts seriously, what a peril, what an empty peril for someone as experienced as myself! Not for me, such doubts, so often the product of pride, the Devil's first weapon, of a striving to be holy.

The priest prayed briefly, still mocking himself for a day of such useless self-reproach. He felt the bumps in the figure on the end of his rosary with sly irony. You were ill last night, he told himself, and it deranged you briefly and gave you delusions of spiritual struggle.

To prove to himself how well he had exorcized his demons, Gabriel went straight downstairs, looked up the Institute of Baroque Music in the directory, and when he contacted Oliver, invited himself round for an appraisal of the passages in the diary describing the spinet Andrew da Rocha built for the emperor.

He went back upstairs to collect the papers, and for a moment hesitated in the room. Then he opened the desk's central drawer and picked out of it a prism of rock crystal which he always kept there. He held it to the window; it sparkled, and he ran a finger over its polished facets feeling with pleasure the light grooves of the Chinese characters engraved on one side. He smiled and slipped it into his pocket.

Rosie met him at the bottom of the stairs. He hurried away from her anxiety, but she told him that Paula had telephoned for him, and Mr Wang had inquired after the musical bird. Gabriel thanked her and moved to the front door.

'You will talk to your brother, Father, won't you? He needs you, you know,' she said, working her shiny hands together against her chest.

'Really?' said Gabriel, noting Rosie's concern without much interest. 'Yes, later,' he added, and left.

128

❧ CHAPTER 9

Paula looked with disgust at some seagulls outside her window. They lurched in flight, slipping down the airstreams and braking against the draught with oversized webbed feet as if they feared to fall. What were they doing so far upriver and inland, anyway? Brown-nosed scavengers who had mutated till they and a few starlings and sparrows were the only birds capable of living off the refuse of cities. They mewed self-pityingly above her window and beat their wings as they snatched at the husks and rinds a neighbour was offering them. Paula glared at them from her desk, remembering how she had once ridden into Liverpool by train and seen seagulls in packs like jackals preying on the town's wastes, where a few bulldozers feebly churned, trying to reduce the heaps of rubbish in their jaws. Above them, enjoying the rich harvest in their wake, the gulls circled and cried.

Paula frowned and pulled at her hair. 'Fuck Dejanira,' she said aloud, 'and Fuck E for Electra and F for fuck and S for shit.' She screwed the cap back onto her pen with a vicious twist of her wrist and rocked backwards on her chair. A moment later, she snapped to her feet in one movement and crossed the room restlessly. One more effort and she could finish Hercules. But in her present mood, she might ruin the whole drawing. She ruffled her hair impatiently and then flattened it over her ears. Feeling her ears, she scooped the wax out of them with her little finger, liking the sharpness of her nail against her skin and then eyeing the yellow rim under it with interest.

'Damn it!' she said aloud. She knew from experience that

when heated with frustration and anger as she was today she could destroy a week's work with a single ugly stroke of her hand across the paper.

What shall I do? she asked herself, moving irritably about the small flat. She plugged in the kettle to make a cup of coffee, and then noticing the half dozen half-drunk mugs lying around, a film of greying milk on their surfaces, pulled the plug out again. A bath? she thought. The hot water was switched off – it was the middle of the day, and besides, she'd already had a bath that morning and one the night before. She could always clean the flat. Under the bed there was slut's wool which, whenever she flung the duvet over, scurried about the floor. She could go to the launderette, and watch clothes tumble over and over.

Paula collapsed on to a chair with one movement again of her long limbs and covered her face with her hands. She would go shopping. Yes, she would go out shopping. She was wearing a faded skirt of silk velvet she had found on a barrow in Brick Lane market one Sunday morning. It was deep cobalt blue, and she had afterwards embroidered it with flowers in silk thread she had bought in an old ladies' needlework shop. The assistant was taken aback when Paula yelped with pleasure at the drawers of rainbow-coloured skeins, arranged in sequence of colour, like a chemical breakdown of the components of light. The iridescent range rivalled even watercolours and moreover, Paula exclaimed, running a skein through her fingers, there was the firm fine texture of the silks, like bright clean hair. She had bought three dozen colours to use all over her clothes, on the edge of her jeans, on the back of her denim jacket, on her silk-velvet skirt. The assistant serving Paula, a gentle middle-aged lady with long nimble fingers, laid aside some crochet she was working to ring up her purchase and put the silks in a bag. She moved warily, scared by the young girl's enthusiasm which she had noticed reached an almost hysterical pitch.

This had taken place four or five months ago, when Paula's affair was running out, leaving an emptiness in them both. The colours and the soft suppleness of the silks had touched something, and Paula's extreme rejoicing in them was caused by this movement of quickening in the middle of the aridity of the past months when she had lain in bed next to John, wanting him to touch her and make love, wanting to touch him and make love, yet full of fear that they would try and she would be dead. For in her mind's eye she saw herself as bloodless, an animal hung up to bleed white so that it can be fittingly consumed. When John touched her, it was worse, because her dead rawness became dry as dust. So they had lain side by side, clutching each other like the shipwrecked, babying each other with words to make it better, which of course it never did.

Paula's revivification after her purchase of the silks had been brief, but for a few days embroidering with them had been therapy and had helped her, she was sure, to decide to take the flat. She had not thought of leaving the home where she and John had lived, but the decision had suddenly been simple to make, and John had not struggled against it.

She had made several decisions after that, because after two years of the sleepy formlessness of life as created by John, she found herself hungry for order. The first had come upon her when she let herself into the empty flat on her own with her own key during the early days of her life there, and could not find the light switch. It is my own flat, she thought, not by right of ownership, but mine by right of exclusive occupancy (for the time being at least). Soon every switch will be familiar to me, and to me alone. I could have a secret life here if I wished, I could keep a hundred cats or a hundred lovers or eat cream buns all day long, and nobody need know. I can make use of my time as I want, without interference. I could even put the clock on my time, and no one else's. This was the positive side of solitude, but she was not used to being on her own.

She remained flung in the chair, inert, head buried in her arms. The resolution that had followed quickly on her adoption of autonomy had filled her with a giddy kind of elation. She would choose her own company and seek it out for herself. Women were brought up to accept or decline, but not to offer or express inclination themselves. Taught to bask in the interest of others, they forgot to find out where their own interests lay; feminine pride was so nurtured that telephone calls had to be incoming and not outgoing – at least where the opposite sex was concerned. Her mother was the prime example of this, thought Paula. She accepts everyone whom she attracts without judgement or discrimination. She appears a dominant woman because of the men who flutter in the arc-light of her person. But this was the quintessence of weakness, the feminine position of dependence. Paula shuddered when she thought how her mother failed to keep a grip on the course of her life, how she threw herself with enthusiasm into dud plays and dud men who spun around in her magnetic field for a while, and then became so much space junk hurtling about the stratosphere.

The resolution to avoid her mother's situation and impose her will on her own life had however made Paula's newfound solitude more exacting than it already was for the thousands of other single young women in London. She sometimes went to parties given by old friends from art school. They were happy to see her alone because John had been a difficult bastard, or so they told her in their clumsy attempts to cheer her up, forgetting that when they themselves had experienced rupture, disparagements of the vanished lover only increased the hurt. Paula went out to the cinema and to Ronnie Scott's and ate pizza and hamburgers and drank quantities of overpriced plonk with different men who worked in newspapers or in advertising or dealt in various kinds of tat or more superior tat. But in practice, with dead dragging still deep inside her she did not initiate anything herself. She acquiesced to the invitations until for want of responsiveness on her part they petered out one by one. She was relieved, not distressed; in spite of the fierceness of her opinions, she hated being impolite, and she could hardly fail to know after the last months with John, that when it came to sex, men were as delicate and vain as women were supposed to be.

Recently she had gone out with a classmate from art school. She had always made a point of being friendly towards him, because he was so scraggy and timid, and so she let him follow her into the flat for some coffee at midnight. After he had drunk several cups and she had watched him, she said, 'I'm sorry, but I must go to bed now.' He had thrown her a look of such appeal that dumbly she had replied, shaking her head, 'I'm sorry, Tom, I just can't.' She would have liked him to be someone to whom she could say, laughing, 'I have a kind of female impotence', but she knew he'd feel bound to offer to cure her and she didn't want to go down that path. 'Why?' he had said, his drawn face whitening as he put both hands clenched on the table. 'Everyone else does, why not me?' She looked at him in horror, and he continued, 'Why does it never happen to me?' Then ashamed of the tears rising in his eyes, he shook himself to his feet and left, slamming the front door. For a few minutes after he had gone, Paula trembled with cold. She was surprised that she was so frightened.

Of course humiliation could happen on both sides. Once another man had driven her home and, on arriving at her door, had leaned over and pulled her towards him, placing his dry lips on hers and pushing his wet and chilly tongue through her teeth. He performed this as if it were his automatic duty, and Paula nearly gagged. Later, in the safe emptiness of her flat, she burned with shame that she could give anyone the impression that a try-on was expected of him. And she was again humbled when she realized how close she had come to the fear of the hunted, in spite of her fine resolution to be the hunter, when she could find a trail.

A psychologists' survey in a newspaper revealed that the average among students was 6.25 friends each. Paula had snorted viciously when she came across the passage: 6.25 friends! The figure belonged to fantasy, it existed beyond the selvage of any reality she knew. Yet the number, so crammed with the stupidity of statistics, lay like salt in the raw pit of her stomach, as if her lack of friends – the absence of that magic 6.25 – were a wound in her very entrails. God damn it, she cried out inwardly.

So another resolution had followed Paula's attempts to give structure to her private world. She decided that she would concentrate on the immediate connections she already had – her family. The experiment with her parents was not proving very successful. But she loved Francesca with simple love, and she now had great hopes of Gabriel.

Last night, the second time that week she had spent the evening at her father's house, summoned by her mother to the family's council of war ... She lifted her shoulders, hugging herself, and rose slowly from the chair. Teresa and Jerome, she moaned. The blind, the deaf, the dumb.

Yes, she would go out shopping. Eyeing the wheeling gulls with renewed loathing, Paula noted rain. But she dismissed the thought, pulled on her jacket and a pair of boots and jumping on to her bicycle made for the High Street. As she pedalled she flung her head back to feel the sharp April breeze through her hair and dangled one hand by her side, ignoring the churning traffic around her.

'Where's your pride?' Teresa had said the night before, her large black eyes gazing lustrous at Jerome who, sweating hard, was telling her in great excitement about the showdown at the *Review* that afternoon and his victory of persuasion over the staff. 'Can't you see you'll have to step aside? It's the story of Old Wolf, Young Wolf, I swear to you, my darling.' Teresa's voice was sharp and knowing. She turned to Paula and said, 'The trouble is, your father has never grown up. He still thinks the world is at his feet the way it seemed when he was young. He still thinks it's a kind and tender place full of poetry and love and light when in fact as I know, and you know too, it's up to here in envy and jealousy.' She gestured with her fine flashing hands above her head. 'Ready to drown everybody in time. Especially the old. It's the law of nature, darling, you must see.' She looked appealingly at her husband, as if she were humouring a child, and then at her daughter for approval. Paula looked away. Her father murmured softly,

> 'They flee from me, that sometime did me seek
> With naked foot, stalking in my chamber.
> I have seen them gentle, tame, and meek,
> That now are wild, and do not remember
> That sometime they put themselves in danger
> To take bread at my hand . . .'

Paula flinched from him too. His glasses were misting with emotion.

She struck down hard on the pedals of her bike, forcing herself up the hill towards the High Street. A police car whistled by and turned at full tilt into the police yard. 'Road hogs,' she muttered.

Her father, still sweating freely, had looked crumpled as he leant forward over his glass of claret to talk to his wife, to draw her to his point of view. 'I can't believe it. Why? Why? The

Review's success is due to me. I created it. It's my paper, and it always has been my paper. I ... fashioned it.' He raised his two stubby hands which he could no longer spread flat and looked at them. 'I ...' he faltered, and Teresa snickered, 'You are an innocent, Jerome my darling. You have no conception of the hardness of the world.' She got up from the table and walked into the sitting-room to turn on the television.

Paula stopped, threw her leg over the saddle and running, pushed the bike across the road towards an antiquarian bookshop she knew and liked, because it specialized in nineteenth- and early twentieth-century illustrated books. She fought away her memories of the night before and stood looking at the shelf of bargains on the pavement. Eric Linklater: *Juan in China*. My father might like that, she thought. But no, he's bound to have it. She went inside.

The thought of her father brought her back unwillingly, and she stood in the shop, gazing blankly at the cabinets of books. When the Ten O'Clock News had begun, Teresa had called Jerome and Paula gathered close to watch. The announcer promised, 'The latest developments in the story of the *London Review of Books*'. Paula listened in a daze to the disasters that had befallen the globe that day, while the weight of anxiety in her stomach grew in pain and intensity. Then her father appeared on the screen. He was coming out of the doorway of the office opposite the British Museum and he was waving away reporters so that his hands seemed white and oversized, like a clown's. But he was laughing good-humouredly behind his gestures, and his loud bluff voice could be heard saying, 'We have had a very good talk, my staff and I, and everything has now been explained. Everyone is satisfied, I think.' Then he bustled away down the street and the television camera followed his sturdy figure half-walking, half-running towards the tube station with his jacket flapping open over his bottom. Jerome squirmed as he watched, and wiped his mouth with the back of his hand.

The reporter said, 'But things at the *Review* are not as calm as Dr Namier maintains, Mr Ian Holmes, assistant editor, told the Ten O'Clock News team.' The screen focussed on Holmes, in the studio, in a bright green shirt. 'Ian, are you satisfied with Dr Namier's explanation?' asked the reporter. 'No, frankly,

I'm not,' said Ian, deliberately picking the Gauloise out of his mouth. 'I'm frankly dissatisfied.' He leant back coolly in the tubular steel chair, laying both hands on the arms, and described how Jerome had met all the staff's queries with pusil-lanimous and self-serving vagueness and that he as a result had offered his resignation, which Dr Namier would be receiving in the morning. 'I can no longer work for a journal that poses as independent when it is in actuality a political tool.' His eyes searched the camera's eye as if he knew Jerome were out there beyond it.

The newscaster reappeared. He described the character and background of James Cunliffe, the *Review*'s chief backer. But Paula did not hear a word he said because she had eyes and ears only for her father. He was making for the television, like a wrestler on the attack.

Paula in the bookshop turned over the pages of an edition of *Ondine*, illustrated by Arthur Rackham. She looked at the watercolours coolly, for she admired him without liking him. She put the volume back and took down *William the Bad* by Richmal Crompton. This artist at least had wit, she thought, looking at the plates with amusement. 'William calls the kettle black' ran one rubric. Paula smiled briefly.

When James Cunliffe had appeared on the screen – Paula had always found him dull and odiously vain – Jerome became quiet again and stopped, foursquare, arms on his hips, in front of the set. Head hooked forward, he watched his friend in silence; but as James spoke, Paula at her father's back could see the bellicose thrust of his shoulders slacken and his spine slump in defeat. Yet she did not see it happen, so much as feel it, sitting as she was behind him, unable to speak, unable to move. Oh no, drawled James, he would on no account be selling or surrendering any part of his shares in the *Review*, which he had founded; he was proud of the journal's record and achievement; the matter of the CIA funds was a minor blemish, but no *mea culpa* was needed from him. What was needed now that it had all come out into the open was a change of direction, a new hand at the tiller. Of course, he said, his handsome face puckering, he was in no position to comment on that at this moment.

'Your friend,' Teresa spat at Jerome. 'You see what I mean. It's a bloody awful place, your world. It ought to be mocked more, not followed.' She picked up a box of beads from a necklace she was rethreading and moved closer to the lamp to see so that her face was half in darkness but her hands in her lap brightly lit. Paula looked at the rooted stance of her father, then across at her mother. Her mother glanced up at Jerome, and Paula saw a spasm cross her shadowed face. The beads fell from her knees in a tiny, tinkling cascade. Then Jerome fell too, crashing down on the sofa, his strong heavy frame racked with sobs of anger and rage.

Paula held *William the Bad* in her frozen stare. In her mind's eye she watched her father's heaving body. She was terrified of his tears, terrified and ashamed and helpless. The sequence blurred: Teresa enfolded the bulk of him in her long thin arms and cradled him, cooing and cajoling as if he were a baby, her early sharpness and malice gone. Meanwhile sounds of gunfire burst from the television set. But Paula was out of the house and running hard, down the hill until her gasps brought her to a standstill. Why hadn't Gabriel been there? He would have helped, he would have seen that it doesn't matter, that Daddy will be all right.

She let *William the Bad* fall from her fingers on to the table and stood in unseeing silence in front of the bookshelves. After a few seconds, the movements of the assistant behind her brought her back to herself, and she walked slowly out of the shop.

Poor Daddy. There was nothing more to say. Poor Daddy. He had been unlucky in his friends, that was for certain. She wouldn't be, though. She felt listless and frustrated again and eyed the shop windows with indifference. Spending money would only afford a temporary relief. The pleasure of dumping packages on the kitchen table and undoing them, folding the paper bags and the tissue paper and snipping off the tags and labels, hanging up the clothes or putting the books by her bed, smoothing things into drawers, all that would soon be undone by the guilt and the fear about the money. Paula shook her head. The mood had passed, thank God.

She noticed then that the man walking in front of her down

the street had one shoe off and one shoe on. He moved in consequence with a syncopated motion, as if listening to a beat playing in his ear alone; his one sandal flopped against the pavement to mark the rhythm, and his basket banged against his leg in answer. Paula laughed suddenly, and overtook him, keeping her face down to hide her smile. But on second thoughts, she turned and grinned at him and nodded, and he, after a moment, laughed back.

Paula looked about her and tried to wipe the previous night from her mind. It was a grey day, and the light of London flattened the buildings. But through the uniform and shadowless drabness a throng of people moved, scattered across the streets and pavements around her like a flock of gaudy coloured birds settling on a sudden instant flowering in the desert. She took in the vivid faces and the vivid clothes with wonder. The shoeless man behind her had long tow-coloured hair, which fell gaily down his red-checked woollen lumber jacket; a girl in front of her struggling with a child in a babywheeler wore a long Indian cotton skirt striped in blue and green and mustard under a short flared grass-green coat, and pulled down over her ears and her child's were identical multi-coloured knitted caps with earmuffs and a pattern of dolls dancing round the crown. Mother and child had cheeks glowing from the sharp air that morning. Matisse, thought Paula. And in London, where there's no light to speak of. A couple strolled past rolling against each other as if in the street too they must retain the intimacy of body next to body, key into lock, they had in bed. They too were splashes of colour: the man's sweater a blackberry purple, his boots made of patchwork leather; the girl in a tangerine rough camel cloak from Morocco with a long cowl cross-stitched in black hanging down her back – the tassel bobbed as she moved. It seemed to Paula as if all the bazaars of the Orient had been raided for this north London High Street scene where the shoppers were on their way to the rich man's wedding feast.

The couple walked past Paula and noticed her rapt attention. They met her eyes candidly but without a smile, returning quickly to their mutual self-absorption. How each group was entire of itself, thought Paula, forming a single bubble in the great convection that is sucking the whole gaudy and glittering mass up the hill into shops and out again, each bubble separate from the other, and yet part of the seething city, the vessel in which they stream and swell. This crowd, so playful and expensive . . . She stopped and smiled as a hearse swept by up the street with a surging procession of huge black cars behind it. The boots of the vehicles in the cortège were open, so that everyone could see the piled wreaths inside. There's no point, no point whatsoever, Paula told herself, scuffing the toe of her boot with her heel, in thinking about trivial personal things when all this huge expenditure of energy is happening all around. Here were children bright with health and mothers with the figures of dancing girls and purses filled and bulging to buy. Here were some people who had never experienced want or struggle and obstruction. What was the point of thinking of other things? Wasn't it mad to be sad in such an effervescence?

Frowning hard to keep back the tears blinding her, Paula turned into a herbalist's and bought Francesca a bar of special soap and herself a small pot of rosemary. As she bicycled back home with the rosemary in her basket she leant forward to breathe in its perfume. 'Damn it, damn it,' she whispered fiercely to herself as she pedalled. 'All is damn well all right with the world.'

❧ CHAPTER 10

Gabriel entered the Institute of Baroque Music and found himself in the middle of a crowd of tourists. One of them, taking Gabriel for an attendant, asked him authoritatively, 'And what is this?' letting fall a shower of pot-pourri petals back into a china bowl in the hall. Gabriel looked down on him, a small man, checked his natural haughtiness and smiled benignly. 'It smells sweet, why don't you try it?'

The house was filled with a strumming and twanging and jangling of instruments as the party of tourists tramped through the Institute. One child banged out chopsticks on the seventeenth-century virginals, and a man testing a clavichord shook his head and condemned it for lack of volume.

Where was Oliver? Gabriel left the ground floor and walked upstairs, where he heard the successive notes of a scale being played insistently as the strings were tightened or slackened under the tuner's tools.

Oliver was bent to the harpsichord in a small wainscoted room on Gabriel's left. His hand was under the lid, turning a key to tune the instrument. The bridges on which the strings rested curved away from him in two graceful and complementary parabolas, and the golden veneer of the pearwood of the instrument's case gleamed.

Gabriel felt at once possessed by harmony. Oliver did not stop or move when the priest entered the room, but smiled at him with his slow merry eyes, piercing Gabriel down deeper, to his dream. He stood beside the harpsichord and waited, glancing out of the window, and feeling self-conscious. A family came into the room but they clustered quietly round Oliver with exaggerated tiptoe steps, fingers to lips urging one another to hush. Oliver smiled up at them as well and continued up the register. When he reached the top, he settled himself and played a few bars of a piece, letting the music fall in rills round the room. Gabriel looked down at the garden, where a single white lilac tree stood, a drift of spring snow against the freshening green of the lawn. Oliver came up to him.

'Very good to see you,' he said, 'let's go. I wanted to go out, and besides there are too many people here.'

He jumped down the stairs and, pulling a sweater over his head, reached the front door where he turned to watch Gabriel descending more slowly.

'Come on,' he said with energy. 'We'll go out on the Heath. There'll be no one there.' He threw his fair hair away from his face and held the door for Gabriel.

The older man was about to protest and raise the subject of da Rocha's craftsmanship as an instrument-maker, and to remind Oliver he had come to consult the library, but the words did not form themselves and docile, he followed Oliver out and down the lane that led to the pond and to the sandy path towards the blasted willows. Although he followed Oliver's rapidly-moving figure gaily enough, he felt on the verge of profound embarrassment. In Oliver's presence he felt as if the boy – for Gabriel, forty years older than Oliver, saw him as a boy – might do something altogether extraordinary from which Gabriel would have to dissociate himself, like cut a caper or sing a song aloud, and Gabriel would have to turn his face away and say, 'I'm not with him.' For he had become connected to him, implicated in him, so that anything Oliver did might have the power to embarrass him. Because such sensitivity does not cancel attraction but rather strengthens it, Gabriel found that his anticipation of embarrassment sharpened the pleasure he had in Oliver's company and fastened him closer to his side.

Oliver stopped and ran back to Gabriel. 'I'm going too fast for you,' he said apologetically. 'But for a man of your age you look tough and lean.' He pushed at Gabriel's ribs with his hand. 'Thinness, that's what matters.' The look in his eye had a certain gleeful edge to it, as if he were congratulating himself on Gabriel's interest in him.

They walked together more slowly towards the trees and Gabriel found himself confiding in Oliver the horror of each summer when his hay fever was so bad that a jelly of mucus sometimes formed over his eyes. Oliver looked at him sidelong and brushed his hair out of his eyes again, baring what seemed to Gabriel a childishly smooth pale forehead. 'It's all in the mind, you know,' said Oliver, tapping his temple. 'People who are ill like you, it's because they're crying out for something else. It's a distress signal, the body shouting, Gimme, gimme. But you're not listening, or you don't know what it's telling you. You should really learn to play something. Whenever I'm ill I sit down and play until the fever's at rest inside me. It works, you know.' He looked earnestly at Gabriel. 'It's the truth.'

'You are fortunate,' said Gabriel drily. He was cross with himself for listening at all to Oliver's modish pseudo-metaphysical claptrap. Curtly, he outlined to him the complex physiology of his long illness. As he argued with Oliver that his complaint was beyond his control, he began to relent, and soon, smiling a little, was describing to him how, when he was fourteen years old, he had been convinced that two armies were butchering each other in his grandmother's garden, wielding hacksaws and battleaxes. Hearing the screams of the victims from his bed, he rang the bell again and again for the nurse, and when she came, begged her to order the armies to stop fighting, because he himself was too weak to leave his bed and shout at them from the window. The nurse tried to console him, but she returned later with a priest.

Gabriel's long seamed face became almost youthful as he said to Oliver, 'That was the first time I really felt the goodness of a priest! He blessed me, and quietened me, the war in the garden came to an end, and I fell asleep.'

'There you are,' said Oliver with a triumphant twinkle in his light eyes. 'I told you it was all in the mind.'

They had reached the hollow beech.

'Look at her!' said Oliver. 'Look at the power and the age and the beauty of her.'

Gabriel was surprised. 'My niece Paula is very taken with this tree too. She tells me she has drawn it many times.'

Oliver turned on him fiercely. 'This tree is not an it. She

is, well, she is all *she* and nothing else, the matrix, the womb.'
He laid a hand on the scarred bark and stroked the smooth
black skin inside the hollow. 'Once when I was alone here I
crawled inside and went to sleep inside her.' He looked keenly
at Gabriel, and added in an undertone, 'It was beautiful, more
beautiful than anything, lying there at the bedrock of it all.'

'Nonsense,' said Gabriel, tolerant.

'You Catholics,' said Oliver, 'I think you're the most down-to-
earth practical people I know, in spite of all the holy water and
relics and stuff.'

'If you went to a Catholic church now,' Gabriel interposed,
'you would find it very simple, simpler indeed than most of the
Anglican churches in England.' He was serious. 'We have become a practical church, it's true.'

Oliver walked away from him into the trees beyond and flung
his head back, looking up at the branches. 'Look,' he said softly.
'The leaves are opening.'

Gabriel followed his glance and shuddered. The branches
above his head were interlaced against the light – it was in just
such a wood that last night he had run.

'No,' he muttered involuntarily, and Oliver, noticing his con-
straint rejoined him quickly. 'Come on then, Father,' he said
mockingly, and looped the older man's arm in his. 'We'll soon
find out what causes all these illnesses of yours.' He laughed,
nodding. 'We will, I swear.'

Gabriel shook his head, but did not withdraw his arm. It was
years since anyone had treated him with such familiarity, and
although he knew Oliver was teasing him, he did not feel
mocked. Oliver's energy and his ease, the life that raced through
him made Gabriel happy. The young man did not suffer from
one drop of the twin contemporary sins of accidie and tepidity,
and the priest argued to himself that Oliver's zest and brightness could help to overcome his own habitual cynicism. Gabriel
wanted to reach out and touch him, just as a sick man holds a
doctor's hand in the hope that healing power will flow from his
fingertips. It did not occur to Gabriel to ask why Oliver should
give him his time – he was used to the attention of others.
But he did worry – and then quickly dismissed the worry from
his mind – why the holiness of the flesh radiated from every
movement Oliver made and from every curve of his smiling

lips. He clung to his feeling of joy as he followed the boy who was swinging down the path in front of him, who seemed to have nothing on his mind other than staying in his company. The rhythm of Oliver's life seemed to the priest to have an un- forced, unpremeditated quality that was absent in his own strictly organized day. Oliver had slipped into Gabriel's world without effort, with gaiety; a cuckoo who sets up camp in another's house and cheerfully takes the bread out of his mouth, but in return brings in the spring with its cry. Gabriel saw only the spring, not the usurper; he wanted Oliver to ban- ish the staleness in his heart and fill him with admiration for the arrangement of God's universe. Gabriel forgot the anger and the pain he had experienced that morning at his desk, when he had rebelled so violently against the use of material images to excite religious devotion and the crucified body of Christ had seemed to him a cheap device to sublimate love. In the grey out- door light and seeing the new leaf, he no longer felt oppressed and his earlier fears seemed foolish: the created world had been conceived in all its perfection in God's imagination and each tree and plant and creature found its form and disposition through Him. With a human soul like Oliver, who seemed to have pierced the outer skin of the visible world to some music of the inner ear beyond, he, Gabriel, could renew his experience of the love of God without anxiety or guilt.

The young man was leading the priest over the Heath where the fields run down to a small permanent gipsy encampment. Gabriel put his hand in his pocket and smiled as his fingers found the lump of rock crystal he had taken from the drawer of his desk. 'Oliver,' he said, using his name gently for the first time. 'Look at this.'

Oliver Summers picked up the piece of rock crystal delicately, trying not to film its shiny facets with his fingertips. He held it up before his eyes against the sky's grey banks of cloud. It was cut and polished so finely that it seemed insubstantial, the very emanation of the spectrum itself flashing with rainbow rays of purple and gold and flame. Oliver ran a finger over the Chinese characters, and then, with a baffled look, handed the prism back to Gabriel and turned away.

Gabriel was silent for a few moments, hurrying down the path behind him towards the road and exit from the Heath. Then he took a sharp breath and said, 'I rarely have difficulty expressing myself' – his manner was formal and Oliver stopped and listened to him with a serious air – 'but this piece of rock crystal is important to me in many ways. My father bought it in the great street of antique shops, *Loi Lu Chan*, in Peking. It is a very rare piece and he could hardly believe his good fortune when he saw it on a tray with other knick-knacks of no interest. He gave it to me for my twenty-first birthday – in 1929. No . . .' Gabriel waved away Oliver's look of concern. 'That's not what's important. It's this.' He pointed to the inscription. 'That says, "This crystal is a piece of the true material of heaven. I, Ch'u Tai-su, wrote this poem." Then it gives the date. Ch'u was an astronomer, poet, painter, a true Superior Person in the Confucian tradition. He profoundly admired the Jesuits' learning. I did some research into his life when I was given the prism, and I found the record of a conversation that he had had with another Jesuit, a colleague of my friend da Rocha. Ch'u and the Jesuit Father had been discussing the nature of the heavens.' Gabriel told Oliver how the Chinese scholar had maintained that the stars floated freely in infinite space. 'That was the ancient Chinese view – which as we now know is correct,' he added. 'We do not know what the Jesuit himself thought was true. Galileo's telescope and its discoveries – which showed the accuracy of the traditional Chinese theory – had been first heralded by the Jesuits in Rome but then condemned by the Church. Maybe the Jesuit Father in Peking did not know of Galileo – though I myself doubt it – but anyway he was obedient to the Holy Father and he instructed the Chinese scholar in the Ptolemaic idea of the universe.' Gabriel described how the earth was suspended at the centre of nine concentric spheres, and how on the eighth or penultimate sphere, the fixed stars were set like so many jewels in a crown. 'These spheres laid one inside the other were made of crystal, it was said, which is how man could see through each planetary sphere to the fixed stars beyond.'

Gabriel caught the momentary look of vacancy on Oliver's face. He breathed deep, but could not check himself. Two high spots of colour glowed on the pale priest's cheekbones, but he pressed on, taking the piece of quartz from his pocket again and standing it on his palm. He knew no other way to communicate the intensity of his emotion than through the special channel of expression he had used for many years of domination: teacherishness. The cloth of priesthood had freed him from the accusation of pedantry or pomposity by the general, and so there survived in him now this teacherishness, his heart's bane, like aphids choking new growth in May.

Oliver was smiling at him in a puzzled way. 'The Chinese scholar was dazzled by the Jesuit's superior command of geometry,' Gabriel was saying, 'which he used to press his argument. And as a tribute to his false teacher, he inscribed this piece of quartz with the words, "This crystal is a piece of the true material of heaven," as I said.' Gabriel, drawing a sharp breath, held it out to Oliver. 'Take it,' he said. 'For a time, you keep it.'

Oliver's transparent skin coloured and he pulled at his fair hair. He was flattered by Gabriel's desire for his company, but he disliked sentiment.

'No,' he said, looking down.

'Yes,' said Gabriel. His voice was firm, and Oliver, suddenly brightening and smiling his slow smile, took the prism from him. With a cheerful nod of his head but without looking at it he slipped it straight into his pocket. He was deliberately casual, trying to put paid to Gabriel's earnestness.

Gabriel found that he could not explain why he wanted Oliver to have the crystal. The boy's cheeriness checked him. Yet I would like to tell him, thought Gabriel with unaccustomed poignancy, although he might not have understood. There was a connection between what Oliver made Gabriel feel and the image of the crystal piece of the sky. The Church's adherence to the Ptolemaic universe revealed the fundamental concreteness of the Catholic faith: the heavens were made of rock just as analogously God was made of blood and flesh and spittle and sweat. The Chinese imagination, on the other hand, thought Gabriel, is abstract, and therefore the Chinese universe is insubstantial and in their cosmology the stars swim in bright and empty air, just as their god is energy itself, the life force, abstract, without form or substance, not a personal god. Oliver is an image from the concrete Christian world – he has reminded me of the presence of God's spirit everywhere, in human beings, palpable and apprehensible, like the crystalline heavens.

❦ *CHAPTER 11*

Paula was travelling to the West End by taxi because her Uncle Gabriel had insisted that he could not abide the tube. They were on their way to Mr Wang's antique shop in a back street on the shabby border of Soho and Covent Garden in order to return the singing bird in the golden cage.

It was the beginning of May, and with reckless optimism the workers of central London were exposing their arms and necks to the first feeble sunbeams of summer.

'Will it be hot in Sicily?' asked Paula, noting the undress on the pavement.

'I think so,' said Gabriel wearily. He was not looking forward to the Sicilian trip at all. He did not want to leave London or his book. Apprehension seized him at the thought of neglecting his writing for a month. A whole month. He calculated again the portion it represented of his life, and clutched tightly at the strap. Moreover, Jerome had been foisted on him. As a companion! he exclaimed inwardly in irritation.

It had all been decided by Teresa, who for once had misgivings that her acting prevented her ministering to her husband. When Nanny told her, with some excitement, that Gabriel was off to Sicily in the near future to investigate a certain vision of Our Blessed Mother, Teresa suddenly conceived the idea that the whole family should go with him, herself excluded. She offered Paula and Francesca and Tilly the fare; Gabriel had grimaced at the prospect but felt that after his brother's defeat at the *Review*, he could hardly complain.

'Jerome must get away from it all,' Teresa had told him. 'And they won't get under your feet, not if they all go. They'll

147

entertain each other.' She plucked at his sleeve, crafty, and added, 'It's like adultery, though you wouldn't know about that, of course. The public humiliation matters more than the thing itself. Jerome must get away from people's sympathies and gossip and chatter about the rights and wrongs of what he did or didn't do.' Gabriel agreed reluctantly. But he had been extremely relieved when Francesca said that Tilly would not be well enough for the trip and she wanted to stay in London anyway. Although she disliked accepting such a present from her mother, Paula had yielded because she felt obliged to help her father. In the circumstances her mother's solution was the best. As for Gabriel, he was pleased because he knew Paula would look after her father.

Jerome, presented with the *fait accompli*, assented sheepishly. He had been docile over the last two weeks. Teresa had supervised his letter of explanation and resignation to the *Review*, excised the tetchiness of his tone and replaced it with phrases of regret that blamed no one. She had sent one copy to the paper's staff, one to James Cunliffe (with an icy message of her own appended) and another to *The Times*, which had printed it at the bottom of the front page in an article sympathetic to Jerome's plight and filled with praise of his editorship. This had gratified Jerome, avid for vindication. But he felt dull when he thought of going to Sicily with his brother – Gabriel's company always grated on him. Paula on the other hand was brimming over with expectancy.

In the taxi, she could draw little out of her uncle, and the pauses between question and answer gradually lengthened as they rode into the West End. Paula was aware that her father and herself were probably unwanted company on Gabriel's expedition, but she was determined that he would not regret it. She would act as a buffer between the two brothers and keep the peace, and she was excited by the thought of seeing Gabriel at work as a priest. So she decided to ignore Gabriel's silence by her side and his evident lack of enthusiasm for the Sicilian trip. In the end, she thought, he will be pleased we came with him.

The windows of Wang's shop were grimy and the once-gilded letters of its name on the glass door were half effaced. A few large pieces of blue-and-white were displayed, alongside a splendid ceremonial urn. Paula paid the taxi and then pushed open the door for her uncle. The tongue of a dud bell sounded. She held the door as Gabriel, clutching the package in which the musical bird was wrapped, passed through. When the door swung to, the cracked bell sounded once more.

At the back of the single room a curtain moved and the stooped figure of a Chinese emerged. The atmosphere was thick with smoke, and before he let the curtain fall, Paula caught sight of a plump young redhead lying on the sofa in the cubicle behind. The antique dealer himself looked very old; he had long grey hair swept back from a domed forehead, from his long chin sprouted a few long whiskers, and his papery hands, yellowed from tobacco, were crowned with finely shaped talons that intensified his resemblance to a sombre and aged bird of prey. He folded his hands calmly over a nearly concave chest, and bowed slightly.

'Ah, Father Namier,' he said, clicking his tongue softly on his palate so that all the consonants sounded liquid as vowels, 'it is a long time.' His mouth smiled, revealing blackened teeth, but his eyes remained serious, and his face showed no wrinkles. Paula wondered how if she were to draw him she would manage to convey the great antiquity of his appearance.

'Yes, Wang,' said Gabriel, 'and as always I am deeply grateful to you.' He looked around the crowded shop for a space to put down the bird. Wang moved forward with dignity to lift a pile of drawings and woodcuts from a heavy mahogany chest and place them on top of another huge pile of papers.

'It delight you?' he asked, eyebrows rising straight on his forehead, as he pointed at the bird with his cigarette.

'It did,' said Gabriel, with a small smile.

'If you do not want it, I offer to V and A, or maybe British Museum.' Wang shrugged.

Gabriel laughed. 'You know I could not afford it, Wang.'

Wang nodded. 'You are priest,' he said softly. Paula strained to decipher his liquid pronunciation. 'You forsake worldly possessions. But I must live from trade. Your brother?' Again the eyebrows shot up.

'No,' said Gabriel. He would like to have discussed buying the bird with Jerome and prompted his brother's ready generosity. But the opportunity had not presented itself over the last two weeks. Gabriel sighed.

'I shall enjoy it on exhibition,' he said. He removed it from its box and set it tinkling and trilling again. 'It is a fine piece of craftsmanship.'

'It tell lie,' said Wang, smiling. 'It sing happiness and laughter. That is all lie.' He stabbed the air with his cigarette in Gabriel's direction. 'Was it made by the man who you write about?'

Gabriel spread his hands. 'It could have been,' he said, wistful. 'I wasn't able to check. There are no signatures on such objects, no records.'

Paula was picking her way through the shop. In a large celadon vase on the floor she found a bundle of scrolls tied together with ribbons. She looked over her shoulder at Wang, and he urged her with his long-taloned hand and mirthless smile to explore and open them.

Paula began to unroll one. Under her fingers a grey tinted watercolour of cloud-capped peaks rising mistily over a curving river unfolded. In one crevice, half concealed under a canopy of willow fronds, stood a small open-terraced house where a man in voluminous robes sat writing with a brush.

Wang came towards Paula on slippered feet. 'That is Wang Hui, The Dragon Cloud Pavilion.'

'It's beautiful,' said Paula.

'You read the inscription, Father Namier,' said Wang, puffing on his cigarette and eyeing Gabriel sidelong.

Gabriel demurred, then came over and studied the characters running down the left side of the scroll. Slowly, his lips moving, his eyes passed down. 'Clouds . . . rise up to heaven . . . It is the picture . . .' He stopped and chuckled. 'It's a quotation from the Book of Changes. "It is the image of waiting. Thus the superior man eats and drinks, is joyous and of good cheer. I, Wang Hui, wrote this in my fifty-seventh year in the garden of the Dragon Cloud Pavilion." He was a sensible man, I expect, who retired to a garden.' Gabriel looked well pleased with himself.

'Yes,' said Wang. 'Who understood that in pursuit of antiquity only knowledge is found.' He held his cigarette to his lips and through the smoke said to Gabriel, 'The Classic of Changes is a wise book, Father Namier.'

'So it is,' said Gabriel.

Paula rolled up the scroll again and tied its ribbon. Then

curious, she turned to Wang and asked, 'Can you do it? Will you do it for me?'

Wang nodded slowly.

'I shan't participate,' said Gabriel, good-humouredly. He was proud that he had construed the inscription so readily and gratified that he had placed the quotation. Such ease was not always the case with him, though he was reluctant to admit it to others.

'Come this way, if you please,' said Wang.

He lifted the curtain, and held it while Paula and Gabriel passed through. The room beyond was nothing more than an alcove, and it too was piled with documents and *objets de vertu* and vessels. The atmosphere was saturated with tobacco, mingled with a cheap and lively perfume of lilies of the valley wafting from the ample body of the redhead on the sofa. She shifted as Paula and Gabriel entered.

'May I present to you my daughter, Jacqueline. She is gladness in my declining day. She will make tea.'

Wang spoke to the young woman with reverent gentleness. Paula was astonished: the desiccated old Chinese and the frowzy girl belonged to different worlds.

'Can do,' said Jacqueline in an American accent. Edging forward from the sofa, she grasped a stick leaning against one of the pieces of furniture crowding the room and pulling on it, raised herself to her feet. Then Paula saw that under the hem of her patterned dress, she wore calipers on her right leg. They gleamed, heavy and metallic. Paula reddened, ashamed of her sour thoughts, and flattened herself against the wall in order to leave Jacqueline as much space as possible to manoeuvre in the tiny room. But the girl's movements on her stick were nimble, and from inside a small chest she produced a tray with delicate blue and white thimble-sized cups, a small teapot and a brightly enamelled canister of tea. She set a kettle on a primus which was perched on the edge of another piece of furniture, and swivelled on her stick to gaze gravely at her father's guests.

Wang indicated with a wave of his long hands that Gabriel should sit beside him on the sofa and Paula draw up the chair to the small table and sit down facing him. Paula caught Gabriel's eye; Wang intercepted her plea, and said suavely, 'Jacqueline is the victim of car accident. The driver—her husband

– dies. By good fortune – it is destiny, circumstance bring us together and I have no children, so I adopt her. She is mine. Father Namier knows, I tell him before.'

Gabriel nodded impatiently. The air was stifling behind the curtain. He lit one of his own Turkish cigarettes to dispel the fumes of Wang's tobacco and the girl's heavy flowery perfume, and inhaled slowly. He knew the story of Wang and the American girl, but he had forgotten it. It did not interest him much.

Wang handed Paula three coins from a small glazed jar on a shelf above his head. They were Chinese copper cash, verdigris-ed with age and pierced by a square hole. At his instruction, she threw them on the cloth covering the table, and Wang marked a line on a piece of paper after each throw. Paula felt tense; as the first trigram was completed – from bottom to top, two broken lines and one unbroken – she felt unwillingly bound by Wang's intense gaze on her. She threw again three times: first an unbroken, *yang* line, second, also *yang*, but a changing line, third, a broken line, *yin*.

'*Hsien*,' said Wang, 'The hexagram of Wooing.'

His slurred syllables flowed uncomprehended over Paula, who could think of nothing else but Jacqueline and her life behind Wang's curtain. Wang talked to Paula of influence and joy and keeping still to remain at the heart of things. He told her the hexagram judged that her perseverance would succeed and that taking a young man for her husband would bring her good fortune.

Paula stretched out her legs and crossed them as he spoke. Then, remembering Jacqueline she quickly tucked them under her chair. She drank her thimbleful of tea hurriedly, glad of its freshness in the asphyxiating room.

'The image,' continued Wang, 'is a lake on top of mountain. Lake gives water to mountain, mountain collects cloud and feeds lake, which grows. So the forces have power to influence each other.' The words meant little to Paula. The idea of wooing was at least positive, but the mention of marriage irritated her. She was disappointed.

'There is a further image,' said Wang, pressing the words to her attention. 'Lake can only form in mountaintop if mountain is hollow and receives and retains water. So wise man is empty, and is not closed to thoughts of others. So the superior man encourages others to come to him and receives them openly.'

Gabriel, who had been smoking, eyes closed, now leant forward with interest. 'The Book of Changes is always full of good advice, my dear,' he said complacently. 'I have always followed its philosophy that one should remain open to the ideas of others.'

Paula looked at him, gaping for a moment. He brackets himself with the 'wise man' and the 'superior man' as a matter of course, she thought, and for a moment recognized that this revelation was a warning to her. But she chose to ignore it.

'Let's do yours,' she said. She was bored with her hexagram. 'Let's see what it tells you.'

'No,' said Gabriel. But his tone was not firm, and Wang handed him the coins, smiling his sad smile. Gabriel took them in his palm and closed his hand over them. 'You know what the Emperor K'ang-hsi said about the Book of Changes, don't you?' He addressed Wang, with a gleam in his eye. Wang's lids drooped in assent. 'But let me hear again, for he was a wise man.'

'K'ang-hsi said, "I have never tired of the Book of Changes, and have used it for fortune-telling, and as a source of moral principles. The only thing you must not do, I told my court lecturers, is to make this book appear simple, for there are meanings here that lie beyond words." ' Gabriel threw the coins six times on the table.

'*Ta Ch'u*,' said Wang, softly. 'Aaha. It is apt. "The Taming Power of the Great".' He tapped the two trigrams on the paper in front of him. 'For a man of God, it is apt. I think Confucius comments so: "When innocence is present, it is possible to tame. But holding fast to heavenly virtue is prerequisite of innocence, and innocence of course is indispensable for holding on to pristine heavenly virtue." ' Wang's eyes glittered and his grey brows shot up. 'Is that not wisdom?'

Gabriel's mouth pursed in amusement. 'You think me innocent?'

'As a man who renounces many things,' Wang waved at Jacqueline, 'you are.'

'But children are only important to a Confucian master like

you,' replied Gabriel, ironic. 'It is no hardship for me to go without.'

'It is the book which judges you innocent, Father Namier,' said Wang gravely.

Paula looked into Wang's smooth face and then at her uncle beside him. 'And then?'

'The young are too impatient. The meanings that lie here run too deep for quick and agitated minds.'

Paula coloured at the sting. 'I was only interested,' she muttered.

'The Judgement says,' Wang began again, unhurriedly, 'perseverance will bring good fortune. Not eating at home brings good fortune, and you have great success if you cross the great water.' Though Wang's syllables were becoming less intelligible as he recited, Paula caught the end of the sentence. 'Ah,' she exclaimed. 'Sicily.'

'You must not be so literal, my dear,' said Gabriel, kindly.

'I suppose not,' said Paula, but she stored it up as a good omen. Wang continued to expound the hexagram, with more illustrious reflections on Gabriel's character. He took the lines one by one. 'You have nine at the beginning,' he said. 'This first line is strong. It is in its proper place. It would like to advance, but two strong lines above obstruct it. It means clearly, "Danger is at hand." ' Wang paused and his long hands fluttered. 'Father Namier, you must not expose yourself to danger,' he admonished him. 'It is a changing line in your hexagram, and it is strong.'

Gabriel shrugged his shoulders and put out his cigarette with a rapid and contemptuous gesture. 'As a source of moral principles, the Book of Changes is rich. But when it resembles the tittle-tattle of Madame Sesostris on Brighton Pier, I'm afraid, my dear Wang, that it is nonsense.' He smiled thinly. Just as he had been susceptible to the flattery in the oracle's words, he was sensitive to its criticisms, Paula noticed with surprise, and again ignored the warning about her uncle's character.

Wang stood up slowly at the table and spread his thin hands on his chest. 'So, Father,' he said softly, 'we pick and choose. What pleases us, what displeases us. But the Book is not like that. The Book is not courtier.'

Paula looked at both of them, anxious. Gabriel looked down

at the table and, after a pause, said coldly, 'We've found your readings most interesting.' He got to his feet. 'Most interesting.' He was not placatory, so Paula added quickly, 'Yes, absolutely. Thank you so much. I was fascinated . . .' Her voice trailed off.

Wang held the curtain for them to pass. Jacqueline pegged her way out after them, wrapping them in a cloud of her scent. She placed a hand on Paula's elbow and leant to her ear. 'It always tells the truth. It knows,' she said. 'It told me just about everything that was gonna happen just like it did. You think about what it told you.'

Paula said, 'Yes I will.' She was longing to break away from the shop's closeness, compacted of dust and scent and smoke. Besides, she had already forgotten what her hexagram had said.

'How disagreeable it was in there,' said Gabriel, starting fast down the street and pulling out a large white cambric handkerchief to blow his nose.

'I'm afraid Wang was offended,' said Paula.

Gabriel did not reply, and Paula wondered why he was so stiff and unrelenting. He was annoyed with himself for getting involved in a fortune-telling session, but he found it difficult to admit that he was in the wrong, and did not like to explain the reasons for his behaviour to others. Yet perhaps he should have told Wang and Paula, he thought, that his interest in the working of the Book of Changes was academic – it had been the subject of one of the most bitter controversies among the Jesuits in China. But Paula did not look as if she questioned his participation. He looked at her as she strode along beside him, lessening her step now and then to fall back to him, and felt a sharp pleasure in her liveliness. It reminded him of Oliver. He asked her, with a beam of affection in his eye which she quickly noticed, 'What do you think of your fortune?'

'Don't you disapprove?' she replied.

'What did you think of it? I want to know,' he asked again, indulgent. 'Then I'll tell you what I think.'

Paula told him she was more interested in Jacqueline, and begged him to describe what had happened to her. She was disappointed when Gabriel said he had forgotten.

'How could you?' she cried.

Gabriel lifted his thin shoulders. 'When you reach my age, and you've met so many people, they soon cease to be of interest, you know.' Then he remembered Oliver again, with a stab of wonder.

'Your fortune seemed more apt than mine.' Paula continued with a laugh, 'Actually mine fitted you better than me.'

He made an effort to talk to her as he would have done to Oliver, because for a moment she had reminded him so sharply of him that he felt she was a representative from the same world. 'Telling the future is impossible, and the attempt foolish,' he said deliberately. 'But it is undoubtedly true that the Book of Changes often opens the mind to new ideas and provokes fresh thoughts about a situation in which one finds oneself.' He faltered. 'It's a stimulus, a guide, like the Meditations of St Alphonsus on the Stations of the Cross. But because it is so hermetic, it is open to a far wider range of interpretation. Fate, the divining of fate is not for us. Or rather . . .' He looked at Paula solemnly, 'not for me. I once told you – do you remember ? – that the Jesuit astronomer Adam Schall told the emperor that the spots which had appeared on the face of the sun were Buddhists conspiring against him. He could see the hand of God in natural portents, without a qualm. And later, there was a quarrel, a very fierce quarrel, between my friend Andrew and another Jesuit in Peking about the Book of Changes. Andrew thought it a superstitious, pagan work, but the other priest, a Frenchman called Joachim Pernet, maintained that its morality was without fault. Pernet was prepared to cast the *I Ching* and discuss the hexagrams with the Emperor K'ang-hsi, but Andrew wasn't. So they quarrelled, and the emperor was angry, because he declared that the Book of Changes was above all a work of philosophy and not a mere manual of clairvoyance.'

They were standing in the street, and Gabriel was talking rapidly, his hands pushed down into his worn black pockets and his sallow cheeks flushed with excitement. Paula was aware of passers-by stepping down into the road to get by, but she sensed that Gabriel was saying something he did not want interrupted.

He looked her hard in the eye, and said, 'It is the old, old problem.' Then he laughed. 'If God is almighty, then any event, in the weather or the stars, or any accident, like the throw of a coin, lies within His knowledge and His power. The Bible itself is full of natural prodigies which express God's will. Andrew was certain the throw of the *I Ching* was occult nonsense – and dangerous; but Adam Schall could read the stars to suit the Church's purpose with a clear conscience, and Pernet discussed hexagrams with the emperor.' Gabriel shrugged again and, with an unusual gesture, ran his hands over his head. 'I don't know any more, my dear, you see.'

It was a huge confession, and Paula shrank from it. She looked at Gabriel's small eyes, tired and red-rimmed and pouched. I should like to kiss him, she thought, so she leant up to his cheek and put her lips gently against it. Gabriel looked surprised, as if he had previously not been aware that she was there, and then smiled wanly. Looking into her wide-apart eyes divided by that central anxious crease, he thought, For her, and for Oliver, and perhaps for many of them, the world is in a state of flux and their conception corresponds to the Book of Changes. It isn't patterned or rigid or organized, but ebbs and flows, in waves, ungoverned, ungovernable. They see order in disorder, they have no need of an ordainer. There is complexity, but not chaos; multiplicity, but not confusion. They see their lives and the life of everything else as a series of haphazard and incomprehensible accidents, and it doesn't bother them at all. Oliver isn't uncomfortable in his world without God, and neither is Paula.

His hand was resting on Paula's arm, detaining her. The shadow over his eyes lifted and the corners crinkled.

'My dear,' he said. 'A friend of mine, an American scholar, has been working on a new translation of the *I Ching*. He has come up with some interesting renderings, but there's one in particular you might like. You remember Wang mentioned "Perseverance" to both of us. The word occurs in the judgement of almost every hexagram. My American friend went back to the root of the ideogram and discovered it was composed of "Divination" and "Cowrie shell". Money, you know. It probably doesn't mean "perseverance". It probably means, "Pay the diviner." The earliest form of "Cross my palm with silver." '

Gabriel laughed, very dry. And Paula, hearing again that note of cynicism habitual to her uncle, chuckled, happy that the trouble in his mind had abated. She left him with an easy salute. 'Your Holiness,' she said, turning on her heel.

❧ *CHAPTER* 12

During the few days left to him before his departure for Sicily, Gabriel was working long hours, sustained by the image of Oliver which constantly moved and lived in his mind, like a dancing figure in a magic lantern, and by occasional conversations and meetings with him in which Gabriel felt lit up by the powerful longings Oliver's company stirred in him. So he worked fast and well during this period, rewarding himself for a good morning's labour with a short visit to the Institute.

Gabriel ran his eye over his own annotation to a passage in da Rocha's diary. The year was 1688 and Andrew, previously Verbiest's assistant at the Bureau of Astronomy in Peking, had been appointed to succeed him as Director, with the title 'Exploring Teacher of the Mysteries of Heaven'. 'As director of the Bureau,' Gabriel had written, 'Andrew was responsible for the compilation of three annual calendars. The first recorded the lunar months and was circulated publicly throughout China; the second predicted the movements of the planets; and the third, which was exclusive to the emperor, described the conjunctions of the moon and the planets in the forthcoming year. He was also responsible for predicting eclipses, and sent a report every six months to the emperor which gave the exact time, degree and duration of forthcoming eclipses for every capital of every province in China. This document remained secret, so that portents could not be improperly interpreted by different factions to serve their ends.

'The Director of the Board of Astronomy also supervised three tribunals. The mandarins of the first tribunal were required to assemble and watch every eclipse. As the shadow appeared, they knelt down, bells were rung, drums beaten and gongs sounded for as long as the eclipse lasted, in a ceremony intended to help the star in its ordeal. The starclerks of the second tribunal observed the movements of the heavens each night, and recorded them in their annals; the officials of the third tribunal were responsible for public works and gave the hour of the night to the watchmen in the capital, who rang bells to inform the people. Visitors to Peking always complained of this pitiless night-time pealing.'

The year 1688, thought Gabriel, was crucial. He began making notes on the best way he could pull together the crises that had beset Andrew. Andrew's discomfort over his position as astronomer in the Chinese court was increased by a growing tension in his relations with the Emperor K'ang-hsi. As Director, he felt more acutely his personal responsibility for the naming of auspicious and inauspicious days, and his conscience troubled him. He argued with himself in the diaries, trying to persuade himself that 'the emperor has in truth abandoned Chinese superstitions, I do believe'. K'ang-hsi continued to demand prognostications from the Bureau, but, wrote Andrew, 'Although it is true that the emperor has not hitherto abolished this bureau, it is because a principle of policy guides him, in order to maintain the peace and safety of the empire, whose citizens are still plunged into the darkness of ignorance and believe in the stars. The prince himself does not place any faith in the bureau's reports ...' Andrew's tone was pleading. 'The choice of lucky and unlucky days is made after he has sent his orders to the tribunal, and its resolutions always agree with the time he has decided upon beforehand. Thus it is evident that he himself has no belief in such superstitions.'

In 1688, five Jesuits arrived to swell the tiny mission in China, sent in answer to the Peking Fathers' impassioned pleas. Two priests, including Father Joachim Pernet, remained in Peking and began to instruct the emperor daily. It was Pernet who was to become Andrew's trial.

Gabriel was enjoying himself, continuing to make notes, ringing the numbers of the paragraphs and setting down the ideas in neatly indented lists: *Topic A*, *Topic B*. He had now reached *Topic C*, and was summarizing the politics of the situation:

'1.   Arrival of new Fathers strengthens China mission; spontaneous success with K'ang-hsi.

2. But. They are French. Loyalties of Jesuits established in Peking lie chiefly with Portugal. French side with Dutch, whose ambitions in the Far East make them Portugal's natural enemy.

3. Andrew feels bound to his King (Port.) and his country's interests, and threatened when two French Fathers, including Pernet, appear to be gaining great ascendancy over emperor. Tension, because:

4. Andrew at first is joined by them to continue instruction of K'ang-hsi and Heir Apparent in the sciences, but soon (May? June?) French Fathers commanded to come on their own so that Andrew can devote himself wholly to preparations of calendar at Bureau of Astronomy.

5. Andrew's jealousy.'

No, thought Gabriel, this is a new topic. He wrote *Topic D.* and began again:

'1.   Andrew's jealousy.

2. K'ang-hsi asks Pernet to translate Euclid into Manchu, which he has quickly mastered, and speaks "with a good accent".

3. Andrew feels his influence and that of older Portuguese Fathers on the wane, and criticizes Pernet and the other French priests for using methods to win the emperor's attention which he himself practised, i.e. a. constant reference to Chinese classics; b. flattery of Chinese traditional wisdom.

4. Andrew's vehemence overwhelms all his brotherly feelings towards another SJ and he attacks Pernet.

A microcosm reflecting the violent rivalries that blighted China mission as a whole and led to its undoing.'

Gabriel turned to the diaries, and began writing his commentary on the dispute between the French and the Portuguese Fathers. 'In 1697, for the first time since 1685, da Rocha was not summoned to accompany the emperor into Tartary for the spring expedition. If he had been asked, he would have tried to excuse himself, pleading old age and creaking bones; but he was wounded that he had been overlooked.

'That spring K'ang-hsi was once again moving against his old enemy Galdan, the leader of the Zungar rebels, whom he had fought the year before. Joachim Pernet returned from the spring campaign with many stories that pricked Andrew to the heart.'

Gabriel consulted the diaries and checked his translation: 'My respected Father Pernet,' wrote Andrew, 'has returned with many measurements he has taken for the map of Mongolia that the emperor has commissioned. He has nothing but words of praise for the prince's splendour and person, and avows that he rivals the Sun King himself in brilliance. His magnanimity surpasses the bounds of comprehension. Father Pernet described to us what happened in the emperor's tent when the fighting was over and the victory was his. Galdan's warriors had been defeated, and Galdan, an enemy worthy of the great prince, had committed suicide with poison. Father Pernet had the story of that night from a bondservant who was present. How I wish I might have seen it with my own eyes!

'It was in this wise. Dantsila, nephew of Galdan, was captured by the emperor's men as he was fleeing south to Tibet with the ashes of his uncle. K'ang-hsi summoned him to his tent. He ordered the guards to loose the bonds Dantsila wore round his wrists, and then to stand aside. Then he summoned him to come towards him, and indicating a cushion by his side, bade him sit down with him and share his evening meal. All his attendants were standing, but the hostage Dantsila sat, sulky as a wrongly punished child, and would not eat. He cast fierce looks at the assembled company, and seemed as proud as a fallen angel from heaven. So the wise emperor, seeing the unbroken spirit of his enemy, found the stratagem that would tame him more readily than whip or bridle. He pointed to the meat on Dantsila's dish, urging him to eat. He would not, so the emperor smiled and nodded his head, as if to say "I understand," and taking his own ivory-handled hunting knife from his belt, handed it to his enemy.

'Thus did that greatest and wisest of emperors – a true Solomon of justice – show his trust and restore the honour of his enemy. And Dantsila was won to his service, for he now waits on the emperor faithfully, and has been given a prince's title.'

Gabriel smiled with pleasure as he worked on the translation of this story, one of the vivid glimpses into K'ang-hsi's character provided by the diaries. How he wished, like Andrew, that he had been there and seen it with his own eyes. Gabriel made a note to himself on a pad where he jotted queries that he should look up elsewhere what happened to Galdan's ashes, which Dantsila was smuggling away, over a thousand miles to an honourable burial in Tibet. Had K'ang-hsi's generosity been extended to them?

But he would postpone that piece of research for the time being, because he wanted to turn to the central crisis in the relations between Pernet and Andrew, the quarrel over the use of the Book of Changes. Gabriel began itemizing the events that led to the dispute: 'At the beginning of their tutorials together, the Emperor K'ang-hsi informed Father Joachim Pernet of interest in the Classic. Pernet was intrigued, because of all the Chinese books, the *I Ching* is the most gnomic, and its interpretation in the light of Christian moral philosophy had not been attempted by eminent predecessors like Ricci who had commented on the Classics. K'ang-hsi also knew how to appeal to the Jesuit Father's vanity: "Even though some of the Western methods are different from our own,' he declared, "there is little about them that is new. The principles of mathematics all derive from the Book of Changes."

'For four years,' Gabriel continued, 'Joachim Pernet worked on an exegesis of the *I Ching*, and he often discussed the meanings of the hexagrams with Emperor K'ang-hsi and tried to elucidate their spiritual and moral content. His conclusions were startling, and a philosophical school was founded on his analysis. It was called Figurism, and it enjoyed a brief life. Leibnitz, with whom Pernet corresponded at length, was almost persuaded to embrace it.

'The Figurists like Joachim Pernet set out to prove that the Book of Changes expressed the ancient law of Israel in symbolic form. Pernet argued that the Chinese in antiquity had known the one true God, and that their knowledge of Him had been expounded in the Classics. These however had been damaged by continual war, upheaval, fire and flood, and the texts had become distorted, especially by the commentaries that had later been attached to them by teachers like Lao Tzu, the reputed author of the *Tao Te Ching*, and Buddhists who traduced the truth of the classic books. "The great and wise Emperor

K'ang-hsi," wrote Pernet, "would never have permitted our holy religion to take root in his dominions if he had entertained the least doubt that the fundamental maxims of the Christian religion, which flow from the law of nature, and are its perfection, were contrary to those of the ancient Chinese; for if the Chinese Classics are considered in their genuine purity and according to the principles established by the ancient sages of China, *free from those additional corruptions inserted by their modern doctors, they will be found to agree altogether with and be identical to the law of nature*."

'Pernet argued that all passages from the *I Ching* that were tinged with polytheism or pantheism could be eliminated because they were later accretions that adulterated the original, and the pristine text of the Book of Changes could be reconstituted, whereupon it would appear a Christian book. The long-standing tradition that held the Confucian Classics to be guides to political and social good behaviour was dismissed as a fundamental misapprehension of metaphysical, inspired works.'

Gabriel chuckled to himself. He enjoyed Pernet's boldness.

'But allegorical exegesis did not satisfy Biblical scholars or religious philosophers of his time, and Pernet had to provide strong historical evidence to support his claim that the Book of Changes contained the Ancient Law. He and two colleagues in China, enthusiastic "Figurists", conflated several famous "lawgivers" to arrive at a single historical personage. They argued that the Chinese ruler Fu Hsi, the alleged creator of the trigrams of the *I Ching*, was probably not Chinese at all, but Greek; and that he was in fact Hermes Trismegistus, the magus himself, whom they then assimilated to Zoroaster of the Persians and Enoch of the Hebrews. This fabulous man of wisdom from the East had received the Ancient Law through the sons of Shem, Noah's son who settled the Mediterranean islands and Asia Minor after the Flood. (See Genesis 10:2–5) The law as transmitted from Shem's sons to Fu Hsi–Hermes Trismegistus became corrupt among their descendants, and would have been entirely lost to the peoples of the East, if it had not survived in symbolic form in the mystic trigrams of the *I Ching*. The trigrams, or "figures", contained the Law of God and the covenant God made with Noah after the Flood, translated into hermetic symbols to protect the knowledge from further destruction.

'The Figurists' premise was perhaps not altogether unreasonable, since orthodoxy then demanded a literal acceptance of the Book of Genesis. All mankind, with the exception of Noah and his progeny, was drowned in the Flood, so the inhabitants of the globe are all Noah's descendants, and could have inherited his knowledge of God's covenant with Noah and the promise of a redeemer to his forebear, Adam. It therefore became imperative for the Figurists to reconcile Chinese and Biblical chronology. (Footnote: Chinese tradition ascribed Book of Changes to legendary date in third millennium BC, i.e. before Flood, as then dated by Biblical scholars. But Pernet and followers not defeated by discrepancy. Combing Greek Fathers and Septuagint, they discovered Greeks' chronology differed from Latin Vulgate. According to latter, Adam created 6600 BC; but according to Septuagint, possible to argue Creation took place 5500 BC. Generally believed Flood occurred in year 2348 of Creation. Pernet able to demonstrate that Fu Hsi, creator of trigrams, began reign in year 2548 of Creation (2952 BC). If Adam made 5500 BC, not 6600 BC, then Book of Changes no longer written before Flood but about two hundred years later. Pernet declared firmly, "We know, from the certain proofs of scientific inquiry, that the whole world was drowned in 3152 BC, and that Noah died in 2908 BC, and so regarding the Book of Changes, created by Fu Hsi, who began to reign 2952 BC – no problem . . .")'

Feeling that he had demolished the historical objections to his thesis, Pernet then argued that the Chinese Classics resembled Christian philosophy because revelation had been handed down to them, in a strong body of writings, not because the Chinese had arrived at similar ethics on their own. Gabriel continued, 'His conviction led him to excesses of speculation. Andrew da Rocha scoffed at them bitterly, but could not dissuade him. "Father Pernet", wrote Andrew, "looks at the character for Mountain, (*Ken*) which is the fourth trigram of the *I Ching*, and perceives the Mount of Calvary where our Blessed Lord was crucified." ' Gabriel laughed.

When Paula arrived at Admiral's Walk that evening around

six o'clock, the priest was well satisfied with his day's work. For a single day, disturbing doubts and passions had been successfully kept at bay. Pernet's adventures were so absurd and so entertaining that Gabriel could not feel endangered by them. Andrew rebelled against Pernet's enthusiasm for the Book of Changes, just as he had against Buddhism. The irony was, Pernet's use of typology and his cabbalistic procedure again had more in common with the mystical religions of the East than with the Jesuits' favoured Confucianism; when Pernet attached his commentary to the *I Ching* he was following in the same tradition as the Taoist teachers whose commentaries he excised so contemptuously. But Gabriel was not as personally worried by Pernet's quandary as he was by Andrew's.

Andrew had refused to expound a hexagram when the Heir Apparent requested it. He suddenly declared that the *I Ching* was contrary to his faith, and he would have no more to do with it. He nearly lost his head for that act of conscience, thought Gabriel, lighting a cigarette, and unbending his thin legs, stiff from working all afternoon at his desk. Of course, Andrew was longing for martyrdom, so when K'ang-hsi ordered him to recant, he vowed he would rather die than accept the *I Ching*. The emperor pointed out that he had always showed the Christians the utmost consideration, and would like them to heal their differences. He had once refused the Great Lama's request to have a portrait painted by one of the Fathers, because he knew they would find the task disagreeable. When a lady of his court had wanted to learn the spinet, he had considered erecting a screen or even disguising her as a man, but had rejected both ideas altogether because he respected the priests' scruples about women. But what really angered the emperor was the Jesuits' dissension amongst themselves.

Gabriel shook his head, and inhaled contentedly at the spiced cigarette. The difficulties female neophytes caused in China! The Fathers were not allowed to have any contact with women. 'Woman threatens us perpetually,' wrote one Jesuit. 'Neither the youth nor the adult, nor the old man, nor the wise nor the brave nor even the saint is ever safe from woman, this universal enemy ...' St Francis Xavier exhorted his men never to speak to a woman alone in private unless he were confessing her *in extremis*. Gabriel closed his eyes with amusement. They must have been hot-blooded men, full of youth's ardour: temptations of that sort have long passed me by.

All at once he remembered the Hilary Term of 1927 – how old was he then – nineteen, twenty? A girl with red hair like his grandmother's but lopped straight across her forehead, came up to him in the High and asked him the way. He was going in her direction, and for a few moments they walked on together, one slackening his pace, the other quickening it, so that they should not seem to be together. But then she had laughed, a deep gurgling happy laugh, and tossed her head so that her short hair swung across her cheek. Gabriel laughed with her, and said, 'We do seem to be going the same way . . .' So they walked on together. She was the daughter of a history lecturer at Worcester, and she had just been in Yorkshire with one set of relations and was going to Cornwall to stay with another. Gabriel remembered this because the stab of unhappiness her proposed visit to Cornwall provoked in him only ten minutes after they met startled him by its sharpness.

She talked a good deal at great speed which matched her step though she wore ridiculous shoes which were then – and always are – the fashion. Helena. Helena Roberts. I wrote her reams of poetry, Gabriel thought, his lips curving fastidiously. I tried to make her understand my view of the perfect ideal woman, but she was impatient and she stopped reading the poems and she stopped tossing her head and chattering and was always sad when we met. Then there was that day in the summer, when we went for a walk on Boar's Hill, and sat down on the ridge overlooking the town. There was a green haze hanging in the air, so warm, so intense it was almost tangible, and everything was buzzing around us in the trees and the undergrowth. The grasses' ears were nodding, heavy with seed. The grass! That's what did it.

Helena took Gabriel's hands in hers and lifted them to her face and ran them over her eyes and nose and lips which she parted to kiss his fingertips one by one, and then down; her shirt was made of silky stuff, it had something embroidered on the pocket, over her heart, initials, he could feel them under his fingers and the warmth of her body through the silky fabric, and the shallow contours of her tiny breast and the blood underneath racing like mad. She pulled his arms round her to hold the narrow column of her waist and held her own small hands over them and lay back on the buzzing grass so that he came down with her. His own heart leaped and his limbs stiffened and he wanted her so that the pleasure in pain of it blazed through him. She said his name many times, hoarsely, and she kissed him, opening her lips. It was with extraordinary surprise that he tasted the salt of her saliva on his tongue.

Oh, but I couldn't breathe, thought Gabriel, squirming in his chair at the memory, I couldn't breathe. It was the grass and the time of the year, and I was heaving.

Gabriel buckled above Helena and, flinging his arms out, clawed the ground, and fell gasping face down in the grass, 'What is it?' Helena screamed. 'What is it?'

Gabriel shook himself. No more. In those days he did not have an inhaler to help him overcome such attacks. But the thought of Helena still made him smile. No more of this now. Tomorrow he would tackle Andrew's denunciation of Pernet to the Holy See, his attempt to secure Pernet's condemnation by the Sacred College of Propaganda in Rome.

His eyes darkened at the quarrel. Pernet had counter-attacked with equal viciousness, accusing Andrew of entertaining an unnatural fondness for his Chinese servant. Gabriel shook himself again, drove away the face of Oliver in his mind, and looked over at Paula, who was bringing in a tea tray. He smiled at her absently, wondering why he was seeing so much of her. It never crossed his mind that Paula was seeking his company. But she was surprised to see Gabriel's rare wide smile, and she grinned back and asked him how his day had been. He told her the story of Galdan's nephew and the emperor's knife, and she exclaimed with pleasure. The late spring evening was light and grey-green, the limes outside the house tasselled with tight buds that held the full promise of summer's scent, and Paula felt a creamy contentment inside her rise in anticipation. Yes, she thought, Sicily will be fun.

❧ *CHAPTER* 13

The station at Selinunte looked as if it had been set down in a chalk quarry, so dusty and so white was the single chipped office on the brief platform and the road that wound away up the stony hill. Paula got out first and turned to take her father's suitcase and then her uncle's as they handed them out from the high railway carriage.

In the white sunlight, she was aware of the cypresses' dark shadows cut out against the whiteness with a precision of line unknown in the diffuse English day. Their three figures, crumpled and damp from the train-ride, stood with their shadows and waited, blinking in the strong sunshine, until another figure robed in black jumped up from the only bench in the office and came towards them, hands extended in greeting. His face was shaded under a wide hat; only his outstretched fingers shone white.

'*Benvenuti a Selinunte*!' he cried as he puffed up to them on small feet, his black shadow running alongside.

'*Il padre Valentino?*' asked Gabriel, holding out a stiff hand. 'We are tired.' The parish priest nodded and was introduced to Jerome and Paula. 'I hope you have made arrangements at the hotel,' said Gabriel anxiously. '*Si, si,*' said the priest, smiling broadly at them. 'How well you speak Italian,' he added.

Gabriel shrugged. He was exhausted, and he did not speak Italian well, but as both he and Jerome had spent a part of the war in Italy they had a smattering.

Jerome held a handkerchief to his brow, and then to his mouth. Paula could see he was in a dangerous mood. He had been silent for over an hour, ever since the train had come to a standstill twenty kilometres south of Castelvetrano, with a mere five more to go before reaching Selinunte. They had waited patiently for twenty minutes, while Jerome had continued the long conversation – the long soliloquy – he had held ever since they had left the airport and got on the train. The torpor which had held him, as if by a spell, in London had suddenly vanished and he was full of a maddened gaiety that incited him to a jumble of memories, reflections, ambitions, recalled sometimes with laughter, sometimes on the verge of tears. Paula knew a few of the stories, but others surprised her and brought her father into a sharper and different focus. She realized that as far back as she could remember, Jerome had always been an old man, and the very idea of his youth astonished her. But his monologue, however cheerful and heroic, filled her with discomfiture: she understood that it was part of the long process of assessment, the painful reckoning Jerome was making of his life after the end of his career as editor of the *Review*.

He was charitable about colleagues he had previously delighted in betraying at social gatherings with spiteful and witty anecdotes; but himself a victim now, he used honey on his tongue. Envy still flowed through his recollections, Paula thought, like a dangerous undertow in a river that cannot be seen on the surface. She recoiled from it, wishing she could stop her ears, because such talk exposed her father's vulnerability as she had seen it the night of the television announcement. 'Of course,' Jerome would say, 'Samuel was never quite alpha plus, in spite of that early brilliance.' Or John, or Harry, or Maurice. He would bat his hands together with energy and then, following the strand of men who had shared his Oxford career with him, return once again to 'that dreadful little chemist who has made my college a product development centre for ICI'.

Jerome listed exploits, achievements, arguments that he had held with distinguished men, accolades from others even more distinguished. He explored further back, before his university career, before the war, when he was bursting with ambitious hopes, a young correspondent on *The Times*. 'Shanghai in the Thirties,' he said, his eyes bright behind his glasses. 'What a lesson in human morality! The Japanese stuffed the genitals of prisoners into their mouths and left them out to rot like that, for us to see when we came in again after they left . . . The rats ran round the bar while we ate next door in the restaurant at the Majestic in the International Concession . . . One night, an actress who lived there – a pretty young thing – was so tight she fell down the lift shaft and killed herself.' He ran on. 'But when I got a scoop I didn't use any low tricks. No, not like that fool Evelyn in Abyssinia who tried to go one better on his colleagues and filed a story in Latin so that they wouldn't understand. But the sub-editor didn't understand it either. Ha!' Jerome brought one hand down on the other, and carried on, looking at Paula. 'I hope, darling, that you will never see war. It drives men mad, every faculty of judgement is impaired and every normal emotion turned inside out.'

'I *have* seen it,' interrupted Paula, with self-hatred, 'on television.'

'It's not the same,' said Jerome, ignoring her tone. 'Now Gabriel, he was brave. You wouldn't think it, to look at him, but he was. In spite of the asthma, and all that, he stayed with the troops.'

Gabriel waved two long fingers in his brother's direction. 'No, no, Jerome,' he said quietly, and went back to his book.

But the whole congeries of the Namiers and their history was to be ordered in Jerome's relentless memory. He put his hands together on his knees and rocking back against the upholstered and antimacassared seat, looked out of the window and continued, 'When Tripoli harbour was blown up, Gabriel was out on the quay straight away administering communion and extreme unction. "Here's your immortal soul, and yours, and yours." ' Jerome laughed with a touch of bitterness. 'The Protestant padre was under a table in the mess room. "Is it safe to come out now?" That was his cry to the wounded.'

'It was my duty,' said Gabriel. He had not found it heroic or difficult. He found his dreams now a far greater ordeal than the dying around him that day. 'The cries of the wounded', he said, closing his book momentarily, with a finger marking his place, 'are indescribable. No one could ever tell you what their screams are like. I shall never forget it.'

'That doesn't come across on the telly,' said Paula, sharp. 'But David says so too.'

'You know,' said Jerome, looking hard at both of them,

'the bodies of women float on their backs, but men float face down. I saw them – dozens of them – moving slowly downstream in the Whampoa.'

The others were silent; Jerome's relish in the cruelty of his memories was painful to see. Taking advantage of their silence, he pursued his inexorable course backwards through his life, contrasting himself and Gabriel, jolting his brother's memory now and then, and always interjecting the protest that no, his life had not failed altogether. This theme beat under the main flow of his talk like the punctuating throb of the double bass in a jazz quartet, almost imperceptible, yet providing the necessary frame for the music. Paula wanted to bring the sound to a stop, and tell her father it wasn't necessary to make this inventory of events that had made his life worthwhile, because she and Gabriel knew and loved and appreciated him. But she also knew that he had to list them for himself, to staunch his recent wound. Besides, his pitiless demand for attention from herself and Gabriel united her with her uncle and gave her a feeling of delightful complicity as together they tolerated and humoured her father.

Inspired by the sight of the Sicilian landscape around them, Jerome talked of the campaign in Italy, which he had seen in '44. He was in the middle of telling Paula – Gabriel was doggedly reading and trying to ignore the combined irritations of the stationary train and Jerome's garrulousness – that what he had most disliked amongst his duties as an officer had been the task of reading the letters of his men. 'I had to,' he was saying, 'in case they mentioned something delicate, a place or a time or a plan of some sort. It was unbearable.' He frowned and looked down at his hands. 'The banalities men write. Sad, sad. The things they say to their wives and sweethearts. Always the same, and always trite and sentimental. It made one despair somehow of the human heart. The expression doesn't amount to the feeling, I know. But somehow the love they felt was cheapened by the cheap words they used.'

'Oh no,' protested Paula. 'That's disgusting. You're being utterly snobbish and elitist. Poets don't have finer or deeper feelings than others just because they are able to say it better.'

Jerome coloured. Paula had touched on another disappointment. 'No,' he said coldly. 'They are just able to express them memorably.' He looked out of the train and shot to his feet. 'Hasn't this damned train started moving yet?' he bellowed.

Gabriel's eyes left his book. 'Patience,' he said, with good humour. 'This is Italy, you know.'

Paula leapt up, anxious to check her father's temper and said she would find out what had happened.

She made her way to the front of the train, where, by craning her neck round, she managed to discover that the train had run over two cows. The owner, gesticulating over the bleeding carcasses, was in tears. Paula understood that he was insisting that he could not lose his valuable cattle, so a butcher had been summoned and had just arrived to begin the task of cutting up and jointing the animals where they lay on the tracks. The finished pieces were being passed up to the policeman and the guard and other locals who had gathered out of curiosity; they in turn handed the meat over to the owner, who, brushing the sweat and tears from his face, was piling it into his van parked by the railway line.

Jerome swore when Paula, choking with laughter, gave him this information. Gabriel smiled quietly over his book. An hour later, the train set off once more for Selinunte, but Jerome did not speak again.

At the station, there was a problem with the car, a Fiat 500, which could not carry the three Namiers, the parish priest, the driver and the luggage all at once. Paula was anxious that they should not leave Jerome behind on his own, as the neglect would compound his anger. Padre Valentino and Gabriel volunteered to stay behind at the station and wait for the car to return.

The Fiat's tyres spun in the white dust, blowing it up on either side as they ground up the hill and then on to the tarmac road towards the village. The lemon groves, hung with fruit like illustrations to a book of nursery rhymes, stood in rich red soil, with neat dykes and conduits dug round their trunks. The air under their bright leaf appeared cool as ice, but the trees themselves looked as vivid and vibrant as blood, thought Paula, in the bleak calcimined whiteness of everything else. As they drove down towards the sea and into the stark village, the driver pointed and said something. When he saw they did not understand, he repeated it louder and again louder. Jerome shook his head, frowning hard, but the man did not stop talking until they reached the small *pensione*, painted ultramarine blue, that stood above the harbour and the rattan awnings of the fish market. Underneath the freshly painted letters saying '*Pensione della Madonna dell' Oliveto*', Paula noticed the fading capitals of the former *Pensione Bella Vista*.

She chuckled and pointed it out to her father. He nodded and his lips tightened. They passed over the terrace into the cool shuttered interior of the entrance hall. A ladder of light fell precisely aslant the chip-marble floor from the jalousied windows. Paula felt she had stepped into an old photograph, and that colour had been bleached out of Sicily like clothes faded from prolonged washing. She stood with her father, striped by the light in the hall, and waited while the driver roused the signora. She appeared at length, in slippers and pinafore, and briskly welcomed them, smiling up at Paula, who was a good foot taller.

'*Che bella fanciulletta!*' she said to Jerome, taking her eyes off Paula. '*Come è bellina.*'

She shuffled off up one flight of stairs and they followed. Paula's room and her father's were distempered and plain, with narrow beds like monastic pallets and a small washbasin and cupboard. Pleased, they decided to wash and meet downstairs later. Jerome's mood had improved. On his way upstairs he had caught sight of an excellent cold table, set with pale pink shrimps in lemon and garlic, a large dish of crusty *parmigiana*, and another of generously stuffed tomatoes.

As they awaited the return of the car, Gabriel listened in silence to Father Valentino's rapid summary of the marvels that had befallen his parish. The Pope had sent his blessing to the three little Marias, surely a sign of great hope for their cause, he said, spreading his plump hands and then clasping them together and looking upwards as if in prayer. The Archbishop of Syracuse, although he had not yet given his much-desired approval to the visions, had consented to say Mass on the fifth anniversary of the Virgin's first appearance in the olive grove. This was a major step forward, and would Father Namier please do the village the honour of staying for it? The event was taking place on 31 May, the feast of Our Lady's Queenship – which explained why the children saw her wearing a golden crown surmounted by twelve stars.

Father Valentino smoothed down his long black robe with his two hands flat on his breast and looked into Gabriel's eyes. 'The children are the instruments of God in this,' he said eloquently. 'Especially the elder, Maria Pia. We are the happy recipients of unaccountable graces here in Selinunte, where nothing of note has happened since Hannibal laid it waste over two thousand years ago.' He spread an arm to embrace the countryside around and shook his head wonderingly. 'Here in Selinunte, Father Namier. You shall see.'

Gabriel followed the plump priest's conversation with difficulty, trying to translate in his head as he listened and thus missing long sections of his effusions. But those parts of the story which he was able to catch were already familiar to him from the material Father Superior had given him in London. Seated beside a man who believed so firmly, with such gaiety and respect, Gabriel felt conflicting emotions: his usual scepticism battled with trust in the man's simplicity. He yielded to the latter because he was tired, and let a slow fuse of enthusiasm light within him, the first stage, he knew from experience, of involvement in a problem.

He looked out across the carious expanse of earth and track in front of them and wondered if he would attain in Selinunte that illuminated space of the mind he craved, with a centre so translucent and so infinitely permeable that he could fall into it. Then neither ascent nor descent would hold any meaning; he would be suspended in a crystalline space of light and air, ringed with a corona of flame: flame, the perimeter of pain through which he, burning still, had to pass to reach the lambent core of translucency. Sometimes, he was plunged into this pale fire while writing; more rarely, and not for a long time now, he had been able to reach it through meditation and prayer. Perhaps here, he begged, I might find a simple, holy, pure place.

He hoped for a moment that this village, if truly hallowed by the Virgin's presence, might give him reprieve from the attachments that both tormented him and gave him such intense joy, and with a flicker of delight, then hurt, he thought of Oliver and saw his face lit up. Like a seraph, he thought with rebellion. He lit a cigarette. The wheel turned and turned, always bringing him back to his point of departure. Because when he thought of the Madonna, he thought of her as Leonardo painted her, against the pinnacles of the river gorges, attended by that angel with the slow-curving smile.

Gabriel's eyes were sore from the journey. He took out his handkerchief and dabbed them and blew his nose to free it of dust.

'The light', he said to Padre Valentino falteringly, 'is very strong. We are not used to such strong light in England.'

As he said it, he made the connection between the dazzle beyond the shade in which they sat, and the hopes he had entertained of finding a bright truth in Selinunte that would irradiate the darkness in which Gabriel had found himself recently. How naive of me, he said in self-reproach, and relapsed into a detached frame of mind.

'I do not know how long I shall be able to stay,' he said, and added abruptly, 'When can I talk to the little girl, Maria Pia?'

'Tomorrow,' said the priest. 'I have told her.'

Paula strode on to the terrace in a flowery dress cut for a woman three times her girth. She had bought it from a market stall, and her studied gawkiness made the floating frock, with its aura of matronly teatimes of gossip and complaint, seem a thing of wit and comedy. She found her father writing, seated with two Camparis before him. He had also changed into Mediterranean dress, and was wearing cream canvas shoes and a short-sleeved shirt. His arms and ankles were stained, as if by tannin, with large liver spots and the hair on them was white. Paula had noticed similar stains on his hands before, but had no idea how far they had spread over his body. His feet were swollen and the skin parched and flaky. At his neck, the full colour of his face and mouth drained away, and under his open collar Paula could see the loose double fold of flesh hanging from his chin down to his dry pale chest where again his hair grew hoary-white. Paula was afraid. Had he been so old the last time she saw him in summer clothes? His feet especially made her wince with pain, for blue and scarlet thread-veins ran under the tender bulbous surface.

'I'm writing to your mother,' Jerome said.

With an effort, Paula laughed. 'You know she can never read your writing.'

'I want her to forward my post.'

'But you're meant to be on holiday. Away from all that.' Paula was gloomy. She sat down beside him and waited, still filled with horror at his appearance. 'Daddy,' she said, 'let's go and explore.'

'Tomorrow,' said Jerome, and added as if he had divined her thoughts, 'Your old father has had quite enough for one day.'

The light beyond the awning that sheltered them glittered on the pale sands of the beach. The setting sun hit the sea aslant, catching its silent surface, ridged like hammered metal. It was the beginning of the evening, the end of the shuttered afternoon. Fishermen left the shadow of their boats' hulls to sit in the sun, but the few figures on the beach did not animate the frozen sea or the empty bleached shore.

Paula remonstrated, 'But we must go out and see the village.'

'You think I'm made of sterner stuff than I am.' Jerome did not look up from his letter.

'You're such a good guide,' said Paula, playing with the end of her belt.

Jerome chuckled. 'Remember when we all went to Greece? It must have been our last holiday *en famille*.'

Paula sighed. She had stirred a new set of recollections. 'You were lecturing,' she said dully.

'Yes, it was all free. I had to give three lectures on the influence of Greece on Eng. Lit. Ha! What a sinecure. They wanted "Burning Sappho" and I gave them Cavafy. Very fine stuff it is too. But the organizer or someone summoned me to his cabin and said, "Doctor Namier, that's not what we had in mind. It's all right with me, I'm broad-minded, but the old gentlemen — and the ladies! — they don't like it, Doctor Namier." '

'I didn't know.'

'Oh yes,' said Jerome, his eyes gleaming behind his glasses as he looked at her. 'Someone had complained. "I have not left Nebraska to come to Greece and listen to pornography." It was the boys with the silken handkerchiefs that did it. "But their only aim ..." ', Jerome closed his eyes and recited,

> ' "The touching of hands over the handkerchiefs;
> The coming close of their faces, by chance their lips;
> A momentary contact of the limbs."

'Well, it was too much for the Hellenophiles. But we enjoyed ourselves, didn't we, darling? We walked around the boat, talking, do you remember, you and me and Francesca?'

'Yes,' said Paula softly. 'I was twelve and I liked the stiff young men in the museum with their curly hair and wonderful pelvic muscles.'

'Did you?' said Jerome, with a chuckle. 'And the young girls, in their transparent dresses which cling to them because the sculptor wetted them so he could see better?'

'Yes,' said Paula. 'Sexy Greeks.'

'There was a steward on the boat you bewitched. He called you Artemis and pointed to the moon and said he'd give it to you if it weren't yours already.'

'Did he?' Paula echoed his pleasure. 'I'd forgotten.' She paused. 'You cried. I remember that.' She added with emphasis, her upturned eyes smiling into her father's, 'I nearly died of embarrassment.'

'Did I?'

'You were standing in an amphitheatre somewhere giving a lecture ...'

'The Theatre of Dionysius in Athens. Yes, I remember now.'

'On ... what was it?'

'Not Cavafy.' Jerome smiled. 'That episode was over. I was being good for the benefit of the Nebraskans.'

'Byron?'

'Yes, I think it must have been.'

'You were reciting, as usual, and tears came gushing out of your eyes. I didn't know where to look. God, parents are embarrassing people.'

'*The Isles of Greece!* I did give it to them in the end. It's stirring stuff.' He bent down over his glass and began:

> 'Fill high the bowl with Samian wine!
> Our virgins dance beneath the shade ...'

'Daddy,' said Paula, 'You'll only do it again.'

'And why not?' said Jerome. His glasses were already misty. Paula submitted, swallowing her drink quickly.

> 'I see their glorious black eyes shine;
> But gazing on each glowing maid,
> My own the burning tear-drop laves,
> To think such breasts must suckle slaves.'

'Oh God, that rhyme,' Jerome groaned, laughing, and went on.

> 'Place me on Sunium's marbled steep,
> Where nothing, save the waves and I,
> May hear our mutual murmurs sweep;
> There, swan-like, let me sing and die:
> A land of slaves shall ne'er be mine –
> Dash down you cup of Samian wine!'

Jerome opened his eyes wide. They shone with feeling. 'Of course, Byron was prophetic.' He looked down ruefully into his empty glass and then at Paula, with a tender smile, 'Another, darling?'

'Yes,' she said, smiling back at him. She thought, Daddy can be appalling – sometimes.

❧ CHAPTER 14

The cottage where Maria Pia and her mother lived stood at the end of the village beyond the olive grove in which the Virgin had appeared; where the asphalt road came to an end and the chalk-white scree took over. The dry leaves of the olive trees rustled against each other in the fields on either side, showing their silver undersides. Father Valentino opened the door and ushered Gabriel into the dark front room.

A woman came forward and greeted the two priests with a shake of her head. She had a handsome, full face, but her mouth was narrow and strong furrows outlined her expression of discontent. Her dark eyes moved continually, scanning Gabriel rapidly, up and down.

'Maria Pia,' she called and, undoing the ribbons of her apron, folded it and laid it over the back of her chair. '*Prego*.' She gestured to other chairs.

'Donna Anna,' began Father Valentino.

She shook her head again, and closed her eyes, as if she did not wish him to say more.

Gabriel returned her earlier scrutiny, and she did not flinch, but her eyes travelled over his face again. Uneasy, he looked around him. For a Sicilian parlour, the room was startlingly empty. He had expected china souvenirs, elaborate velvet flowered cloths with fringes over the furniture, vases of dried or plastic flowers. But there was nothing, not even an ashtray, and more surprisingly, no image of the Madonna.

The door opened, and from the shadows Maria Pia moved swiftly into the room; coming straight up to Gabriel she held out her hand with a wide smile that showed a gap tooth in the middle and lit sparks in her eyes. She was heavily built like her mother, with the same light colouring at the centre of dark irises which gave her eyes a similar hunger, although they did not move so restlessly. Donna Anna was stern, but the daughter radiated good humour and jollity, and she bubbled with a stream of delighted compliments and thanks. She grasped Gabriel's hand firmly, and when she released him she continued to stand in front of him, holding her hands up and making quick gay gestures, her eyes dancing, and her head held on one side.

Her mother's eyes flickered over her, nervous as the needle of a compass. But when the two priests and Maria Pia began discussing the procedure of the interview, she left the room on quiet feet.

Gabriel had prepared questions, and after discussing them with him, Father Valentino had rendered them into Italian, which he would translate into Sicilian if Maria Pia had any difficulty understanding Gabriel's accent. Similarly, if Gabriel had difficulty, Father Valentino agreed, with a worried air, that he would attempt to translate Maria Pia's words into Latin. They both hoped this would not be necessary, and Gabriel was taping the interview so that he could go over it later. Maria Pia, far from shrinking from the machine, lighted on it with zest and threw her head back with a long laugh when he played back a passage to test the sound.

To Gabriel's surprise, Maria Pia did not collect herself when he began questioning her about the visions. She addressed him with respect, but did not drop her voice to a prayer-like monotone. She prattled on as noisily and as rapidly as she had when she greeted him, with flights of merriment and loose waving of her arms and hands throughout. But her movements did not communicate anxiety to Gabriel, because throughout their meeting she remained still from the waist down, her ankles neatly crossed and her pleated brown skirt smoothed down over her knees. Her repose and the quick frankness of her replies impressed Gabriel; there was no professional piety or conspiratorial appeal to shared 'special graces' from God in the case of Maria Pia.

'Yes,' she said, laughing, the Madonna had reproached her once for her free and easy manners and told her to take the chewing gum out of her mouth when she came to the olive grove. At

Gabriel's raised eyebrow, she spread her hands. '*La Madonnina* always talks like that to me, very simply, like my sister or my best friend. Sometimes she tells me of grave matters but at others she is gay. I asked her – that was a time when the others were with me – if she liked my new haircut. She smiled at me. You have never seen such a smile, Father. It lit up my whole body.' Maria Pia pointed to her feet and then slowly traced the contour of her limbs with her finger and held out the ends of her hair. 'From head to foot, all over, I burned with the brightness of it, like charcoal when it has been well soaked and well laid and the flames have died down leaving a really hot bed of coals to cook on. That was how I felt when she smiled. "Yes," she said, "I like your hair." I could not live without the sweetness of that smile now that I have felt it. But that was not the first time she smiled, Father. And not the last,' Maria Pia's face calmed and she turned her eyes up in anxiety, 'I hope; but I have not heard from the angel who comes to announce the Madonna's visits.'

For three hours, Gabriel remained in the cool dark room with the fifteen-year-old girl and the parish priest. Maria Pia did not flag, but pleaded tiredness from time to time when her clarity about the exact day, the words exchanged and the precise sequence of events was clouded.

She was a star witness, there was no doubt about it, thought Gabriel. She described her visions with the timing and assurance of an athlete executing a special feat, with the conviction of vivid experience. Unerringly, and without apparent cunning, she avoided the traps he set for her, as when he asked the same question twice in different ways or changed the words he attributed to her.

'Father,' she would interrupt, with a wave of her hands, 'I said . . .' or 'The Madonna said . . .' or 'No, that was not the way she meant it . . .' or 'I told you before, Father' (slightly impatient, a wrinkle of wonder in her forehead at his muddle-headedness). She had the word-perfect memory of an illiterate, everything committed, classified and garnered without a single scribbled note or reminder. But was it memory? he wondered. He was here to find the answer. Memory or fantasy, there could be no doubt that it had happened for Maria Pia and that the distinction, if she was making it up, had dissolved long ago.

Gabriel elicited the story in Maria Pia's own words. One evening five years ago, in the season when the olive harvest ripens, Maria Pia and two friends, both younger than herself, called Maria Concetta and Maria Gabriella – here, Maria Pia pointed happily to the coincidence – were playing ball in the lane before the evening meal, and it flew right over their heads through the air and landed over the wall somewhere among the olives. All three jumped over and began looking for it, but it had been a long dusty day and it was shady and pleasant under the trees, so they stayed, fooling around and shaking the branches until the berries rattled down on the dry earth, and they giggled and gathered them up to take home. 'Only I didn't,' said Maria Pia, 'because Mamma would not have been pleased. They were not our olives.' They knew they were doing something wrong but were thoroughly enjoying the mischief, when an angel appeared.

'He was small, not tall like in the paintings, and he had curly hair and looked like a thirteen-year-old with short wings and a very cross face.' Maria Pia drew a line across her forehead. 'He frowned so. We were very afraid and froze, but he told us he was Michael the Archangel and that the Mother of God was coming to talk to us. We were immediately filled with repentance for what we had done, and we went down on our knees. I said to the others, "We must pray." So we recited a Hail Mary and then another, and, when we had finished the second, the Madonna stood before us.'

The Virgin appeared wearing a loose white robe with a blue cloak and a golden sash : there were roses round her head and on her wrists and between her toes. She looked about eighteen years old, in Maria Pia's opinion, but the others thought she was older. 'But it is only because they are younger,' said Maria Pia, tolerantly. The Madonna was serious at first, and told them they must say their prayers with more attention and behave better towards their parents and their teachers. 'Of course,' said Maria Pia, *La Madonnina* knew everything about us, so that we felt transparent before her.'

'Transparent?' asked Gabriel. The young girl's ingenuousness aroused his curiosity. 'Transparent?' he asked again, and she looked him in the face with her full luminous eyes. 'Yes, Father. It is frightening at first, but then it is wonderful because it makes *La Madonnina* seem so close. There is no need to say anything or explain. She knows.'

Gabriel nodded. 'The first message?'

'Yes,' said Maria Pia. 'When I came out of my trance, I repeated it to myself again and again so that I should not forget the words. She said, "I am *Mater Ecclesiae*" – she said it like that, and I did not understand it until later. "But the Church is turning away from me and from my son and many priests are taking the path to perdition." ' Maria Pia forced her tongue round the words, marking the difference between phrases learned by rote and the spontaneity of her normal discourse.

'Yes, yes,' interrupted Father Valentino. '*La via della perdizione*. It is very grave, Father.' He shook his head solemnly. 'We must listen to the Virgin's warning.'

Gabriel asked Maria Pia about her ecstasies, and the girl spread her hands and said quietly, 'It is something that overwhelms me, that is too strong. Sometimes it comes when I do not want it to, when I am in the street and people stare and think I'm mad. I feel her presence, and a dazzling light fills me to the brim and then I cannot walk, because I feel my soul fly up and my body is like a dead weight behind it.'

'Yes, she falls, and the other little girls too,' said Father Valentino, 'and the strongest men cannot pick them up because their limbs have become so rigid and their weight so heavy.'

'But there are different ways she comes to me, Father.' Then, looking suddenly shy, she paused.

'Go on,' said Gabriel, kindly.

'I sometimes think – please don't think I'm silly – that it is like the nets the fishermen cast into the sea, what the Madonna does to me. Some days when she comes she casts the huge heavy net that sinks to the bottom of the ocean floor and trawls for huge fish like the tunny and the cod. Then the whole of me is caught and I cannot think of anything; I cannot even say to myself, I must remember this and what she is saying, because I am deep down in nothing but the sweetness of her . . .' She stopped and reddened suddenly for the first time since their colloquy had begun.

'*Si, si.*' Father Valentino shook his head wonderingly and cooed, '*La piena dolcezza della Madonna.*'

183

'Continue, please,' said Gabriel, coaxing. He was taken aback by the urgency of his interest.

'But then at other times, even during a vision when we have a long conversation and people tell me I have been "gone" for nearly an hour, I am not plunged in so deep, I do not fly away into space where everything comes to . . .' She hesitated, then said, 'To nothing, I suppose. I can still hear what people around me are saying, and I can carry out their wishes, give the Madonna rosaries and holy pictures for her blessing, and I can even think of stupid things.' Gabriel reminded himself as he listened that he must not forget Nanny's rosary, which she had given him to bring and collect Our Lady's special blessing. Maria Pia laughed. 'Sometimes, I find myself thinking things like, If this goes on much longer I shall be late for supper and Mamma will be angry.'

She paused, thinking, then said, 'Like this I feel that the Madonna has only cast a fine floating net with a close mesh, like the one our men here use at night to catch sardines. It does not sink very deep, but it hauls all the hundreds of thousands of little fish which shimmer and glint in the dark, the way that part of my mind filled by the Madonna sparkles with the light she sheds in the shadows.'

Maria Pia's face shone, and she began to speak fast and breathlessly until both priests remonstrated together that Gabriel could not keep up with her. 'Sometimes,' said Maria Pia, shyly clapping one hand over her mouth, '*La Madonnina* enters a tiny part of me. I feel her slip in and wait patiently inside, not in front of my eyes, but somehow *behind* my eyes.' She paused. 'I do not see her then the way I see you now, the way I do when she comes to the olive grove. I cannot put out my hand and touch hers and kiss them. But it is still more real than a dream. This third kind of vision,' Maria Pia straightened herself and looked serious, 'I think is like the fishermen on the breakwater. They sit for a long time, with a single rod dangling in the water. They are connected to the sea by this cord and now and then there is a tweak, and ah, a fish, or perhaps not . . . But it is pleasant, and they are in touch. So the Madonna stays with me although we do not speak, and I continue to do all the things I have to do – washing, ironing, shopping.'

Gabriel sat back in silence for a few moments. Father Valentino observed him unobtrusively, but Maria Pia's open gaze rested frankly on him. He was pricked by envy. He longed to plumb her contentment and find her assurance and faith, even though he had many reservations about her experiences. He felt exhausted and he wanted to listen to the tape and to compose his thoughts. So he looked at her and nodded with approval, then stood up to go. Against his better judgement, he said, 'There is a growing apostolate for *La Madonnina* in my country . . .'

Maria Pia leaped to her feet and threw both hands in the air. 'I am so happy. And the Madonna, too, she must be so happy.'

As they moved to leave the room, the door clicked open and silently Donna Anna reappeared. Both priests thanked her; Gabriel asked her for an interview. The lines round Donna Anna's mouth hardened and her flickering eyes held Gabriel's for a moment. She agreed, with a cold nod of the head.

As they walked back into the village, Gabriel recalled the literature which had described Maria Pia's simple life with her mother in their cottage. 'They take in sewing and make clothes for the villagers . . . Donna Anna is an accomplished seamstress.' Foolishly, he had taken the information as it stood and had not thought to enquire further. He turned to Father Valentino. 'The mother, what does she feel about her daughter's visions?' he asked.

Father Valentino sighed and shrugged. '*Poverina*!' he said. 'She is a little crazy. You saw her eyes, how they look?'

'What do you mean?' Gabriel was impatient.

'She is just a little crazy, that's all. And jealous of the attention paid to Maria Pia.'

It was Gabriel's turn to shrug. 'I did not get that impression. She seemed to me a woman of some substance, to be reckoned with, and she certainly did not try to compete for our attention . . .'

'No, she withdraws and sulks.'

Gabriel snorted. 'I think you are attributing the lowest motives to the mother without giving me any reasons.' He paused, and asked rapidly, 'Isn't the mother's lack of involvement important? Isn't it possible that she knows some things she would not like everyone to know, that she disapproves of her daughter's claims, and that Maria Pia is not altogether telling the truth?'

At these words Father Valentino stopped walking, and, his eyes bulging, seized Gabriel's arm and shook his head emphatically. 'No, no, Father, it is not so. I will tell you.' He dropped his voice to a confessional whisper. '*La Anna* is not a *signora* at all.' He looked at Gabriel and nodded meaningfully. Gabriel responded blankly, and so, squeezing his arm even more tightly and pressing his mouth close to Gabriel's ear, Father Valentino said, 'She is a *signorina*.' He backed away, waiting for this to make an impression.

Gabriel burst out laughing. The shocked plump face of the parish priest made it even funnier, and he wiped his watering eyes and coughed to disguise his mirth.

But then, in the silence as they began walking back over the chalky path towards the village, Gabriel thought it over and became sombre.

'Surely illegitimacy is common in Sicily?' he asked.

'Unfortunately.' But Father Valentino was hurt, and would not continue.

'Why is Donna Anna still embittered?'

'She was specially unfortunate,' replied Father Valentino curtly.

'How?'

The priest did not answer.

'Who was the father?' pursued Gabriel, with urgent curiosity. Valentino lifted his plump shoulders. '*Chi lo sa?*'

'What happened to her? How did she manage?'

'Many helped her,' said Father Valentino slowly. 'In Sicily, that is our way. But Donna Anna is stubborn, and she will not bend her will.'

It was clear that the parish priest was not going to say more. Gabriel resolved to ask Donna Anna herself; and, if that failed, to talk to the villagers who would all know her story. So Maria Pia was a bastard, he thought. It was interesting.

❧ *CHAPTER* 15

Gabriel found Jerome and Paula sitting together on the terrace of the *pensione*. He was staying in the presbytery with Father Valentino and he had not seen his brother and niece since their arrival in the village. During the interval, Jerome and Paula had explored the Greek ruins on the promontory overlooking the estuary and their interest in these and other local sights had promoted an alliance which ranged them together and made Gabriel the odd man of the group. Paula was disappointed and resentful that Gabriel had avoided their company and immediately questioned him closely about the visionary and the progress of his investigations, concealing her disappointment because of her interest in the apparitions.

Laconically, Gabriel told her of his interviews and, under Paula's persistent interrogation, described Maria Pia's metaphors for the three degrees of visions she had experienced. His tone was flat, and communicated the information without excitement.

Jerome nodded. 'Good. Down to earth, taken from her immediate surroundings. Nothing literary or affected, which I like, I like it a lot. It reminds me of Teresa of Avila, doesn't it you?'

Gabriel pursed his lips. 'Almost uncannily. But as you say, it derives from her first-hand experience. She is certainly genuine – giggles and all.' He closed his eyes in the evening sun and ordered a drink. 'She is illegitimate, Jerome,' he added, blowing out the smoke of his cigarette contentedly. 'Does that signify something to you?'

'A love child,' said Jerome. 'How appropriate.'

Paula frowned. 'It must have been hard for them, in Sicily of all places.' Gabriel said nothing. 'The villagers and pilgrims don't seem to mind. The church is full of candles and pictures hung up on the wall in front of a very crude painting – quite a good primitive in its way – of the Virgin in the olive grove with three little girls at her feet. Some grisly things too. Photographs of sores and wounds and smashed cars, big thankyous written on them. Miracles, I suppose?'

Gabriel's mouth twisted. 'Allegedly.' He paused, 'I said the little girl was genuine enough, but not that the visions of Our Lady were. There is a distinction, I believe. The visions might even be the work of the Devil – in the seventeenth century that was a popular view of the dangers of "special graces" and St Teresa herself worried that her experiences might have an unholy origin.'

At Paula's aghast expression, Gabriel chuckled. 'Don't worry, my dear,' he said, 'I'm not going to report our little visionary for a witch. Besides, there is no stake nowadays.' He paused, his smile vanishing. 'I feel the clue lies with the mother. And perhaps with the two other little girls. We shall see.' He sipped at his drink with a satisfied look. 'At least it's turning out more interesting than I had expected.'

At this, Gabriel was reminded of London and so was Jerome. Gabriel felt a wringing of the heart as he thought of Andrew's diaries lying unattended in his desk drawer, and the neglected manuscript. When it was so urgent to finish it! Thoughts of his age and his weakness brought him back to Oliver, and with a stab of love-longing he remembered the young man sitting at the harpsichord playing while a thin veil of rain glistened through the window behind and the notes coolly cascaded through the room.

Jerome too felt a rush of pain when he remembered London, and the shining and tranquil evening scene around him in Sicily lost its delight. He had written a few careful letters in the mornings, while Paula still slept: one to James Cunliffe had cost him a special effort. He had given James his present address, but had doubts as to whether he would reply. He was already agitated with anticipation, and stood at the *pensione* window each morning, stalking the postman with his eyes.

The two brothers sat in the quiet of the twilight thinking of the different men whom they loved in their different fashions, although both would have shied from such a word. But Paula thought with sympathy of Maria Pia, living with her mother at the end of the village, almost cast out beyond the boundary as if to symbolize the social stigma. She had been disgusted by the cheap and grim mementoes and thank-offerings she had seen at the shrine, but she was fascinated, and a part of her was deeply impressed. The trustfulness displayed by the men and women who had decorated the shrine made cynicism seem at best unkind, and the naive colouring and clumsy execution of the *ex voto* artefacts appealed to the inverted aesthetic code that Paula sometimes followed. The visit to the church had not stirred any remnant of the little faith she had had as a child, but it had moved her for other reasons. The distinction between the truth of the visionary and the truth of the vision meant nothing to her: the Virgin Mary had no independent or objective life in Paula's mind, and therefore she did not even consider the possibility that the Virgin had appeared in Selinunte in person. But it did seem sufficient to her that when an individual believed in all sincerity that she had kept company with the Madonna, she was expressing a truth, her truth, and others should be free to believe it if they chose.

Paula had been impatient to see Gabriel and to hear about Maria Pia. His taciturnity at first disappointed her, but she knew it was his habit, and she still trusted him to reveal more to her as a friend than he would to others, in spite of their lack of contact of these past few days. So she began, 'I was really quite impressed by the faith of the people in church. All the candles lit with hope and prayer, by people who obviously believe enough to work a miracle sometimes by themselves, psychosomatically – if as you're implying the Virgin didn't really appear to the girls. Don't you welcome that much faith at least?'

'It depends where it is placed,' commented Gabriel languidly, without opening his eyes or turning his face away from the setting sun.

Unconsciously, he had let Paula slide back into the neutral slot she had filled in his mental image of his brother's household. For a time she had acquired important definition in Gabriel's mind because she became a model and possessor of the vitality and spontaneity he needed and was seeking, and in England he had enjoyed her company because she seemed to him a female counterpart of Oliver. He had used her as a substitute for Oliver, or as a guide to the way Oliver, as her contemporary, might think and feel. Paula could not know that. For a time, her need had become embroiled with Gabriel's very different need, and there was no way she could know that their two needs had never been in accord.

Here in Sicily, Gabriel assigned Paula back to her father; he associated her with the irritation he felt that his present mission had been taken over as a Namier family rescue cure. But above all, her presence grated on him now because she reminded him of Oliver when Oliver was not there in person to release him from the pang of his desire to see him.

So when Paula continued, hastily and inarticulately, to ask Gabriel about the visions of the Virgin, Gabriel overlooked her tension because he had banished her from the private world he had once or twice allowed her to enter, and he spoke to her with cold animus. 'But the Virgin here,' he said, 'might be the figment of an over-excited adolescent's imagination. Maria Pia herself is a self-confessed hysteric, who falls down in trance, with a fixed beatific rictus ...' Gabriel opened his eyes wide and pulled the corners of his mouth apart in a mask-like leer. 'Like this,' he said. 'And her limbs become rigid. This may or may not be the effect of a divine gift.' He was impatient and sarcastic, but Paula continued to tackle him.

'But the woman she sees – is there anything wrong with what she says or does?' She spoke hesitantly; the right phrases were difficult to find, because her uncle was being so dismissive.

Jerome, noticing that Gabriel's lips were twitching with irritation at Paula's questions, interrupted. 'I think', he said with forced good humour, 'that there should be visions for everyone, of everything. Divine light should dazzle us from every privet hedge in Surrey, and not just from romantic olive groves in villages filled with Grecian ruins. The Madonna should stroll in Hyde Park looking like a Raphael come to life; St Peter should rattle his keys beside the men's bathing pool in the Heath to reassure the high divers. I think the Church, Gabriel, with all due respect to you, is wrong in setting out rules and organizing committees to examine the claims of visionaries and the miracles they perform. Of course miracles occur if people believe they will – that is true of all religions everywhere. Of course visions have taken place when people say they have seen them. Unless they are professional charlatans. But this girl plainly isn't.'

'Yes, yes,' said Paula, lighting up. 'Each of us carries his own paradise inside him. It can't come from outside, so it doesn't matter if Maria Pia saw the real Virgin, like I see you now, because she really saw what she really thought was the real Virgin.' Paula laughed. 'Anyway you might not be here for all I know. I might be imagining I'm seeing you.'

Gabriel's mouth tightened as father and daughter leaned towards him in excitement. Paula now realized that the balance in the group of three had altered. In the train Jerome had been the outsider, while Gabriel and Paula listened to him and indulged him. Now Gabriel was the subject of the combined observation of herself and her father. Gabriel shifted in his chair and said nothing, but slowly continued smoking and avoiding their eyes.

Seeing him silent, Jerome pursued, 'We do not have to experience the supernatural to see God. It's around us everywhere, and you – you experts from the Vatican and elsewhere – you shouldn't deny it and circumscribe it and put fences up around it and say this is so-and-so's special preserve and tell people what they may or may not feel for themselves. Why couldn't the little girl find her angels and her Madonnas when and where she likes? It reminds me of the Book of Taliesin's marvellous words about falling snow, that "the angels were at their white joinery in heaven, and the saints were plucking their geese". David Jones, the poet and the painter, you know . . .' He beat one hand against the other and looked at Paula apologetically, realizing from her smile that he was once again reciting. But he persisted, 'When David Jones quoted that, he said, "It is important to be anthropomorphic, to deal through and in the things we understand as men – to be incarnational." ' Jerome chuckled. ' "To know that a beefsteak is neither more nor less 'mystical' than a diaphanous cloud." That's why I like this little visionary, with her plain-spoken Madonna and her talk of fish-hooks and nets. She sees the holy in the ordinary – that's the best thing, the most poetic thing about Christianity, Gabriel, surely?'

Gabriel did not reply. His face was sour, and he coughed.

After a few moments, he said coldly, 'Neither of you understands anything about metaphysics. You, Jerome, are making an elementary mistake: the girl's visions have no relationship to romantic pantheism. You both speak about things you know nothing about, and I'd rather not discuss them. Let's go and eat.'

Paula was silent, in deep dejection about her hopes of comradeship with her uncle. He had scorned her in cold anger and had lost all interest, it was obvious. The brief moment had passed when he had turned his sharp dark eyes on her to elicit her opinion, as he had the night they walked on the Heath, and when they went together to see Wang. She felt crushed and cheated. With a childish impulse, she wished she were back in London, working in solitude in her flat.

Paula was the only female at the small gathering of tables under a trellissed vine in the local restaurant on the quayside. The men looked at her as if they were swallowing her alive. The three Namiers ate at leisure, in spite of the scrutiny; Jerome and Gabriel discussed the quality of the local wine that all three were drinking in great quantities. Gabriel judged it lacked vitality, but was pleasant. Towards eleven o'clock the fishermen came in with the catch, and a heavy briny scent wrapped them like a sea breeze. They were noisy and curious and soon the Namiers found their table had grown to accommodate several young men and two older ones.

Jerome always liked an audience, even if only a quarter or less of what was being said was comprehensible to both sides. He offered the men a drink; most of them took beer. Gabriel sat back, silent. The leader of the young men was red-headed. The sun and wind had blistered his face and hands so that they were covered in purplish-brown patches where the skin showed through like new bark under the old. His features were coarse but animated, his neck thick, his head round, and he scanned the three Namiers greedily. But his eyes rested with particular avidity on Paula, who returned his look with the thin-lipped smile of a nurse over a sick-bed. He bombarded the three of them with questions, and when they grasped what he meant Jerome or Paula alternately tried to reply. They explained who they were, and where they had come from. Then the redhead asked Paula how old she was, and when she said 'Twenty-three' he shook his head and asked why she wasn't married yet. Paula pulled a wry face at him, and protested that she did not want to marry. He scratched his burned hands and looked down.

One of the two older men at the table laughed heartily, and the younger man looked across at them in anger, his light skin colouring. His companion, who sat close beside him, whispering, was slight and dark with hair that lay stiffly against his head from the salt contained in it. It was to him that Gabriel, moving forward to lean on the table, addressed his questions, asking him what he thought of the visions of the Madonna.

The young fisherman did not answer; the older man at his shoulder interrupted with a laugh, 'It is very good for business. Not now. You see, the village is empty. But in August! Ah then, the buses come from Catania, from Palermo, from Syracuse, from Rome, from Dublin, yes, from Dublin.' His neighbour nudged him and added with a smirk, 'It is a blessing on our village, Father.' This man is sly, thought Gabriel, he's guessed I'm not on pilgrimage. He nodded to him and proceeded, but in an undertone.

'I am puzzled by the attitude of Maria Pia's mother. She does not seem eager . . .'

The young man turned up his eyes. '*La disgraziata*,' he said.

The two older men heard him, and one flared up, 'Donna Anna has made reparation for the past, and anyway the girl – *non ci entra* – it does not affect her.' The old man joined his hands and pointed the tips at Gabriel. 'Father,' he said, 'this is the greatest miracle since Lourdes . . .' An uproar broke out around the table, but he raised his voice and went on. 'Here, here in Selinunte. The Madonna comes, once, twice, three times and more, and gives us serious instructions and tells a pure young girl how we should change our lives for the better, and then people spread scandal about her mother to cast shame on her. It makes me hang my head, Father, that such abominations happen . . .' He scowled at the sly young man and downed his beer. Then he shook his head sorrowfully and looking Gabriel in the eye said, 'Donna Anna has suffered very much, Father. But some priests are not good men like you.'

The group around the table hushed, and Gabriel, Jerome and Paula were immediately aware that a taboo had been breached. The sea could be heard paying itself out in smooth slow ripples along the beach below the wharf. The redhead was hunched over his wine, cupping it in hands rusty from the enemy sun. Idly, with the wine blurring her responses, Paula looked at him, liking his roughness and his ugliness and the vulnerability of his obvious lust.

Gabriel said to the old man, 'What do you mean?' He bowed his head, paused, and looked up. 'You are an important man, Father, you have come a long way to see the graces that have been conferred on us.' He spoke ceremoniously, using rhetorical flourishes that made him sound pleasantly outmoded. 'I shall tell you what everyone knows, but will not say.' He looked around the company challengingly and frowned. 'The father of Maria Pia was our parish priest. Not this one . . .' (a flicker of a smile) 'of course. No, the one who was here sixteen years ago is now a *Monsignore* in Messina. May it please God to find a way to forgive him! He asked for a transfer as soon as it happened and Donna Anna accused him. There was no investigation of Anna's claims, and if there had been she would not have been believed. But we in the village, we all knew. It is true. *La Chiesa*, Father, in Sicily had its own way, its own justice. But Donna Anna has not forgiven the Church, and she says she will never repent.'

The redhead rubbed his big hands through his hair. '*La putana del prete*,' he scoffed, looking at the old man. 'The priest's whore. *Che stronza*. What an idiot.'

The old man turned on him in anger, but the redhead persisted, mulishly. 'Your Anna,' he said heavily. 'Your wronged Anna . . .' His face flushed and he got up, clattering his chair to the ground.

The sly young fisherman followed him quietly, and as they walked away the old man looked at Gabriel and tossed his head back and raised one hand in deprecation.

Paula knew that she had incited the red-haired fisherman's sudden violent anger against women; she knew by the heaviness of his look that he had wanted her badly and hated himself for wanting her, and that by inflicting a return look on him she had fed his frustration and sullen rage. The knowledge of this simple power excited her, and she drank down more wine and addressed herself to Gabriel.

'Do priests often give women babies?' she asked, looking at him archly over her glass.

'Perhaps they do in Italy.' Gabriel was curt. He felt no compassion for Donna Anna. His mind was chasing a thread towards an explanation of the visions, and he was not concentrating on what Paula was saying nor the spirit in which she said it.

'I think it's fucking awful,' she shouted. 'God, it's awful being a woman in a Catholic country. First you get knocked up by the local representative of God almighty, and then you get dumped.' She snorted viciously. 'And that fisherman. He looked as if he'd rape me, given a chance, he hated women so much.' She giggled and covered her face with her hands.

Her father looked anxiously at her, eyes benign behind his glasses. He cleared his throat, and was about to speak, when Gabriel interrupted in a terse tone. 'Jerome,' he said, 'take the child home. She's had far too much to drink.'

Jerome looked worried. 'Darling,' he said. 'And on top of the sun all day, too. You're not used to it.'

Paula shot Gabriel a look of hatred, her eyes dark and full with rising blood. 'I'm not a child.'

Gabriel laughed. 'That kind of remark proves it, my dear,' he said lightly. 'You'll grow out of violent emotions when you reach my age.'

'You never had any,' spat Paula, as her father took her elbow and began leading her away from the silent group around the table. 'You just want everyone around you to do what you want, and you never do anything in return.' Tears rose to her eyes and choked her last words.

As her father guided her over the lumpy sand and chalk of the road, she stumbled in the pretty sandals she had put on for the evening, and he once let her fall to her knees in order not to wrench her arm too badly. She came up again and held her fist tightly against her chest. It was full of sand. Fiercely she said to him, 'I can feel this sand. I can feel it there. I want to stop being alone. I want to feel people, things, like I can feel this. It's such hell, day-to-day life.'

'Darling,' said her father gently, 'you've got lots of friends.' But he knew his words were futile.

'It's not that,' she said. She was calmer now, after her outburst. 'I know, address books full of names and numbers. Oh yes. Lots of people. But you're still alone with them . . . I want to connect, in some way that isn't through doing the same work, or borrowing the butter from upstairs, or . . . sex, of course. I want to grip someone without any of those things that usually, by chance, because there's nothing better, put one person in touch with another. I thought with Gabriel . . .' She paused and squeezed her father's arm. 'You see I thought with him, because he doesn't belong to anyone, being a priest, that we could be friends for the sake of it, and not for a purpose. Do you see? But I was wrong.' She let the sand drift out of her opened fist, and then smiled wanly at her father in apology for the self-dramatization of her gesture.

'Never mind, darling,' said Jerome lamely. 'I think friendship is often more wounding than love. It can be, anyway, because one doesn't expect to be let down, while with love . . .' He patted her arm which was linked through his. 'It won't seem important to you later.'

'What?' Vehement, she turned on him. 'It does matter. That's the whole point. It matters very, very much. None of us can see beyond what's right there to touch and feel and grasp. We just accept what's lying around, like Mummy and her queer friends . . . Now the girl here, she's probably fed up too and she didn't want to be alone either. So she saw something else, something fabulous, which she used to stop the separateness, the unconnectedness . . .' Paula stopped and pulled at her hair till it stood out in tufts. 'But don't worry, I'm not going to start having visions.' She laughed, though the frown did not leave her forehead. 'Rats, Dad,' she said. 'Never mind.' And she turned up the stairs into the *pensione*.

'You'll be all right, darling?' he asked. 'I must just go back for the bill.'

At the restaurant, Gabriel wondered what had provoked Paula's tantrum. He had rarely seen eyes so loaded with hate as hers. He doubted that she was upset about Donna Anna's misfortunes, and he did not consider that he personally might have inspired her outburst. Gabriel had the kind of egotism that blinded him to the reactions he aroused in others, so that even the love they might bear him slipped past unrecognized. He dismissed Paula from his mind and spoke again to the old fisherman who had stayed in quiet dignity at the table.

'Your wine is rather strong,' said Gabriel.

'Yes,' said the old man. 'And she is young, too young.'

He resumed the story of Donna Anna, telling Gabriel how she had turned against the Church because she was told she must confess and beg forgiveness for her sin. 'But it cannot be a sin,' she had said. She had tried to prevent Maria Pia attending Mass and taking her first communion. His stately manner gave his words the atmosphere of an ancient fable, as if he were remembering a village story of struggle and heroism heard in his youth.

'The girl, Maria Pia, she is courageous,' he said. *'Tenace.'*

'Yes,' said Gabriel. 'She has character.'

When Jerome rejoined them, he said decisively, 'I think we should pay and leave.' He signalled to the kitchen, and a child came forward for the money. Jerome paid, but his anxiety about Paula stopped up his customary sense of grievance at Gabriel's stinginess.

The old fisherman rose slowly and took his leave with courtesy. When he had gone, Jerome spoke bitterly to his brother.

'You have upset Paula dreadfully – why?'

'She drank too much.'

'No, Gabriel, it's not only that. She was counting on you.'

Jerome's portly bulk stood before Gabriel's stooped black-clothed figure at the exit of the restaurant. Gabriel lifted his thin shoulders.

'God almighty! Sometimes, Gabriel, you are the end. You are flesh and blood, at least I suppose you are, but when you strike your damned superior attitudes I could imagine you were made of something else. You remind me of Graham Greene's bastard of a typical conscience-stricken Catholic who's holier than the Pope himself, except that you don't seem to suffer from remorse. What is it Orwell said about *The Heart of the Matter*? Yes, that Greene always implied that Catholics alone know the meaning of good and evil. I was brought up a Catholic too, but its acid hasn't bitten into my soul, thank God, and it hasn't bitten into Paula's either. We don't pretend to any special hold on grace, and your cloth doesn't entitle you to, whatever you might think.' Jerome paused, his eyes gleaming. Through Paula he had managed for the first time to tell his brother what he had thought of him for years.

Gabriel cast his eyes down, and kept his hands in his jacket pockets. He was not going to protest. At his silence, Jerome, feeling he had scored some kind of victory and wishing to conciliate, said in a lighter tone, 'Paula saw you as a friend. She thought that coming here – you would have lots to say to each other. God knows you're your own man and no one else's, but you should have a heart for the girl. She trusts and admires you, it's written on her face, and you have snubbed her and ignored her.'

Gabriel muttered through closed lips that he was sorry if he had been the cause of her distress. Then he added that she should learn to control herself, and, suddenly heated, said, 'She knows nothing about religious matters, and she was offering opinions . . .'

Jerome broke in, 'She was only interested, Gabriel, and you were making things damned awkward. You could have explained . . . She would like to know more. You're too harsh.'

Gabriel's small black eyes fastened on his brother's milder bespectacled gaze. 'It was not harshness, it was a just assessment.'

Jerome sighed. He, so prone to rage, saw the ugliness and the emptiness of anger in others all too easily. Turning up the steps of the restaurant into the road, he said slowly, 'The curious thing is that you're a priest, yet you have no feeling for religion. I have, and Paula has, though we haven't any belief. That's why we rather like the story here, the visions and whatnot . . .'

'Religion', countered Gabriel, very drily, 'is not a question of feeling, but of intellect.'

❧ CHAPTER 16

Father Superior had not requested a comprehensive report, so Gabriel was keeping it succinct. He had discovered much since his first interview with Maria Pia, but he had been discreet, and had not revealed his doubts, so the village still treated him with a reverence that in some cases amounted to fawning. Many believed devoutly in the visions – a procession to the olive grove led by Maria Pia (where she duly held out Nanny's rosary for a blessing) had been affecting in its sobriety, thought Gabriel. But he decided not to wait for the bishop's fifth-anniversary Mass.

When he went to interview Donna Anna, she sat stock still in an armchair, her ankles together, her hands folded and immobile in her lap, her eyes scanning Gabriel up and down, all over, until he felt she had a hundred eyes he could not escape. Gabriel never considered the company he kept associated with him; he usually felt apart, elsewhere, sheathed as if in the shield-like halo that marks off the Redeemer in the apses of old churches. So he rarely held intimate conversations; his talk revolved round themes and issues, but did not reflect his personal life. He recognized that his remoteness drew others and dominated them, but he had never understood that when he relaxed and became less distant with people who were accustomed to his detachment, he could often charm them as he had charmed Paula with his confidences that night on the Heath.

But Donna Anna vexed him, because she took everything personally. With her fierce restless look and her short answers she accused him in person, along with every other priest, until

Gabriel wanted to look behind him, and redirect her gaze at Father Valentino, to take the brunt of it no longer, to shake his head and say, 'No, no, you cannot blame me.' He knew however that to do so would amount to admitting his contamination, and he restrained himself. The conversation was stilted, and brief.

Of Maria Pia, her mother said: 'She is good, but foolish. You saw for yourself how she is.' Of the girl's visions, she would say almost nothing, but when Gabriel pressed her to give an opinion, she looked at him hard and said, 'Maria Pia's visions are full of sweetness, light and gentleness, roses and blue ribbons and angels with curly hair.' One hand unclasped itself from the other, and she gestured stiffly round her parlour, 'These are things Maria Pia will not find with me, here in my house. I do not have a mind for such things.' She returned to her frozen position again and would say no more.

Gabriel, twisting under her eyes, resumed his questioning. He was irritated, almost flustered, and it crossed his mind that the Inquisitors must have been sorely tried by their recalcitrant subjects.

Eventually, Donna Anna said slowly and thoughtfully, 'I have chosen to live with my sin and to refuse the love and the forgiveness of God offered to me by . . .' Two stiff fingers indicated the two priests, 'by men like you.' She was deeply sarcastic. 'I do not feel sorry. I liked my sin, and I liked the man who sinned with me. I will not withdraw that, whatever has occurred since.'

Father Valentino's figure shrank further back in the room behind Gabriel.

'Do not pray for me,' said Donna Anna fiercely, as the parish priest surreptitiously brought his rosary to his lips to kiss the crucifix. She got up from her chair. Gabriel looked at her stern, thick-set figure. He thought, My God, she's only thirty-three, it's terrible. He felt unusual respect for her, and stood up and said, 'The love of God is always there, it surrounds you and fills you, even though your heart is closed.' He faltered over the Italian, and Father Valentino hurriedly came to his rescue.

Donna Anna did not react. Gabriel resumed a more natural tone. 'Besides, there is some question as to what is a sin . . .'

He noticed that her flickering eyes darkened, as if to warn him, You are not to try and take that from me as well.

She opened the door for them, and as she did so, a square of blazing light fell sharply on the tiles of the austere room. Blinking, Father Valentino and Gabriel stepped out into the road. When they turned round to make their formal farewell, Donna Anna's figure was blotted out by the dazzle in their eyes. Then the door shut, and they began to walk in silence back to the centre of the village.

During the next few days, Gabriel also interviewed the two other little girls, both now fourteen years old, who had seen the first three apparitions of the Virgin with Maria Pia. Father Valentino had been apprehensive, and had claimed that it was not necessary for Gabriel to talk to them. His bright plump face perspired as he hurried along beside Gabriel on the way to the second young seer's home, explaining that they were not such reliable witnesses as Maria Pia. In the case of Maria Concetta, gasped Father Valentino, her father was an out-of-work *dolce far niente* playboy – and a Communist of course, he added. He had beaten his daughter soundly every time she mentioned the visions of the Madonna. As a result, she was now too frightened to talk of them, and the beatings had distorted her memory. She would probably deny her earlier testimony, if only in fear of her father's lash.

'Surely you should stop such things? You should report him to the authorities.'

'What would that achieve?' said Father Valentino. 'He would only thrash his wife and all his children together if he thought they had been telling on him. The man rules in his house here, more's the pity.' His mouth turned down helplessly.

Father Valentino proved to be right: Maria Concetta, in a thin newly washed cotton dress, white socks and shoes, and a ribbon in her curled and neatly parted hair, stood before the two priests while her father lounged sullenly in a chair beside her. Her mother made an anxious appearance from the kitchen every now and then, but her husband dismissed her with a jerk of his head, and she withdrew, hunching her shoulders.

Maria Concetta stood and said, 'I imagined it. I did not see anything, but Maria Pia told us it was the Madonna and we should pray, so we did.'

When Gabriel asked her what she had experienced in trance, a spasm of terror crossed her pinched small face and she said, 'No, it's not true.' Gabriel asked if he and Father Valentino could remain alone with her. A plea trembled on her lips, but her father, shifting heavily in his chair, said with thick good humour, 'Why, is there something a man cannot hear in this story?' He patted his daughter's shoulder. 'I don't think so, ahah, *bimba*, do you?'

Gabriel left soon after. He still believed that the child had fallen enraptured in the olive grove, thinking she had seen the Virgin. She was lying when she denied it.

The parents of the third child, Maria Gabriella, were on the other hand exemplary, Father Valentino reported. They had ten children, of which Maria Gabriella was the fourth; they were devout and modest and hard-working; they considered the matter of the visions an incomprehensible and unsurpassed blessing to have befallen their house. Gabriel found Maria Gabriella to be a placid, well-developed child who looked five years older than she was and had almost nothing of interest to tell him. She smiled a lot and invoked God and the saints in the conventional words of a school prayer-book. The only flash of real feeling she communicated was when she came to Maria Pia. In all her stories, Maria Pia was the heroine, a bright inventive leader in the games the three of them had played together before the visions put an end to the fun of their tiny gang.

Gabriel began to compile his report for Father Superior, setting out the material in front of him on the plain wood table in Father Valentino's spare room. He first marshalled the evidence of the three girls' ecstasies in the olive grove. Maria Pia naturally emerged as the strongest, and the testimonies to the intensity of her raptures were plentiful and sincere. Pious men had pricked her while she prayed and she had not flinched; but when she emerged from her trance she rubbed the spot and wondered how she had received the hurt. Several strong men testified that they could not lift the light young girl in her state of ecstasy. None of the evidence differed from other apparitions past and present that Gabriel had examined for *Vision and Prophecy*. He knew too that the phenomena were to be found in almost all other religions.

He discussed the participation of the two younger girls, listed the alleged miracles performed at the shrine since the visions began, and outlined the criticisms and warnings pronounced by the Virgin. After this, his tone altered, and he began to write with more urgency. 'I believe that the young girl Maria Pia is the victim of delusions. I am sure that they do not emanate from any evil source. She is certainly not "possessed". But she is not aware that they are delusions. A psychiatrist could therefore judge her condition better than I. But I should like to make plain certain features of her position which in my belief invalidate her visions and render impermissible any devotion to Our Lady as she appeared here.

'1. Maria Pia is the illegitimate daughter of a local priest, who has since been removed from the village. (It seems he has been promoted.) Her mother consequently nurses a morbid grievance against the Church, and clings to her "sinfulness", as she sees it, as to a badge of identity. She has tried to prevent Maria Pia taking the sacraments and going to church.

'It is my considered opinion that this explains the strictures against the laxity of the clergy that Maria Pia has heard from the Virgin. I do not think they have any relation to the present unrest among younger priests. Indeed, regarding your original enquiry, I do not think that Maria Pia knows very much about Vatican II, or its recommendations, or the controversy that has ensued. The message of the Virgin concerns Maria Pia's father, whom she has never seen but knows is a priest.

'2. Illegitimacy brands the mother and the child in a small village like Selinunte. They are cast out, and live on the margins of respectable society, not at its centre. It is pertinent, for example, that Maria Pia and her mother's house is on the outskirts of the village, as if they should not occupy even geographical space at its heart.' (Paula had pointed this out to Gabriel.) 'In Father Chambercy's seminal work, *Magic, Witchcraft and Centralization in France*, 1572–1789, with which you are familiar, he argues convincingly that tales of demonic possession, or of "special graces" including ecstatic falls, voices, imperviousness to pain, flourish in areas where local identity and autonomy are being eroded; poor, backward areas sliding back into an even more primitive form of existence because the revolution in contemporary living is leaving them behind. Claims to an active spiritual experience attempt to redress the loss and give importance to a place and a people who are steadily losing position and being destroyed.

'In my view this provides a model for the situation of:
a. Selinunte. This is not the place to go into the economics of the village, but it is poor, primitive, the people live mainly by fishing, and it has a grand and ancient past (of which the inhabitants are proud). It is losing its young men to the bigger cities and consequently dwindling in size, wealth and influence. In short, it is a place in a state of decay.
b. Maria Pia. She has been displaced in the social order partly because she is illegitimate, and partly because her mother is obstinate and insists on living as a pariah. The family therefore occupies a weak position in the structure of village society. Maria Pia's visions assert her challenge to that society, her attempt to be reintegrated at a higher level.'

Gabriel then drafted his conclusion, commending the piety of many villagers at the shrine during the ceremonies. 'It is however sad but necessary,' he went on, 'to disabuse our English flock and, through the official channels, to inform everyone concerned as swiftly as possible that this stimulus to devotion is spurious.'

Gabriel laid down his pen, satisfied with his work so far. He walked to the wash-stand and poured out some water into the china basin and splashed his face. The white dust of Selinunte was irritating to his sensitive eyes; the cold water soothed the lids. He felt that he had put his case with conviction, and he was certain that he had come to the correct decision about the visions. The trouble was – and a shadow crossed his complacent mood and deepened the lines round his mouth – that he was not sure what he would have felt if the visions of *La Madonnina* had proved authentic.

He patted his face gently dry with the small white linen towel Father Valentino had provided, and held it against his eyes. My God, he prayed, please take away these misgivings that torment me all the time. Jerome and Paula fingered this sensitive spot when they teased me on the terrace the night Paula was drunk. I couldn't discuss it with them because I was afraid.

Gabriel felt the fear rise in him again, and he did not take the towel from his face. What was it Jerome had quoted? Yes, that falling snow was angels plucking their geese, or the white joinery of the saints in heaven. Something like that, some lines that meant that God was everywhere, manifest in all creation. Then why should miracles or visions be necessary? Why these extraordinary encounters with the supernatural? That was the point Jerome was making. Gabriel remembered their conversation, and found himself agreeing that it was ludicrous to have to believe that the Virgin herself appeared, in order to validate the vision. Why shouldn't a child's dream be equally powerful?

Gabriel took the towel from his eyes and blinked hard; then he folded it methodically over and over and hung it carefully on the side rail of the wash-stand. He would try and pray to chase the thoughts away. But his heart was dry, and would not open. His eyes scanned his breviary, his fingers threaded his rosary; he persisted, knowing that he was suffering loss of faith like a haemorrhage.

That evening he recited his daily Mass in a side chapel in the church. It was unattended, so he said it in the old way, in Latin, and some of the dryness left his soul till through the comforting and familiar patterns of the sacrifice he was able to reach once more a territory of the mind where he could scrape some water from the stony ground.

Sensuality! he groaned inwardly. It isn't the sensuality of this world that's stained, but the sensual experience of the other world. He had never sinned in the flesh by deed; his concupiscence led him into pride, not into venery. But how deep was his iniquity, his profound doubt that the bodily senses could belong in any way to the divine. Like K'ang-hsi, he found himself scorning the idea of the Incarnation. Had not St John of the Cross himself warned against visions like Maria Pia's because they came through the senses? Gabriel tried to prise the words loose from his memory. 'And it must be known that, although these things may happen to the bodily senses in the way of God, we must never rely on them or admit them, but we must always fly from them, without trying to ascertain whether they be good or evil; for the more completely exterior and corporeal they are, the less certainly they are of God. For it is more proper and habitual to God to communicate Himself to the spirit ... than to sense.' Gabriel thought over the last two sentences in despair. What were the Crucifixion and the Resurrection if not mysteries communicated to the sense? What was Christ's birth in the flesh and death in the flesh and rebirth in the flesh but an exterior and corporeal mystery communicated in an exterior and corporeal way? Maria Pia taking the Virgin's hand and kissing it, wasn't she like Thomas who probed Christ's wounded side?

Saint Teresa! thought Gabriel, how I once longed to be granted your knowledge of divine love, the piercing pain when the angel plunged his great golden spear into your heart so that it penetrated to your entrails and the sweetness was so severe it made you moan. This child here in Selinunte mocks your language with her laughing echoes of your raptures. *La piena dolcezza della Madonna*.

Gabriel continued to pray, with his head in his hands, his elbows on his thin knees, sitting in his shirtsleeves and his old black trousers on the edge of his white bed. 'Give me something other, Holy Queen, give me the peace that passes all understanding, give me light, only light, a pure circle unshadowed by the carnal taint that darkens our language of spiritual experience, and through language the experience itself and taints our intimacy with you.' Gabriel bowed his head further between his hands. 'Forgive me, forgive me. I know ...' He could not say Oliver's name, not even to himself, so he passed over it. 'I know he's a warning to me. Teach me to understand and overcome it. He smiles and smiles at me in my memory and tells me my nature is utterly fallen, but dearest Holy Lady he fills my heart with gaiety and gentleness and love, and it turns me away from you and from your gentle son my saviour.'

What is he to me? Or I to him? Nothing. Gabriel thought of Oliver and cursed him. He's shallow, insubstantial, a half-formed personality, nothing but a child, leading a disorganized, haphazard life, believing trees have souls. Gabriel almost snorted. What a foolish old man I have become, he thought, that I can't free myself from such a simple and empty obsession.

The consolation Gabriel had found a month before when he prayed after his dream of the hunt did not come to him now. His waking life from day to day in Sicily resembled the nightly torture of an insomaniac, like a man bound to a wheel, chased eternally by a stream that turns and turns it till it always comes back to the point where it began.

Jerome also was preoccupied, but found that he was relieved when he did not receive a letter from James Cunliffe: at least James didn't have the effrontery to try and explain or excuse himself. But Jerome faced the return to England with apprehension: he had no idea what he was going to do. Never before in his life had he been without full-time obligations to a wide range of people and business.

He remembered how, nearly forty years ago, he had stood on the quay at Southampton, blindly asking the hustling porters where he could find a most important packet that had been sent to him via this ship, from China. He had not dared say, 'My father's ashes.' It had been unbearable, the thought of the mass and power of Henry Namier diminished so utterly, to a lost parcel on a crowded quay. Gabriel had not come to meet the ship. He had not time, because then as now (as ever), his work had been so time-consuming and all-important that he could not spare the afternoon. 'I'll come to the ceremony, of course,' he had said. 'But there's no need for both of us to go, is there?' So Jerome had stood alone, plucking at the edge of his hat in pain as the parcels were thrown in heaps. And then a voice behind him spoke his name, and informed him solemnly that the captain was waiting to hand over his father's remains. Of course, it had been stupid of him to think otherwise. But the anxiety that he had never proved himself to his father during his lifetime had blotted out his common sense.

Now, every time he imagined himself spending the day at home, without an office to go to, he felt mounting resentment against his brother who had taken over his study. If he asked Gabriel to move, he could imagine the conversation: 'Now that I'm not going to the *Review*, I'd like my study back.' Gabriel: 'But what for, Jerome, are you writing anything?' Jerome frowned to himself. Yes, Gabriel would be likely to say that. And the bitter part of it was that Jerome did not have any plans for writing.

Paula noticed her uncle's eyes shrunken in their sockets

behind puffy sacs but she did not enquire after his health. Her only comment came when he told them that he had concluded his investigations by condemning Maria Pia's visions. 'But what will happen to her now?' She was upset that the young girl would be discredited. 'What about the faith of all those people – does that mean nothing?'

But she knew her remarks would receive no reply from Gabriel. Since the evening in the village with the fishermen, he had hardly spoken to her or Jerome. For Paula, the Sicilian expedition had represented a chance to pursue her ideal of gratuitous friendship. In her expectations, she had figured as the cornerstone of the triangle of herself, Jerome and Gabriel. She had looked forward to supporting her father, and to regulating the tension between the brothers by drawing from Gabriel the vulnerability and gift for friendship she had glimpsed on the Heath. She now saw the complete folly of her ambitions. Gabriel had retreated into aloof superciliousness, and for two weeks she had been the object of her father's most assiduous solicitude. She had kept him company as they made excursions in hired cars or on the local trains, while Gabriel pursued his investigations. Her drunken scene had turned her into the patient when she had wanted to be the doctor, and her father was playing the role of nurse with delight. 'You are *en pleine beauté*, darling,' he said to her one morning, when she came down to have breakfast with him on the terrace. She met his praise with sulky irritation, exactly as she had done ever since she was fifteen, and she hated herself for it. Her father would say, 'I wish you'd have some cake. They look so good. I mustn't, but you should. You don't eat enough, darling.' Or, on another occasion, his eyes gentle behind his glasses, 'Are you all right for money? I know you're independent, and I'm very proud of you, but I'd like to send something to your bank ... I'm thinking of transferring some stocks anyway. It's good for me for tax reasons, so why don't I send them to you?' Or, 'There's so much furniture at home, and Teresa complains the house is cluttered. Would you like the desk in Nanny's room? It's good, not very good, Victorian, well made. I know she has no use for it ...'

Paula responded miserably to all her father's offers, shaking her head dumbly and tugging at her hair, disliking herself more than she could bear for her inability to deal with his concern and to be either firm or grateful. She realized that, having become the dependent, the weakling, the sick man of the trio, she was fulfilling a very deep need in her father, a need almost greater than his appetite for literary success; but the position shattered the proud image she had made of herself and humiliated her. But Post-John, Phase Two, as she now called the period she had entered, meant that she would no longer try to impose her will on circumstance. She would no longer plan or strive. She would not make resolutions of any kind but, like an automaton, would accept whatever happened to her.

'You live too much in your head, Polo,' David had told her the day before he left for Vietnam. It was what John used to tell her too, but more unkindly. 'You want to be in control all the time, of everything. You can't bear the event you hadn't planned for. It can't happen because you didn't make it happen. You're like a child thwarted from going on a picnic by the rain. Why does it have to rain, you cry, when I want to go out on a picnic?' Now Paula would listen to them both, and she would yield and bend and go with the flow.

Her thoughts turned again to Gabriel; once in London, in the days when they were closer, he had said that the Taoists considered water the image of the highest good, because water is submissive and weak and yet can wear down the hardest stone and metal, and because it always flows downwards, seeking the lowest level. Christian mystics on the other hand believe in the will overcoming nature: their characteristic image is a mountain with rugged sides and the painful struggle towards the distant summit, the stumbling and the falling on the climb.

I will be base and without volition like water, thought Paula, and find my own level. Then she smiled to herself and tapped her head lightly. There I go again, she thought, willing and deciding everything as if I were in control.

Paula hid her injury from Gabriel as well as she could; Jerome hid his fears from her out of solicitude and from his brother out of habit. Gabriel for his part was too engrossed in his own pain to notice either of them.

CHAPTER 17

The foyer of the theatre had been cordoned off by policemen. Huge cars disgorged members of the audience who had paid twenty guineas each to attend the charity première of *South Pacific* in aid of the Society of Needy Orphans Overseas, alias SNOO. Francesca slipped quietly through the crowd and found a red and gold pillar where she waited for Wayne Dupree, who had been designated her escort for the evening by Teresa. Francesca looked gravely at the leaflet a girl with mild eyes had handed to her at the entrance. At the top in bold letters it said, 'REMEMBER CAMBODIA?' I do, I do, thought Francesca, David just about got out alive.

The group in which the girl stood carried a few home-made banners; the police encircled them but had not joined arms, because the demonstrators looked defeated, not aggressive. Members of the first-night audience, some smiling with gratified vanity, others scowling in a pretence that the attention of the fans in the crowd was disagreeable to them, passed over the carpet on the pavement and gathered in the foyer, uttering shrill cries of greeting and recognition.

Francesca waited. She was the only Namier in England on Teresa's opening night, so she had had to come. Ever since David's departure, she had resolutely kept her mind on the ordering of domestic matters, planning each day's work-load with meticulous care. 'Fetch prescription. Buy toothpaste, Uhu glue, paper towels, water softener.' She made lists every night, and checked them off the next day if accomplished. If not, she transferred them to a new list.

Now she had been jolted from this pleasant, isolated, waking sleep and reminded of the existence of a world beyond Tilly and herself. Dressing for the occasion had brought tears of vexation to her eyes. A pile of discarded clothes lay strewn about her bedroom; every type of dress she tried seemed to give her too defined a personality, when she wanted to be invisible. But the babysitter approved when she saw her. 'You look fabulous, Mrs Clark,' she had said, admiringly. The girl was about seventeen, thought Francesca; she did not like leaving Tilly alone with her. Against the pillar, Francesca's clear face flickered anxiously.

Above the hubbub she heard a shrill 'Darling' and turned to find Wayne skipping towards her in a silver cowboy shirt with fringes on the sleeves and over the chest, and platform boots with diamanté heels.

'Don't I look super, darling?' he said, wriggling his shoulders so the fringes shimmered. He was wild with excitement. 'And look!' He pointed to his lapel where in sloping silver letters, a brooch spelt out, 'GAY DOG'. 'OOoohee!' he cried. 'I'm so excited I'll have to go to the little boys' room all through the show.'

'I hope not,' said Francesca drily. 'We're in the middle of a row.'

'It's going to be great,' said Wayne, as they fought towards the bar. 'It's going to be terrific.'

Francesca had a double whisky. Then she asked about her mother, and Wayne spread a hand on his chest. 'An artist, darling, like I say, a true artist. She'll really give it to them. It's great, just great that I can sit out front with you tonight, but I hope the boys will be OK without me, I really do. No, there's absolutely nothing to get fussed about, Teresa'll slay them.' His eyes were darting round the company and his fingers wiggled at several other members of the audience. 'Isn't this smashing?' As the curtain went up, he took Francesca's hand and held it tight.

The musical's designer was a disciple of Lavish Naturalism, and the audience gasped and applauded at the set: a street in Saigon, choked with Hondas and bicycles, children on the backs of some, on the bars of others; shops saying 'Massage Parlour', where reed-like girls in silken sheaths peeped round doorways, and street vendors spread contraband goods on khaki ground-sheets in front of them; GIs milling about in an assortment of button-laden uniforms and graffiti-inscribed caps and boots – Francesca recognized a grotesque replica of one of David's photographs. The soldiers swaggered and smoked and goosed the girls, and then, of one accord, froze and turned and flung out an arm in file. An uproar of applause greeted the GIs as they slapped their thighs and squatted on their haunches and brought their fists down on the saddles of the Hondas. 'There is nothing like a dame!'

Wayne dimpled with delight. The throng of GIs parted and his pressure on Francesca's hand became almost unbearable, for Teresa stood revealed centre stage in black Vietnamese pyjamas, lolling against a ramshackle booth. A sign above her head said, 'BLOODY MARY'S SALOON BAR, GIS WELCOME'. It swung slightly as the set silently moved forward to the front of the stage. Francesca lifted her eyes quickly to her mother's face and dropped them again. She felt stiff with terror. Her mother was sure to do something dreadful. But no, pleasant throaty sounds followed one upon the other without a stumble and the spotlight played dramatically on her white face and hands and the shiny folds of her costume. The GIs moved in to surround her, belting out, 'Bloody Mary is the girl I love.'

The audience clapped tumultuously, and Wayne whispered to Francesca in excitement, 'These radio mikes are far out. What a sound!' His eyes glittered now like his clothes. Francesca's palms were wet, so she extricated her hand from Wayne's and folded them in her lap. Now that her mother's entrance had passed without mishap, she was able to look more attentively at Teresa and note that the long black glossy wig suited her small-boned face.

By the interval it was obvious that the audience was loving it. Francesca, drinking another double, heard all around her exclamations of delight at the pace, the movement, the singing, the acting being tossed from one decorated face to another. 'Making it Vietnam works so well,' commented someone behind her. 'It makes it so up-to-date, don't you agree?' Wayne did not notice Francesca's silence; he was busy flicking his silver fringes.

There was a note in the programme declaring that fifty thousand babies were fathered by US servicemen in Vietnam. Francesca read it and her lower lip quivered. The madness of it. So that was why SNOO had agreed to accept the proceeds of the première. She shut her eyes as her mother screamed abuse at the lieutenant and did not open them again until the curtain fell. She was more glad than she would ever be able to express that David was not there.

Teresa was presented with an enormous bouquet. She smiled radiantly at the audience and extracted a rose to throw at them. The actors turned on their heels after the third call, nodding to each other as they reached the wings, as if to say, 'It worked all right, didn't it?'

'Come on, darling, let's make tracks,' said Wayne, pulling Francesca by the hand out into the street, round the back and past the doorman with a quick 'OOooee' and then up the stairs into Teresa's dressing-room.

'Great, darling, just great. You slayed them!' Wayne fell on her cheek, cold cream and all, and hugged her till she wept.

'Oh it's so good, it's so good, it's so good,' she said. 'To hear them all out there having such a good time.' She was clutching her wig in one hand as the tears rolled down. 'Hello, darling,' she said to Francesca, 'I hope you liked it.' She gestured to the bottles in the basin. 'Come on, open the champers.'

She peered at her reflection in the bright bulb-framed mirror. 'If only your father had been here! He could have seen me as I really am, at my very best. Isn't that right, Wayne darling? Not that snivelling neurotic he has to live with, but me, the real me.'

'Yes, it's a shame,' said Francesca softly, taking the tooth-mug of champagne Wayne offered her.

'I was good, wasn't I? Darling, say I was good,' said Teresa, looking up at her daughter.

'Yes, of course, Mummy. You were wonderful.'

'Oh, children are always hopeless. They never like anything one does.' Teresa was in too good a mood to mind.

Several people put their heads round the door and cried congratulations to Teresa; several more, seeing the champagne, stayed. Kuo, who had played Teresa's daughter, glided in, led by the lieutenant who was her lover in the musical, and smiled gently at Francesca. She was even more flower-like in real life, and Francesca noticed a certain sharp set to her mother's jaw as she caught sight of Kuo's beauty in her mirror.

'What shall it be, kids?' called out Wayne. 'Luigi's? Or something a bit more posh for the occasion?' He took Teresa's arm firmly and began walking her out of the dressing-room. Francesca, seeing them together at that moment, realized how serious and sincere Wayne's protection of her mother was, and she felt more kindly towards him.

The group tumbled down the stairs out into the street where the air, still fresh with the bite of spring, made them shiver after the heat of their dressing-rooms. Chattering, they scurried round the block and descended on Luigi's with its walls papered with signed photographs. Teresa's had been taken several years ago, and she covered her face coyly when she saw it.

Francesca ate without appetite, watching the others indifferently. As soon as she could, she turned to her mother and asked if she had heard from Sicily. Teresa broke out of her excited conversation and leaning back in her chair, spoke behind the lieutenant's back.

'Your father telephoned this morning to wish me luck. Christ, the line from Sicily was like trying to listen to drowned Ophelia!' Seeing Francesca's serious expression, she composed her face and added, 'It's going a treat, apparently. Jerome's looking at all those ruins he gets off on; you know, darling, Greek temples and so on.' Francesca wondered at how extraordinarily silly her mother became in theatrical company. 'Gabriel has discovered a new saint, but she turns out to be a fraud in his opinion, though your father and your sister are utterly enchanted with her. They're all well, anyway.' She paused and turned back to the table. 'But the best news,' she said loudly, 'is that my husband has been partly vindicated of all that ridiculous CIA shambles. The *Review* is in a state of collapse, because they can't get anyone – anyone decent that is – to edit it unless that snake Cunliffe gets the boot. Everyone at last realizes he's the real culprit. They're all locked in murderous strife, like proper intellectuals and the *Review* has missed one issue and if it misses any more it'll be ruined.'

'Good,' said Francesca.

'Any news of David?' said her mother, kindly.

'I had a letter this morning.' Francesca did not say more, and her mother, knowing her daughter's privacy of mind, did not enquire further.

When Francesca had finished eating, she got up, kissed her mother and walked slowly towards the main street to get a taxi, refusing the offers of Wayne and the lieutenant to help her. When she got home, she kept the taxi for the babysitter and then went in to Tilly to listen to her steady breathing for a few moments in the dark room. She picked her up and hugged her, pressing her lips to the child's warm forehead with its powdery and peppery smell and rocking backwards and forwards while Tilly half opened bleary eyes and curled herself into the contours of her mother's body.

Francesca left the room with the child sleeping against her and picked up the letter – the only letter – she had received from David since he had been away. 'Listen,' she said to her child, 'listen.' She began reading the letter aloud, slowly and quietly, hearing David's cadences in every word.

'Darling Frog, I just got back from a terrible day,' it began. She turned over the airmail sheets (there were three of them) feeling with pleasure the fine crinkly paper between her fingers. She imagined the room in which David had written it, with lizards asleep on the ceiling or going gup-gup-gup swallowing flies, as he had once described to Tilly to make her laugh. She tried to think herself into the heat of the tropics, to remember the shape of his head under her hands when she held him like that to kiss him, as she liked to do because contact made her feel closer to the thoughts he always entertained of countries and people so far removed from herself and her child. As she read, forcing her voice to savour the words of the letter, she fought back tears of jealousy that he sounded so excited, so occupied, so happy. But she had long ago stifled the reaction, How could he feel like that, in that place? And so with brave articulateness she finished: 'Funny Froggy, I miss you and wish I was back with you. Kiss Tadpole for me. Love from David.'

Francesca smoothed the sheets back into the envelope, covered with gay stamps of flowers and fruit. Then she took herself and Tilly to sleep together in the bed she shared with David. She curled the child into the crook of her body and listening to her softly taken breath, held on to her warm, firm form, still vigorous in sleep, where dreams made her clench her fists and strike out with her feet.

❦ *CHAPTER 18*

Gabriel had not yet seen Oliver. It was his first day back at work in his brother's house, after almost a week spent discussing his experience in Sicily with Father Superior and organizing his draft report into a form in which he could present it. He had wanted to discuss with Father Superior the deeper implications for his own faith of his attitude to Maria Pia, but he had found he could not broach the subject of his own personal doubts. He needed to conceal them, because he feared that Father Superior might forbid him Oliver's company, and he longed to see him again. I'll visit him once more, he thought, and then I shall talk to Father Superior. So he resumed work on the diaries, re-entering his book at a later point in Andrew da Rocha's life.

'In 1696, the Pope, reacting to the emperor's edict of toleration, appointed a vicar-general and a bishop to each province of China. Naturally, the newcomers were not subject to Jesuit authority, and men like Andrew da Rocha feared that the fragile edifice of understanding and respect that the Society had built would crumble at the rough and often high-handed measures of the new Christian missionaries. Charles Maigrot, Bishop of Conon and Vicar-General Apostolic of the province of Fukien, was the most dangerous trouble-maker of all in Andrew's eyes. Even before his landfall in China, Maigrot had declared himself an implacable opponent of the Jesuits in the arguments that raged about the Chinese rites.

'The controversy grew in intensity as more voices joined in the debate. Dominican theologians argued that the Chinese word *T'ien* could not be applied to a supreme and heavenly power, because it denoted the material sky. When the emperor made his annual sacrifice to Heaven, *T'ien*, he was nothing but an idolater adoring the material creation.' Gabriel looked out of the window at the withering lilac blossom, and remembered his crystal prism and its inscription. He thought, Yes, of course, the Christians could not understand how the Chinese held the heavens to be apprehensible to the senses and an abstract concept of spirit or being at one and the same time. The Jesuits came near to the Chinese way of thinking, but because of the Church's authority – think of Galileo – they could not deny a literally material sky. But their critics lived more strictly within traditional dualism, and the distinction between spirit and matter was reflected for them in the distinction between the sky and Heaven. Gabriel thought of Oliver and his lips twitched. If he pressed on today and managed a good day's work, he would go and see him later. It had been over a month. He smiled to himself a little sadly, yearning for Oliver's blitheness to work its way into his spirits again, yet hoping he might have become immune to it and free.

'The effect of outside criticism on the Jesuit community in Peking was strengthening for a time. The Fathers closed ranks in the face of the menace; the Portuguese forgot their struggles with the French; Andrew da Rocha buried his grievance against Joachim Pernet, and Pernet forgave him for the reprimand from Rome and did not press sordid charges against Andrew. All their energies were concentrated on winning their case for the Chinese rites.' Gabriel pulled one of the volumes of Andrew's diaries towards him, and opened it at a marker. After an absence of over a month, he was finding it difficult to recapture the involvement he had felt before he left. He dabbed his eyes, and thought angrily of Maria Pia, who had diverted him. Yet his experiences in Sicily and the debate in China were woven together on the same warp: they both raised questions about the nature of God's manifestation on earth.

Gabriel again wiped his eyes and, sniffing loudly, mopped his nose. Pollen. It was swarming now, he knew, like a plague of live creatures, the count rising and rising until it had reached a height worthy of front-page reports. Gabriel's lids and nostrils pullulated as if a thousand insects, each with a thousand legs, were creeping over his tearducts and down his nose. He snorted fiercely, trying to soothe the itch, and putting away his handkerchief, reapplied himself.

The drama which had finally rung down the curtain on all hopes to convert China had been the embassy of the Papal Legate, Cardinal Maillard de Tournon, Patriarch of Antioch. Gabriel wanted to make his embassy the subject of the penultimate chapter of his book. In 1705 Pope Clement XI sent Tournon to China to investigate the procedures of the Jesuits. Gabriel lit a cigarette. Although it was not his habit to smoke while working, he found the fumes deadened the nasal irritation for a time. He began marking places in Andrew's diaries. How the recriminations and rancour had built up! Tournon the Legate, a young invalid, elevated through his august family's connections, arrived in Peking, and shortly afterwards accused the Jesuits of usury, bringing forward Chinese witnesses who professed to be the victims of the Fathers' rapacity. Then the League heard reports of the quarrel between Pernet and Andrew, and introduced spies into Andrew's house to observe his relations with his servant. Gabriel's mouth twisted, and he placed another marker between the pages. Tournon took down the testimony of one of the Fathers' underlings about Andrew's 'unnatural relations' and sent a despatch to the Sacred College of Propaganda in Rome, denouncing Andrew da Rocha as unfit to hold holy office. But the Jesuits were loyal to their own against the intruder: Tournon's messenger was intercepted and the letter did not reach Rome. Gabriel chuckled: the Legate was a guest of the Jesuits in Peking, and it was naive of him to suppose that his dictation was not overheard and reported. From then on, Andrew and his colleagues were to give the Legate no quarter, nor he them.

'His Eminence told me', wrote Andrew with singular vehemence, 'that when the demons left hell to come to Peking, they could never have done Religion and the Holy See more harm than we have done. "I counsel you to leave China," he said to me, "you, and all the Fathers of your Company." Dear God, as You are my judge, when I heard those words, I Your servant was filled with the anger of the righteous that possessed Your

Son when He drove the money-changers from the temple. We, the allies of the Devil! No rather, he, the Holy Father's Legate, who seeks to undo all that we have accomplished with his haughty and ignorant decrees.'

How sad, thought Gabriel, is the conviction of a man who knows that his course is doomed. Andrew was whole-heartedly committed to the cause of the Jesuit Order, but deep down he recognized that he and his colleagues would eventually be condemned by the Pope through the agency of his Legate, and that, as Jesuits who had taken a special vow of obedience to the Holy Father, they would have to yield.

But before the inevitable collapse, the Fathers were to score one notable victory: the public humiliation of the Legate and his train. Gabriel laughed sympathetically. In 1706, on 30 June, Charles Maigrot, Bishop of Conon, arrived in Peking, summoned by the Legate to assist him with arguments against the Jesuits and the emperor. Maigrot was the Legate's natural choice as advocate because he had decreed in his diocese that the Confucian rites could not be performed by Christians, and that the words *T'ien* and *Shang-ti* could not be used to mean God. He had also condemned the view that the Chinese Classics contained nothing contrary to Christian dogma and moral principle, and had therefore forbidden their use in missionary schools. When he arrived in Peking, the emperor was preparing to leave for Tartary; he therefore ordered Maigrot to follow the court to the palace beyond the Great Wall, at Jehol in Manchuria.

'The emperor's lofty brow was creased with anger such as I have rarely witnessed in the great prince,' reported Andrew. 'For usually, I cannot admire his mildness enough. He commanded me from the throne to accompany him to Tartary at once. Then he said, and his words still pierce me like burning arrows, "Such dissension between you Christians cannot be inspired by the Lord of Heaven, but by the Devil who, I have heard you Westerners say, leads men to do evil since he cannot do otherwise." Then he dismissed me and I withdrew, shamed that such a wise and mighty ruler should perceive the contentions that divide us.'

But Andrew's grief at the political turn the encounter between K'ang-hsi and Maigrot was to take did not dim his delight in the scene of Oriental splendour that the emperor laid on for the Pope's advocate.

'Jehol, 4 August 1706. The emperor gave audience this morning in an outside pavilion erected in the shade of the orchard at his palace here north of the wall, the pleasure gardens of Jehol. The scenery displays the grandeur of nature as tamed by man's wisdom: strangely shaped rocks are placed on the skyline to enchant the eye and the scent of the *ilha muke* trees the emperor has imported from Ninguta to delight him cling in the heavy summer air, fragant as I remember the spikes of lilies of Europe in July. His throne stood on a silk-lined dais, screened from the heat of the sun by an awning of gleaming yellow. Hanging embroideries on either side showed the imperial symbol of the five-clawed dragon pursuing the fiery pearl of knowledge and immortality. Such a sight should strike respect into the heart of any man, but His Grace the Bishop of Conon is obdurate.

'Maigrot was led before K'ang-hsi. He kowtowed, then stood at the foot of the emperor's throne. Three of the Fathers, including myself, stood in attendance on his left, and we gazed at the bishop who had come to challenge our endeavours. We took no pains to disguise our shame and disdain.

' "Tell me," said the emperor to the bishop, "can you understand our sacred Classics?"

' "A little."

'The emperor's grave countenance showed some surprise. He asked the bishop what he had read and what he remembered. Answering, Maigrot stumbled awkwardly over the unfamiliar language. We would have mocked him with our laughter had the situation been less damaging for ourselves. The emperor with quiet impatience turned to us and, nodding, indicated he wished one of us to interpret. We were reluctant, for we feared that later we should be blamed for altering words to suit our ends. But we agreed, and Pernet and I took the task in turns.

' "Explain", the emperor again addressed the bishop, "what you have found contrary to the Christian religion in our sacred Classics." His Grace demurred: he could not accept, he said, that a pagan king should judge Christian doctrine, for the Pope alone was arbiter. Father Pernet omitted the slur "pagan" in his translation, yet still the emperor frowned deeply. He pointed to the four large characters blazoned above his throne. "Read them," he ordered. The bishop attempted it. The emperor, having listened to his clumsiness, spoke slowly. "You are mistaken. You have recognized the first character, but you have not read the others correctly." He paused, and when he spoke again, his words were bitter. "If you cannot understand the meaning of four characters, how is it you can expound our books? Our scholars spend fifty years studying to accustom themselves to the contents of the Classics."

'His Grace the bishop looked humbled for a moment, but then he rallied, and his answer was filled with impertinence. "If the Chinese themselves take fifty years of study, it is not surprising that a stranger like myself cannot explain a few Chinese characters."

'The emperor smiled a small smile. "If I had as little understanding regarding your affairs as you have regarding ours, what would you think of me if I wished to direct and govern them?"

'We stirred uneasily during the exchange, for the emperor's shadowed face threatened the years of careful labour we have spent in China. We tried to catch the bishop's eye and cut his insolence, but he kept his face turned to the emperor and did not waver. Confronted with such contumely, the emperor bent forward slightly from his throne and, raising one hand, tapped the armrest angrily. "Before Father Ricci and his companions came to China, no one had even heard of the Incarnation, or of the name you give to God, who was certainly not incarnate in this country. I have told you that Heaven and the Lord of Heaven mean the same in our language, and that we honour Confucius as our master, without any other goal but the expression of our gratitude for his teaching. As for the tablets of our ancestors, we do not ask them for honour, nor for happiness. These are the three points with which you disagree. If these opinions are not to your liking, you must leave my country. You have not come to found and establish your law, but to destroy it, and in consequence, if the cause of your religion is ruined, you can only blame yourselves."

'The emperor waved his right hand, and declared the audience at an end. Two eunuchs led the bishop away. He had not looked once in our direction. When he had left, the emperor stepped swiftly from the dais. Doubt and anger clouded his still features, and we his attendants could not do otherwise than let him depart in silence. But a sigh, torn from our lips involuntarily, hung in the heavy air under the fruit trees and as it reached his ears I saw his spine stiffen. I wanted to fall on my knees before him, but I knew that any further loss of dignity on our part would contribute further to the undoing of our holy cause. So I have spent half the night in prayer, and have vowed never to leave off the hairshirt I wear until the day Christianity is accepted in this empire.

'All night I have pondered with growing grief the days when the emperor would send his gentlemen to enquire about the condition of souls in the other world, about heaven and hell and purgatory, the existence of God, His providence, and the means necessary to salvation, so that God seemed to move his heart after an extraordinary manner and to affect it with those holy doubts that usually precede conversion. But that happy moment has never come, and when I stood and watched His Grace the Bishop of Conon chastised for his great folly, I despaired – my God, forgive me! – that it would ever come at all.'

Gabriel put his head in his hands. Andrew had been right to dread the truth of the emperor's words. After the interview with Maigrot, the cause of Christianity in China was lost. Maigrot himself was held for four months under house arrest in the French Jesuits' headquarters in Peking, tried in the emperor's presence, and expelled from China. Cardinal Maillard de Tournon, the Legate, retreated to Canton where he issued a formal decree banning the performance of the rites and following Maigrot's guidelines in other respects. The Portuguese Bishop of Macao, who was sympathetic to the Jesuits' views and conscious of their power, arrested Tournon for flouting the authority of the King of Portugal by proclaiming laws in his territory at Macao without his ratification. After long months of harsh treatment, Tournon died in prison in 1710, of apoplexy.

But by then, thought Gabriel, Andrew da Rocha was already dead: he did not see the undoing of his life's work. After the disaster of the Papal Legation, the Emperor K'ang-hsi decreed that all Christian proselytizers should present themselves to Peking. Only after a formal acknowledgement of the legitimacy of the rites to Confucius and the ancestors would missionaries be issued with letters patent permitting them to practise their calling. 'How do we know,' declared the emperor, 'that there are not others like the Bishop of Conon, stirring up commotions among the people and rashly condemning our doctrines and customs although they do not understand them? I wish to purge my empire of these foolish and turbulent men.'

What an impossible dilemma! Gabriel felt Andrew's sorrow keenly, as if it were his own. On the one hand the Legate, acting for the Pope, condemned the rites; on the other the emperor made the rites a condition of Christianity's survival in China. It killed Andrew. He was found dead in his bed by his favourite, his servant, on 30 October 1708. And in that same year, K'ang-hsi had the court exorcized because he believed the Heir Apparent had been bewitched, and then ordered the deaths of the men whom he took to be Taoist sorcerers. The wisest and most Christian of emperors! Gabriel exclaimed to himself. How little the Jesuits' patient strivings had achieved.

Gabriel pushed the diary away from him with relief. It was after one, and he could stop for a break. After lunch he could do two hours' annotations on the debate between Maigrot and K'ang-hsi at Jehol that summer nearly three hundred years ago. He wiped his nose. Did they have hay fever in Manchuria? he wondered. If only Maigrot had not been such a twaddle, perhaps the outcome might have been different and the emperor might not have turned against Christianity in the end. But hypotheses are absurd, mere wishful thinking. In 1722 when Yung-cheng, K'ang-hsi's son and heir, acceded, everything was finally lost. He soon issued a decree condemning Christianity altogether, and in it he singled out the mystery of the Incarnation as 'a trick to fool the simple' and the intervention of God in human affairs as unworthy behaviour on the part of the Supreme Being. Then Yung-cheng proscribed the religion because it opposed filial piety and the ancestral rites. So the Jesuits had been correct in their assessment. Gabriel thought of Maria Pia's simple faith in the real and physical intervention of the Virgin in her life, and he sighed. He yearned for the vivid, solid, absolute experience she had had, but he knew it would always elude him.

By four o'clock, when Gabriel was walking on light feet towards the Institute of Baroque Music, he realized that the whole momentum of his day had sprung from his promise to himself that he would see Oliver again. He had not driven himself so hard to make up for lost time in Sicily; he had not kept his back bent, his head down over the diaries because Andrew da Rocha fascinated him; he had not concentrated in order to overcome the singing in his head and the burning in his nose and eyes. It was true he had worked for a combination of these reasons, but above all he had laboured because he could then reward himself with a few moments in Oliver's company. It was a trade-off with God, he recognized. His self-disgust almost made him turn back; but he thought, for perhaps the hundredth time, What harm is there in it? The attachment is not evil in itself, and it will not go away if we don't meet.

So the priest happily deceived himself as he stepped over the threshold into the Institute. He walked into the first room, where he had heard Oliver play the day of the glistening rain, but it was empty except for three sunbeams which passed through the square panels of the tall windows and made a precise chequerboard on the carpet. Gabriel blinked, and crossed the hall to another room. A middle-aged woman stood behind a desk, selling the catalogue and postcards. 'Is Mr Summers here?' Gabriel asked her.

The woman smiled softly. 'Why, no, Oliver is on holiday.'

'On holiday?' Gabriel blurted, and then realized that his violent tone had frightened the woman. He added, attempting a more casual manner, 'Oh yes, is he? Where?'

'Oh, the Lake District,' she said. 'Or maybe Norfolk. He usually goes to one or the other. He'll be back in a week or so. He needed a holiday.' She spoke indulgently, gazing into Gabriel's sore red-rimmed eyes with concern. Two spots of high colour had appeared in his sallow cheeks.

'Yes, I'm sure,' said Gabriel, not moving.

'Did you want something special? Perhaps I . . . ?'

Gabriel brushed aside her offer and turned away. But at the front door he stopped, and instead of leaving the Institute, walked swiftly upstairs. He took the first flight too fast, and rested at the landing, his lungs heaving. When he reached Oliver's study, his heart leaped within him, for he felt the boy's nearness, in his books, in a white heavy-knit sweater flung off on a chair, in his desk untidily strewn with papers. Gabriel went to the desk to write Oliver a note asking him to telephone as soon as he returned. The words of the woman downstairs cut him; her knowledge of Oliver – 'He usually goes to one or the other' – suddenly excluded Gabriel from Oliver's familiar world. But his pain was fast turning to anger as he jibbed at the evidence of Oliver's autonomy and independence. The boy was his possession, almost his invention; because he led such a persistent existence in Gabriel's imagination, Gabriel no longer believed that Oliver was entitled to a separate life beyond the images that he entertained of him. The Lake District, or Norfolk! He knew nothing of them, of Oliver's 'usual holiday', and his ignorance filled him with a bitter jealousy. Separation from the loved one can be tolerated when his or her movements can be traced in the mind, and Gabriel in Sicily had imagined Oliver in London, playing at the harpsichord, walking on the Heath. Now he realized his mental tracking of Oliver's day had been false, and the warm bright images he had cherished were blotted out as lies.

He looked over the heaped desk for a piece of clean paper, and his eye lighted on a sheet filled with a familiar black jagged script. His sore eyes burned and he rubbed his head as he looked at it, transfixed. 'My dear Oliver,' it began. His letter. The one he had written to Oliver from Sicily, in which he had surpassed himself in delicacy of expression, and communicated confidences with gentleness and a touch of wit, so as not to overwhelm him. His letter, four pages of himself, thrown here on the desk along with Oliver's bills and circulars for anyone who came in to read.

Gabriel's heart pounded painfully, and he put away his pen. He would not write Oliver a note. With quivering hands he pulled his letter from the sheaf of papers, tore it up and put the fragments in his pocket.

Pride, he thought, pride is the enemy.

❧ CHAPTER 19

'*Capot*,' boomed Jerome, 'is the French word for French Letter.'
He rubbed one hand on the other. 'An American in Paris. His
wife dies and he hasn't got anything to wear for the funeral. So
he goes to the hotel manager, and asks him . . .' Jerome put on
an execrable French accent, knowing that everyone in the
room knew he spoke the language perfectly. 'He asks him,
"*Estke je pur avour ung capeau noir?*" The hotel manager raises
his shoulders and says . . .' (Here Jerome dropped the bad French
and gesticulated gallically) ' "*Ah, monsieur, c'est bon, ça, un
capot noir, mais quand-même . . .*" The American explains why
he needs a black hat. "*Vous savez, monsieur,*" he says, "*c'est
parce que ma femme est morte.*" "*Ahaha!*" cries the hotel
manager, raising his eyebrows and kissing his lips, '*vous Améri-
cains, quel sentiment! Quelle délicatesse!*" '

Jerome laughed loudly, rubbing his hands together, palm
onto fist. Since his return from Sicily, the thrust of his reminiscences had become wilder and more manic, although he had
found that London society's fickleness had already turned
around the prevailing wind. A chorus of despair at his leaving
the *Review* now filled his correspondence. He was gratified
but he had not found peace of mind. '*Capot!*' he exclaimed,
chuckling over the word, and everyone laughed with him.
Except Gabriel.

It was Teresa's birthday (her fifty-third, and she had been
tearful all day), and when the show came down she returned
home with Wayne to find the rest of the family gathered,
waiting to celebrate both this and David's return from Viet-

nam. The curtains of the sitting-room were open, and at eleven o'clock, after an immaculate June day, the last light was dying in the summer sky beyond the inky outlines of the trees. A window onto the small front garden stood ajar, and the warm air blew in, gently lifting the edges of the curtain and lightening the pall of cigarette and cigar smoke. Rumpled leaves of tissue paper and discarded ribbons from Teresa's birthday presents and the crushed and torn remains of crackers gave the discreet sitting-room a reckless atmosphere which grew as more wine bottles joined the empties on the tables and the floor and the Namier family sprawled on the carpet and in the soft deep armchairs at the other end of the room from Gabriel.

Gabriel had remained distant all evening, and no one knew why he stayed at all. But their revelry had soon made them forget him, so that his silence failed for once to dampen their high spirits. He sat away from the group near the harpsichord, by the window that stood ajar, at a table set with a chessboard. He was playing both sides of the game, very slowly.

Wayne said, 'I know another.' He giggled and looked round the room. 'I was at a party, and a man flashed. Oooee. A girl turned round and she looked at it, and quick as a flash ...' Groans interrupted him. 'Sorreee, didn't mean it, anyways, just like that, she says pointing at him, "Oh my, just look at that. It looks just like a penis, only smaller." ' Wayne bent forward, hugging himself with laughter till his head almost touched his knees.

Teresa picked up the theme. Spreading a hand in the 'oyez, oyez' gesture of the music hall, she cried aloud, 'A man propositions a girl at a party, right? They're going upstairs, and on the way she says to him, "I think I ought to tell you that I'm a Lesbian." "Yes?" he says. "And how is Beirut these days?" '

Jerome ignored the others' stories. Their laughter dying down, he began again. 'There once was a Frenchman, who made love to a girl he found drowned on a beach. When the gendarmes picked him up, they said, "But she's dead." And he replied, "Oh, I thought she was American." '

'Oooh,' shrieked Wayne. 'Nasty. Macabre.'

Paula looked at her father, wondering at the turn his stories were taking, but she laughed, because like the others she had had a lot to drink. Then David said in a small dour voice, 'The trouble is the fucking Americans in Vietnam don't use contraceptives. They can get them wherever and whenever they want, they're in slot machines in every mess and they're free. But they don't fucking use 'em, and why not?' He raised his voice and mimicked a big crude buck GI. ' "Because, man, I'm going out there to get my balls blown off and I want to leave something of me behind. Get it?" ' He dropped back into his own deliberate voice. 'Fucking bastards.'

Teresa stabbed the air with a thin forefinger, accentuated by a large silver ring. 'Darling, you'll have to come and see the show. You'll love it. We tell it like it is, just like you said, all about the bargirls exploited by the GIs.' She was emotional and her voice shook. 'Leaving them with coffee-coloured babies. Perhaps we could adopt one, darling, what do you think?' She looked up at Jerome from where she was sitting on the floor, straight-backed and cross-legged. 'Maybe a Vietnamese baby would be as beautiful as Kuo. I'd love to have another baby to look after. I did love it, you know.' She looked around the room, her black eyes brimming with tears. Both her daughters avoided her gaze.

'What a fucking hype!' said David. 'Your show! Huh. Singing and dancing and it makes everything better, oh yeah.'

'Heavy, heavy,' muttered Wayne, eyeing Teresa with concern and reaching for her hand to pat. 'Darling, I know how you really feel, in there.' He tapped his chest. 'Teresa is a real person, David,' he said, wheedling. 'She doesn't get her kicks watching babies being blown up.'

'Oh God,' said Paula, as David went white with anger. Francesca put out her arm to restrain her husband.

David dropped his fist. 'Shit, there's no point fighting people like you, if you are people, that is. You're just . . .' His voice was thick with rage. 'You're just parasites, scum.'

'Oh baby,' cried Wayne, wriggling. 'Scum, scum, look up my bum.' Teresa giggled nervously.

'In my house,' said Jerome, getting to his feet and walking up to David until he stood over him, 'no one talks like that to my wife.' He was rubbing his hands and his eyes gleamed.

Paula drew her breath sharply. 'Daddy,' she said, trying to restrain him.

David looked up at Jerome. He smiled crookedly, and said, 'You're right, old boy, I apologize.' He held up his hand, mocking Jerome with his eyes and his fake plummy voice, 'I'm sorry, your wife has a heart of gold. I swear to it, scout's honour.'

'You are an insolent hooligan,' said Jerome. He still held his empty brandy glass in his hand and his body was swaying. 'When I think that you are married to my daughter . . .'

It was Francesca's turn to plead. 'Daddy, please,' she said in a small voice. 'David doesn't mean it, you know he doesn't. He just gets very worked up about Vietnam, and you would too if you'd been there like him. It's not a joke for him, you must see that.'

Jerome stood rooted, looking from her to David and back again. Everyone waited; it was the moment, as each of them knew, when his temper might abate or explode anew. David got slowly to his feet as they waited, and moving noiselessly as if in a room full of sleepers, laid a hand on Jerome's arm with gentle fastidiousness and said quietly, bending his face down to the ear of the shorter man, 'I really meant no offence, to you or to Teresa. I'm jumpy, that's all. The Frog will tell you.'

Jerome closed his eyes and nodded, setting his lips firmly. 'Yes,' he said, and clasped David's arm. He turned away. David went on, assuming a chatty tone of voice, 'The worst thing I think is a pretty well-known thing but we don't give much thought to it, and that is that a wounded man can feel the pain in the limbs that he has lost.' He held out his fist to Jerome, palm up. 'A man can feel the agony of the moment when he was shot up, years after his arm was amputated.'

Paula shuddered. 'We sit here slanging each other uselessly when there's so much horror about.' She pulled at her hair.

'Polo, what can we do about it?' said David, 'Fuck-all.'

'That's what's so awful. I do nothing about it. What's the point of drawing or painting. What good does it do?'

Wayne gave a groan. 'For Christ's sake let's avoid that number, "Why am I in the world and think of the starving millions." ' He turned on his stomach on the carpet, and looked up at Teresa between cupped hands. 'Do your thing as well as you can, that's your contribution to the state of mankind, isn't it, pet?'

Teresa nodded silently, looking at Jerome who was standing abstractedly in the middle of the room, his hands cradling his balloon glass. David, following Teresa's eyes, addressed his next remarks to Jerome personally, with kindness. 'One of the correspondents in Saigon had a good word for all the maundering liberals who go on about the state of the world.' David paused, and chuckled briefly. 'He called it Afghanistanism.'

Jerome nodded, to show he was listening.

'Afghanistanism', continued David, 'means worrying about what's going on in Afghanistan instead of worrying about your own back garden. It's feeling responsible for everyone out there in Timbuctoo or Tierra del Fuego and not caring for your own mother or wife or whatever.'

'But you don't want to repress the idealism of youth,' protested Jerome in a mild tone. His flash of anger had died. 'And that must be based on each man considering himself a citizen of the world. "No man is an Island entire of itself; every man is a piece of the Continent, a part of the main ..." ' He paused.

'Go on, darling,' said Teresa in her richest and most cajoling voice. 'I love that piece.'

' "If a clod be washed away by the sea, Europe is the less, as well as if a promontory were ... Any man's death diminishes me ..." '

The others joined Jerome and recited with him, ' "Because I am involved in Mankind; and therefore never send to know for whom the bell tolls; it tolls for thee ..." '

Jerome paused and then, pleased that the attention of the room had returned to him, said lightly, 'Hemingway was a ruffian of course, with a ruffian's sentimentality, and he picked up that quotation because it's a resonant cry to a kind of global patriotism. The spirit of the *Internationale*. That is what young people feel, but when you get to my age,' he laughed sourly, 'you know Voltaire was right in the end, and each man is an island, alone and drifting at sea, and the only thing to do is to cling on and cultivate your garden.' He sighed.

'You're not like that, Daddy,' Paula remonstrated. 'You're not cynical at all.'

'You're wrong, darling,' he said, and his eyes suddenly

231

twinkled. He waved a hand loosely over the assembled company. 'You can't let the death of others – real or spiritual – diminish you. I've cultivated my garden, and here it is, and I'm proud of it.' He looked at his wife and his daughters, but they kept their eyes down, afraid of his sentimentality.

Paula said at length, 'I don't know why we say the things we do.'

'Yes,' said Francesca, shaking her long hair over her shoulders, 'we've drunk too much and we're like rats in a cage turning on each other, and Gabriel is the scientist outside the cage watching us and taking notes.' She turned her head towards the table by the window. The others laughed and followed her look.

But Gabriel had gone.

'The experiment was too much, even for the scientist,' said Paula.

'Strange,' said Teresa, 'Gabriel's offhand, but not that offhand.'

'He must have used the window,' said David. He laughed and caught Teresa's eye. In that moment the words they had exchanged earlier were forgiven. 'Like in a play, Teresa,' he teased her.

CHAPTER 20

Gabriel stumbled down the sandy path towards the splintered willow trees in the hollow, and then on, with the lights of the gypsy encampment on his right, towards the beech grove on the rise and the shelter of its broad trees. He no longer aspired to the light, but shunned it, sore-eyed as a bat at noon. It was the high-fever season for him, he knew, when pollen loaded the air and assaulted his lungs and nasal passages, but he sought out the pain and the danger in loathing for the Namiers he had left behind him, with their chatter and their smutty laughter and their triviality when he, Gabriel, was suffering such abominable torments. That he should pay such a penalty of emptiness and anguish when lesser men lived bathed in love and wreathed in smiles and wrapped in secure faith and knowledge . . .

The priest in his old black suit hurried on towards the darkness of the wood. The translucent summer night was now denser with shadow, but the lingering radiance on the rim of the hill above pierced through his tired vision as if it were the naked sun. Sirius, the single star bright enough to defeat the lightness of the night, needled his brain when he glanced upwards. He longed for cool darkness, deep cool darkness to extinguish the burning in him, but he loved the fire as a stigmatic loves the bloody holes in his hands and feet. He pressed on towards the Heath in his quest for that sweet flood of peace he had felt there twice before, when with Paula he had been penetrated by the closeness of Andrew by his side, when with Oliver he had been brimful of expectation. But now hatred. He hated his mess of a book, he hated Andrew's failure and the destruction of the Jesuits' hopes in China, he hated Maria

Pia for her fraudulent, winsome sincerity, he hated Oliver for taking possession of him. He hated them all. Together they had dismantled the firm and unassailable structure of his life that he had assembled for over thirty years. With God the cornerstone. He shrank into his jacket and wrapped it about himself angrily. Hidden God!

The thin man stumbling over the rough grass in the hollow laughed a dull laugh in his throat. He too would hide in the darkness and find there the oblivion that would halt the ebb-tide stripping him more naked each day. What had the poet of Cold Mountain written?

> 'Days and months slip by like water
> Time is like sparks knocked off flint . . .'

He would arrest the flying lathe so that the burning of his heart and mind should cease. He turned his sore eyes to the sky and thought, Dear God, what have I done that everything I believed should feel so hollow now?

In the copse the summer foliage thickly dressed the trees, and a warm and humid smell rose from the mulch that yielded softly to his tread. The interwoven branches overhead screened the sky, and the trees tossed as the wind soughed through them. From the ground, Gabriel heard their restless complaint like the boom of the ocean in a seashell, and the pitch and creak of the branches reminded him of a yawl carrying too much canvas in a freshening breeze. Take me away, he asked. But when he looked up, the trees above seemed still, even statuesque, and only their sighing told him of their ceaseless harassment.

Gabriel began to walk more slowly, catching his breath and listening for the susurrus of the leaves as they flurried in the night. The ground was growing harder as elm and poplar gave way to beech; and then he found himself in the beech grove beside the huge cleft tree he realized he had been aiming for: he wanted to look at it again and absorb some of its strength. He stood in the dark wood and his breath came more lightly, and as it eased he heard footsteps behind him. For a moment he thought, panicked, The hounds again . . . the chase, the angel's hunt. He waited, listening to the fast beat of his heart. The footsteps paused and he thought, Foolish old man, dreaming again.

A voice behind him said: 'Eh, sir, 'scuse me, got a light?' The words were spoken reedily, with sarcasm.

Gabriel wheeled round in the darkness. Two boys leaned against each other, chins up, hands dug into their pockets.

Across the pool of darkness that divided them, he said, 'Yes, I think so.'

They strolled forward, rolling their hips, keeping their hands pushed down. Gabriel found his lighter and noticed with anger that his hand shook as he held it out and pressed it. A spark flew off the flint, but did not ignite. For a fraction of a second the boys' faces gleamed. Gabriel pressed the lighter again, and the flame flared. They came up close, clinging to each other, and thrust their faces up into Gabriel's.

He saw that they were very young, with a dark down on their cheeks and upper lips that had not yet seen a razor. They wore their hair so short the pink scalp showed through. Their eyes flicked from side to side nervously, mocking him. One spoke, drawing his lips back in a sneer. Gabriel could feel his breath on his face, but he stood his ground, determined he should not seem afraid.

'Perhaps he wants a fag,' said the first boy, cocking his head on one side and sliding his eyes sideways.

'Yes,' said the other. 'Perhaps he does want a fag.'

'Yes, a fag,' his companion echoed sing-song. 'Come on, give over.' He jerked his head in the direction of the lighter.

Gabriel put it back in his pocket. 'No, I don't think so,' he said politely, trying to control the quaver in his voice. He moved to turn away.

'No you don't.' The clinging figures split in two and each took Gabriel by an arm.

'Aren't you a bit far from your pitch?' the first said, cooing in Gabriel's face.

'If you're looking for trade, it's back there.' The other thumbed with his free hand over his shoulder.

Gabriel tried to pull away from the grip on his arms, but the first boy kicked his shin and he nearly crumpled to the ground.

'I . . .' he began.

'You what?' smiled one boy as he drew both of Gabriel's arms behind his back.

Gabriel drew his breath sharply, 'I would like . . .'

'Yeah,' said the other boy who was slowly and methodically turning out Gabriel's pockets. 'You'd like what . . . ?' He showed his tongue.

'Rough trade. Rough trade,' chanted the other. 'That's your line, you dirty bastard, isn't it?'

'Take what you like,' gasped Gabriel, abject. He shrank from the boys, but no longer struggled. A greater fear grew inside him as the stranglehold on his throat drew tighter and tighter and throttled his breath.

The boy rifling his jacket threw down his breviary in disgust without looking at it, then found his rosary. He put it over his head.

'Pretty, ain't I just?' he said, mincing in front of Gabriel and twirling it. Then he dug into Gabriel's pockets again and finding the torn squares of the letter to Oliver tossed them over his shoulder. They fluttered on the smooth hard ground of the grove, and scattered. Gabriel lurched in his captor's grip when he saw the white fragments dance on the earth, but soon he forgot them, even forgot the boys who attacked him, because he was fighting to breathe. His nostrils dilated, he threw his head back and struggled to release the air exploding his lungs. As his gasps became harsher, he thrashed about in the boy's arms.

'My puffer,' he hissed. 'Please give me my puffer.'

'Your what?' said the boy holding him, placing his chin on Gabriel's shoulder and speaking with mock sweetness again. 'You'd like what?'

'His poofter,' shrieked the other, laughing. 'Poofter wants his poofter.'

The boys' jeering was less committed; the frisker had taken Gabriel's watch and was now going through his wallet. He pulled three pound notes from it and angrily tossed it away.

'Let's split,' he said sullenly. Then, jerking his face into Gabriel's, 'Mean ponce.'

When the boy let him go, Gabriel fell forward on his knees and the earth clogged his fingernails where he clawed it. He could see his puffer, a white spot in the darkness a few yards away where the boys had thrown it, and fighting for breath he began to crawl towards it. He was blowing hard through his nose, as he fought down the swelling in his chest that was suffocating him. His eyes bulging, his ribs heaving to his hoarse abrupt exhalations, like a terrorized animal thrashing and panting in a hunter's net.

Gabriel felt the sweat drip into his eyes as he dragged himself on. But the chequered shadow of the leaves now covered up the white spot he was searching for. He caught his knee on a straggling root and the pain shot through his kneecap up into his spine, and his face struck the earth under the huge beech. It was moist with dew but still retained some of the warmth of the June day, so Gabriel stayed there, cheek and chest to earth.

The face of the afflicted priest sank down. He forgot about the white inhaler and his hands loosened their grip.

'Fairy', chanted the boys from the woods as they ran off. 'Fucking filthy fairy.'

❧ CHAPTER 21

Jerome sat in his study where Gabriel had worked, absorbed in Gabriel's manuscript. A shaft of the afternoon sun fell slanting across the bookshelves, illuminating the microscopic teeming of the indoor air, and falling across the spare form of Nanny Murphy who with methodical movements was clearing out the contents of a chest of drawers into a series of cardboard boxes. Now and then she sniffed, and her mouth worked as if she wanted to say something, but she remained silent and her eyes dry.

Jerome's attention wandered from the papers in front of him. 'What was Gabriel doing on the Heath at that time of night?' Teresa had asked in exasperation. 'What a fool! Didn't he know that you can't go wandering about like that in the middle of the night, especially at his age and in his state of health. It beats me, it really does.' 'Hush,' Jerome had replied, taking his wife by the arm, 'you're upset and that makes you angry, but you must try not to speak of it like that. Paula feels responsible. She's got some damned fool notion that she put the idea into Gabriel's head. You must talk as if his death was something that would have happened anyway, that he was ill, and old and was about to die.' 'Why should Paula feel that, I wonder?' said Teresa. 'I don't understand it. What could she have to do with it?' Jerome shook his head. 'She was very fond of Gabriel. She loved him.' 'So did I,' said Teresa, 'I thought he was maddening and uptight and difficult as hell and much too cerebral for me, but I did, and I don't feel guilty.' 'It isn't the same,' said Jerome wearily.

He bent his head again to his brother's work. He was finding the sequence of events difficult to follow, and he was not sure when to turn from Andrew's diary in one pile of manuscript to Gabriel's annotations and chapter introductions in another. He was enjoying the material, but he noticed that there had been a great deal of confusion in Gabriel's thinking, and that he had never gained control of the sprawling structure of the book. Gabriel was far too deeply involved in the character of his protagonist, thought Jerome, to keep the distance that is necessary for good historical judgement. And Gabriel's own writing was loaded with nostalgia for China. It was extraordinary how powerful the romantic pull of the place remained for him. He chuckled to himself, strumming on his hand to the rhythm of some lines of Bret Harte's:

> 'Which I wish to remark,
> And my language is plain,
> That for ways that are dark,
> And for tricks that are vain,
> The heathen Chinee is peculiar . . .
> Which the same I am free to maintain.'

He stifled his irreverence, for Rosie's sake.

For although Jerome was not a vindictive man, he was happy that his brother was no longer a paragon, just as, even though he was not a malicious man, he was more perplexed than distressed by the horror of Gabriel's lonely death on the Heath. To discover that Gabriel, so controlled and decisive, so apparently certain of himself and free from the ordinary human needs for kindness and friendship, should have stumbled out into the night amazed his brother.

As soon as Jerome heard the news from two policemen first thing the following morning, he had known that he must finish Gabriel's book. The resolution filled him with a warm feeling of magnanimity: he would make it a great work, a great memorial to his brother. But he was only able to reach such a decision because the manner of Gabriel's death had emptied Jerome of the envy he had felt all his life and rendered the brothers Namier equal. Gabriel's violent end released Jerome from a shadow that had fallen across his actions for fifty years. He now felt like a hunchback who is straightened, or a convict who has only seen the trees in the exercise yard suddenly let loose at Kew Gardens in July, or an oak, once choked by mistletoe, after the pruner's saving shears have passed. Jerome's exhilaration set in and stayed. His own failure was wiped out by his brother's death, his own temperamental inability to obtain respect was cancelled by the revelation of Gabriel's state of disturbance. And by editing and finishing Gabriel's last work, he would dominate his brother in the final and most important hour, the years after death when reputations are made.

After the revelation of the CIA's role in the finances of the *Review*, Jerome had been the focus of London malice, but he knew that it was Gabriel's turn now, and that his brother's adventures were a richer subject of speculation for the gossip-mongers. He was delighted that his own misfortunes had been completely overshadowed by his brother's. It was ironical, he reflected, that Gabriel could eclipse him, even in scandal. But he did not mind. Also he could now watch the decline of the *Review* from a position of innocent hauteur, as James Cunliffe tried to appoint an editor who would retain the opinion of literary London. Jerome huffed with glee at the mess; although he minded that the journal he had founded should collapse, he loved his amour-propre more.

His self-love had undoubtedly been given a fillip by Gabriel's death. But Jerome was convinced that the rumours that surrounded it had no substance; for as long as he had observed him closely, his brother had been ascetic in everything but wine and tobacco. Jerome would have reproved angrily anyone who so much as intimated any scandal about his brother, but he understood very well the world in which he and Gabriel had moved, and he knew that denials would not scotch the rumours, and that Gabriel's eminent standing had been undone by his death in the darkness of the Heath on a fine summer night. Of course, many people would feel sympathy for the man killed by violence, and would shake their heads about the rising crime among the young and worry that they too might be mugged. Others would feel sorry for the priest, imagining his struggles with himself before he yielded to ignominy and temptation and sought clandestine meetings. There would be a few voices, thought Jerome, who would declare Gabriel innocent of lust. But he knew that all

London had tittered with glee when the Society put out a statement that Father Gabriel Namier, sj, had died of suffocation after an asthma attack probably caused by the violent emotional stress of a robbery, and that he was an insomniac who had recently made it his habit to take long walks on Hampstead Heath in the hope that the exercise would tire him out and help him sleep. 'Tire him out, indeed!' Jerome could hear voices whooping with laughter.

It was Paula who told the two Fathers who came to visit Jerome that it was her fault, that she had prescribed walking on the Heath for Gabriel's sleeplessness and had gone walking with him and made light of the dangers. 'I told him', she said, distraught, 'that women were safer there than men. But he can't have understood what I meant. He lived in a world of his own, and it was always difficult to know how much he was taking in. He knew so much about some things, you couldn't tell how much he grasped about others.'

'Innocence', said one of Gabriel's colleagues, a priest with white hair and sunken cheeks who chain-smoked during the visit, 'is a part of wisdom. Christ loved the little children, though their understanding is limited. Maybe Father Namier shared their outlook on the world.' He tried to look as if he meant what he was saying, and swallowed. 'Where there is inner purity, there can be no defilement, whatever men may say.'

Paula's eyes had filled with tears, and Jerome hurried the two priests out, thanking them. A week had passed since then, a week in which time had crept by as stealthily as the growth of a swelling bud. Throughout it all, Paula had become the focus of everyone's concern. She asked if she could help Nanny and her father go through Gabriel's papers and squatted on the floor with the notes scattered around her, staring at them with burning cheeks.

'I turned away from him after Sicily,' she said, 'I hated him. Oh, God, why was I so mean? Why didn't I understand the way he was, and go on trying?'

'Darling,' said Jerome, pleased that she did not pull away from him sulkily and that he was able to take her hand and stroke it. 'When you get to my age, you will realize that the worst part of any death is the remorse you feel afterwards, at all the cruelty and the neglect and the thoughtlessness, the lost opportunities and the lack of love. I was in despair after my mother's death, and my father's – not because I loved them, but because I felt I'd failed them as a son. You will have to learn not to brood on that, but to think of Gabriel at his best, when you were friends.'

Paula pulled at her hair and fought her rising tears. 'I wish I'd cared for him like I wanted to. But he made it so hard. He would suddenly become all cold and distant, and leave me feeling like a deb going gush gush gush, with my mouth open spouting rubbish.'

'He did that to everyone,' said Jerome quietly. 'It was part of his strength as a personality. Gabriel was a powerful character, as you know.' He thought to himself, But not powerful enough to dominate me from the grave.

Nanny sniffed loudly behind Jerome and he remembered the manuscript on his knees. She made a gesture at the chair he was sitting on. 'Move it over, please, there's a dear,' she said, 'I must clear everything that has to be sent back to the Fathers.'

Jerome moved obediently, but continued to think of Paula. How he wished he could iron out the frown that permanently creased her forehead between her brows. Yet without it, he thought lovingly, she would not be my Paula.

He began reading, finding himself hunting tiger with the emperor in Manchuria. Nanny turned round from the desk, where she was sorting out the contents of the drawers, and said, puzzled, 'I can't for the life of me find that piece of rock crystal Father liked so much. You know the one, your father gave it to him.'

Jerome got up. 'Of course I know it. How very odd. Perhaps it was in his pocket when he was mugged. Gabriel was very attached to it.'

'Yes,' said Rosie, 'he told me it was one of the few things he kept, personal things that is, after he was ordained.'

'It is strange,' said Jerome. 'The police had better know Gabriel might have had it on him.'

Across the green slopes of the Heath that hazy midsummer afternoon Paula sat at her desk. She was trying to draw a portrait of Gabriel before the memory of him faded, but likenesses had never been her strong point, and although she could still see his long thin Crivelli face with its hooded small bright eyes and seams of tiredness running from nose to mouth, she could not transfer the image on to the paper in front of her. All around, the flat was in chaos, clothes and books and dirty mugs and bedclothes flung about. Disorder, Paula felt, was a small tribute to the dead.

When the telephone rang, she had fallen asleep with her head cradled on her arms over the desk.

'It's Oliver, Oliver Summers.' He spoke brightly, sounding quite different from the mournful voices of condolence that had sought Paula over the past few days. 'I must see you.'

Paula was surprised. She did not know him, except by sight. But his energy made her straighten her shoulders and inject a corresponding warmth into her voice. She said, 'Of course, but why?'

'I'll tell you when I see you,' he said, without emphasis, so Paula felt trusting, but curious. 'Can I come over now?'

'Well. It's rather a mess here,' Paula began.

'I'll be over right away,' said Oliver decisively. 'Twenty minutes.'

Paula washed her face and pulled her hair in place over her forehead and ears, grimacing at its greasiness. Dirt and disorder, tributes to the dead.

When she opened the door, Oliver, drawing quick breaths after his rapid walk across the Heath, walked straight past her into the light of the back room where she worked and then turned and looked at her.

'Are you all right? Your father told me you'd taken it badly.'

'No, no, not really', Paula shook her head. The glow of health from Oliver's flushed cheeks invigorated her instantly. He threw his hair back out of his eyes. 'You're very pale.' he said. He looked around, gathered up a few dirty mugs and walked through to the kitchen. 'I'll make you some tea, that'll restore you.' He looked over her empty shelves and laughed. 'Not very domesticated, are you?' He found the teabags and plugged in the kettle. 'No chance of any milk, I suppose?'

'No, 'fraid not,' said Paula, 'But there's Marvel.' She let him minister to her, surprised at his forthrightness in a flat he had never seen before.

Oliver moved quickly, tossing the teabags into the pot and swirling them round, then pouring out the tea and dripping some honey into the mug. 'Medicinal,' he said, smiling at Paula.

Paula sat with her head in her hands at the kitchen table and sipped at the tea slowly. She realized as she did so that she had not eaten for a long time. Oliver drew up a chair opposite her, and putting a hand in his pocket he drew out Gabriel's engraved crystal and put it on the table between them.

'Your father is looking for that,' he said.

'What is it?' It sparkled where it lay and she ran a fingertip over its polished facets.

'It's a Chinese prism. It belonged to Gabriel, and he gave it to me.'

Paula frowned. 'I didn't know you knew him.'

He said, 'Yes, but not well. We went walking on the Heath.' He spoke clearly, without embarrassment, but his light eyes looked straight into hers, aware of the importance of his words.

Paula's eyes opened wide. 'You did?' she said.

'Yes,' he said, with less blitheness than before. 'We passed the tree where he was found.'

Paula picked up the crystal. Her pulse was racing. 'And Gabriel gave you this?'

'He wanted me to take it. For a time, he said. It seemed important to him, so I did.'

Paula looked at the characters bevelled into the crystal. 'What does it say? Do you know?'

'It says that it's a piece of heaven. At least that is what Gabriel told me. It was some kind of a sign to him, but I didn't understand.' Oliver laughed lightly and pressed his fingertips on the table, rocking on his chair on its back legs. 'He could be very weird sometimes, as if there was something churning inside him which he couldn't get out. He was in one of those moods when he gave me the prism. I didn't want to refuse because I could see that it meant a great deal to him. I used to feel that one day he would tell me something very important to him, and that he would be able to tell me because I didn't belong to his usual world, and didn't share any of his beliefs. But he never did.'

Oliver tipped his chair back to the table and held Paula in

his curving bright smile. His soft candid tone struck her ear a little false, and under her ribs a danger signal began to beat. 'It's difficult for me now.' His eyes were dancing. 'I just went round to your parents' place and asked if I could do anything to help, and your old man was giving a description of this thing on the telephone. He hung up, and said in that hearty way of his, "What could a lot of young thugs want with a K'ang-hsi crystal prism?" I could hardly say, "Oh, talking of that, I happen to have it on me," could I?' He chuckled softly, and eyed Paula's mug. 'Drink up, before it gets cold. You're looking half dead with tiredness, you're so pale.' He paused, and then added, 'You see, Paula, no one knew that Gabriel used to come and see me, and I knew that he didn't want anyone to know, because once when I was at your father's house, he said hello to me, but politely, as if to warn me to keep my distance, which was very different from his way with me when we were alone.'

Oliver got up and leaned back on the sink, looking at her. The constriction in Paula's heart was painful. She kept her head down over her mug, looking at the crystal in front of her, scared that Oliver might notice her turmoil. She thought, I did not have anything to do with it after all. I played no part, I'm not to blame. She felt light-headed with the freedom of it, with hunger, with the laughter she wanted to let explode from her belly and fill the room till it shook. She looked up and across at Oliver, and she understood as she took in his slight, graceful body leaning against her kitchen sink. She thought, This boy, he was the cause. This boy like a thousand others in London. Attractive, casual, open, pretty, with a nice smile. She ran her hands through her hair and chuckled. 'Oh Gabriel,' she said aloud.

The revelation of her own inconsequence made her vibrate with joy, and when she looked again at Oliver she smiled in his face as gaily as a child at a conjurer when a dove bobs up bright-eyed behind his coloured handkerchief.

Knowing his presence now to be a presence that had entranced her uncle, she ran her eyes over him with quiet curiosity that grew rapidly in intensity, as she thought, Did he? Did they? What happened between them? She followed the curve of Oliver's lips to the corner of his ear under the falling blond hair and wondered at his epicene delicacy.

She caught his eye, and a gleam of glee born of his ready opportunism lit him up and he smiled slowly back at her, without parting his lips. Inside, she felt the wick of appetite catch, and she thought, Why the hell not? It's been so long. With this one? She almost shook her head, thinking, No, he's too willing. There'll only be that nothing afterwards when we cannot think of anything to say to each other and the memory of our closeness stands between us like a window pane. Yet through him she would reach out and hold Gabriel again. So she chuckled and looked back at Oliver. She could see him taking her in, a pale skinny girl with gangling limbs and spiky hair that could do with a wash, but she knew that it didn't matter to him in the least. She understood the particular pattern that trapped her, and Gabriel and Oliver; that she had been irrelevant to Gabriel, just as he had been irrelevant to Oliver. She smiled again, her face and eyes speaking suddenly of her inner resolution. She thought, the changes really have tumbled through the particular lock that is my life. These are the shaken patterns of the *I Ching* – moments when the flux stops and falls into shape, when the pattern of clouds show a tree, a monster, a face.

He said slowly, coming towards her, 'So please, will you take it back and say that Gabriel gave it to you?'

'Yes, I will,' said Paula softly, 'I will.' She picked up the prism and left the kitchen. Oliver followed. She put it on her desk in the afternoon sun, so that the iridescence exploded inside it and shot rainbows round the walls.

'Look,' she said, pointing at her attempted portrait of Gabriel. 'It's not quite right.'

She quivered with anticipation at his closeness. 'I know,' she said, under her breath. 'But it doesn't matter.'

'No,' said Oliver, turning his face to hers.

She did not move away. She thought again, Why the hell not? I use my head too much. So she let him hold her. Again she thought, I played no part in it after all. Her ecstasy of innocence when she smiled full into Oliver's eyes made him crow aloud. She found it strange, but she liked it, and he bent towards her and kissed her mouth. He said, 'Nothing like it, really.' She returned his kiss, but without closing her eyes, because she wanted to look at Oliver, and remember Gabriel.

PRINCIPAL EVENTS IN THE
LIFE OF ANDREW DA ROCHA, S.J.

1645   Born in Oporto

1654   Birth of future Emperor K'ang-hsi

1661   Emperor K'ang-hsi succeeds to the Dragon Throne

1664   Andrew enters noviciate in Lisbon

1667   K'ang-hsi assumes government of Empire

1669   Ferdinand Verbiest, SJ, appointed Director of Bureau Astronomy in Peking; Jesuits ordered to rectify Chinese calendar

1673   Andrew arrives in Peking. Appointed Verbiest's assistant at the Bureau of Astronomy

1685   Accompanies K'ang-hsi to Tartary

1686   Andrew begins daily instruction of K'ang-hsi in Mathematics, Geometry, and Astronomy

1687   Verbiest dies, and Andrew succeeds him as Director of Bureau of Astronomy

1688   Jesuits from France arrive in Peking

1692   22 March. K'ang-hsi issues edict of toleration of Christianity in China; missionaries and clergy of different orders establish themselves

1696–7   K'ang-hsi's northern campaigns against the Zungar rebels under Galdan

1704   Andrew refuses to expound the *I Ching* with K'ang-hsi

1705   The Papal Legate, Cardinal Maillard de Tournon arrives in Peking. December 31. Audience with K'ang-hsi; informs him that the Pope has ruled against the performance of the rites to the ancestors and Confucius by Christian converts

1706   Charles Maigrot, Bishop of Conon, debates the rites question with K'ang-hsi at Jehol; K'ang-hsi orders every

Christian to carry a certificate saying he accepts the Confucian and ancestral rites

1707 Tournon issues Edict of Nanking, declaring rites superstitious

1708 K'ang-hsi believes the Heir Apparent has been bewitched; Andrew da Rocha dies

1717 K'ang-hsi prohibits preaching of Christianity and orders deportation of missionaries working outside the court

1722 K'ang-hsi dies

1724 Emperor Yung-cheng his son forbids the practice of Christianity in China, deports all missionaries to Macao

1736 Ch'ien-lung succeeds; proclaims death penalty for preaching Christianity, but retains Jesuits at court for other purposes

1742 In the papal Bull *Ex quo singulari* on July 11, Benedict XIV forbids the Jesuits to continue their mission in China

1773 The Jesuit Order is suppressed by Pope Clement XIV

✖ ACKNOWLEDGEMENTS

Andrew da Rocha, SJ, and his Diaries are imagined, but the circumstances of his life are historically authentic. I would therefore like to acknowledge my debt to the following works:

Bettinelli, Giuseppe, *Memorie Storiche della legazione e morte dell' eminentiss. Monsignor Cardinale di Tournon. Esposte con monumenti vari ed autentici non più dati alla luce.* 8 Vols (Venice 1761)

Bouvet, Joachim, SJ, *L'estat Présent de la Chine en Figures* (Paris 1697). *Life of the Present Emperor of China.* Trans. J. Crull (1699)

Carton, L'Abbé, C., *Notice Biographique sur le Père Verbiest Missionaire à la Chine* (Bruges 1839)

Extrait de la Relation de Pékin le 30 Octobre 1706, touchant l'entretien qu'eut Mgr. Maigrot avec l'Empereur de la Chine. Ms. Bibl. Nat. Fonds Fr. 9093

du Halde, J. B., SJ, *Description Géographique, Historique, Chronologique, Politique et Physique de L'Empire de La Chine et de la Tartarie Chinoise.* 4 Vols (Paris 1735) (Especially for *Voyages en Tartarie du P. Gerbillon, Missionaire Français de la Compagnie de Jésus à la Chine 1688–9*)

Jenkins, R. C., *The Jesuits in China* (London 1894)

Lecompte, Louis, SJ, *Memoirs and Observations made in a late Journey through the Empire of China.* (London 1697)

Lettres Edifiantes et Curieuses, écrites des missions étrangères, nouvelle édition (Paris 1781)

Needham, Joseph, *Chinese Astronomy and the Jesuit Mission: an encounter of cultures* (The China Society 1958)

Pfister, Louis, SJ, *Notices Biographiques et Bibliographiques sur les Jésuites de L'Ancienne Mission de Chine. 1552–1773.* Variétés Sinologiques No. 59. (Shanghai 1932)

Pih, Irène, *Le Père Gabriel de Magalhaes. Un Jésuite Portugais en Chine au XVIIe siècle* (Doctoral thesis, kindly lent by the author)

de Prémare, François, SJ, *Vestiges des Principaux Dogmes Chrétiens Tirés des Anciens Livres Chinois.* Translated from Latin by A. Bonnety and Paul Perny (Paris 1878)

Rowbotham, Arnold H., *Missionary and Mandarin: the Jesuits at the Court of China* (Los Angeles 1942)

Spence, Jonathan, *Emperor of China, Self-Portrait of K'ang-hsi.* (London 1974)

Tournon, M. le Cardinal, *Patriarche de'Antioche, Visiteur Apostolique, avec pouvoir de Légat a latere à la Chine. Anecdotes sur L'Etat de la Religion dans la Chine.* 2 Vols (Paris 1733)

Travels of Certain Learned Missionaries of the Society of Jesus into Divers Parts of the Archipelago, India, China and America (London 1714)

Verbiest, Ferdinand, SJ, *Lettre écrite de la cour de Pékin sur le voyage que l'empereur de la Chine a fait dans la Tartarie occidentale.* (Paris 1684). ed. J. F. Bernard. *Epistola Rev. P. Ferdinand Verbiest Vice-provincialis Missionis Sinensis*, SJ *1678 15 Aug. Ex curia Pekinensi in Europam ad socios missa* (Paris 1684)

Walker, D. P., *The Ancient Theology. Studies in Christian Platonism from the Fifteenth to the Eighteenth Century* (London 1972)